Practicing Normal

Studio Digital CT, LLC
P.O. Box 4331
Stamford, CT 06907

Copyright © 2016 by Cara Sue Achterberg

Story Plant Paperback ISBN: 978-1-61188-244-5
Fiction Studio Books E-book ISBN: 978-1-945839-01-6

Visit our website at www.TheStoryPlant.com

First Story Plant Printing: June 2017

Printed in the United States of America
0 9 8 7 6 5 4 3 2 1

Practicing Normal

Cara Sue Achterberg

THE
ST●RY
PLANT

For Linda, my first friend, first neighbor, and always my first call—love you Lou.

"Do not think that love, in order to be genuine, has to be extraordinary. What we need is to love without getting tired."
– Mother Teresa

KATE
≈≈

Waving to Jenna as she waits at the bus stop, all I can think is, *Please let her go to school today and stay in school all day.* Jenna is such a smart girl; I don't understand why she doesn't apply herself to her studies. She could be anything. A doctor, even. I was a nurse, but Jenna is smarter than me. Of course, that was twenty years ago. Before I married Everett. Before Jenna and JT were born. Before we ever lived in Pine Estates.

I was the one who chose the house. Everett thought it was pretentious, and it was. All the houses on our end of Pine Road were pretentious. But it was the nineties. Everyone was building McMansions and taking out ridiculous loans to pay for them. Everett had just left his job as a police officer for the job at FABSO (Family and Business Security Options).

We needed to start a new life. We celebrated the new job and didn't talk about the fact that things could have turned out very differently if his captain had chosen to bring charges against him. Instead, he recommended Everett for the job at FABSO and made it clear Everett would be wise to take it.

I remember lying in bed holding Everett the day he turned in his gun and his badge. He was devastated. Being a cop had been Everett's dream since childhood. "All I've ever wanted to be is a cop. If I can't be a cop, who am I?"

"You're a father and a husband. That's so much more," I told him. He didn't say anything about it again. He got to work. He made something of FABSO. And he's tried so hard to be a good dad.

I don't remember much about my own dad, and whenever I asked my mother she would say, "There's nothing to remember about that louse except that he was a louse." When I pressed her later, after I'd grown up, she'd said, "It doesn't matter now. He didn't want to be with us enough to stay."

All that bitterness can't hide the fact that when my father left, he apparently took my mother's heart. She's spent the rest of her life alone. Except for me. And Evelyn. Although, once Evelyn left home, she didn't come around much. These days she visits Mama on Saturdays, unless she has something more pressing to do, which is most weeks. Mama annoys her. I suppose I do too. We don't fit into Evelyn's shiny, perfect life.

When I first met Everett and told Mama about him, she was skeptical. "A cop?"

I told her how he'd wanted to be a cop since he was a little boy, the same way I always wanted to be a nurse. I gushed about how he told me I was beautiful and how he said he'd been certain about us the first time he saw me. Mama said, "Men will say whatever it takes, Kate. When will you realize that?" But I knew she was wrong about Everett.

I met Everett in the ER. I was treating a patient who was high on coke or meth or God knows what. He was lean and riddled with track marks, his strength coming from whatever drug was flooding his body. I didn't recognize him as one of our regulars—the ones who showed up like clockwork in search of pain meds. This guy was out of his mind and covered in his own blood from where he'd scratched his thin skin. Another nurse helped me attempt to strap him to the gurney with the Velcro holds, but he was out of his mind and reached for the needle I was about to use to sedate him. Everett was nearby at the desk filling out forms and heard me yell. In just moments, he wrestled the junkie to the ground and held him still as I plunged the needle in. When the man finally collapsed, Everett lifted him back onto the gurney and secured him.

When he turned and looked at me with his green eyes, the same eyes Jenna has, I knew I would marry him. I told him that on our second date. He laughed. I've always loved his laugh.

When Everett started at FABSO, he made nearly twice the salary he'd made as a cop. I didn't need to work any longer. It was our chance. I would stay home and take care of our happy family in our beautiful house in Pine Estates. It was our new start. I thought we belonged there.

When I open the door to Mama's house, she's already calling for me. She may be losing her mind, but her hearing hasn't deteriorated one bit.

"You're late!" she scolds.

"Sorry, JT had a hard time picking out a shirt to wear today."

"He's not a baby! I don't know why you put up with it."

I smile at her. No sense taking the bait. "You're right, Mama."

"You've always been so indecisive. I swear if I didn't tell you what to do next, you'd stand there like a statue."

"Good thing you're so good at telling me what to do," I mutter as I go to prepare her tea.

Mama wasn't always like this. When Evelyn and I were little, she was our whole world. She baked homemade cakes for our birthdays, and elaborately decorated them with whatever we were currently obsessing over—Tinker Bell, Barbies, guitars, or, for Evelyn, a computer one year, and the scales of justice the year she announced she was going to be a judge when she grew up.

Mama read to us every night. I remember snuggling into the crook of her arm, even when I was too old to be doing it. Evelyn would be on her other side and our hands would meet on Mama's flat tummy. I loved the stories with a happy ending, but Evelyn demanded that she read "real books." She wanted mysteries and thrillers instead of the children's books Mama picked out at the library. So Mama began to read Nancy Drew, but Evelyn went to the adult aisle and picked out John Grisham, Tom Clancy, and Stephen King. Mama tried to read them to us. She'd come to a part that she felt was too racy for us and she'd hum while she skimmed ahead til she found a more appropriate section before beginning to read again. This drove Evelyn nuts. She'd pout and complain, eventually stomping off. Mama would return the books to the library unread, but it wasn't long before Evelyn was old enough to have her own library card and checked them out for herself.

In the mornings, Mama would braid our hair, pack our lunches with tiny handwritten notes, and walk us to the bus stop for more years than was appropriate. When Evelyn reached high school, she demanded that Mama stop, but she still followed us with her car and waited to be certain we got on the bus safely.

Now that I'm a mom, I know it couldn't have been easy raising us alone. As she's gotten older, she's gotten difficult. But I put up with her increasing number of quirks because I feel I owe her. Evelyn doesn't see it that way, but then again Evelyn doesn't feel she owes anybody anything.

"Here you go." I hand Mama the bitter Earl Grey tea she likes over-steeped with no sweetener.

"I've already missed Phillip," she says as I help her out the door to the back porch. She spends most mornings there, talking to the birds that frequent her multiple bird feeders.

"Who's Phillip?" I ask, mostly to make conversation. She loves to talk about the birds.

The look she gives me is just like the one JT gives me when my random "Wow" comes at the wrong time in one of his lengthy soliloquies on his current obsession. "Phillip is the male cardinal who has begun stopping by each morning. He comes over the fence from the southeast. He's usually here before the chickadees move in and take over the birdbath."

I look at the crowd of birds fighting over the seed at the feeder. They all look the same to me. "I've got to take care of a few things at home after I run JT to school; I'll be back at lunchtime."

"Always leaving me!" she complains. "You can't even spend five minutes with your mother."

I'd protest, but there's no point. She sees things the way she needs to see them. Rewriting history is one of her specialties. I've been listening to her do it all my life. When Everett and I took the kids to the beach last summer, she said, "Must be nice! I've never had a vacation." Yet, I remember several summers when Mama took Evelyn and me to the same beach we were headed to. Or when I graduated from nursing school, Mama said, "I've always said you'd make a fine nurse," when, in reality, she'd been telling me for years that I could never be a nurse because I was so weak at chemistry. She thought I should have considered something in business—like being a secretary. She's been spinning her stories of Evelyn's escapades, my mistakes, and my father's general louse-likeness for so long, she probably believes them as gospel truth. They are, I suppose, at least to her mind.

I hurry home, hoping JT has finally decided on a shirt for school. We're going to be late if we have to argue about it.

JENNA
≈≈

I wave to Mom as she drives past on her way to Gram's house. I don't know why she drives. It's a perfectly nice day and Gram only lives a couple blocks up the street. She lives in the old part, where the houses are pretty much all one-story brick numbers with window boxes full of plastic flowers. Old people live there. Or young people without much money.

Our end of the street is for the rich people, not that we're rich people. We just pretend to be. Everett—my dad—makes decent money, I'm pretty sure, but nothing like the money Mr. Braddington pulls in. I should know. I spend plenty of time in the Braddingtons' house. And today, that's where I'll go just as soon as my mom's car is out of sight, but before the bus pulls up to take me to school.

I don't see the point of school. Bunch of idiots there. And not just the students; the teachers aren't such a bright bunch either. It's a waste of my time. I'm sure I'll catch hell for it from Everett, but I can't stomach the jerks today. I grab my backpack and double-time it to the Braddingtons' house.

I know it's empty. On a day like today, Mrs. Braddington will be on the golf course teeing off. Wells and Tiffany will have already left in Wells' fancy corvette, headed to school. I don't know why they go to the public school. I'm sure the Braddingtons could afford the Country Day

School. Wells is a junior, like me. He's a big deal on the football team. And a state-ranked wrestler. Plus, he runs track. The guy is your all-American dream, if that's what you're into.

Tiffany is a freshman. She made waves when she started at Cramer High. Everyone knows she modeled for J.Crew as a kid. She's cardboard pretty and already hangs with the mean girls in my grade. I guess she's too good to be an actual freshman.

I've seen the pictures of Tiffany in the J.Crew catalogs. They're blown up poster-size and plastered all over the Braddingtons' house. There are pictures of Wells, also. In most pictures, he's holding a trophy. He's always been beautiful, too. That's how I think of all of them—the Beautiful Braddingtons. Alliteration, see? I wasn't snoozing through English class last week.

The Braddingtons have an alarm system, but it's easy to get around. The control box for the alarm system is in the garage, which has a cat door for their overly obese cat. They've had to enlarge it twice. The cat happened into the right family. It's diabetic and Mrs. Braddington gives it shots every day. I've seen the meds and the instructions on the counter.

Getting into the Braddingtons' is easy as pie. I'm small enough to get through the cat door. I found their security code the first time I stopped in, but even if I hadn't, I could easily disarm their system since the box is right there next to the door. I could simply pull the wires to the phone and power. I don't need either.

I learned how to disarm home systems from following Everett around on his job when I was little. He works for a security company. He's even made geeky YouTube videos. In one of them, he dresses up like a repair guy and shows a customer how a burglar could easily break into his house. He overacts ridiculously, as if he's some Hollywood star. They still use that video on cable channel advertising.

Embarrassing for all of us, but Everett actually watches it pretty much every time it airs.

Today at the Braddingtons' house, I fix a big bowl of ice cream—Peanut Butter Swirl—and take it to the window seat that looks out over the backyard, which includes a fancy outdoor kitchen, a pool shaped like a tennis racket with a hot tub on the handle (you can swim between the two!), and a golf tee with an enormous backstop. The Braddingtons also have the biggest bird feeder I've ever seen. It looks like an old-fashioned hotel with a tin roof and dozens of balconies where the feed comes out. A neon sign on the top of it says, "Fly Right Inn" and holds the extra bird food that automatically refills the feeder whenever it gets low. My gram would probably kill to have a feeder like that. I've thought about stealing it for her, but then the Bs would figure out someone's been here.

Gram is crazy about birds. As in, she's so crazy she thinks she can talk to birds and they talk to her. I like to mess with my mom sometimes and say shit like, "Maybe she *can* talk to birds. How would we know—we don't speak bird."

"That's ridiculous, Jenna. No one talks to birds."

"Sure they do. People talk to birds all the time." Which is true, right?

"Your grandmother is getting old. She's confused. She cannot communicate with birds."

"I just think we aren't experts. It's possible. People talk to dolphins all the time."

"It's not the same."

"Sure it is."

"It doesn't help your gram to encourage it. She's struggling to keep her mind sound as she ages."

This is Mom's way of saying Gram is going nuts. Mom should know since she spends every day over there taking care of her. If anyone's crazy, it's Mom. She has no life because she has to be there to feed Gram all her meals and clean every possible speck that ever lands in her house, or Gram will start yelling about the mess. She's better off outside talking to the birds. Her yard has a ten-foot privacy fence, about fifteen bird feeders (that Mom fills EVERY day), and four birdbaths. If I were Mom, I'd park Gram out there first thing in the morning and come back after dark to roll her back inside.

I finish up my ice cream and take my English book to the chaise lounge in the sunroom. That's my favorite room in the house. Before I go, I'll wash my dishes and put everything back the way it was, reset the alarm, and slip back out the cat door. Maybe today I'll visit the seven dwarfs over at Ms. Cassie's place.

KATE
≈≈

I've just finished cleaning up Mama's lunch dishes and settled her down for a nap when Everett calls.

"You need to get over to the Braddingtons' house."

"What? Why?" I ask. Susan Braddington and I aren't really friends. They live across the street, but I've only been in their house once. Back when we first moved in, I tried in vain to get to know Susan. The Braddingtons are the only family with children on our end of the street. Our kids are nearly the same ages and, when we moved in, I imagined us becoming best friends, sharing mornings at the bus stop and afternoons at the Braddingtons' pool.

Susan has always been pleasant enough, politely refusing every invitation I made. Sometimes I wonder if it's because of JT. The one and only time I've been in their house was the day JT got upset about something I can't even recall. He was probably about four. He'd run blindly across the road and up their driveway. I'd chased after him, but he was fast. Finally, he tripped over the low stone wall that banks their driveway. His knee was bleeding. It wasn't a big deal, not really, but Susan Braddington heard him crying and came out to help. She invited us in to wash the cut, but when she approached JT with a can of first aid spray, he began shrieking and kicked a dent in their drywall. I tried to explain, but it was impossible over JT's screaming, so I picked him up and carried him home.

I sent Everett over to offer to repair the drywall, but Susan insisted there was no need. Since then, the

Braddingtons always wave whenever we see each other, but they never stop, never chat. Why in heaven's name was Everett insisting I had to go there now?

"I don't know, but Jenna is there and so are the police!"

"Oh my God!" I drop Mama's soup bowl in the sink with a clatter. So much for Jenna going to school and staying there.

"What is it?" screeches Mama.

"I'm trying to reach one of my buddies at the department to figure out what she did and what can be done," says Everett.

"Katie! What happened? Don't ignore me!"

"I'll go there, now," I tell him.

I grab my purse and tell Mama, "It's nothing. Take your nap. I'll be back in time for dinner." I can hear her calling to me as I race out the door.

As I drive to the Braddingtons' house, I try to apply some lipstick, glancing in the rearview mirror. My hair looks terrible, yanked into a haphazard bun this morning while arguing with JT about his shirt. It'd taken nearly the whole morning to get him dressed and then over to the school. He'd insisted I walk him in, even though that was one of the skills the teachers wanted him to master by now—walking into the building by himself.

He'd refused to even get out of the car alone.

"If you make me, I'll have an MI," he'd said. JT, like most kids with Asperger's syndrome, has an obsession. Currently, it's emergency medicine. He streams medical dramas nonstop and throws medical jargon into his conversations. Because I was an ER nurse, I know that an MI is a myocardial infarction.

"You won't have a heart attack because you walk into the school building alone. You can do this JT. You're too old for me to walk you in. Besides, you're over an hour late."

"Only because you made me take my stupid pills. They're unnecessary and dangerous."

"You have to take your meds before school. They help your focus. We've talked about all of this."

"Those meds make my BP go sky high."

"They do not raise your blood pressure, but you are most certainly raising mine."

JT smiled then. He'd done it. Found a way to work his newest code into the conversation. "There's no need for a BMW!"

Most days, I'm willing to play his game. It's harmless really, and, besides, he's expanding his knowledge base and his vocabulary. Mrs. Fall would be proud. BMW stands for "Bitch, moan, and whine." I'm not even sure which program he'd picked the term up from. It might be from one of the paramedic blogs he's been following.

"There most certainly is going to be a reason for me to have a BMW if you don't get your tail into that school."

JT grinned. "Today, just today, can't you go with me? Otherwise, I'm AGMI."

I couldn't help but laugh. AGMI stands for "Ain't Gonna Make It." He explained that to me last night. I'd never heard it before, but I suppose text messages are increasing the number of acronyms medical personnel use.

"This is the last time," I said, and got out of the car. When JT reached for my hand on the sidewalk, I shoved it in my pocket, even though I wanted to hold his hand as much as he wanted to hold mine. The school counselor's voice rang in my head, *It's really not appropriate for a twelve-year-old boy to be holding his mother's hand when he walks in the building. That's what we're working on here, Mrs. Turner. We're trying to help John Thomas learn to function in a regular classroom.*

I drive up the Braddingtons' curvy driveway as fast as I dare. A police car is parked in their turnaround. The house is the same distance from the road as ours, but the driveway is twice as long, snaking back and forth with that expensive stone wall guiding it. Before I can ring the bell, Susan Braddington opens the door.

"Kate, hello. Sorry to see you under these circumstances." Her face is made up perfectly, and she smiles at me in the cautious way she does whenever we run into each other at the school or the store and I say, "We really should get together."

"Uh, yes. Hi, Susan." I stammer, glancing past her into the empty foyer. I don't see Jenna. "This has something to do with Jenna?"

"I'll let the officer explain," she says, and leads me down the hall to the cavernous kitchen. Jenna is sitting on a stool at the counter, looking bored.

I don't know if I should hug her or not. Has something happened to her or to Susan? I place a hand on Jenna's shoulder and feel her shrink away from it.

"What's going on?"

"You're Mrs. Turner?" asks the officer. He looks much younger than Everett. He might have worked under him at some point years ago. I notice the brown-stained fingers as he holds his notepad. A smoker. Everett would never have shared a car with him. He can't stand smokers.

"I am." I hate that I'm trembling. Authority figures tend to reduce me to an anxious puddle. Maybe that's part of the reason Everett still has such an effect on me physically. Even if I'm furious with him, I can rarely resist him in the bedroom. It's silly to be so nervous because I know that this officer is really just somebody's son or husband dressed up in a uniform that has to be dry cleaned every week. The badge glares at me. I try to focus on the officer's face, smooth as if he's just shaved or is too young to need to.

"Did you know your daughter was not in school today?"

Was that what this was about? Relief washes over me. Maybe Susan found Jenna and knew she was supposed to be in school. I wish Susan had just called my cell phone. I wrote the number on the invitation I'd sent them at the end of summer. I'd invited the Braddingtons for a cookout, but Susan never RSVP'd. I couldn't bring myself to call and ask if they were coming. That seemed too desperate. I don't know why I care about being friends with them. Maybe it's silly, but I've always dreamed of living in a neighborhood where the neighbors got together for cook-outs, traded recipes, and watched each other's pets when they went on vacation. Pine Estates looks like such a friendly place, but we've been here eight years and I have yet to find any friends on this street. Still, I haven't given up hope. I know these things take time. Everett doesn't understand this. "Why would you want to be friends with them, anyway, up there in their big house on the hill with that ridiculous driveway?" When they didn't show up, I took the extra burgers I'd made to Mama's to freeze for easy dinners in the microwave.

"Mrs. Braddington came home and discovered your daughter crawling through the cat door of their garage."

"Oh?" I can think of no other response. I'm stunned. Why would Jenna want to get in their garage?

"Well?" asks Susan, clearly expecting me to give some response. All I can hear is Everett's voice. *Don't you know what your own daughter is doing?*

"I'm sorry. I thought Jenna was in school." I turn to Jenna. "Why were you in the Braddingtons' garage?"

Jenna shrugs.

"What happens next?" I ask the officer, not meeting Susan's accusatory eyes.

"I've written a report. I'll have to file that. Is there anything else that will turn up when I run her information through the system?"

"I don't know." I say this because I don't. I know that Jenna had gotten in trouble a while back for sneaking into an electronics store and watching television, but Everett said he'd taken care of that. Jenna hadn't taken anything or broken anything getting in, so there wasn't a real crime he'd said. He'd even seemed somewhat impressed that

Jenna could do it without tripping the alarm system. He'd grilled her on how she'd gotten in.

"Well, Mrs. Braddington is reserving the right to press charges depending on whether Mr. Braddington discovers that anything is missing from the garage."

"I don't know what he keeps in there," explains Susan, crossing her arms and frowning.

"So, can I take Jenna home?"

"For now, but we may need you to bring her down to the station if there are charges."

Jenna gets up from the stool and walks silently past me.

"I'm really sorry," I say to Susan. "I don't know what she was doing here. It won't happen again. I promise."

Susan Braddington says nothing to me. Instead, she takes the officer's arm. "I really appreciate your prompt response. It's good to know we have such excellent police coverage in Pine Estates."

"No problem, Ma'am."

I let myself out. Jenna is walking across the Braddingtons' expansive, expensive lawn. At the bottom, she stops to kick a beautiful blooming yellow mum, scattering bright petals across the grass. I could yell at her, but that wouldn't help. If Susan Braddington saw what she'd done, she'd probably be even more upset than she was about finding Jenna in her garage.

Back at the house, Jenna parks herself on the couch, surfing through the channels on the television.

"I'll drive you to school now. We can talk about this when your father gets home."

"There's no point in me going." Her tone is one she might use with a young child.

I sigh. "There's still an hour left."

Jenna doesn't respond. She stares at the television. I don't know what else to do. Everett will deal with her. I drive back to Mama's. I left laundry in the washing machine.

≈≈

Walking in the door with JT later, I can already hear Everett and Jenna going at it.

"What the hell is the matter with you? Answer me! Are you a frickin' zombie or something? You can't answer a simple question?"

They're in the living room. Jenna is right where I left her nearly three hours earlier. On the couch with remote in hand. Only now, there are empty glasses and dishes scattered on the coffee table. So she's moved, at least.

Jenna stares straight ahead. She pauses her movie in deference to her father, or maybe because she can't hear it above his screaming.

"Let's talk about this later, when everyone's calm," I say, clearing the dishes from the coffee table.

"Don't touch those dishes! She can get her lazy ass up and take them to the kitchen! She might not want to answer my questions, but you're not her damn maid."

At his words, Jenna gets up and picks up the only dish I'm not holding. Without looking at either of us, she goes to the kitchen.

"Yelling at her doesn't work," I say to Everett. He knows this as well as I do.

"No, you're right, it doesn't. Maybe I should beat her ass," he says, and stomps out of the room. I know he doesn't really mean that. He would never hit our children. We talked about that years ago when I was first pregnant with Jenna. Back then, it seemed so simple. We would love our little girl. She would love us. How difficult could that be?

The screen door slams behind Jenna. I watch her go and am relieved to see her settle on a swing in the backyard. She sways back and forth slowly, her feet dragging on the ground as she positions her ear buds and selects music from her phone. At least she isn't prowling the neighborhood.

I find JT in his room, lying under his bed. Only the bottoms of his feet are visible.

"Hey, what did you want to show me?" JT had been insistent that he wanted me to see something when we got home.

"Is Daddy done yelling?" His voice is muffled.

"I think so, for now. He's pretty upset."

"What about?"

"Nothing big. He's just frustrated with Jenna."

"'Cause she won't tell him why she breaks into houses?"

"What? How do you know she breaks into houses?"

JT emerges from beneath the bed. "She told me."

"She told you?"

"Yeah. I wanted to go with her, but she said that wasn't a good idea. But she brought me something once." JT goes to his closet. He pulls out a box from behind the pants and jackets hanging there. He likes to wear coats that fall below his knees, and has amassed a collection of them.

He opens the box and pulls out a hospital bracelet. He holds it up for me to see. I can just barely make out the name. *Baby boy Asher.* The bracelet belongs to the Ashers, a couple who live two houses up from us. I barely know them. I did take them some bread when they first moved in and then a set of bibs when they had their baby. They never even sent a thank you note. I guess they're busy. Both parents work, so they aren't home very much. When they were away this past summer, they hired Jenna to feed their fish and bring in their mail.

"JT, this doesn't belong to us. It's probably very special to the Ashers."

"So?" He pulls the bracelet close to him. "Jenna gave it to me. It's from a real hospital!"

I don't know what to say. Everett will go ballistic if he finds out. Why would Jenna steal their baby bracelet? Maybe the Ashers gave it to her.

I remember why I'd come to JT's room in the first place. "What was it you wanted to show me?"

JT grins and runs to his desk. He opens his backpack and pulls out a stack of papers. They're medical charts with the names cut off the top.

"Where'd you get these?"

"Mrs. Fall at school. She let me have them. I have to read them out loud to the other students." His teacher has been working on getting JT to speak in front of the other students. He flat out refuses to talk at school, only answering questions when the teacher takes him in her office or the other students are out of the room. Clever woman to use medical charts, although I have to wonder if it's ethical.

"Wow. Where'd she get those?"

"Her dad used to be a doctor. All these people were bagged and tagged a long time ago."

"Do the charts explain how they died?"

"Nope. They're just boring exam notes. Some are hard to read, but Mrs. Fall is explaining cursive to me."

"What did the other students think?"

JT shrugs. "I don't know. I wasn't watching them."

"I'm really proud of you for reading out loud." I give him a hug. "Dinner will be ready soon."

"What kind of macaroni?"

"Probably the wheels."

JT smiles. Food is another issue with him. He only eats pasta at dinner. I've gotten pretty good at hiding various forms of proteins in the accompanying sauce. There was a time when the pasta could only have butter on it. Breakfast is always oatmeal with brown sugar. Lunch is a cream cheese and jelly sandwich. I've long ago given up trying to force other options on him. The doctor says that's all right because everything is enriched these days. I've got bigger battles. Like keeping him in the regular public school. We can't afford the private school he belongs in.

After dinner, Everett takes my hand and leads me out to the porch swing. It's been our nightly ritual since we attended couples counseling last year. In the beginning, it felt stilted, but now I look forward to this time. I like hearing about Everett's day. Tonight, though, I'm anxious to check on Mama. She's been more agitated than usual lately. Still, I want to know what Everett found out at the police department.

"So, Georgie told me that Susan Braddington called them. Apparently, she pulled in just as Jenna was starting to climb out of the cat door. She drove the car bumper right up against the door, trapping Jenna. She could have killed her! Stupid woman. She claims she couldn't tell that she was a kid."

"We can't blame her. What was Jenna doing in their garage?"

Everett makes a face. "You really believe she was only in the garage?"

"She hasn't said otherwise."

"She hasn't said anything!"

"You shouldn't scream at her."

"Jesus Christ, Kate! Are you just going to blindly defend her until she's locked up in juvie? We have to do something! Take something away; punish her in some way. We can't just act like it didn't happen. She needs to answer for this."

"What do you propose?"

"I think we should tell her we're going to take her to a shrink if she doesn't start talking to us."

"She'd never talk to a shrink!"

"Exactly."

Everett is good with plans. I don't have any better ideas, so I agree.

JENNA
≈≈

It was stupid to get caught, but Mrs. B believed me when I said I hadn't been inside. I watched her check the alarm system. She really believes it keeps people from just walking into her house. Stupid woman. That must be where Tiffany gets it.

After dinner, I walk down to Ms. Cassie's place to visit her cats. She isn't home, but she never is. She works with dead people. Actually, people about to be dead. She's a hospice nurse. Why would anyone want that job?

Ms. Cassie has seven cats. I asked her once what their names were and she said, "Oh, they don't have names. I don't want to get too attached." I wonder if she doesn't bother with her patients' names either.

I named the cats after the seven dwarfs. Dopey's my favorite. He's black and white like a cow. He actually comes when I call him. Ms. Cassie doesn't usually lock her back door, and tonight I walk right in. I find the tuna in the pantry. There are three cases in there. I don't know why Ms. Cassie doesn't buy regular cat food. That would be a lot cheaper. I grab four cans and take them back outside. They all share pretty well, except Doc. I have to give him his own can, or he'll chase the others away and eat it all himself.

I hang out with the cats and look up my homework on the school website with my phone. Not much. A few math problems, a few more chapters of *Grapes of Wrath* (which I already read). Quiz tomorrow in bio. I won't have to fake my own note either, because Mom already said she'd write an excuse note. She doesn't want to get a call from the truancy officer again. That guy is some kind of grumpy.

It's dark when I head home. I have to wait until Everett's in his room on his computer and Mom and JT are streaming the latest *Grey's Anatomy*. I walk straight up the middle of the street. The moon is full, big, and yellow, so it's easy to see where I'm going. As I get to our end of the street, the houses are further apart so it's even darker. I'm almost to our place when I hear a movement in the bushes next to the Ashers' house. It's not an animal. I freeze and listen. The movement stops.

I can hear my own heart beating. I'm thinking whether I should make a run for it or wait to see who it is. Finally, a shadow steps out of the bushes.

"Hey, Jenna."

It's Wells.

"Hey," I say. What the hell is he doing out here? He should be up there in his perfect house with his perfect family working on his perfect SAT scores so he can go to the perfect school and get a perfect life.

"Heard you broke into our garage today."

I'm tempted to correct him and tell him I actually broke into his house, but I don't want to incriminate myself, so I don't.

"I was looking for a screwdriver."

"Right," he says, and steps closer. He really is hot. I'm not saying that because I'm a typical stupid girl who likes jocks like Wells or anything. He's just really good looking in the classical sense. Like if there was a definition in the dictionary for the words "hot guy," Wells could be the picture they'd use. He actually has razor stubble and his sandy blond hair, even at this hour, is tousled just right, like some salon chick sprayed it into that position. Maybe she did. I don't know Wells so well. Ha. More alliteration! Well (again!), actually they're homonyms.

"Whatever," I say and start to leave. Hot as he is, he's giving me the creeps.

"Wait! You don't have to go."

"You want me to stay?" That would be bizarre.

"Sure," he says. "I had to get out of my house. My dad wouldn't shut up about Harvard."

"You're going to Harvard?" I knew Wells was pretty smart. He's in a bunch of AP classes, including my English, but I didn't know he was that smart.

Wells shrugs. "That's where my dad went so he wants me to go there. The only way I get in is as a legacy student and that'll be a stretch if my SAT scores don't improve."

"Do you want to go to Harvard?"

Wells shrugs again.

"Where are you going to go?" he asks.

I laugh. "Me? I'll be lucky to get into HACC." HACC is our local community college.

"Why do you think that? You're smart."

This time I shrug. "I don't go to class much."

"I thought you just had some kind of medical condition."

I laugh. "Yeah, I'm allergic to school."

"School's not so bad."

"The building's fine. It's the people I hate."

"That's kind of harsh."

"Can't be helped. If they weren't so stupid, I might feel differently."

"Does that mean you hate me?"

I put my hand to my chin and look him up and down, like I'm thinking about it. "Maybe."

He laughs. It's a nice laugh, not the one I hear him use when he's in the back of my English class with his football buddies. It's softer.

We see the approaching headlights of a car at the far end of the road.

"See ya around," I tell him. I gotta get back and walk Marco. Marco's my dog who is mostly deaf and nearly blind. Everett hates him because, just like his kids, Marco's not living up to Everett's expectations for a good pet. He can't chase a ball he doesn't see. I've tried to tell Everett this, but he still tosses tennis balls for Marco and gets annoyed that he doesn't fetch them. Sometimes he runs in the general direction of the throw, but he rarely makes contact with the ball.

"Yeah," says Wells, trotting up the perfectly manicured lawn of his house. "See ya in English."

KATE

≈≈

I'm exhausted. I've listened to JT dissect the entire episode of *Grey's Anatomy* we just watched—pointing out the inconsistencies and blatant mistakes. Even though we've watched probably dozens of episodes by now, it still bothers him that the surgeons don't wear goggles like they would in real life. Today's episode was yet another rare brain surgery and JT is practically shrieking in frustration. I try to get him to speak at a reasonable level. It's a constant battle, but the more excited he gets, the louder he gets.

I know Everett is downstairs in the kitchen, probably fuming over Jenna. The last thing he needs is JT complaining about everything the surgeons did wrong in a high shrill, voice loud enough to be heard up and down the street. Even after JT has gone through his bedtime routine (brush teeth, take bath, line up shoes and socks for tomorrow, pet Marco, feed his fish, and pull his shade—in that order), he can't settle down and needs to run through the entire episode's failures once again. I'm trying to be patient. I know he has to do this or he'll never go to sleep, but I'm distracted knowing that Everett is waiting downstairs for Jenna with his grand plan to rein her in. Threaten her with the psychologist, and meanwhile instill a curfew that I'm fairly certain she won't follow, and that can't be enforced because most nights Everett works late and won't be here to do it and I'll be at Mama's putting her to bed.

After JT goes to bed, I join Everett in the kitchen. The dishwasher is running, but the sink is piled with dirty pans from dinner. I set to work on them, and Everett recounts for me his frustration with Jenna.

"It's like she just doesn't care. I don't understand that. She has it so good. When I was a kid, my dad would beat my ass if I pulled a stunt like she did today. And why did she do it anyway? It's like she wants to cause trouble. She wants to piss me off."

"I don't think she did it to make you angry," I say, but Everett can't hear me and he continues.

"I'm so fucking sick of her shit. She takes everything for granted. Maybe it's time we took a few privileges away. Her whole generation thinks they're entitled to whatever the hell they want and screw the rest of us. There's no respect. That's the bottom line. She has no respect for anyone."

I know he has a point, but at the same time, I don't think Jenna is disrespectful. She's a thoughtful child. Always has been. Maybe the real problem is that she has no friends. When she was little, I scheduled playdates every weekend, but ever since middle school—when it became taboo for your mom to set up playdates—she's been by herself all the time. I've tried to encourage her, but she claims she doesn't like any of the kids at her school. That seems impossible. There must be some nice children there. I worry that she's lonely and her acting out today was a plea for attention. Maybe I need to spend more time with her.

When Jenna comes in, I try to focus on finishing up the dishes and stay out of it. Everett is at the table with his arms crossed. Jenna doesn't make eye contact with either of us. She opens the refrigerator and takes out an apple. Her pointed nonchalance is baiting Everett. She grabs Marco's leash from the hook.

"I'm just gonna take Marco out," she says, snapping the leash on Marco, who has been tailing her around the kitchen. He is devoted to Jenna and, even though he can't hear anything and his vision is going, he seems able to sense her presence. He can be sound asleep in the living room, but will leap to his feet and sprint for the kitchen the moment Jenna appears.

"Hold on just a minute, young lady." I cringe at his tone and I see Jenna's shoulders clench. I wish that Everett could hear himself. He talks to Jenna like she's still six years old, but she's sixteen now and sometimes it feels like she's already got one foot out the door.

"I'll be right back," she says, opening the door. Everett stands up and strides for the door, slamming it and narrowly missing Marco's pointy nose, which was already headed out.

"Before you disappear again, we need to talk."

Jenna rolls her eyes. She leans against the wall and crosses her arms. "So talk," she says. Marco sits at her feet and watches her with his blurry eyes. I can't help but smile at his devotion.

"Let's all sit down," I say, pulling out a chair for Jenna and reaching for the jar of dog biscuits on the counter. I give two biscuits to Marco and sit down next to Jenna.

Everett lets out an exaggerated sigh and sits down across from us. I try to shoot him a warning glance. I wish he could explain his plan without talking down to Jenna. He presents plans all day at work. Plans for keeping people safe and buildings secure. They love him at FABSO. Being a former police officer, he's well-versed in the criminal mind and is an expert at adapting security plans in light of new threats. That's what this is to him—a new threat. Getting Jenna to behave is as simple to him as a good plan. He's probably already put together a power point in his head. I've always admired that about him, how he can see things so clearly. He's certain he knows how to fix this.

"I'm guessing that this isn't the first time you've been in the Braddingtons' home," he says.

Jenna looks up at him, raises her eyebrows in acknowledgment, but says nothing.

"How'd you get in?"

Jenna picks at her nails. She reaches down and scratches Marco, who has finished his dog biscuits and is intently gazing in my direction, hoping for another. She shrugs. "It was easy. The box is in the garage."

"Did you re-alarm their system?"

She nods.

"What'd you take?"

"Nothing."

"I don't understand," I say. "Why would you break into their home?"

"'Cause I can."

"But you were supposed to be in school!"

"School's stupid."

"I've had about enough of this attitude of yours," says Everett, his voice rising. "You are not to cut another day of school."

Jenna lets out a snort and shakes her head.

"You think we can't make you go?" asks Everett, leaning towards Jenna. I want to pull him back. Can't he see how threatening he is? Everett is such a large presence. Years of weightlifting give him a bulk that intimidates, even if much of it has gone soft as he's aged.

"You can't," says Jenna. Her face is unreadable. Why does she always have to taunt Everett? And why does he always have to try to force her to behave? They never used to fight like this. When Jenna was young she adored her father. And he thought her the prettiest, smartest child ever. She followed him around when he was home, asking him questions about his day. She probably knows more about what Everett does at FABSO than I do.

I think she's been angry at him ever since that woman. I've tried to explain to her that husband and wife relationships are complicated and that Everett and I love each other and I've forgiven him, but when I tell her this, she looks at me like *I'm* the child. As if she knows more than

I do. I know it's simply the confidence of being a teenager. I remember thinking I knew more than my own mother did, too.

"Oh, I think we can. 'Cause if that truancy officer pays us another visit, you're going to find yourself going to juvie. I've been in that place. They lock you in and you stay in. I made a few calls today. Found out we don't even have to wait for the truancy officer. We can commit you *ourselves*."

Jenna looks up at this, alarmed. I do, too. What is Everett thinking? We didn't talk about juvie. We talked about a psychologist. We are not going to put Jenna in juvie. I watch as Jenna forces disinterest, taking a bite of her apple and reaching down to pat Marco again. I truly can't believe he would really put her in the juvenile detention center. God knows what kind of kids are in there.

"You done?" asks Jenna.

"For now," says Everett, smiling smugly.

Jenna gets up and takes Marco out.

"You wouldn't really lock up our daughter?" I ask the moment she is gone.

"I would. I've had about enough of her self-righteous bullcrap. She needs to learn a lesson. It might be the best thing for her."

"She could get hurt in there—even raped. I won't let you do it. What about the psychologist?"

"Kate, you need to let me handle this. You are too easy on her. I've thought about it, and talking to some shrink isn't going to change anything. What she needs is some discipline."

"I won't allow it. There has to be a better plan. Maybe we all need some space. Maybe she could go live with Mama. She could help me with her. Maybe what she needs is more attention and some responsibilities. They could be good for each other."

Everett laughs. "Oh, that's a great plan! Then she'd be free to shake down the entire street and flunk out entirely while she makes your mother lose her mind even faster. What she needs is a firmer hand, not more freedom."

"She's not a little girl anymore. I worry if you keep threatening her, you'll push her away."

Everett shakes his head. "You're always too soft on her. That's half the problem. She knows she can run right over you."

I open the dishwasher to let the steam out, and begin wiping the counters. Everett doesn't say anything more. I glance at him checking his phone for email messages. He smiles at one and I wonder if it is from a woman. I feel sick to my stomach at the thought.

Everett sees me watching him and I turn back to my work, lining up the sugar and flour canisters neatly against the backsplash. He gets up and stands behind me, one hand on my waist, the other hand massaging my shoulder. "Ready for bed?" he asks. He kisses my neck. How does he switch gears so quickly? I'm still worrying about Jenna, wondering what I will say to her when she comes back in. "Hmmm?" he murmurs in my ear. I feel something inside of me give out. I'm too tired to fight with him. He'd never put our daughter in Juvie. He's just trying to make a point.

Later, after we've made love, I lie awake staring at the swirls in the plaster ceiling. Why do I still doubt him? He loves me. This can't work if I don't believe him, trust him. Hasn't he just shown me how much he loves me? He promised it would never happen again. And I do believe him. I have to.

≈≈

In the morning, I'm surprised to find Jenna at the breakfast table. Maybe Everett was right. Maybe she does need a firmer hand.

"Good morning," I say, touching her on the shoulder as I pass.

Jenna says nothing. She's reading the paper and eating cereal. Marco sits patiently at her feet, waiting for her to give him the milk in her cereal bowl when she's finished. The dog is as round as a barrel. All the table scraps can't be good for him.

"I'm headed over to Mama's. JT is sorting his socks. If he comes down, will you remind him that I'll be back by seven?"

Jenna nods, without lifting her head.

≈≈

Later that morning, I walk JT to his classroom, but don't hold his hand, which causes him to twitch and brush against me repeatedly.

When we reach the classroom, I turn to him. "I'm so proud of you JT. See? You don't need to hold my hand! We'll try it like this again tomorrow."

"It didn't feel right, though."

"That's okay, the important thing is you did it."

While JT begins his morning rituals, I pull his teacher, Mrs. Fall, aside and ask if it would be all right if I stay to hear JT read his charts. He was up early this morning practicing, and I know he's excited about reading them to the class.

"Of course, that would be fine," she says, but I can tell she isn't thrilled about it. I switch off the ringer on my phone and hang my purse in one of the cubbies. I wave to JT who smiles at me as he arranges his pencils and books on his desk.

There are only three other children about JT's age in the classroom. I'm disappointed to see that two are definitely nowhere near as high functioning as JT. A girl with red curly hair pulled back in a haphazard ponytail rocks in her chair and stares at a mobile hung strategically near an air vent. The brightly colored birds twirl in circles each time the fan clicks on.

Another child, presumably a girl, but the hair is cut so short it's hard to tell, wears a helmet complete with facemask. She wanders on a repeated path in the back of the room, muttering to herself. The only other child is Tucker. JT calls Tucker his friend, but that only means that he doesn't scream at Tucker if he sits too close to him. I've tried to contact Tucker's family to arrange a few playdates, but haven't had any luck so far.

Tucker lives with a grandmother who doesn't drive. Tucker's Asperger's is pretty mild. He is obsessed with space travel, chews his nails completely off when he is anxious, and talks overly loud, like JT. It's rumored that he will be mainstreamed after Christmas. I want that for JT, also, even though I worry about the other children. Most of the time, JT doesn't realize that they make fun of him, but as he approaches adolescence, he seems to be reading their behaviors more. I know it's a good sign that he's paying attention to other children, but it means he might get his feelings hurt, too.

When it's JT's turn to read, he smiles at me and follows Mrs. Fall to the front of the room. She motions for him to turn to face the other students, which is basically just me and Tucker as the other girl has gotten up now and is standing in front of the bird mobile while the other child continues to wander in the back of the room. JT holds the paper up in front of his face, blocking his view of us, and reads. For once, his voice isn't blasting and at times it even seems to carry some inflection. He has no trouble with complicated medical terms, reeling them off like a doctor. When he is finished, Mrs. Fall prompts him and he says, "Any questions?"

Tucker and I are the only ones watching him. Tucker shakes his head, and says loudly, "I have no questions." He probably knows a lot about medical terms since he listens to JT recite them every day at lunch. JT looks expectantly at the back of the room where the wandering student has increased her pace and is now waving her hands next to her ears.

I can't help myself. I raise my hand. JT's eyes grow large and he points at me. "What's your question?" he bellows.

"When a chart says that a 'CBC' was ordered, what does that mean?"

"You know that," says JT flatly.

"But everyone else doesn't," I say and nod towards the girl with the mobile.

"CBC. Complete blood count. An all-purpose blood test used to diagnose different illnesses and conditions."

"Oh," says his teacher. "How interesting."

"And what about 'NPO,' what does that mean?" I ask.

"NPO. Nothing by mouth. The letters don't match because it's actually from the Latin, *nil per os.*"

I smile. My smart boy. I'm about to ask about ALOC, but Mrs. Fall cuts me off.

"Very well done, JT. Now, let's hear from Tucker."

I suffer through Tucker's slow monotone recitation of an old newspaper article about Apollo 13. It seems to go on for hours. When he finishes, I clap more out of relief than appreciation, which makes the redhead still staring at the mobile begin to wail.

Mrs. Fall escorts me to the door. JT gets up from his seat and rushes over to hug me good-bye. I remember the pediatrician who first diagnosed JT. He said that JT might never be affectionate in the traditional manner, but he was wrong. JT is more than affectionate. He hugs me several times a day, sometimes even when I'm only leaving the room to go start dinner.

"You have a good day. I'll see you this afternoon," I tell him.

"You have a good day. I'll see you this afternoon," he recites back and then laughs. He finds mimicking to be hilarious. It's the only thing that makes Jenna lose patience with him. Otherwise, she's amazing with him; almost over-protective, really.

When I get in the car, I notice I've had seven voice mails from Everett and ten from my sister Evelyn. What? This can't be good. I dial Evelyn's number.

"Where the hell are you?" Evelyn screams.

"At JT's school, why?"

"You can't answer your phone?"

"They make us turn the ringer off when we're in the classroom. What is it? What happened?"

"Oh, nothing, just Mother almost burned her whole house down."

"What?"

"No worries. It's under control. Luckily a neighbor saw the smoke and called 9-1-1."

"Is she okay?"

"She's fine. She ran outside to rescue her birds. When the firemen got there, she was stumbling around on the deck shooing birds that weren't even there. They had to drag her out of the yard."

"And the house?"

"Mostly it's smoke damage. She turned on the teakettle but forget to put water in it. Burned the bottom off of it, but there doesn't look to be any real damage other than the stove and the microwave above it."

"Thank God." I'll have to start unplugging the stove whenever I leave. Mama rarely tries to do anything for herself anymore. It's not that she can't; I'm pretty sure she simply prefers to be dependent on me. Evelyn thinks we should put her in a home, and this latest episode will likely make her even more determined. Heaven forbid Evelyn take any time out of her day for her mother.

"Look, I've got to get back to court. Can you meet her at the hospital?" asks Evelyn.

"They took her in? I thought she was okay."

"She was screaming and rambling about the birds. They had to put her in restraints and sedate her. I think they just took her in to cover their butts."

"I'll meet her there. What about the house?"

"Can't Everett deal with that?"

We've been over this, but Evelyn likes to conveniently forget the fact that Everett will no longer have anything to do with Mama or her house. It's my fault, really. Mama has told me since the day I married Everett that he will leave me. And, in a weak moment, I told her about Everett cheating on me with that woman Charlene. I was upset and I didn't have anyone else to talk to. Besides, Mama's been through it herself; I thought she might be more sympathetic. One of the very few facts I know about my father is that he cheated on my mother before he walked out of our lives.

Mama had seemed almost giddy when I told her about Everett and Charlene, and now every time she sees Everett, she can't help but remind him of his mistake. The last time he went to her house to fix a broken toilet, she held her tongue until he was leaving.

"There you go, Ma'am, all fixed up," he said as he slammed his toolbox. She stood in the doorway watching him like he was one of those prisoners on the side of the road cleaning up trash in an orange jumpsuit.

She didn't say anything as he sidled past her in the doorway.

"Thanks, babe," I said and kissed his cheek.

He was almost out the door, when Mama muttered, "How dare you cheat on my daughter!"

"Excuse me?" said Everett, hand on the door and I thought, *Just leave, just leave, just leave.* But he didn't.

"I can hardly stand to look at you. You're a louse, just like him." This time her voice had found its footing and she leveled her eyes at him, daring him to disagree.

Louse is what she's always called my father. As in, "If it weren't for that louse, I wouldn't be trapped in this tiny house on this miserable street." Mama moved to Pine Estates soon after we moved here, but she couldn't afford one of the new houses and had to settle for the cozy rancher Evelyn's real estate agent was selling.

"Gee, Mildred, you're welcome. Next time call a plumber!" Everett slammed the door as he left and a picture fell from the wall. The nail that held it clattered after it, bouncing across the hardwood floor and coming to rest in the fringe of Mama's area rug. We both stared at it.

I know I can't ask Everett to help with Mama's house. He's made it clear he won't budge on the issue. Early last spring, I tried to convince him to take a look at her furnace and he refused, even though it meant me lugging space heaters over there to keep her warm until the repairman could come out.

"You know she's just saying to you all the things she wishes she could say to my father," I explained.

"But I'm not your father," he'd insisted.

"She can't help it. She's still hurt. When she's yelling at you, you *are* him. Can't you just see it that way and ignore her?"

"No, I cannot. That was forty years ago! It's about time she moved on."

"Please. It's not so easy for her."

"I won't go over there. She says these things in front of our kids. Again and again. Pretty soon they're going to believe it."

I don't know why he can't get past this. *Is he still cheating?* Is that why he can't dismiss Mama's ramblings?

"You know Everett won't have anything to do with Mama's house," I tell Evelyn.

"Well, maybe he could make an exception since she won't be in it."

"I'll ask him, but what if he says no?"

"Jesus, Kate, what is he, like two? Ask him to be a grown up."

"That's not fair!"

"Fine. If you can't handle this, I'll call somebody. See if I can get them out there today. Don't bother precious

Everett. Wouldn't want him to go out of his way for family or anything!"

"He's not like that!" I insist, but Evelyn has hung up. I put the car in drive and head for the hospital.

JENNA
≈≈

Tiffany and Wells were on the bus this morning, which was weird. Maybe his car is in the shop. At the bus stop, Tiffany didn't look at me. She spent the entire time texting on her phone. Wells said, "Hey," and then ignored me. The only other person who gets on at our stop is a seventh grader. She's usually there ten minutes early. I don't know her name, but she lives in the brick house next door to Wells and Tiffany. They moved in about a year ago. They have a fenced yard and a nasty dog, so I've never been in their place. It's not that I'm afraid of the dog. Dogs like me. But her grandmother lives there with them and is always home. At the bus stop, the girl-whose-name-I-don't-know always has earbuds in and never makes eye contact. She doesn't talk to Tiffany or Wells either, so I don't take it personally.

The bus finally shows up and Wells motions all of us to get on before him. Such the gentleman, right? I sit in the middle, behind two girls who giggle through the whole ride. Their conversation is too stupid to even bother listening to. Most everybody is either looking at their phones or listening to music, so the ride is generally quiet, except the two idiots in front of me. Because Wells is gracing the bus with his presence today, there's a ruckus in the back where he is welcomed with guy-talk and testosterone-charged goofing off. The driver actually stops the bus at one point and glares at them. They only laugh.

45

The bio quiz is easy. School is stupid. As always. I cut out after lunch. It's only two miles to our street from the school, so I walk home.

When I get to our neighborhood, I have to walk in backyards because I just never know when my mom will be driving back and forth to Gram's house. Gram lives near the beginning of the street in the old part. I think about stopping in. She never asks why I'm not in school. Probably because she's basically not all there anymore. And if she did, all I'd have to do is distract her by saying something like, "Hey, isn't that a new bird on your big feeder?" and she'd be off on a monologue about the exciting lives of the birds in her backyard. I really hope that isn't what I have to look forward to when I'm old.

Some days Gram is really sad. She says nobody cares about her and she'd be better off dead. Sad shit like that. It's depressing. She's all alone all the time, besides my mom. Aunt Evelyn hardly ever comes to see her anymore. She and Gram had a big fight last Fourth of July. It was something about my grandpa, whom I've never met. He took off when Mom and Aunt Evelyn were kids. Apparently, he contacted Aunt Evelyn last spring and she's been talking to him.

When I asked Mom about him, she said, "He isn't a part of our lives." End of story. Everett got mad when I said I wanted to meet him. So talking about him is taboo. I plan to quiz Aunt Evelyn about him when I see her at Thanksgiving. I wouldn't mind having a new grandpa. Maybe he wouldn't be as nuts as the rest of my family. Maybe there's a reason he took off.

We don't see Evelyn very much. She's a big-time attorney and lives about an hour away, out in the ritzy part of the county. She divorced my Uncle Josh when I was pretty young. I don't know what happened to him. Aunt Evelyn says he wasn't "husband material." Whatever that means.

As I approach Gram's house, I see a firetruck and some firemen on her porch. Her front garden has been trampled.

Mom always plants it with mums this time of year, as if Gram is ever going to go out there and see them. For the past year, she's refused to leave the house except to go out the back door to see her birds. And even then she can't see anything because she had this crazy ten-foot solid fence built around it. I did say the woman is nuts.

I need to be sure Gram is all right, so I talk to the fireman. I tell them I'm her granddaughter.

"Yeah, old lady made it out. Burned the bottom out of a teakettle. House is fine except a little smoke damage and the stovetop. Microwave above it might be toast, too."

"Is she in there?" I ask.

They shake their heads. "Ambulance took her to Mercy. She was pretty worked up. They had to sedate her."

I can imagine Gram was freaking out. I call Mom to make sure Gram is really okay.

"How did you find out?" asks Mom.

"It doesn't matter. Is Gram okay?"

I hear Mom sigh. Gram must be fine. "She's going to be fine. She's resting now and they want to watch her overnight."

"I bet she won't be happy about that."

"Probably not, but they know how to handle these things. You need to get back to class."

"I will. The bell hasn't rung yet. Is Aunt Evelyn there?"

"She went to the house when it happened, but she had to get to work."

"Is Dad there?"

"No."

"So, you're there by yourself?"

"I am, but it's fine."

"I could come."

"No, you couldn't, because you can't miss anymore school. Now get to class!"

"Jeez, okay, I'm going."

"Jenna?"

47

"Yeah?"

"Thanks for wanting to be here."

I don't say anything. My mom can be all right sometimes.

"Yeah, okay, see ya."

I hang up. Now I feel kind of guilty for cutting out of school. But nothing else was going to happen. English class is a snoozer. Gym is pointless, and the teacher in Intro to Sociology won't even notice I'm not there. He said at the beginning of the semester, "With this being last period, I'm sure many of you involved in sports will be missing class periodically. I won't count that against you, but you're responsible for getting the assignments and completing anything you miss."

I told him I'm a cheerleader. I figure that'll cover me all year. I do have to be more careful, though. I think Everett is just a blowhard, but you never know. He was a cop and he's got connections. He might just send me to juvie if it came down to it.

I decide to go see Ms. Cassie's cats. I've been there like fifteen minutes and I'm lying in the grass watching them eat their tuna when Ms. Cassie opens the back door. Wow, she's sneakier than I am.

"Hello, Jenna," she says, as if she didn't just catch me snooping in her yard and feeding her cats, which she must know means I've been inside her house.

I look up, but don't move. I never want adults to think they scare me. 'Cause they don't.

"They were hungry," I say, nodding at the cats.

"Thanks for feeding them." She sits down at the little metal table on her porch.

After a while, the silence feels weird so I say, "Aren't you usually at work?"

She smiles. Pushes her hair back off her forehead. "I needed a break. Aren't you usually at school?"

Touché.

"I needed a break," I tell her.

We both watch Sneezy cough up a hairball.

I've always been curious about Ms. Cassie's work. Mom says she's a hospice nurse, which means she watches people die every day. That seems pretty sick.

"What's it like when someone dies?" I ask.

She looks at me and takes a deep breath. She picks a few dead leaves off the plant on the table in front of her. "What do you mean?"

"I don't know. Do they cry? Does it hurt? Does something happen when they die—like in the movies when there's a big whoosh of air or something?"

She smiles. Shakes her head. "It's pretty rare that the patient cries. It's my job to help them with the pain, but it's not always possible." She grimaces.

"Do they know they're going to die?"

"By the time I'm involved, that's the general consensus."

"Isn't that pretty depressing?"

She sighs again. "That's not what it's about. It's not about me. I'm there to help the patient die as well as they can. And I'm there to help the family accept that and be a part of the patient's care."

"Wow. I bet you've seen some pretty gruesome shit."

She laughs when I say this. "I have seen some pretty gruesome shit."

She doesn't say any more. Maybe she saw some gruesome shit today and that's why she needed a break. I get up from the grass.

"I like your cats," I say.

"I can tell," she says.

"See ya."

She waves, but doesn't move. It's kind of cool that she didn't care that I was there. She didn't freak out like stupid Mrs. Braddington. I should go over there today just because I can. I would, except I don't much feel like it anymore. Between Gram's accident and thinking about

Ms. Cassie's depressing job, I'm feeling kind of bummed. I go home and flip on my favorite show, *Merlin*. I stream episodes until Everett comes home. He had to pick up JT since Mom's at the hospital. This should be good. JT doesn't like change in his routine, which is pretty much the biggest understatement of this exciting day.

KATE

≈≈

My phone rings at 4:35 p.m. Everett. This can't be good. I glance at Mama; she's sleeping. There's a small trickle of drool rolling down her chin. I use a tissue to wipe it away before answering my phone in a whisper.

"Hey, everything okay?" I know it isn't, or Everett wouldn't be calling. Out the window, I watch as a custodian rolls a dolly loaded with orange bags of medical waste to a waiting truck. Just being in the building, observing the daily ebb and flow of a hospital, calms me. I miss the hospital. It feels more like home than home. I know when Mama finally wakes all hell will break loose. This makes the quiet feel rare and delicate. This morning in JT's classroom seems like days ago. I hear JT now in the background as Everett speaks. He's having one of his tantrums.

"No, everything is not okay! He's flipping out! All I did was tell him he could have cereal instead of a blueberry Pop-Tart for a snack."

I'd planned to go to the grocery store today. I knew we were running out of Pop-Tarts. JT's whine turns to tears.

"Let me talk to him."

I'm helpless as I listen to Everett shout at JT. "Here! Your mother wants to speak with you. Stop crying! It's your mother!" There's a commotion and then JT's sobs grow louder.

"He won't take the phone. I can't deal with this shit. When are you coming home?"

51

I've never understood why he can't be a little more patient with JT. He was a police officer, for heaven's sake. That's a profession that requires mountains of patience.

"Try again," I say evenly. I know he's doing the best he can. I can picture the scene at home. JT is probably lying on the tile floor under the breakfast bar with his hands over his ears, sobbing and kicking his feet at anyone who comes near.

"He won't let me near him."

"You'll just have to wait it out then. He'll calm down. Is Jenna home?"

"Yeah, she's comatose on the couch watching her stupid show."

"See if she can help."

"Doubt she can leave her little self-absorbed bubble to assist me here, but I'll ask."

He hangs up without saying good-bye. The hospital seems even quieter. I listen to the steady breathing of my mother.

JENNA
≈≈

Of course JT flipped out. You'd think after twelve years with the kid, Everett would understand that. It's almost like he wants to pretend that JT is normal, and when he does something like this, he acts like it's such a big surprise. JT drives me crazy too sometimes; but he's my little brother, right? Can't change that. Besides, he's so frickin' smart and funny. Other kids think he's weird because he talks in this loud, high voice and uses medical slang, but they just don't get it. They are so stupid. I'm fairly certain that JT and I are Everett's biggest disappointments in life. I'm sure he'd rather be with his girlfriend than here dealing with this.

This afternoon I discovered that Everett's sleeping with some chick he met on the Internet. It wasn't hard to figure out. Our whole family shares one computer because Everett is too cheap to spring for laptops. Sucks for him. I guess he's never heard of "history." I was really just checking to see if he'd actually talked to anybody who works at juvie, which of course he hasn't. It's easy to figure out what he's up to and for a security "professional" he's pretty dumb about his passwords. His emails made me gag.

I go into the kitchen not because Everett is asking me to, but because JT needs me. JT is scrunched up under the counter, holding his ears and wailing. I sit down beside him, he leans in to me and his crying gets quieter. I play a game of Sudoku on my phone while I wait for him to come back from that crazy place he goes to when he can't deal with what is happening in front of him. It's weird that he does this. When he's fine, he's fine. He's cool for a little kid. When he freaks out like he does, people think he's retarded or something, but he's smarter than most people I know. Certainly smarter than Everett, who has gone upstairs to find Tylenol because he now has a headache. He says this like it's JT's fault. He's probably going up there to send another gross email to his gross girlfriend.

After a while, JT lays his head on my shoulder and stops crying. "You wanna play?" I ask him, handing him my phone. He takes it. I love watching him solve the Sudoku in like three seconds. It's crazy how smart he is.

KATE

≈≈

When Mama wakes later, she panics, pulling at the restraints that Evelyn insisted were necessary and looking at me with wild eyes. The frail, frightened woman in the bed bears no resemblance to the mama I grew up with. I pat her hand and whisper, "It's okay, Mama, it's going to be okay," the same way she'd comfort me when I was small and would come home from school in tears because someone had left me out—again. I've never been very good at finding friends. Maybe I depended on Mama too much back then.

I'd come home from school and she'd be there—always—waiting for me, with a snack set out on the counter. She'd listen to the details of my day at PS 46 Middle School, which in truth must have bored her to death. I told her of the pop quiz in social studies or the mean girl who teased me in gym class. Later I would sit at the counter and do my homework as she cooked dinner. She always managed to time dinner to be ready the moment the activity bus rumbled down our street and deposited Evelyn at the end of the drive.

She'd ask Evelyn about her sports, but Evelyn always seemed annoyed at Mama's interest. It didn't deter Mama. She'd ignore Evelyn's sharpness and, eventually, Evelyn would tell her about the game or the practice, knowing the interrogation would continue until she did. It occurs to me that Evelyn, Mama, and I have been playing the same roles all our lives.

I suppose we have always been Mama's world. It was only later, when we became teenagers, that her oddity as a mother became clear. We never went to neighborhood Christmas parties or attended church. We never went to amusement parks or hosted a Fourth of July cookout. Relatives didn't come to visit, although we had an uncle who used to send us each five dollars on our birthdays.

I tuck Mama's blanket under her quivering chin and she closes her eyes.

I guess I was like most kids. I didn't think of my mother as a person, just Mama. To my mind, she had no other life beyond us and, for the most part, that was true. That's what Evelyn doesn't appreciate. Mama's life revolved around us completely. When our father left, she shut out everything in the world except us. We became her world. And now that her mental health is failing, Evelyn just wants to park her in some care facility and forget about her.

Recently, Evelyn's been in touch with our father. I don't know how she found him or why she wants to invite him back into our lives. Mama is the one who was there for us. Mama is the one who gave up everything to raise us.

A cart rattles down the corridor and Mama's eyes open again. She furrows her brows and scans the room, her mind trying to catch up with the events of the morning. She seems even frailer here, swallowed by the whiteness of the room. I touch her shoulder. "It's okay, Mama."

"Where am I?" she cries, whipping her head back and forth.

"In the hospital, remember? There was an accident at the house."

Her eyes rest on the IV in her arm. "That seems unnecessary. I feel fine. I want to go home."

"I'll get the nurse." Mama was a nurse herself. It will be better if a nurse tells her that they're keeping her overnight.

"Hello, Mrs. Watts. Glad to have you back with us!"

"I don't want to be with you at all. I want to go home. Right now!" she says.

"Let's see how that blood pressure is doing." The nurse fastens a cuff around her arm.

"You don't need to make all this fuss. I'm fine, but I have to get home. The birds need me!"

"The birds will be fine, Mama. They can take care of themselves."

"But they'll wonder where I am. I need to go."

The nurse looks at me with raised eyebrows. "My, your blood pressure is a bit elevated Mrs. Watts. I'm just going to give you something for your nerves." The nurse pulls a new bag off her cart and attaches it to Mama's IV.

"I don't want anything! I want to go home!" Mama struggles to free her arms from the restraints. "Katie, get me out of here. Why are they holding me here? What have I done?"

"It's okay. They just want to keep you here for a little while to be sure you're okay."

"But I am okay."

"You breathed in a lot of smoke."

"No, I didn't! Don't be silly."

"Mama, do you remember what happened this morning at the house?"

She looks confused, embarrassed that she doesn't remember.

I pat her arm and readjust her blankets. "Just rest and let them take care of you."

"What about my birds?"

"I could go and check on them," I offer.

"I guess you'll have to if I'm a prisoner here." She sounds defeated, the air gone out of her. "Be sure that Major has plenty of peanut butter on his perch. And refill the bird bath. There've been some crows coming in at night and making a mess of things."

"I will," I tell her, pulling on my sweater. I lean over and kiss her head. "Sleep now."

When I get to the house, I'm surprised that there's only a faint scent of smoke left. Efficient Evelyn has already gotten the place cleaned. There is a note on the counter with their card and a receipt for the new stove. The microwave will need to be replaced. Another chore.

I'm not really here to check on the birds. Birds don't need me or Mama to take care of them. They can take care of themselves. I just need a few moments to myself before going home and facing Everett. I know he will be angry that I wasn't there to deal with JT. He'll be angry that JT had a tantrum I could have prevented if I'd just gone to the store yesterday.

He tries. He does. He used to be more patient with the kids. It was easier when they were little. And he's stressed at work. I know that. And I've been so busy with Mama lately. I don't want to admit to Evelyn that I could use some help, but I could. I won't put Mama in a home, though.

I wander through the first floor. The cleaning crew has done a good job. The house smells of astringent. I open a few windows to bring in fresh air.

I want to believe that Everett and I are fine, but all the signs are there. He's disconnecting from us in the same way he did last year. He's sneaking away to check email and texts, always claiming it's work, but returning in a much brighter mood than he would have if it was only work. He's working later and later, even going in on the weekend sometimes. I want to believe this is because he's working on a big project, like he tells me. I need to believe that. I need this marriage to hold tight.

Growing up without a father around was hard. I don't want that for Jenna and JT. They need a dad. I need a husband. Besides, I'm not my mother; I don't believe that all men are bound to leave. When I was young and Mama would start on one of her bitter rants about men, I'd think:

you're wrong! I looked for examples of love that lasted, choosing romance novels and love stories with happy endings. I watched the Disney princess movies over and over. I wanted her to be wrong. I was certain my life would be different. I would make it different. And my life *is* different. Everett and I love each other.

She's never believed my marriage would work, and hasn't hesitated to say so. When she found out about Everett's affair, she seemed almost giddy, tripping over herself to say, *I told you so*. When I told her we were going to counseling and working it out, she said, "Don't let his charm blind you."

Maybe it did. But I've been in love with Everett Turner for over twenty years. I can't just stop being in love.

I hear the therapist telling me, "Trust is just that—trust. You have to *decide* to trust each other." I feel like I'm facing that decision every day. I do trust Everett. I do. I have to stop being so suspicious. I know he's under a tremendous amount of pressure at work. And I know how easy it is to set off JT. It's just that it's easy to not set him off, too. If you try.

I open a few windows upstairs and turn off the thermostat so the heat won't run unnecessarily. I'd better get home before JT goes to bed or it might set him off again.

JENNA
≈≈

Leaves crunch under my feet as I walk down our street. The world looks overripe, like a peach left out on the counter. Walnuts smack the ground, showering down in bursts whenever the wind kicks up. I duck instinctively, a foot soldier under fire.

I like fall. For some crazy reason, when we go back to school again, I always think, *Things will be different this year*. Only so far, they aren't. The only interesting thing that's happened is that Wells Braddington has made a point of talking to me pretty much every day. He's on the bus in the mornings now. His dad took his keys away until he makes more progress on the practice SATs.

Yesterday, I barely made the bus. I had to run for it, which is always awkward. I'm not athletic. I know I look like a dork when I run, plus my shoes weren't tied and my backpack strap came undone, so halfway there my backpack fell and I had to carry it in front of me, banging against my knees. When I got on the bus, Wells was in the back already, sharing a seat with one of his football buddies, but he looked up when I got on and smiled at me. I scowled at him. Nobody should be that happy in the morning. Especially on the bus.

Today I'm legitimately going to Ms. Cassie's. Yesterday, she stopped when she was driving past me and said, "Since you already know where the cat food is, how about you feed the cats for me after school? I'll pay you twenty dollars a week. Is that fair?"

I would have done it for nothing, but money is good. Her kitchen is spotless today, which is odd. She's not much of a neat-nik. I pull out the cans of tuna and turn to find all seven dwarfs already lined up on the patio by the kitchen door. Dopey is standing on his hind legs, pawing at the glass. I crouch down and smash my face against it, he bats at me. He's tough, that one.

While the cats are eating, I wander through Ms. Cassie's house. There are a lot of books. Mostly poetry, which is cool. I don't understand poetry. I like the idea of it, but it makes no sense. I like writers to say what they mean. There are also books on nursing. I wonder if Ms. Cassie has always helped people die or if at some point she helped them live.

My mom was a nurse. She worked in the ER. She seems happy when she talks about that time. I told her once that she should go back to it, but she said she can't. She has to take care of Gram and JT. I could take care of JT, though. He's easy. He doesn't play any games. If he's unhappy, you know it, and if he's happy, you know that, too.

I hang with the cats for a while and, when I'm about to take off, Ms. Cassie pulls in. Instead of coming in the front door, she walks around to the back.

"Here you are!" she says, setting her purse on the metal table and reaching down to pick up Sneezy.

I hate when adults state the obvious so I throw some obvious back at her. "Here I am," I say.

She smiles, puts Sneezy down, and picks up Sleepy. "I was wondering if you might be able to feed the kitties tomorrow."

I shrug. "Sure, you going somewhere?"

"I'm picking up an extra shift tomorrow."

It's none of my business, but I ask anyway. "I didn't think you worked on Saturdays."

She smiles. "This is a special family. I'd like to be with them tomorrow."

I think about this. Why would she want to be there unless the patient is about to croak? "Is he going to die tomorrow?"

"*She* might. It looks like it."

"Do you always have to be there when someone dies?"

"No, but this one is kind of special."

I frown. Who'd want a job where everyone you like dies? Seems a bit masochistic. Or maybe she likes watching them die. I squint at her. She's sitting now and has three cats in her lap. You never know about a person. She might be a regular sicko.

"How do you know she's going to die?"

She sighs and sets down Dopey (he's pushy) to pick up Doc. "You really want to know?"

I nod.

"It's different with everyone, but most of them show a few definite signs."

"Like what?" I really want to know. My gram is old. She says she's dying. She almost burned her house down last week and I asked my mom if she did it on purpose. Mom looked at me like *I* was the nutcase and said, "Of course she didn't! Why would you think that?"

I don't visit Gram very often anymore because, when I do, it's a real downer. She says shit like, "You could at least sit with me. I'm going to die soon. Any day." But then she's still there the next week, and when I do sit with her all she talks about are the birds in her backyard. I asked her once what she was like before she got so old. We were doing an assignment for history class and I had to interview someone who was at least sixty. She's like seventy-something.

She talked about being a nurse, the same way Mom does, like it was the best part of her life. Then she talked about Mom and Aunt Ev. I asked her about my grandpa, but that set her off. It usually does. She said, "Why would you want to know about that louse?"

She said they were better off without him. I don't know the whole story there, but Gram sure does hate him. So I asked about my mom when she was my age, and Gram looked at me real hard. She said, "She was a lot like you, actually. The boys couldn't stay away." Relatives are kind of biased like that. I could have told her that the boys had no problem staying away from me, but I let her believe what she believes.

Then she told me my skirt was too short and that was the real problem. "You shouldn't show them so much. Your mom was the same way. Always wanting the boys to notice her. And she had this one boy—his name was Jonathon. He was such a nice boy. I don't know why she didn't marry him. Then she wouldn't be stuck with your father." Gram frowned. I could tell she was thinking about Everett. She hates him. I think he hates her, too, so it works.

That day Gram didn't talk so much about dying, but most days she does. I don't think there's anything really wrong with her. She fell a few years ago and broke her hip, and ever since then she's like a *really* old person. She even has a walker, but she refuses to use it. She'd rather complain and make you help her. She was much nicer before that happened. I can't remember if she always talked about dying or not.

I don't think she's really dying just yet, even though she says she is. Still, I'd like to know what to watch for.

Ms. Cassie sets Doc down and he walks right over and jumps on my lap. She gets up and goes inside for a glass of water. When she returns, she sits down and looks at me very seriously, like she's checking to see if I'm still paying attention.

"When hospice is called in, the patient is no longer receiving treatment because either the doctor says it's not recommended or the patient has had enough."

"They just give up?"

"Sometimes the treatment is more painful than dying."

This makes no sense, but I don't say anything. It sounds like Gram could rock a hospice situation. She's certainly had enough.

"My job is helping the family care for the patient through the final stages of life. I try to be an advocate for the patient and do what I can to ensure that they are comfortable and not in any pain."

"Do you have to change their diapers?" Ms. Cassie looks at me, surprised. Gram is always saying to me that soon I'll be changing her diapers, just like she changed mine. Sometimes she laughs when she says it, like her dying is going to be a party for us all.

Ms. Cassie nods. "Sometimes, but a lot of the time family members take care of those needs. I do what the patient and family need me to do."

"But how do you know this patient you have now will die tomorrow?"

"I don't, honestly. But there are a few signs that tell me it's likely."

"Like what?"

"Why are you so interested in this?"

I shrug. "My gram's really old. She thinks she's about to die."

Ms. Cassie looks concerned. I almost smile, not because I'm happy Gram thinks she's about to die, but because Ms. Cassie's worried about me now. Most people don't give a shit about kids who aren't their own, but she looks like she really cares, like she'd rush in and help out if I needed her. This makes me feel good. I know that seems childish, but I like Ms. Cassie. I want her to care.

"Is she sick?"

"No, not really. She's just nuts."

"Dementia? Alzheimer's?"

"I don't think so, just nuts."

Ms. Cassie takes a drink of her water and thinks about this. "So why does she think she's about to die?"

I shrug. "I don't know. Maybe she wants attention."

"A lot of elderly people are lonely."

"She talks to her birds."

Ms. Cassie takes this in, but doesn't say anything.

"So what are the signs that someone's about to croak?" I ask. I do want to know. If Gram's about to bite it, I want to get out of there.

"Sometimes they start talking to people they can't see. Then they begin to sleep all the time, and the pauses between their breaths can grow lengthy."

"Is that what's happening with your patient?"

She shakes her head. "No. Mrs. Massey is calm and she sleeps mostly. There have been pauses between her breaths for a few days now. But today, her hands, feet, and knees are growing cold. That means the blood flow is slowing to those areas. Her body is shutting down. It could only be hours. That's why I picked up another nurse's shift for tomorrow—so I can be there."

"Are you always there when they die?"

"Not always, but this family is special. I've been working with them for a few months."

"Wow. Took her a long time to die."

Ms. Cassie smiles at this. "It did," is all she says. Then she gets up. That's my cue. I set Doc back down and pick up my backpack.

"So, you'll take care of the cats?"

"Do you have a cell phone?" I ask.

She looks confused, but nods.

I hold my hand out for it and she fishes in her pocket and hands it to me. I program in my cell number. It's easier to do this for people, especially adults, than to spell your name and number. Less chance they'll get it wrong. I hand her phone back to her.

"Now you have my number. Just in case she doesn't die right off. Call me if you need me to take care of the cats longer."

"Thanks, Jenna," she says. "That's really helpful."

"No prob," I tell her.

"And good luck with your gram. Let me know if I can help in any way."

"Thanks!" I say. "That's cool of you."

"No prob," she says, and smiles at me.

KATE
≈≈

Lying beside Everett, feeling the weight of him beside me, I wonder if other men are different. The only other person I've slept with was my high school boyfriend, Jonathon, and sex with him was always momentary, focused on his satisfaction. I was young, but not so young that I didn't know enough to want more. Mama loved Jonathon, but she only saw his good looks and family money. She liked his manners.

Everett is a romantic. I know it sounds clichéd, but I'm certain that no other man could love me as he does. I was meant to love Everett, and he to love me. I knew it from the moment I met him and I've never doubted it, not really. Everett says what he did with that woman, that Charlene, was him just scratching an itch. He didn't love her. Not like he loves me. I don't think I could be with another man.

I listen to his soft snores and wonder if Everett really is different than other men. When he holds me, sometimes he'll whisper that he loves me so much it hurts, or he'll say that he never knew he could be this lucky. There will be tears in his eyes and a catch in his voice as he says these words. Would another man's hand on my hip make me shiver with anticipation as Everett's touch does? Would another man kiss my eyelashes and tell me how the candlelight picks up a hint of purple in my blue eyes? Would he run a hand back and forth across the curve in the small of my back and tell me I'm perfect?

Tonight, lying in each other's arms, after we have made love so intensely, he whispered, "You deserve so much more than I am." My world is always righted by Everett's love. He reaches a place inside me that no one else knows. What we have is a once-in-a-lifetime love. No dalliance, no itch-scratching, can take that away.

If my mother had experienced that kind of love with my father, could she have found a way to forgive him instead of spending a lifetime with her anger? Despite all the ways that she was a wonderful mother to me, her bitterness colored my world growing up. She raised me to be skeptical of men, but Everett's love taught me otherwise.

My mother was wrong.

Once, she found a stack of romance novels I kept hidden in my bedroom to read late at night with a flashlight. She threw the books in the trash. "Why would you read this garbage? It's fiction—fairy tales! Men don't act like that unless they want something. You need to understand that!"

Everett rolls over, his knee shoving me further towards my side of the bed. He takes up a lot of space. I climb over him to get a glass of water. When I return, I burrow under his arm and he pulls me to him. He kisses my shoulder and wraps a hand around my breast, but soon he is snoring again. I'm lucky to have a man like this. *Aren't I?*

He can't be fooling around. He told me that was over. If he was fooling around, I would know it. I'd sense it in how he touched me. He loves me. I know that. I just have to trust.

≈≈

In the morning, Jenna is already gone when I get up. Saturdays, Everett sleeps in. JT is planted in front of the television, watching reruns of *Emergency 51*. When the program ends, he comes into the kitchen and waits at the counter.

Saturday mornings mean pancakes with raspberry syrup. JT once said the red syrup was like blood. Jenna had laughed, but Everett thought it was a sick thing to say. "What's wrong with him?" he'd asked me after JT had gone upstairs. "Why can't he be a normal kid?"

"I think it's pretty normal for an eleven-year-old to think raspberry syrup looks like blood," I'd told him.

Today, JT pours raspberry syrup on his pancakes. He smiles at me, his eyes twinkling. "I like a lot of blood," he says, giggling.

"Would you like to come with me to take care of Gram today?"

His face clouds over. I know he wants to be with her, but ever since Mama came home from the hospital, she's been acting strangely. She isn't as patient with him or with any of us. He needs people to be consistent. His grandmother has always loved his visits. She'd listen to him for hours, asking good questions and laughing when he repeated a joke she'd heard him tell a hundred times.

She's always been his best audience, but now she grows impatient. The other day she said, "You already told me about that one, JT, don't repeat yourself!" And when he tried out a few of his new jokes, she starred at him blankly. When we were leaving, JT reached for her hand. They've had a secret handshake for years, but instead she said, "You can't give your grandmother a hug? What's wrong with you?"

JT is not a hugger. At least not beyond me, Everett, and occasionally, Jenna. Shaking hands has always been his routine with Mama. When she realized hugs could set him off, she'd made up a secret handshake for the two of them. "There's no reason to hug people," she said to him back then. "A handshake is plenty."

Mama has grown more paranoid than ever since the incident with her stove, insisting that I staple the drapes to the walls around the windows so no one can see in. "I don't want them coming back and carting me off again."

I finally had to call Evelyn and insist that she help. I know where this will lead, but I'm hoping I can convince her that a home is not the answer. Maybe she would agree to hire a nurse to come in a few times a week. Not that Mama will likely allow it. Evelyn's supposed to drive down today and bring lunch so we can talk about it.

I was surprised she agreed so readily to the visit. "That'll work," Evelyn had said. "I've been wanting to talk to you, anyway. I have some very interesting things to tell you about Mama and our father."

She knows I'm not interested in seeing our father, but now I'm afraid to know what she discovered. I'm afraid of how she'll use it against our mother.

Evelyn has always argued with Mama about our father, as if she knew him. She's younger than me, so I'm certain she has no memories. The very few I have are sketchy and fogged over by time. She was relentless in asking Mama about him when we were young. She'd ask and Mama would say, "All you need to know is that he's not a part of our lives." Evelyn would push and Mama would become frustrated, finally declaring, "Evelyn, let it go! I am not going to talk about that louse!"

One Christmas, as we set up our tiny artificial tree, Evelyn said, "If Daddy were here, we'd have a *real* tree!"

Mama laughed. "That's how much you know. Your father never wanted a Christmas tree; said they were a waste of money. The one time I bought one, he hacked it to pieces and burned it in the fireplace. Said that was a better use for it. We've had this plastic one ever since."

But in one of the few memories I have of my father, he was coming through the door with a fresh-cut tree. Mama was yelling at him about the needles that were falling on the floor, and he was grinning from beneath a plaid cap. I remember him whistling as he set it up. But maybe I'm imagining that. I was young when he left.

Evelyn has even fewer memories, yet she has always wanted to believe that Mama drove him away rather than he left. "I'd leave someone who hated me like she hates him," she'd say.

I'd try to rationalize. "I don't think Mama hated him until he left."

When I was eight, I wrote a letter to my father. We were doing a unit on correspondence at school and were supposed to choose a relative who lived far away. Mama was angry. "Why would you write to him? He doesn't care one bit about you." I insisted she mail it, and she said she would. I never did hear back. At the time, it seemed like further proof that my father didn't love us, as Mama said, but when I was older, I realized Mama probably never mailed it. I doubt she knew where he was.

When Jenna comes home from taking care of Ms. Cassie's cats, I ask her to keep an eye on JT while I run over to Mama's.

Mama is in a better mood than usual this morning. It's probably due to Evelyn's visit. I fix her tea and toast and get her settled on the back porch to visit with her birds. She seems better today.

"Evelyn will be here in a little while. She's bringing lunch."

"It's about time! I guess she's too busy with her fancy life to bother with her own mother."

"Now, Mama, that's not fair. Evelyn was the one who came to the house when you had that trouble with your teapot." Mama refuses to admit that she nearly burned her own house down. She blames the teapot. Says it was faulty.

"Don't remind me. She's probably the one who told them to cart me away!"

"The paramedics took you to the hospital because they were worried about smoke inhalation. That's standard procedure. Evelyn didn't have anything to do with it."

Mama scowls. "Well, she didn't try to stop them!"

I leave her with the birds and go inside to start some laundry and run the vacuum cleaner. I don't want Evelyn

70

to think I'm not taking good care of our mother. Not that she seems concerned. Mama is more an obligation to her. But if the house is a mess, it only strengthens her argument for institutionalizing Mama. I run the vacuum back and forth over the clean room, trying not to think about what news she's drummed up about our father. I just hope it doesn't upset Mama.

When Evelyn arrives, Mama is dozing in her chair on the porch and I'm reading her paper next to her, ready to resume the conversation we were having before she dozed off. Evelyn motions me back inside.

"I've got to talk to you," she whispers, her eyes wide with excitement. I'm certain this can't be good.

I close the door quietly, so as to not wake Mama.

"She's been much more difficult since the fire," I tell Evelyn.

"Sit down. This might be a shock."

Evelyn's drama is irritating. "What?" I can't imagine her shocking me. I've grown up with a front row seat for all her drama. Ever since she dumped her husband Josh, I've tried to keep a distance. I don't understand her capacity for cruelty. She takes up too much space in every room she enters. I always liked Josh. He made Evelyn bearable. He was fun and never took life too seriously. He was good for her, tempering her intensity. They'd only been married seven years when Evelyn declared him "emotionally inaccessible" and "chronically unmotivated." I still have no idea what that means. At the time, Everett said, "That means Josh knew to get out while the getting was good." When I asked her about it, she said, "He's a child who has no idea what he wants to be when he grows up."

Josh vanished from our lives so quickly, it was like he'd never been here. Everett tracked Josh down when I wouldn't stop talking about him. Apparently, he lives in California now and has remarried. Good for him.

It's Saturday, but Evelyn's makeup is perfect, her tailored suit ready for court, and her nails freshly created (JT called her fake nails "claws"). Why is she dressed like this to bring her mother lunch? I suppose asking her to help me scrub the singed kitchen cabinets again or pick out a new microwave is probably pointless.

"I've been talking with our father," says Evelyn, with a giddy smile and a glance outside at Mama.

"You've said as much. I don't know why you want anything to do with him. Everett thinks he's after your money."

"He's not after my money."

"Right."

"Kate, listen to me, please!" She takes my hands in hers and leans in. "Our father is not the bad guy Mama made him out to be."

"How can you know? We were young when he left. You were still a baby."

"He didn't leave because he *wanted* to. He left because Mama *made* him. She threw him out!"

"I don't believe it. If that was so, why has she spent her entire life alone? He broke her heart!"

Evelyn smirks. "He had an affair, but when he cut it off and begged her to forgive him, she wouldn't."

"Why should she?" I ask, swallowing the hypocrisy in my statement.

"It gets worse!"

She waits for my reaction, so I take my cue and widen my eyes as if I really want to know, when all I really want is for her to shut up about my cheating father and help me figure out how we can help our mother.

"She said she'd tell the police that he was sleeping with a seventeen-year-old if he didn't leave."

"Well that's worse; that's statutory rape!"

"But she wasn't seventeen!"

"Then how could Mama report him?"

"He said the police would believe whatever Mama told them because they knew her from her nursing days."

"If she wasn't seventeen, then there wouldn't be an issue. There has to be a victim."

"He was young and scared and believed Mama could do it. You know how she was."

"That makes no sense."

"It makes complete sense. Why else would our father leave and never come back?"

"Because he's a cheating, self-centered man who didn't want to be saddled with a wife and two babies?"

Evelyn glares at me.

I roll my eyes, but say nothing.

"He didn't want to leave, but Mama didn't give him a choice. She made him leave town."

"So, where's he been all this time and why is he back now?"

"He's been in the Dominican Republic doing mission work."

"What?"

"He found God."

She says this like it explains everything. "What does that mean?"

"He's been down there working for the last forty years."

"How can you know this?"

"He told me!"

I can see she is enjoying telling this tale and half-wonder if she's making the whole mess up.

"So why didn't he come back? How could we not have heard from him all this time?"

"He said he wrote. But Mama never would have given us his letters. You know that."

"He could have called," I point out, leaning back and crossing my arms. I'm about done with Evelyn's little fantasy of our misunderstood father.

"She changed our phone number twice! Don't you remember that? I had to keep memorizing a new number to sign in at the pool."

I do remember that, but there was always a reason for the phone number change. Everett does the same thing whenever too many telemarketers and pollsters start calling our house.

"Still, he could have at least tried to visit us."

"He didn't have the money to come back for visits. You should hear how he was living! His stories are outrageous. He lived in a dirt shack!"

"But surely he could have found us before now!"

"How? And why? For all he knew, we'd written him off just like Mama did."

I hear Mama stirring and stand up.

"Parents don't give up on their children. They don't." I wonder at the anger I'm feeling. I used to only feel a vague sadness at the idea of my father, but now, thanks to Evelyn, I feel anger. I'm furious, in fact. I turn to go and Evelyn grabs my arm.

"Wait! I'm not finished! He remarried. They were married for twenty-five years, but she died. He's in Florida now. That's where her family lives. It's where she wanted to be buried, so he brought her body back."

"How noble. But this still makes no sense. Why invite him into our lives at this point? It's been nearly forty years!"

"Katie!" Mama calls.

"Let me," says Evelyn. "I have a few things to say to her."

I grab Evelyn's arm. "You can't! She isn't well."

"You know what? I don't care! She's kept us from having a father all our lives. He's not a bad man, Kate. He made mistakes, but he wants to make amends."

I follow Evelyn out to the porch.

"Hello, Mama!" Evelyn sings in her sugary voice, reserved for talking to mentally unstable people on the witness stand, small children, and her mother.

"I was starting to think you'd forgotten me!"

I shoot Evelyn a warning glance and take Mama's arm. "Let's go inside for lunch. Evelyn brought a lovely shrimp salad for you."

"Does it have mayonnaise in it? I don't like a lot of mayonnaise."

"It's from a very nice restaurant. Only a little bit of mayo. It's delicious. I promise," says Evelyn. My head is still spinning with Evelyn's tale and my hands shake as I pour ice tea into three glasses.

Evelyn steers the conversation all through lunch, listening patiently when Mama talks about the birds and turning the conversation back to herself at every opportunity. She won some big case last week. It was in the newspapers, in fact. She's surprised Mama and I hadn't heard.

Evelyn doesn't mention our father at all during lunch and I'm grateful. When we finish, Mama suggests we play a little bridge. "See if Jenna will come over and be our fourth!" she says. For a change, she is very lucid.

I realize I left my phone on the charger at home. When I pick up Mama's extension, it's dead. She's left it off the hook. She's been doing that more and more lately. She says the telemarketers are really spies. "Why would anyone spy on you?" I've asked her. And she nods knowingly and says, "Because," as if that's the answer.

I dial Jenna, already knowing what the answer will be. Jenna dislikes her Aunt Evelyn almost as much as she dislikes spending time inside her grandmother's dark house.

Jenna answers on the first ring. "It's about time! You do realize your phone is here on the charger."

"I've been here, at Gram's, did you try to call?"

"About a million times, but it's always busy!"

"She left it off the hook. Why did you call? Is something wrong?

"JT freaked out because Everett turned on some stupid football game and wouldn't let him finish watching his show. He locked himself in the bathroom and won't come out!"

"Where's your father?"

"I don't know! He got pissed and left. He told JT to stay in the bathroom all weekend for all he cared."

"He won't come out for you?"

"No, he keeps saying that Everett wants him to stay in there all weekend."

I glance in the kitchen at Mama. She is sitting at the table, complaining about how much her knees have been hurting. Evelyn is washing up the dishes.

"I'll be right there," I tell Jenna.

Back in the kitchen, I pick up the dirty napkins and throw them away. "I hate to do this, but I'm going to have to run. Everett got called in to work suddenly and JT's not doing so well."

"What?" cries Mama. "I want us to have a nice afternoon. Just us girls!"

I kiss her head. "I wish I could stay. If I can settle things down, I'll come back. Walk me out, Evelyn." I take a protesting Evelyn by the arm.

When we reach my car, I look back at the house. It's buttoned up tight, according to Mama's instructions. No one could be peeking out since no one can peek in.

"Please don't talk to Mama about him," I plead. "Not without me."

"I came here today to do exactly that! Someone needs to confront her on this."

"What is he expecting, anyway? What have you told him?"

"He'd like to meet us and his grandchildren."

"What about Mama?"

"He says he'd like to see her, too. He's not bitter like she is. It all happened a long time ago."

"Not to Mama."

"Which is why it might be good for her to see him. Maybe she'd realize he's no monster."

"Maybe he is. You've only talked to him on the phone. Maybe Everett could look into his background."

"No!" Evelyn grabs my arm. "Everett does not need to stick his nose in this. Besides, he's not even a cop anymore."

"Once a cop, always a cop. He could easily ask someone to pull some records."

"I'm sure there's nothing to be found. He's harmless. He lives in a condo in Florida and has lunch with his niece every Sunday. He volunteers with Habitat for Humanity. He plays pinochle."

Evelyn looks at me with that look she has, and I know she's going to get her way. When she decides something, she's a boulder rolling downhill gathering momentum and, if you don't get out of the way, she'll roll right over you and never look back.

"Maybe you should talk to him."

"Why?"

"You might like him."

"Maybe."

"I'm not going to put this off, Kate. I'm angry. Aren't you angry?"

"I don't know. She's so old now. We don't know what really happened. He could be making it all up."

"She's not that old. And I do know what happened. What she did was wrong. She needs to know that."

"It isn't so black and white! Why do you always see everything like that? Can't you cut her a little slack? It was a long time ago. Maybe she made a mistake. Or maybe he's lying."

"All my life, all *your* life," says Evelyn, her voice rising, her finger pointing at me, "she's convinced us that he was no good. That all men are no good. They can't be trusted. And in reality, sure, our father wasn't perfect, but he tried! He wanted to be a good man. He spent the last forty years trying to help people!"

"Only those people weren't his children," I say quietly. Surely she sees the irony in this.

Evelyn sighs. "Just like Mama, you can't ever forgive."

"That's not fair. If you want to talk about forgiveness, maybe we should give Josh a call."

"That's completely different. Josh is doing fine. Our divorce was for the best," says Evelyn.

"Well, maybe Mama's was, too."

"You can't possibly believe that! We've had front row seats to her lifelong pity-party. But, you go on home. Continue to do everything she wants—*think* everything she wants, but not me. I'm going to call her on this. Somebody has to."

I get in the car and slam the door. I guess I can't stop her, but I won't stay here and witness it. I roll the window down.

"You don't have to do this," I say.

Evelyn turns on her heel and marches back in the house.

JENNA

≈≈

Once I know Mom is on her way, I vacate the premises. I've had enough of my screwed up family. Speaking of screwing, I'm sure that's what Everett went off to do.

He'd gotten his tools out to take the door off its hinges, like he did the last time JT did this, and then he got a text. Next thing, he puts down his tools and says, "I have to be somewhere." Then he disappears to his bedroom and comes out stinking of cologne.

"Italian shower?" I ask, and he looks confused. He doesn't realize I know.

"Tell your mother I had to go in to work," is all he says.

"What about JT?" I ask.

He listens at the door. JT is humming the *ER* theme music.

"He'll be fine."

That was an hour ago. JT and I have been talking through the door since then. He's recounting the episode he was watching before Everett shut it off. Word for word. He can do that. Who needs audio books?

"JT?" I interrupt. "The Mom-Unit's here. Can you tell me the rest later?"

"I'm not finished," he says.

"Mom-Unit will want to hear it, hold on," I say. JT has called our mom *Mom-Unit* for so long, I can't remember why he does it. I think it started after some math obsession. Anyway, Mom-Unit is the only person he can be flexible with, if you call holding off your tantrum for two minutes *flexible*. Dad-Unit doesn't know how to handle him.

I hear Mom's car door slam and I slip out the back door. Nothing to do today.

I'm hungry, so I decide to find some lunch. I know what Ms. Cassie has in her fridge and it's nothing I want, so I head to the Ashers'. They've always got plenty of food. I don't think either of them really cook; their freezer's loaded with instant food, and the pantry has every kind of junk food created. It's Sherm's naptime; there's a good chance they'll be home, but I go check it out anyway.

On the whole street, I like the Ashers' house best. It's the only house I don't have to break in to because they gave me a key. I take care of their fish and bring in the mail when they're gone, but they never ask me to babysit. I don't think they trust me, or maybe they just feel so guilty about sticking the kid in day care every day that they never go out without him.

In their house, everything's in order. Amy, the mom, must have some kind of fetish about baskets. There are baskets for everything. But I like it. I like how the house smells a little like lemons and also like baking bread. It must have been Sherm's birthday recently because there are balloons floating around the living room ceiling like colorful ghosts. One is tangled around the ceiling fan.

Sherm's about a year old, now, so he's starting to get more interesting. Amy let me hold him once when he was first born. He was tiny and weighed almost nothing. I was kind of afraid I'd drop him, but I liked how he wrapped his little fingers around my pinky and looked at me.

I asked Amy if she'd need a babysitter, but she didn't really answer me. Instead, she grilled me.

"What grade are you in now?" she asked.

"Tenth." (This was last year.)

"Wow, you look older than that. Has your hair always been so . . . black?"

I know she was trying to be nice, but she was freaked out by my hair. A lot of adults are. It's so black it's nearly purple, and I like to tease it into little spikes all over my head. I do it mostly because it freaks people out, but also because it feels cool.

"No, I dyed it."

"What color was it before?"

"Brown," I said, and handed Sherm back to her. "Just boring brown."

"Does it hurt to pierce your ears so many times?"

I figured this interrogation meant they didn't trust me to watch Sherman.

I pull one of the balloons down, untie it, and suck in the helium. Then I talk to the fish in my cartoon voice.

"How're you doing little fishy-fish? Did you have fun at the party? I bet they didn't even let you have a piece of cake. Mean humans!" I sound like a munchkin. Wish I'd thought to record it with my phone.

I look at my watch. It's nearly two—way past Sherm's naptime. I better be quick. I pull out a tub of ice cream, and take it with me to the living room where I'll have a view of the street and be able to see the Ashers if they come rushing back for naptime.

There are new pictures on the mantel of Amy and Nathan and Sherm with some old guy. Probably the granddad. My grandad plays a lot of golf. He's Everett's dad. We hardly ever see him because they live in Ohio. Plus, I think JT makes him nervous, and my grandmother and my mom don't like each other. They'd never admit that, but it's pretty clear. We only see them for Easter and my granddad's birthday. I don't know what makes those days such sacred holidays, but it's cool—I wouldn't want to see them more than that anyway.

I've never met my other grandfather. Mom doesn't even know him and he's her own father. Gram says he's a louse. She loves that word. She uses it for pretty much all men, even Everett. She didn't always think Everett was a louse, but it seems like for the last year or so, while she's been losing her grasp on other stuff, she's been certain about one thing: my father is a louse. I'd have to agree with her.

I try not to think about the woman on the computer with the big boobs. He's probably there right now with his stupid face squished between them, moaning some kind of pathetic shit about how much he loves her, only he doesn't. How could he?

I put the ice cream back in the freezer, grab a box of Cheez-Its, and take off. Maybe I'll go hang out with Ms. Cassie's cats. I'm walking up the street when I hear feet behind me. Wells.

"Don't you have a football game or some other jock thing to do?"

"I got cut."

"Are you bleeding?" I smile at my own joke, but then realize he looks pretty torn up. "Sorry. How'd that happen?"

"Grades," is all he says, and he reaches over and puts his hand inside my Cheez-It box. Pretty presumptuous, but I don't care. Manners are overrated.

"I thought you were going to Harvard. They probably like good grades."

"Nah. That's what my dad thinks."

"I don't know. Harvard sounds pretty good. Better than community college."

"You don't have to go to community college, you know. There are scholarships for smart kids."

I laugh. "I'm not a smart kid."

"Sure you are."

I like that he knows this. "Besides, you have to be *well-rounded*. There's not much on my résumé beyond the Math Squad in seventh grade, and my mom signed me up for that. I'm not really a joiner."

"Just make some shit up. How would they know?"

I make a face. I may be a lot of things, but I'm not a liar. There's plenty of them in my family already.

Wells follows me to Ms. Cassie's. I introduce him to the cats. He likes Dopey best. Figures. She's the cutest one. She's all over him.

"I've never had a cat," he says.

"Why not? You got that monster house. Plenty of room in there for a cat."

"My mom doesn't like them. She says they'll scratch the furniture."

"They might," I agree. That's not really something you should hold against a cat. They can't help it. Scratching furniture is in their nature. Besides, if you let them go outside, they don't do it as much. We can't have a cat because Everett says he's allergic. But he may be lying.

"So, if you aren't going to Harvard, where are you going?" I ask.

Wells shrugs. "I like cars. I thought about being a race car driver."

I don't tell him that sounds like something a little kid would say. Maybe he's not as bright as all that, after all.

"You can get paid to drive race cars?" I ask.

"If you're good. My dad says that's a hobby, not a career."

"It kind of seems like it is," I say. No point beating around the bush here.

Later, I show Wells how easy it is to get into a house like his. We're sitting inside the Bakers' house at the far end of Pine Road, where there's a cul-de-sac surrounded by cornfields. The Bakers are gone to their shore house most weekends. We're lounging on their sectional sofa that takes up an entire room when he says, "You want to get high?"

I'm not into drugs. I figure I've got enough stuff going against me without adding to it. I remember Everett telling me, "Never break more than one law at a time. That's the mistake most criminals make. We caught so many drunk drivers with expired license plates. Or idiots in vans full of stolen shit who run a stop sign." I think Everett would make an excellent criminal.

I shake my head; but Wells pulls out a bag of reefer from his pocket and a little pipe.

"Not in here," I tell him. We go out to their back patio. Now we're only trespassing and loitering, but that's still too many laws for me. When he flicks his lighter, I say, "I gotta run."

"Wait!" he says. "I don't have to do this now. Don't go."

He actually sounds a little sad. If you'd told me that Wells Braddington would be begging me to hang out with him, even a month ago, I'd have said you were cracked like the Liberty Bell, but when I turn around, his blue eyes hit me. Shit, he's hot. I know I said that before, but sometimes people can't help themselves. I sit back down, and he puts away his weed.

We end up talking about elementary school and all the teachers we had, plus the crazy bus driver who didn't speak English. Wells is pretty funny and mostly normal. Funny how we have these impressions of each other and then we're shocked when people aren't what we think they are.

Later we walk back together and, at my mailbox, there's this awkward silence. Like we don't know how to say good-bye. Just then, my front door opens and Mom lets Marco out.

"Oh, it's you," she calls. "Can you keep an eye on Marco?"

"I better go," says Wells. "My dad's probably having a coronary right about now."

"He doesn't know about the football team?"

Wells smiles. "Nope. Told him I was catching a ride to the game and left early. He's probably figured it out by now."

"Shit. That's huge."

"I know. It'll be a fun night at the Braddingtons'," Wells says, smiling that grin that makes weaker girls swoon. Not me. I'm not swooning.

"Good luck," I say. "At least you know how to get in the Bakers' place if he throws you out."

"Yeah, that's good to know."

I watch Wells head up the hill to his house. Marco nudges my leg. "Hey, boy," I say, and bend down to rub his long ears. I don't spend enough time with Marco.

KATE
≈≈

" Jenna?"

The house is quiet. Marco whines near the back door. Jenna must have just left. I knock on the bathroom.

"JT?"

"Jenna left before I finished telling her about my show."

"Can you open this door?"

"But I haven't finished telling about my show."

"I like it better when I can see you as you tell it."

The lock clicks. I open the door. JT is sitting on the floor, leaning against the vanity, his feet pressed against the toilet. I can tell he's been crying.

I crouch down beside him and take his hand. "Why'd you lock yourself in the bathroom?"

"Dad-Unit was mad. He yelled at me."

I lean back against the cabinet and sigh. I wish Everett wouldn't raise his voice at JT. He doesn't like loud noises. Every time Everett starts yelling, JT ends up having a tantrum. Why Everett thought the result would be different this time, I don't know. Everett has got to be more patient with him, but I know JT isn't easy, and he isn't the son Everett pictured he would be. When I was pregnant and found out he would be a boy, Everett went overboard loading up on the baseball and football equipment. "He won't be able to use those until he grows up!" I told him, but I laughed and encouraged him anyway. We'd waited a long time and through two miscarriages for JT. Seeing Everett's happiness filled my heart.

The baseball bat is still in the garage, but Marco chewed up the ball and glove long ago. Whenever I see that bat, it makes me think of those early days colored by joy and anticipation. I understand Everett's disappointment, but I focus on what JT *can* do, not what he can't. He has a brilliant mind; it just doesn't operate the way everyone expects. That doesn't mean there's something wrong with him. It means that people need to stop expecting him to act like other boys. He's not like other boys. Everett has never come to peace with that.

After I get JT settled watching the rest of his show, I make myself a cup of tea. Where is Everett anyway? I dial his number. No answer. What was so important at work that he had to leave on a Saturday afternoon? I need him here. I need to talk about my father and what Evelyn might be telling Mama right at this very moment.

I spend the rest of the afternoon cleaning and trying not to think about what Evelyn is saying or what Everett is doing. Then, JT and I go to the grocery store and I let him pick out three different kinds of pasta. We stop at the library to get the book JT ordered on studying for the EMT exam. I wonder how long this current obsession will last. Maybe he'll want to study medicine in college. When he was crazy about dinosaurs, he'd planned a career in archeology. I know his mind could take him anywhere if he could just figure out how to function in a normal school setting.

He is learning. One of the goals for this school year was for him to become more aware of the emotions of others. Sometimes, when he asks why it's so important to be able to tell if someone is upset with you, I have no answer. Maybe it would be easier to sail through life unaware of the emotions of the people around you. I'm tired of worrying about Mama's mental state, Jenna's anger, and Everett's honesty. Maybe there's an upside to Asperger's.

When we get home, JT races to his room to begin working through his new book. I set a pan on the stove and heat olive oil, crushing a garlic clove in the sizzling oil. I dice onion and pepper; the pungent smells soothe me. I set sausage on the counter to defrost and try calling Everett again. No answer, so I leave a voice mail asking if he'll be home for dinner. Then I put water on to boil for JT's pasta. I study the package of farro I bought. The label makes it sound very simple, but I've never cooked the grain before. I saw it on a cooking show last week while I was at Mama's. I'm probably the only one who will eat it. Everett doesn't like to eat reheated food and will probably just make a sandwich. Jenna will opt for the pasta if she comes home in time. More and more, I find myself eating alone. Some nights I just don't bother eating at all.

I stir the onions and peppers, watching them wither and then glisten in the oil. I do love cooking. Everett taught me to cook when we were first dating. We'd been so happy then, so complete.

Where's the Everett I married? The guy who could always find a silver lining? He taught me to look past what was right in front of me to what could happen—what could be. Like when he lost his job with the police department. Instead of letting the situation drag him down, he'd made the most of FABSO. And look at him now. He's in charge over there. Everett's a survivor.

Why can't he see JT's behavior the same way? Why can't he find the silver lining? If only he could be proud of all the amazing things JT can do, instead of growing so frustrated with what he can't.

I pour myself a glass of wine and drag a stool around to the stove so I can sit while I caramelize the onions. If they burn, the recipe will be ruined. I don't know why I'm so tired, but my legs feel like sandbags. Maybe I have Lyme disease. I read it can manifest in lots of ways, but it also makes a person exhausted and depressed. Am I depressed?

No, I'm not. But sometimes I wish my life was different. I wish I didn't always feel so alone.

And I wish Everett were here instead of God knows where. There was a time when we were inseparable. Everett used to be sure to work the same shift as me. He'd show up at six, just as I was handing off my paperwork to the next shift.

"Keep 'em alive until 5:55," my coworker Ellen would say. Everett would appear a few minutes later, wearing his uniform, a shadow of the new day's beard covering his handsome face, and then Ellen would say, "And if it isn't Prince Charming."

He'd take me to breakfast at some greasy spoon, and then we'd go back to his apartment and make love. When I'd wake up at noon, he would be gone. Out for a run. I'd piece myself back together and slink home. Mama would have plenty to say, but it bounced off me then like rubber. I was so in love. Everett was my hero.

He proposed to me in the ambulance bay. He got another nurse to rush in and fetch me, saying there was an emergency. I ran out to find Everett on his knees, diamond in hand. Everyone on my shift saw me accept, and they cheered when Everett kissed me. It was like a fairy tale.

No, I don't regret Everett, but maybe I regret not trying harder to keep him happy. In the beginning, my world spun around him. It was easy. I was so happy to be out of Mama's house and so grateful that he'd rescued me. Loving him, even doting on him, came naturally. It wasn't until after the kids came that loving him ever felt like an effort.

EVERETT

≈≈

Being with Veronica makes me happy. What's so wrong with that? I deserve to be happy.

There's no happy at my house. Jenna is sullen and angry. JT, well, JT can be happy, but lately everything I do sets him off. Kate's babied him too long. The boy needs to learn how to get along in this world. People aren't going to cater to him forever. He can't explode every time he doesn't get his way.

Kate says she's forgiven me for Charlene, but I don't know if that's true. Sometimes when she looks at me, I wonder if she knows something. Sometimes it feels like she treats me too nice, too polite, like I'm a guest in my own house.

Veronica is the opposite of Kate. She's loud and brash and blond and has these enormous tits—god they're something. And she doesn't care about Kate. She likes that I'm married. She said that makes it more exciting.

Sometimes she'll ask me to describe what it's like to have sex with Kate. If I've been drinking, I can do that, but sometimes it pisses me off because there was a time when sex with Kate was better than anything else in my world. I guess I was young then, and I didn't know anything else; but I do know I was happy. We were happy. Once.

But then that crap started on the force. The captain believed some stupid stoner's story about me roughing him up in the back of the car, and he put all this pressure on me, sent me to sensitivity training, and wanted me to talk to the guy—apologize. Can you believe that shit? So I said, "No,

I've got other options," and tried to get a transfer, but the dickhead got pissed and started calling around.

Next thing I know, I get a call from FABSO and they make an offer I can't resist—better pay, better hours, better benefits, and now I'm the boss. Of course I took it. But I miss being a cop. I was happy then. Kate said she was proud of my new job; she helped me buy a set of suits and ties. You know, I think that was the beginning of the end for us. She was so excited about my new job, made me wonder if she was glad I wasn't a cop anymore.

And then Jenna got older and stopped listening to me, and JT was having all his issues so Kate quit her job and stayed home, which was the greenlight for her mama to start taking advantage of her—calling her over at every hour of the day and night.

Yeah, now I'm much happier when I know I'm gonna see Veronica. The way I see it, that makes it a good thing for everyone. I don't go home all stressed out. Veronica's fun. Much more fun than Charlene, who was psycho at the end there. She actually showed up at our house and told Kate about us. She was pissed that I broke it off, but she was getting crazy, telling me I had to divorce Kate. Telling me she wanted to have a kid with me. I'm no good with kids—that should be clear to everyone.

This afternoon, when JT started flipping out because I turned on the game, it pissed me off. He's seen that show, that stupid rerun about an EMT squad, like a thousand times. He sits there reciting the words right along with the actors. He didn't need to watch it. I'd finished cutting the grass and all I wanted to do was have a beer and watch the game. Why couldn't I do that? I could have missed kick off, waited until the stupid show ended. But why should I have to? It's my house. Besides, the boy needs to learn that he can't have his way all the time.

When Veronica texted, I was ready to get the hell out of there.

JENNA

≈≈

Wells and I hang out together after school almost every day now. He's actually not quite as much of a jock-jerk as I've always assumed. Now that he doesn't have football practice and he doesn't have a car to drive, he rides the bus home with the rest of us peasants. He's supposed to be doing homework after school, but his mom is never home to check up on him.

"How come your mom is never home? She doesn't have a job. Shouldn't she be there waiting for you with the plate of milk and cookies?"

Wells smiles at this. His smile is really killer, but I try not fixate on that fact.

"I don't know what she does with her time, but I think it involves a lot of hair salons, shopping, and getting her nails done. Plus, she's like golf-crazy. She plays every day. She's even on the club's ladies team."

"Tough life she has."

I'm jimmying the door to the Kawalskys' house, and, when it finally gives, I look at my own nails, which are uneven and short. I wonder if he's noticed.

"Where'd you learn to do this?" asks Wells as we help ourselves to Oreos and milk at the kitchen counter. It's raining, or I'd show him the awesome deck they have. It's three layers. 'Course, he's probably been here for parties. I think his mom and Mrs. K are tight.

"Do what?" I ask, licking the middle out of a cookie.

"Break into houses."

I shrug. "When I was a little kid, I used to ride along with Everett on jobs. He showed me how to jimmy locks, bypass security systems, figure out whether anyone's in the house or not. That's important. It would suck to break in to a house and there's somebody in there."

"I thought dogs were the best security system."

"Dogs are easy to get around. Just take treats with you."

"Wow. So you can get into any house on our street."

"Probably. I haven't been in the Wilkinsons' house because the grandmother is there and she never leaves, and I haven't been in that weird red house at the end of the block because it looks like a crazy person lives there."

"Really?" he asks. "How do you know?"

"I don't, but the house is packed with boxes and garbage and all kinds of shit, like the homes on that TV show about hoarders."

"We should break in there." Great. Now Wells thinks he's my accomplice.

"There's no point."

"There's no point to breaking in all these other houses, is there?"

"Yes," I tell him, "there is."

"Like what?"

"I don't know. Oreos. Cats. Ice cream."

"What was the point of breaking in to my house?"

I don't want to tell him that I broke in there the first time because I was pissed at Tiffany. I'd tried to join a four-square game she was playing in elementary school. She'd said, "We don't want to play with you. You're too weird."

So I broke in her house and took a necklace out of her room. I don't usually take anything. That would be stupid. But every now and then something asks to be taken. The necklace had little tiny fake diamonds in the shape of a heart. I thought they were real, but obviously they weren't. Nobody gives their eight-year-old a diamond necklace, not even the Braddingtons. I was sending a message to Tiffany: *You have no heart.*

That first time I broke in to the Braddingtons' place wasn't easy. At the time, their house had the hardest system for me to get around. I'd ended up cutting the power to the house, which is so amateur, but it worked. Later, after Everett installed their new system, it was much easier to get in. Especially once I found their password on the inside of a cabinet. People always write their passwords somewhere. Either that or they hide a key. They can't stand the idea of being locked out of their own house. And it's easy to figure out where they hide keys and codes.

I used to love to go with Everett to all his jobs. Back then, he was like a superhero to me. That was long before he cheated on my mom. Or at least I assume it was. I was too young to see the signs. Maybe he was cheating back then, too. I don't know why my mom doesn't figure it out. She's not really a stupid person. Maybe she doesn't want to know. Or maybe she's too busy with JT and Gram. I don't understand why she even likes Everett in the first place. Anyway, eventually she'll find out about this chick. Everett's making too many mistakes. Maybe he's lost his touch. If men didn't have penises, they'd probably be a lot smarter.

I look at Wells now. He's still waiting to know why I broke in to his house. "I don't know. I guess I was bored."

He seems satisfied with this answer. It's pretty much the reason we're sitting in the Kawalskys' right now.

≈≈

The next Friday, we're back at Ms. Cassie's house. We both like the cats. Wells has Dopey on his lap, and she's rolled over on her back and drooling under his hand. She's pathetic, that one.

"Football game tonight," he says, stroking her under her chin.

"You bummed you won't be there?" I ask.

"I have to go."

"Why? I thought you were cut."

He winces. It's imperceptible, but I see it. Maybe he's not as okay as he says about being cut. "My dad says we're going to go watch, so I don't miss anything. He's working on getting me back on the team."

"Won't that happen automatically, if your grades improve?"

"Probably, but he's trying to make it happen even if they don't."

"Can he?"

"He thinks he can. I guess it depends on how much money he donates to the football program."

"Really? That doesn't seem legal."

"He's a lawyer; so he can make it legal."

I don't say anything. Mr. Braddington seems like the biggest asshole. Really, he's like a caricature of a stupid, pompous father figure. He'd make a great antagonist for any after-school special. The dad who gets it in the end. He creates the illusion of being this great dad and pillar of society when, in reality, he's just your average asshole. (An *illusion* is a false impression as opposed to *allusion*, which would be a reference. We're talking about easily confused and misused words in English this week.)

Wells gets up and sets Dopey on the table. She laps at some rainwater that's still pooled there from the storm this week. Guess Ms. Cassie hasn't been around much. I wonder if one of her patients is circling the drain.

"Anyway, I gotta go to the game. Are you going?"

I do a double take. "You're kidding, right?"

"No. I just thought maybe you could sit with us. If you're going, I mean."

He's serious. Bizarro. It's sort of sweet in a weird way. But I really can't picture me at a football game, much less at a football game sitting with Wells Braddington and his asshole father.

"I think I'll skip that particularly appealing option," I tell him. "I promised JT I'd watch *Backdraft* with him tonight."

"Whatever," says Wells. He actually looks disappointed. I can't believe he thinks I'd consider going to the game. I also can't believe he'd consider being seen with me in public. He's still basically ignoring me in the mornings when his buddies are on the bus, but he sits with me on the ride home when only the losers who aren't involved in sports or cheerleading ride it. I'm not offended by this behavior. It should probably bother me, but I accept (as opposed to *except*, which would mean I'm taking exception to our predicament) Wells and my relationship for what it is—weird. I do take it as a compliment (as opposed to a *complement*, which would mean that Wells completes me rather than is admiring something about me) that he even asked. He's either not that worried about how it will look to be seen with me in public, or he really just wants to piss off his dad.

After Wells takes off, I use one of Ms. Cassie's kitchen towels to wipe down the table and then pull out my English homework. Might as well get it over with while I'm thinking about it.

KATE

≈≈

When I tell Everett what Evelyn has said, he agrees to look up my father Frank. He says he still has connections and it shouldn't take too long. Meanwhile, he doesn't want me to talk to Frank. I don't want to, anyway, so that's not an issue.

Mama acts differently after Evelyn's visit, but she doesn't mention Frank, so I don't ask. She's more easily irritated, and I catch her staring off into the distance with a scowl on her face several times. She talks to her birds more than ever. I'm washing the screens and putting the storm windows back in when I hear her tone change. She sounds incredibly sad. I set down the screen I've just hosed off and watch her. She's gotten up and she's standing near the bird-bath. There's a small, plump gray-and-black bird on the edge of the bath who almost seems to be listening to her.

"I'm telling you, Dizzy," she says. I've never understood how she can tell one bird from another. They all look the same to me—birds. "Life gets away from you."

I watch as Mama wipes her eyes and then draws her sweater tighter around her tiny frame. The little bird flies off and Mama watches him disappear over the fence.

Later, when I'm settling Mama in her recliner with her cup of tea, I ask, "Did Evelyn say something that upset you?"

"What would she say?" Mama is calm now. "It's not like she ever talks about anything but herself!"

I need to know what Evelyn said to Mama. Over the next few days, I leave her messages demanding to know what she's said to Mama, but she doesn't call me back.

At first, I let it go. Mama has settled down mostly. If anything, she's quieter. But I catch her crying one afternoon and she insists it's only from the wind. So, after I've cleaned up the kitchen and waited to hear Mama's not-so-gentle snore, I pick up the phone. Maybe if I call from Mama's phone, Evelyn will answer. She does.

"What did you tell Mama?"

"Relax. I didn't say anything terrible."

"You must have said something. She's acting odd."

"I told her I'd talked to Dad."

"You called him Dad?"

"Yes. He's our father, isn't he?"

"That depends on your definition."

"Oh, don't be so uptight. All I said was that I'd been talking to him."

"And what was the point? Why does she even have to know that?"

"Because I've invited him to come for a visit."

"You what?"

"I invited him for Thanksgiving."

"Why? Why would you do that?"

"Because I'd like to meet him in person. He's pretty excited; even said he might consider relocating up here."

"But he's a complete stranger!"

"No. He's not. He's our father and I, for one, would like to know him. Mama has kept him from us our whole lives."

"She has not 'kept him from us.' He left! He didn't come back!"

"Because he couldn't! Because of her!"

"Oh, c'mon. You know that's not possible. We weren't in hiding. If he'd wanted to find us, he could have. It's that simple."

"Give him a break. He was afraid. And he didn't have any money. He was serving God."

I laugh at this. Evelyn has never believed in God. God is one big joke to her. When Everett and I got married in a church, she laughed.

"A church? Why the hell would you want to get married in a church? It's not as if God is anything more than a figment of people's imagination dreamed up as a crutch to explain all their bad choices and shitty luck."

I didn't even try to explain to her that I felt something when I was in the church. I was being given a new chance. Marrying Everett seemed sacred to me. I'd never experienced a happiness like I did with him. And maybe I wanted to believe in something, even if I didn't know what it was. But Evelyn is the one with the silver tongue and the mind that is always three steps ahead of the rest of us, so there was no point trying to explain it.

"And when did you find religion? I thought God was for the gullible?"

"He was doing more than paying it lip service. He was helping people."

"What else did you say to Mama on Saturday?"

"I told you. I said I'd been talking to Dad."

"And?"

"And what?"

"What else? I know you said more than that."

Evelyn sighs her annoyance. She pauses to tell someone she needs a latte. Finally, she says, "I told her the truth."

"Which was?"

"That I've been talking to Dad and I know that she's been lying to us for forty years."

"And how did she take that?"

"She says he's the one who's lying. But of course she's going to say that. I think she's been lying about it for so long that she honestly believes it."

"Or it's true and he's the one who's lying."

"I don't think so. He even said he'd like to see her."

"Did you tell her that?"

"Yes, but she acted like she hadn't heard me."

"Maybe she didn't."

"Or maybe she didn't want to. What about you? Have you thought about it? Do you want to talk to him?"

"No, I don't."

"How can you say that? He's your father!"

"I don't know him, but I know my mother. She's the one who raised us. She's the one who has been here for us. She loves us."

Evelyn laughed. "If she really loved us, she wouldn't have kept our own father from seeing us."

"We don't know what happened."

"No, we don't, but I think it's only fair to hear from both of them."

"So how did you leave things?"

"She didn't tell you?"

"No, but I can tell she's very upset."

"I told her that he was coming for Thanksgiving and that I wanted us to have a nice family meal together—Dad, you, and Everett and the kids, *and* her."

"You know she can't handle that. She's fragile right now."

"Oh please, she's about as fragile as an elephant."

"What did she say about Thanksgiving?"

"What you'd expect."

"What?"

"That she could not sit at a table with him, and we shouldn't either."

"Why do you have to make this such a big scene? Let her get used to the idea before you throw it in her face! I don't know why you had to even propose it."

"Because it's time to stop pretending we don't have a father. He exists! He wants to be in our lives! You should talk to him."

"I'm not ready to talk to him. I need to discuss this with Everett." Everett still hasn't told me what he's discovered about my father, if anything. He's been home so late, and he and Jenna bicker every night. There's never a good moment.

"Oh, right. Talk to Everett because he'll be so helpful on this."

"What's that supposed to mean?"

"He's the most suspicious person I've ever met. He'll assume that Dad is up to something."

I cringe at her use of the word *Dad*. It sounds so foreign.

"He's a cop. He knows we have to be smart about this."

"*Was* a cop. They took his badge away, remember?"

"He quit."

"Right. Well, you talk to your perfect little husband who knows everything and see what he thinks, and just let me know how many to expect for Thanksgiving."

Evelyn hangs up.

Everett's not perfect. I've never called him that. Evelyn just hates that I have a happy marriage. Nobody's perfect. I certainly am not. But Everett's a good man and he's trying to be better. I know he is.

When that woman Charlene came to our door two years ago, I thought it was the end of my world. But we survived it. As the counselor told us, "When you fix a break the right way, it makes your bond even stronger than it was in the beginning." I wrote his words down and keep them in my purse. Sometimes I read them again when I have my doubts.

I'm not stupid. I still worry about Everett, and I remember how I felt that day. Charlene had just left, taking her vile words and her skintight dress and four-inch heels back down our front walk. I thought she was taking my marriage, too.

When Everett came home from work and I confronted him, he'd begged me with tears in his eyes.

"Oh God, Katie, I can't forgive myself. I never meant for anything to happen. It was the biggest mistake I've ever made in this life. You have to believe me! I'm sick about this. I ended it, that's why she came here. I don't even know how she found our address. I'm so sorry. I could never love someone like I love you. She meant nothing."

I crossed my arms and looked away from him. I didn't want him to see me cry; I only wanted him to feel my anger, my hurt—his betrayal. I'd spent that afternoon preparing to confront him, determined not to cry, but his tears brought mine to the surface. He was sorry. I knew he was sorry that Charlene had shown up, that he had hurt me. But was he sorry that it had happened? I worried that he was only saying what was necessary, but what choice did I have? If I didn't accept his apology, my whole world would crumble. What would that do to JT? To Jenna?

So instead, in that moment, I decided to believe him. Maybe it was the coward's way out; Evelyn never failed to tell me it was, but I think she was wrong. I think it might have been the bravest thing I've ever done.

For months, Everett was the adoring husband he'd been back when I first moved into his apartment and we started our life together. He brought me flowers. He painted our bedroom robin's egg blue, like I'd always wanted, and didn't complain when I signed us up for ballroom dancing lessons. I sewed beautiful new curtains and throw pillows in a soft sage with a watered-down, blue-flowered motif that matched the blue of the walls. I created a new sanctuary for us and, for a while, it really seemed like our love was growing. It was honest and real and raw. And we'd been happy.

He came home every night; we went to counseling together—he even read the book I gave him on living with a child with Asperger's. But the book made him angry. He didn't want to believe there was anything so wrong with

JT that there could be not just a label but an entire book about it.

"I just think some of this is bullshit," he'd said. "JT's not like the kids they write about."

"They're all different," I explained. "That's why they call it a spectrum. Each child is unique and falls somewhere different on the spectrum."

Everett shook his head. "JT is just young. Young kids like routines. They're picky about food. They don't know how to handle their emotions. He doesn't wave his hands around or walk like a robot or talk about dinosaurs. He's just really smart—smarter than the other kids. That's why they don't relate to him."

"JT has his own symptoms. Every child presents in a different way."

"I just think you want to label him so there's an excuse for his behavior. He's smart. Maybe we need to talk to him about this. Warn him that he's getting labeled and he needs to behave better."

"That won't work. I'm a nurse, remember. I know what I'm seeing. JT's reactions are not typical kid stuff. They're too extreme. You don't watch him with the other kids. He doesn't understand them. He can't tell if someone's bullying him or showing a genuine interest in being his friend. He can't read their faces. If we don't help him, how will he ever have friends?"

"He has friends," Everett insisted.

"No, he doesn't," I told him. "Name one."

Everett couldn't.

"You've said yourself that he never looks you in the eye," I continued. "That's classic Asperger's."

"That's classic disrespect. That's what that is. Both our kids are completely overindulged. They need to learn more respect. And it's not just our kids. It's all kids these days!"

I was quiet then. I knew that he was simply frustrated. He was only denying reality because he couldn't accept it. Until

Everett accepts that JT is not a normal kid, he will keep trying to make him one. Sometimes I feel helpless to make things better between them. The more Everett demands, the more JT recedes. These days he avoids his father. He's confused by him and doesn't understand what he wants.

I've tried to help, to explain to JT what his father expects. Sometimes that helps. "Your father wants you to look at him in the eye."

"Why?"

"Because it's a sign of respect."

JT tries, but it's hard and some days he forgets. For him, looking his father in the eye makes as much sense as looking at his wrist or his shoulder or his nose when he talks to him. It seems random and it requires that JT make a conscious effort to do it. No one else in his world demands this, so it frustrates him, I know. But he tries, because Everett is his father. JT is like every kid—he wants to please his dad.

≈≈

A few days later, I call Evelyn. I still haven't talked to Everett, but I don't want Evelyn to start meddling and encourage Frank to contact me. I want her to tell him to leave me alone. Thanksgiving is still two months away. There's no reason to decide now.

"I'm not ready to talk to him," I tell her.

"Just hear him out! Can't you at least listen to what he has to say?"

"What would it matter at this point? We're all grown up. I don't need a father. And Mama certainly doesn't need us dredging up old stuff that was over long ago. I think we turned out fine without a father. He's a stranger to us now. Can't he just live his life?"

"He doesn't want to; he wants to know us. He wants to know his grandchildren."

"No! You invited him back into our family without talking to me or Mama. We don't need him showing up at this point in our lives. We're doing fine without him."

"She's nuts, you know. At some point, very soon, we need to start the process of getting her into some kind of facility."

"We've been over this. I can take care of her."

"I can afford to pay for it, if that's your worry."

"That's not my worry! She's our mother! She raised us. Do you have no sense of loyalty? After all she's done for us, the least we can do is take care of her now."

"After all she's done for us? What? Like deprive us of a father and warp our perceptions of men? Do you know that it wasn't until I was in college that I realized how we'd been duped? Men are not the enemy, Kate. And our father isn't either. He only wants to make up for lost time—be a part of our lives. Are you really going to deprive your children of that?"

I don't know, but I don't tell her this. I'm still undecided about JT and Jenna meeting their grandfather. But I don't like the way Evelyn is shoving him down our throats and using him to hurt Mama.

"I have to go. We can talk about this another time."

"Can I give him your number?"

"No!"

"Fine, but think about it."

"As if I couldn't."

JENNA
≈≈

I've been hanging out with Ms. Cassie more and more. On Friday night, while Wells is at the football game I didn't go to, she makes popcorn and we watch a movie. She's also a huge Jane Austen fan, so we debate the merits of the movie *Mansfield Park* and the book. The movie totally opts out of so much in the name of selling tickets. We agree on this and decide that's what we'll watch next time, just so we can pick it apart. Ms. Cassie doesn't have a streaming service. She watches actual discs. Tonight she has some movie, also set in the 1800s, that I have never heard of.

It's nothing like a Jane story, but I like the costumes and the dancing. When we get to the part in the movie when the heroine's father is dying, Ms. Cassie gets up for a glass of water. When she comes back, I ask, "Did you not want to watch him die?"

She looks at me blankly. "He was sick. It was time."

"Yeah, but it was really sad."

She doesn't say anything.

"Was it too much like work?"

"What? Oh, no. It's fine." She pauses the movie. "Death doesn't bother me."

"Really?"

"It's part of life. A bad death bothers me, but that wasn't a bad death. He was surrounded by everyone who loved him. He knew he was dying. He got to say good-bye. What more could you ask for?"

106

"A few more years?"

She laughs.

"Aren't people pretty pissed when they find out they're going to die?"

She shrugs. "Sometimes, but not often. Most people already know it. It's not a surprise."

"Wow. I just think it'd get pretty depressing being around dying people all the time."

"Actually, many times it's inspiring. Makes me glad for the time I have left. Makes me appreciate simple stuff, like being able to walk into the other room and get my own glass of water."

She clicks the movie back on and I take another handful of popcorn, but now I'm distracted. And curious. I've never seen a dead person. Sometimes when I show up at Gram's after school, she's sleeping in her recliner and she doesn't move when I come in. She looks kind of dead, but she never is. This week I was over there a couple times because Mom had to deal with JT and no one trusts Gram to operate her stove anymore. Death was all she could talk about.

"I'm ready," she said. "I know my time is close and I'm ready to go. In fact, if it weren't for the birds, I might hurry it along."

I looked at her. Shit! Was she talking about killing herself again? She went through that a few years back, when she had to be in that rehab place after she broke her hip. She kept saying she'd be better off dead. Made me promise that if she slipped into a coma, I wouldn't let them keep her alive. I didn't know what to say. That wouldn't be up to me. I just said, "I'll keep that in mind," like my mother says whenever I ask for something she has no intention of giving me.

"Gram," I told her, putting the blanket around her legs the way she likes it, "why would you be in a hurry to leave me and JT and Mom?" I didn't mention Everett since Gram hates him anyway.

She closed her eyes and didn't say anything. I thought playing a little guilt card here would pep her back up, but no dice. So I tried a different tack.

"Besides, then you wouldn't get to see me in a prom dress."

She opened her eyes at this. "You have a boyfriend?"

I laughed. "Not really. But prom isn't until spring. I'm working on something." I almost told her about Wells, but Wells isn't my boyfriend, and just because he asked me to sit with him at the football game doesn't mean he wants to be—it means absolutely zero. He doesn't have a girlfriend, though. He told me. I don't know why he told me. When he did, I said, "Well, good for you!" very enthusiastically, like Everett does when JT tells him something he couldn't care less about.

She scowled. "Stay away from boys. They're not anything you want to get mixed up with. They seem nice at first, but it never lasts. In the end, you'll discover them to be louses, just like your father and your grandfather."

"I'm not sure that the plural of louse is louses, Gram."

"What?"

"I think more than one louse might be lice!" I laughed at my own joke and she scowled some more.

"Bring me that box of tissues and the remote!"

I was still chuckling as I handed the remote to her. "Anything else you need?"

"What? Are you in such a hurry to get away from me? I could be dead tomorrow!"

"I'll have to take that chance!" I told her and took off. I was meeting Wells and didn't want him to think I wasn't going to show up. Not that I cared whether he thought I wasn't going to show up. I didn't.

When the movie's over, Ms. Cassie says, "Are you still worried your grandmother is going to die?"

I forgot I told her about all that shit with Gram saying she was going to die soon. I shake my head. "Not really, but like you said, she might know something I don't. She says she wants to die."

"That's a shame," says Ms. Cassie. "Maybe she's just lonely. Does she like visitors?"

I can't imagine Ms. Cassie visiting Gram. That would just be weird.

"She likes to keep to herself. She even has the curtains stapled to the walls."

"That seems a little ridiculous. And depressing."

"Tell me about it. Everything with Gram is a little ridiculous. But the Conklins across the street keep an eye on the house and they call if anything looks weird. Like last month when Gram almost burned the house down because she tried to make tea."

"Have your parents considered assisted living?"

"You mean an old folks home? That's what Gram calls it. She says only over her dead body, which is funny, you know. Like I said, most everything with Gram is ridiculous."

Ms. Cassie finishes cleaning her popcorn maker. She's the only person I know who makes popcorn in a real popcorn maker and doesn't use the microwave. She doesn't even have a microwave. I read something about microwaves causing cancer. I want to ask her if that's why she doesn't have one, but she's yawning and turning off lights.

"I've got to work early tomorrow. You have any special plans for the weekend?"

Why is it adults always ask if you have "special plans"? What does that mean, anyway? I wish Ms. Cassie wouldn't use that phrase because I think of her as a more-cool adult.

"Nope. Just the same old criminal mischief as always."

She smiles. "Well, stay out of trouble." Another horrible adult phrase. Maybe it's because she's super tired. She yawns again.

"I'll see ya," I say and head out the screened door to the porch. I have to say good-bye to the dwarfs.

"Turn the light out when you go," she says.

"No problem," I tell her.

After I've said *adios* to the cats, I wander the street, hoping Wells will turn up. He doesn't. I sit in the grove of pine trees at the bottom of his front yard and watch his house like a regular burglar. I remember being a kid and being afraid of burglars. They were the scariest thing I knew. There's no action at the Braddingtons, so maybe they're all tucked in tight. I'm about to head home when I see Everett's truck come down the road. What's he doing out this late? I can only imagine. I wait for him to pull in. I watch the lights come on in my house and then go out again. Then I slink home.

EVERETT

≈≈

Ishouldn't have stayed so long at Veronica's. Now Kate will be totally on my case and I'll have to make up some shit about an emergency at work. I was gonna leave, but then Veronica put on that maid outfit she bought from Frederick's and well, shit, when's that gonna happen again? She had the feather duster and everything.

Driving home, I regret that last beer. I probably shouldn't even be behind the wheel. I don't know as many cops as I used to. So many young guys joining the force and they have no allegiance to the brotherhood. Once a cop, always a cop. Luckily, I make it home in one piece.

When I crawl into bed, Kate reaches for me. If I hadn't already done it three times tonight, I would have played along just to keep her from asking too many questions, but there was no way I could get it up again. Besides, she smelled the beer on my breath.

"You've been drinking," she says.

"Just a couple beers after we finished," I tell her, keeping it vague. I roll over like I'm going to sleep, but she doesn't let it go.

"What happened? Why'd you have to go in?"

I sigh. "I'll tell you about it in the morning. I'm beat."

I lie there for a while wishing I wasn't such a dick. Kate is a good woman. She deserves better. I don't know what's wrong with me. I've got to quit this thing with Veronica, but God, the woman is hard to resist. She's built like a house and she's always ready to go and she never asks me about anything. She talks my ear off about the restaurant where she works and she tells me these fucking crazy fantasies she has. If she's had too much to drink, sometimes she'll rant about her ex, but mostly she's just fun. I know it won't last forever. Shit, I can barely keep up. So I got to enjoy it while it lasts.

But I should end it before Jenna says something to Kate. I don't know how Jenna knows about Veronica, but I'm pretty sure she does. I used to love how Jenna followed me around watching my every move. But now it's a liability. She knows me too well.

Most days it seems like she hates me. Kate says it's because she's a teenager, but I think it's more. I think she knows shit. She's always snooping around everywhere and she sees stuff. She's like her old man. I taught her all about the criminal mind. Christ, she could break into any house on our street if she wanted. Putting her in juvie might be the perfect way to scare her straight, but that's off the table now. I'm pretty sure if I had her locked up, even for just a few days, she'd tell Kate about Veronica. She said as much.

Kate was at her mother's and Jenna was cleaning up dinner. 'Course, she was pissed she had to do the dishes, and when I said I was going out, she rolled her eyes. I should have just left, but I am so tired of all her disrespect.

"Don't roll your eyes at me, young lady," I said, as I put my coat on.

"You know, we all have secrets," she said. "Good thing Mom doesn't know yours. 'Course, if you lock me up in juvie, she and I could write long letters back and forth. You never know what I might say."

"What the hell's that supposed to mean?"

She shrugged her shoulders and turned back to the dishes, but I saw her smile. Pissed me off, but I have to give her credit. She's a cunning one, that girl. Gets it from me.

"Just stay out of other people's houses," I told her, and left before she could come back with some smart-ass comment.

I don't know why she was messing with the Braddington house. Those people are loaded. She says she didn't take anything—hope that's true.

If I'd have known kids would be this much of a pain in the ass, I probably would have had a vasectomy back in my teens. Ah, maybe I don't mean that. Maybe. If it's not Jenna, though, it's JT and his crazy obsessions. We should shut off the cable so he can't watch those shows he loves 24/7. But that would probably just set off another of his meltdowns. I don't know what to do with him when he acts like that. He's too old to be throwing tantrums like a three-year-old, and I don't buy that Asperger's shit. He knows better. He's smart. Smarter than any of the other kids at his school. Hell, probably smarter than the adults, too. It's past time he starts acting like it.

KATE

≈≈

When the invitation from Susan Braddington came, I was surprised. We've never been invited to anything at the Braddingtons'. And now we've all been invited for the "Annual Chili Cook-Off." I try not to pay attention to the fact that we've lived across the street from each other for over ten years and this is the first time we've been invited to what is apparently a yearly affair.

When I tell Jenna and Everett about it, Jenna asks, "Why would we go to that? We don't ever eat chili."

Which is true. I've never made chili, and now I've only got two weeks to find the perfect recipe.

"I love chili. That sounds like fun," says Everett. But when I mention that the invitation is for all of us, he insists that we should leave JT at home.

"But the invitation says, the Turner *Family*. JT will have fun."

"JT will so *not* have fun. I don't want to go either. I'll stay here with him. You kids can go," Jenna says.

"No. This is a family outing and we're all going. These people are our neighbors and we hardly know them!"

"I know them," says Jenna.

"You do?" says Everett.

If he spent any time at home, he'd know that Jenna has been spending plenty of time with Wells Braddington.

"Sure. I ride the bus with Wells and Tiffany every day."

"That's true. And when you were little, we shared a bus stop. Susan and I talked every day."

114

I know I'm exaggerating. When the kids were in elementary school and Susan brought them down to the bus stop, most days she was on her phone the entire time. When she wasn't, I'd try to come up with interesting things to say.

"So, I saw that the PTA is going to sponsor an artist in residence! Isn't that exciting?"

To which Susan had said, "I heard it's some old woman who does folk dancing. Really, you'd think they could come up with something that would interest the children."

Another time, I tried inviting her for coffee. "There's a new coffee shop open on Talbot Street. I've heard it's excellent. Would you like to try it out with me one morning?"

Susan answered, "I was just there yesterday. Overpriced coffee, and the people behind the counter have no idea how to make a decent latte."

I know that Susan is a snob, but she's our neighbor. I've always wanted us to be friends. In all those mornings, I don't think I ever managed to engage Susan in one single meaningful conversation. And once Wells was ten, she stopped coming to the bus stop at all.

Maybe the invitation means Susan regrets that we've never become friends. Maybe this is her way of reaching out.

When Everett and I first moved to Pine Estates, I was so excited at the idea of neighbors. The apartment we'd shared up until that day had been above a Chinese restaurant. The only neighbors were the owners and a few of the workers, but no one spoke much English.

Once I stopped working, it was hard to maintain the friendships that had been so important to me for years. My work friends had lives that revolved around the ER and the hospital. When I met them for coffee, I'd listen to their stories; but once they fell into the old banter between each other, I'd have nothing to add. Eventually, I stopped going altogether.

I was trapped in our apartment with Jenna. I loved my baby, but I was lonely. I was sure moving to Pine Estates would bring a new set of friends. I was excited to meet them. As I unpacked and painted, I imagined the people who lived in the other beautiful houses on Pine Road would soon stop by and welcome us to the neighborhood. But no one did. Everett said that only happens in the movies.

I took long walks with JT in the stroller, hoping to bump into someone; but the houses were shut up tight with the central air blasting. The only people I saw outside were hired gardeners, lawn guys spraying chemicals, and the occasional trash collectors.

Even though my days now are busy and full, taking care of Mama and JT, I still feel very much alone. I'm not sure why it's so difficult to find friends once you grow up. I guess everyone already has their "people," and they're too busy to invest in building new friendships. I see women at JT's school or in the grocery store who look like they would make nice friends, but it's awkward. I can't simply invite a stranger out for tea. I guess I've never been the outgoing sort. The few friends I had growing up have long since moved away from here. Everett says it's easy to find them on Facebook, but I'm not looking for virtual friends. Maybe it's me.

The first Christmas we moved here, Everett gave me Marco to cheer me up. "Now you'll have a best friend!" he'd said. Marco was good company, especially when he was younger, but he wasn't the company I really wanted. These days he can't hear anything and he can barely see. Besides, he seems to prefer Jenna's company to anyone else's. Some days I forget he's even here.

He's been peeing on the rug more and more. Last week, Everett said that maybe it was time to take him to the pound. As if that's what you should do when your pet is no longer living up to your expectations. I wanted to say, "Is that what we should do with you when you grow old?" But I didn't. Fights with Everett can go on and on. He always needs the last word.

I secure the invitation to the refrigerator with a magnet and study it. It's beautiful, probably custom made. The red plaid tablecloth pictured on it seems to float right off the page. I run my fingers over it and some of the red color stains them.

After I've gotten JT to school, I stop at Mama's. It's a gorgeous fall day. Maybe today I can convince her to go with me for a walk. The doctor says there is no reason for her to stay in her chair all day. She doesn't even truly need her walker. It's almost as if she wants to be older and frailer than she is. When I'm nearby, she leans on me, gripping my arm tightly with her thin fingers pressing dents in my flesh. We move between the kitchen table, the porch chair, and the recliner in the living room—our daily routes. But when I'm not there, she manages to get herself around. She uses the bathroom and can shower without assistance.

Some days I do wonder how much of Mama's health issues are in her head. Certainly, she struggles mentally. The fact that she won't leave the house is evidence of that. When she came home from the hospital after the teapot incident, she asked me to cover all the windows that faced the road. I knew that covering all the windows was crazy, but I did it because she insisted. It wasn't a big thing and it made her feel safe. Now being at her house feels prison-like, disconnected from everything around it.

Both Mama and Everett seem overly concerned about dangers that never present themselves. That's something they've always had in common. When Everett was still on the force, Mama would grill him on home invasions and carjackings. Watching so many crime dramas on TV had convinced her there were rapists and serial killers on every corner. Crime was rare in our suburban Pennsylvania town, but Everett could enthrall Mama for hours with stories that even I knew were exaggerated. When a small-time drug dealer broke in to the home a few streets away, Everett told her, "The woman hadn't bothered to lock her windows, and the next thing she knows, there's a crack kingpin tearing apart her house." He neglected to mention that the woman was an addict who was passed out cold. I met both of them in the ER when the criminal turned up looking for the victim's hospital room after making bail. Apparently, they were related. Mama would repeat these stories to the other women at the grocery store or the library, adding details that Everett left out.

Back then, I thought Everett's obsession with protection was only an outgrowth of his job and a way to impress Mama, but even now that he is no longer a police officer and refuses to be in the same room as Mama, he is still paranoid about our safety. He installed state-of-the-art locks on all our doors, and had fits when Jenna left them triggered so she could come and go after hours. I'm not sure what he is so afraid of, but I don't dare voice that thought. I've started to believe he needs to do these things—he needs to feel as if he is protecting us. It's his way of showing how much he loves us.

I unlock Mama's door and turn on a light in the dark living room. Then I hide the key back under the planter on the front porch. Mama and Everett would both probably fall down in shock if they knew I keep a key there. I need to make a new one to replace the one Jenna lost, but I never seem to think of it.

At home, there's no key because we use garage door openers or punch in the code. And no one ever uses the front door. We so rarely have any visitors besides Jehovah's Witnesses in their neat skirts and heavy makeup. Some days I talk to them just for the company. Nice young women. Sometimes on Saturdays, they will bring along a tidy young man who wears a tie, no matter the weather. I'm impressed by their dedication but I always toss their literature in the recycling. JT is a voracious reader. All I need is him getting his hands on something that says *The End is Coming*.

"Good morning, Mama!" I call.

Mama is already installed in her chair outside. She's having a serious discussion with the birds. I crack the kitchen window to listen while I make her breakfast. I'm still trying to figure out what she was talking about the other day with the birds. If only *I* was a bird, I might know what's really going on inside her heart.

"I envy all of you," Mama says. "You can just leave. You can just fly away. You aren't trapped here, helpless, waiting." I watch Mama's wrinkled face staring at the sky. Is it sadness or confusion that makes her shake her head and lower it to her hands?

We have yet to discuss Evelyn's news. When I try to bring up Frank's impending visit, Mama acts as if she doesn't remember it or changes the subject. I've known for some time that her memory losses are very selective. She might be choosing to not remember it because she doesn't want to talk about it.

"Here we go," I say as I carry a tray with her tea and toast to the table. Several chickadees that had been resting on the chair opposite Mama fly off.

"I was thinking that it's such a beautiful day we could take a walk. Just up the street a few houses."

"Why would we do that?"

"Because it would be good for you. The doctor said you need to get out."

Mama drops her spoon and it clatters against her tea-cup. "I don't want to go out! Why do you insist I go out? Are you planning something?"

I lean over and pick up the spoon, use it to fish out the tea bag, and set it on the saucer. Then I add cream. "No, Mama. Why would I be planning something?"

"I wish everyone could just mind their own business. Leave me alone. I'll be dead soon enough."

I walk to the birdbath. "It was only an idea." The bath is almost empty, so I pull the hose from the side of the house and fill it up.

"Well, if you don't need anything. I'm going to go home. I have a few things I need to do."

"You go. Leave me here alone," says Mama in a tone that implies that is the last thing she wants. Today, though, I decide to take her at her word.

"Okay, then, I'll be back around lunchtime. You be good."

Mama says nothing. She sips her tea and watches the birds flock to the newly filled bath.

When I get home, I spend an hour on Everett's computer researching chili recipes and choose three that are listed as "Award-Winning Chili." I copy them onto index cards and make a neat list for the grocery store. I'm about to shut it off when an instant message pops up. "Hey Sexy, wanna come play tonight?" The user's name is V. Bowden. What I hope is that this is a message sent to the wrong person. But what I write is, *Go away and leave us alone.*

I'm about to leave for the store when there's a knock on the front door. The Jehovah's Witness girls were here only three days ago. It can't be them. I tiptoe to the door and peer through the peephole at a woman who looks about my age. Her blond hair is sprinkled with gray and cut short and neat. She's wearing jeans and a long-sleeve T-shirt that reads "To Each His Own." She doesn't look dangerous, and I'm certain I've seen her before, so I open the door.

The woman smiles brightly and holds out Jenna's green windbreaker.

"Hi! I'm Cassie. I live a few doors down. Jenna's been looking after my cats."

I had no idea that Jenna was looking after the neighbor's cats.

"Maybe she didn't tell you. Anyway, she left her jacket on the porch. I thought she might need it. The weather is supposed to finally cool off."

I have no idea where Jenna goes when she disappears after school. She could be anywhere. When I do ask where she's been, she almost always says, "Nowhere."

"I'm sorry! Where are my manners?" I finally say, holding out my hand. "I'm Kate." I *have* seen her before. She's our neighbor. She lives in a house about halfway to Mama's. It's an adorable little Tudor cottage, completely out of place on either end of our street. It's always reminded me of the house in the "Hansel and Gretel" story. This is the woman who moved in only a few years ago. I stopped by the house several times, but no one was ever home. That was right after Mama's fall, and since then I just haven't found time to try again. Plus, it seemed like too much time had passed to welcome her to a neighborhood she'd been living in for nearly a year. Still, it was nice that she took the time to return Jenna's jacket.

"So nice to meet you," says the woman, now smiling warmly and taking my hand.

"That's so kind of you to return Jenna's jacket. I hope she's been doing a good job with the cats."

"She's very devoted and the cats seem to like her."

I don't know what to say to this, so I reach for the jacket. I don't want this pleasant woman with the pretty face to leave, so I ask, "Would you like to come in for a cup of tea?"

"I have to get to work, but I did want to inquire about your mother. Jenna tells me that she lives in Pine Estates?"

"She does."

"I'm sorry. I might be talking out of turn, but I'm a nurse and—"

"So am I!" I can't help but exclaim.

"Jenna hadn't told me."

"Well, I haven't worked in quite a few years."

"Actually, I'm a hospice nurse."

"Oh." I can't imagine a job like that. Much too quiet and depressing. I always loved the excitement of the ER.

"Anyway, Jenna tells me your mother is a bit depressed. She's worried about her. I just wondered if she might like a visitor on occasion. I'd be happy to stop in."

"No, I don't think so. Mama doesn't like visitors."

"That's what Jenna said, but I thought it might help. Many elderly people who live alone are quite lonely."

Why would a complete stranger want to visit Mama? I look at her again. Maybe she has an agenda. Everett says that most people who say they want to help you, and aren't getting paid for it, have an agenda.

"I'm sorry, but why would you want to visit my mother?"

"I just thought she might like a visitor. And I actually enjoy elderly people, even difficult ones." She smiles.

"My mother can be difficult."

"So I hear. At any rate, I've offered. Jenna is so great with my kitties, visiting them even when I'm not paying her to. I'm not home very much, so it's nice to know there's someone spending time with them. I only thought I might be able to return the kindness by looking in on her grandmother."

It seems innocent enough. I should probably run the idea past Everett. See if I'm missing something. He would know if I should be worried.

"That's very nice of you. I'll ask Mama if it would be okay for you to visit."

"Great! Just let me know." She starts back down the walk, but then stops and turns. "I really like your daughter. She's a great kid. You should be very proud."

Her words bring tears to my eyes, so I nod. Any response I might have had sticks in my throat. That isn't what most people say about my daughter with the black, black hair, rope choker on her neck, and dark look in her eyes.

"Thank you!" I finally manage to say when she's nearly to the street, but she can't hear me. I watch her walk up Pine Road towards her home. A peculiar woman. A hospice nurse!

EVERETT

≈≈

When I get home from work, Kate is all upset because dinner isn't ready and she hasn't gone to the grocery store to buy all the shit she needs for the chili recipes she wants to try. For the life of me, I don't understand why she even wants to go to the chili cook-off at the Braddingtons' next weekend. They aren't our people. The invitation itself is odd. After that crap with Jenna breaking in to their place, I don't know why they're suddenly opening their doors to us after all these years. Seems suspicious to me, but when I said as much to Kate she accused me of being paranoid.

I'm still feeling crappy about spending the other evening with Veronica, so I offer to help.

"How about I run to the store while you're fixing dinner?"

"Could you?" she asks.

"Sure. Let me just go change."

When I come back downstairs, JT is waiting with his coat on.

"JT would really like to go with you. He wants to pick out his noodles this week. And I gave him the list of ingredients I need. He knows that store backwards and forwards, so he'll be a big help to you."

JT is grinning at me. I haven't had a chance to tell him I'm sorry about Saturday, so I figure this is a good chance to make it up to him.

"Sure, great. We'll be back in a jiffy," I tell her and give her a quick kiss. When JT turns to go, I run my hand over her ass and she giggles. Maybe later I can make things up to her, too.

At the store, JT takes off with the list. I don't know what else to do, so I follow him with the cart. Kate's right, he knows the store well. We've gotten everything on her list and are standing in front of the pasta when there's a commotion at the end of the aisle. A woman has collapsed, and her husband is standing there looking at her screaming, "Oh my God! Oh my God!"

A store employee appears and kneels down by her head.

"Does anybody know CPR?" he yells. I've been trained in CPR like any cop, but I don't want to get involved. The paramedics will be here quick. We're only a block from the station.

"I do," says JT, who is standing beside him. I never even noticed he'd left my side.

The guy looks at him doubtfully, but JT starts telling him exactly what to do in that funny voice he uses when he's reciting something he's memorized.

"Okay, here, you do it," says the guy.

"I can't," says JT. "I'm just a kid."

I know it probably is more likely that JT doesn't want to touch the woman. But the guy tips the woman's head back to clear the airway, just like JT is telling him, and then follows JT's instructions. Moments later, the EMTs arrive, but the woman is breathing again. They are quick to whisk her away. When everyone's gone, JT walks back to me, all grins. I don't know what to say. Sometimes the kid amazes me. I watch as he puts two boxes of the wagon wheel pasta in our cart.

We turn to head to the check out and the store manager approaches us with the employee that performed the CPR. The guy is pointing at JT. "That's him!" he says.

The manager shakes JT's hand. "You're a hero, young man!" He turns to me and shakes my hand, too. "You must be so proud of your son!"

Now, let me say this. In all the years since JT was born, I'm not certain anyone has said those words to me. They've looked at me in pity when I carted him off screaming and flailing from McDonald's because there was mustard on his hamburger or peeled him off the floor at the hardware store because someone started up a weed whacker, but no one has said, "You must be so proud of your son." Ever.

I look at JT. I am proud.

"You saved that woman's life!" the manager is saying. "Jimbo, here, tells me you told him exactly what to do. He'd never have been able to do CPR if you hadn't been there."

JT nods. He says, "You should have an AED in this place."

"A what?"

"Automated External Defibrillator."

"What's that?"

JT looks at him like he can't believe the guy has never heard of it. I know he's wondering if this is a trick. JT has a hard time knowing when someone's pulling his leg.

"Tell him what it is," I say.

"It's a portable device used to induce electrical stimulation to the heart muscle in the event of a potential cardiac arrest."

"Huh? Well, anyway, we'd like to thank you for your help. Let me write down your name."

When he says this, I think, *No way*. If that lady croaks, they could come back and sue us.

"You don't need his name," I tell the guy. "We gotta get going."

"No, really, I think the newspapers would love to have this story!"

The guys is smiling at me like all I want is my kid's name splashed all over the front page. Who the hell wants that?

"Nope. Ain't gonna happen. C'mon, JT, we need to get these things home to your mother."

The guy won't let it go. He follows us as I push the cart to the front.

"I don't understand why you don't want people to know that your son is a hero."

Every register is backed up three deep. I can't stand here and argue with the guy.

"Why can't I tell him my name?" asks JT.

"Yeah, and we'd love to get a picture." He pulls out a phone to take JT's picture. I hold up my hand in front of the phone.

"No pictures." He puts it down.

"At least give us a name. I'm sure that couple would like to be able to thank the person who saved her life."

I can see this guy is not gonna quit. I reach for JT's hand and pray he isn't gonna throw one of his fits. Miraculously, he lets me lead him out of the store.

"But what about our cart?" he says.

"We'll come back later," I tell him.

The manager follows us as far as the door, and then shakes his head. "Let me know if you change your mind!" he calls.

When we get home, JT retells the whole story to Kate.

"I'm so proud! Maybe you'll get your picture in the paper!" she says.

"I won't," JT tells her and looks at me.

"I didn't let them take his picture," I say.

"Why not?" she asks, clearly disappointed.

"Because," I say, and hope she'll leave it at that. But of course she won't.

"Because why?" she asks.

"Because I don't want his goddamn picture in the paper. What if something goes wrong and those people decide to sue us?"

"But you said she was breathing! You said JT knew exactly what to do!"

"That doesn't matter! People are crazy. We don't know them. We don't know what happened after they got her to the hospital."

Kate is angry. We sit down and eat the dinner she's prepared. Jenna comes in midway through the meal, so Kate has to tell her the whole damn story all over again.

"That is so first rate," she says. "You're like, a hero, JT! I'm so proud of you! Maybe your picture will be in the paper!"

"It won't," he says.

"Why not?"

"Dad-Unit won't let it."

She looks at me with a furrowed brow. Here we go; one more reason for her to hate me.

Kate says, "Your father thought it was best not to give them our contact information. Just in case there are legal ramifications later."

"What the fuck?"

"Language," says Kate calmly. In my day, if I'd have said something like that at the table, my dad would have backhanded me so hard I'd be in the other room. Kate says I can't punish her for the way she talks because it's "her only weapon." I think some shrink must have told her that.

"We can't afford to be sued," I tell her.

"Right!" she says in her mocking tone, looking at me the same way she does when she drops comments about Veronica. "Wouldn't want anyone to sue JT for saving her life! That's bullshit!" She gets up from the table and slams out the back door. She'll take any excuse to go run wild in our neighborhood. God knows what she's up to. I'm waiting for it to be something much worse than breaking into the Braddingtons' garage.

Kate clears our dishes and says, "JT, I think we need to celebrate your heroic actions, even if you don't get your picture in the paper. How about we go out for ice cream?"

I'm glad Kate's seeing the wisdom of my decision.

"Great idea!" I tell them. "Leave the dishes. I'll do them when we get back. We need to celebrate our hero!"

JENNA
≈≈

"Everett is such an asshole!" I tell Wells when we meet up at Ms. Cassie's house. She isn't home, so I'm guessing somebody out there is dying right now.

He's standing on the picnic table in Ms. Cassie's backyard with a cat in each hand, holding them over his head. "I wonder what they're thinking right now," he says as he grins at the cats who both look none too sure of his sanity, much like me.

"They're thinking, 'Why doesn't this asshole put me down?'"

Wells laughs and jumps down off the table. He sets both cats down and they crouch there, frozen like they're in shock. Then Sneezy lopes away and Doc peers up at me, hoping I'm going to save him. I do.

"Why is your dad an asshole?" asks Wells, scooping up Dopey and sitting down in the other chair on the patio.

I recount the story of JT saving the woman at the grocery store and Everett not letting the store manager take his picture or even have his name.

"Maybe we should go over there and tell the guy JT's name," suggests Wells.

This seems like a good idea, and I'd do it just to piss Everett off and let JT get some good press for a change, but I couldn't do it to my mom. And really, JT might freak out if people started paying too much attention to him. It's so cool though, that he used all the medical shit

128

he's memorized to really save someone. He's only twelve. That's freakin' awesome if you ask me.

"Nah," I say. "Let's go over to the Ashers' and have some ice cream." They go to church on Tuesday nights.

He's up for it, of course. The guy loves breaking into people's houses. And I like his company.

"So you never told me about the game on Friday. How was it?" I ask when we're hanging on the Ashers' back porch, ice cream cones in hand. I love that the Ashers have real ice cream cones. Nobody else on the street does. Sherm's still too young to hold a cone, so they don't do it for the kid. The Ashers are pretty cool.

"They lost."

"I meant, how was it being there with your dad?"

"Oh, that part sucked. I had to sit with him the whole time. He kept explaining to me what was happening on the field like I didn't know."

"I thought you liked football."

"I do. I just don't like how crazy it makes my dad. It's really *his* thing. I just like playing sports. Football, soccer, basketball, baseball, doesn't matter. But my dad thinks I should be committed to football." When Wells says "committed" he uses a really deep voice to imitate his dad. "He was a big-time football player, even played for Harvard, but that's not really saying anything. Most of the Ivies get their asses kicked by the real football schools."

"That's probably because smart people wouldn't play football."

"Ouch!" Wells says, and takes his ice cream cone and smashes it against my nose.

"Hey!" I laugh. And then Wells leans in and licks the ice cream off my nose. Really. Like with his tongue. I don't know what to say. I just laugh nervously. He's still looking at me, like he's done something amazing. Smiling like an idiot.

"What?" I ask.

"I like you," he tells me.

I know my face is burning up when he says this. I'm glad it's dark, so he can't see.

"I like you, too," I tell him. "But that doesn't mean I have to smash my ice cream on your face."

He laughs and eats his ice cream cone. I wipe the rest of the ice cream off with my sleeve. We talk about school and the Ashers' funny bonsai collection surrounding us. Nathan Asher loves bonsai. He created most of the plants we're looking at. He has all these tiny tools he keeps in a leather pack in their mudroom. I've seen him working on them. It's weird having this normal conversation while the whole time my mind is screaming, *Wells just licked ice cream off my nose!*

By the time I get home, everyone's asleep except Mom. She's sitting in the living room with her glass of wine and her book.

"Hey," she says when I come in.

"Hey," I tell her, and then, instead of going up to my room, I sit down next to her on the couch. Marco jumps up next to me for an ear massage.

"I'm sorry about tonight," she says. "I wish you'd have come for ice cream with us."

The word *ice cream* makes me smile, because oh my god—*Wells licked ice cream off my nose!*

"It's okay," I say.

"Where'd you go?"

"Over to Ms. Cassie's."

"Oh! I forgot to tell you! She stopped by here and brought your green jacket. You left it over there the other night."

"Ms. Cassie came here?"

She nods. "She asked about Gram. I didn't know you'd talked to her about your grandmother's situation."

"I've talked to her about a lot of things." I know Mom wants to know what else, but I don't say any more. I'm tired of my paranoid family who are always afraid to tell anyone else our business. Like anyone would really even care about our business. I try to picture Ms. Cassie and Mom in the same room. I can't. "What'd she want to know about Gram?"

"She wondered if she could visit her."

"She likes old, sick people."

"Gram isn't sick."

I give her a look instead of saying—*Yeah, right, the woman is bat-shit crazy sick.*

"Anyway, I told her I'd ask Gram if she could stop in."

"You're really going to ask her?"

"Sure, why not? It might be nice for her to talk to someone else besides me. And Cassie's a nurse; maybe she'll have some ideas for how we can better help Gram."

"You're a nurse."

"I *was* a nurse."

"You have a degree; doesn't that mean you're always a nurse?"

"My certification is out of date. I'm sure there's been plenty of advances since I was working."

I look at my mother. She looks sad. I want to tell her that Wells licked my nose, but I can't bring myself to tell her, and, besides, you kind of had to be there. She might think it's weird that a guy licked my nose. I smile.

"So is there a boy responsible for that smile?" she asks. I have to give Mom credit. She pays attention a lot more than you think she does.

I nod.

"Can you tell me about him?"

I can't. If I tell her it's Wells, she'll probably freak out and use the information to talk to Susan Braddington. I don't even know why Mom wants to be friends with someone like Susan Braddington. Plus, I don't even know if Wells told her about us. For that matter, I don't know if there even is an *us*. All I've got is the fact that he licked my nose and he said he liked me. But that could mean almost anything.

Wells Braddington goes out with cheerleaders. He's so completely out of my league that the whole thing doesn't make sense. Sometimes I wonder if he's just toying with me. Maybe he isn't serious at all. Maybe he laughs about it with his football friends. I mean, he barely acknowledges me on the bus. He's back there laughing it up with the team, and I'm up front with my headphones on listening to the stupid people around me talking about stupid shit like the homecoming dance. He does sit with me on the bus on the ride home, but that's only because all his friends are at practice. Suddenly, I feel stupid. Why am I so happy he licked my nose?

"Nope," I tell her. "Not yet."

She's disappointed, I can tell. "Well, if you change your mind, I'd love to hear about him. I'm glad you're smiling. I don't see that smile enough anymore."

"Right," I tell her, suddenly wanting to get away from her mom-ness. "I've got some homework to do."

"Okay. Thanks for checking in." She smiles at me.

"Sure."

As I get up, she says, "I love you, Jenna."

"You, too," I tell her.

KATE

≈≈

When I get to Mama's house the next day, she's still in bed. She's moaning, so I rush to her side.

"What is it?"

"I'm dying."

"What's wrong? Does something hurt?" I turn on the light and put my hand to her head.

"No! Nothing's wrong and everything's wrong. I'm just tired of waking up to it."

I sit down. I hate when she's like this. I lean over, pick up a spent tissue, and put it in the wastebasket beside the bed. I sigh.

"Did something happen? What's this about? You were fine yesterday."

"I was NOT fine yesterday! I'm not EVER fine!"

"Okay, but did something happen that upset you?"

"I can't remember. All I know is when I woke up this morning, I knew I was going to die. And I was glad." She closes her eyes.

I don't know what to say. Why does my mother want to die? Has she always been this bitter person and I just didn't see it? I try to remember when she was happy. I'm certain she was happy when I graduated from nursing school, and I think I remember her smiling at me on my wedding day. I can clearly picture her laughing as Everett teased her. And when she came to the hospital after Jenna was born, I saw tears in her eyes—happy tears.

Maybe it started when she moved to Pine Estates. She didn't want to leave the house where we grew up, but the neighborhood around it was getting worse, and after she fell and broke her hip, she'd needed my help. Evelyn had wanted to find a retirement community, but I fought it. Pine Estates was a compromise.

Since then, she's only gotten worse physically. Her balance isn't always so good. I don't remember when she stopped wanting to leave the house. That happened slowly. She came for Christmas dinner at our house last year—oh wait, not last year. Last year she was sick. It must have been the year before that. It's as if she's stuck on some downward spiral and the news of my father has simply sped it up. Why? What is she so afraid of? And why the hell can't we ever just talk plainly in this family? Why can't I ask the questions I want to ask and get an honest answer? Family is supposed to be your safe place—they love you no matter what. Is that only true in movies and on greeting cards?

I open the blinds. Then slide the window open. The sounds of the birds outside and the garbage truck rumbling up the street filter into the room.

"You can't die today. The birds haven't been fed."

Mama opens her eyes. "I can't do everything," she says, but she throws back her covers and inches to the side of the bed. I position her slippers and she slips her feet into them. She says nothing else as I wait for her to use the bathroom and then help her out to the porch.

When she has her tea in hand, I let her direct me in filling the feeders, being certain the thistle goes in the finch feeders and the black-oil sunflower seeds are loaded in the others. Then she says, "The birds won't come visit if you're out here with all your nervous energy."

"I've got to go run a few errands, anyway. I'll be back later with lunch."

"That's right, go on and leave me. I don't blame you."

I kiss the top of her head. "You'll be fine. I'll be back before you know it."

≈≈

I need to go to the grocery store and buy the ingredients Everett and JT abandoned last night. I only have four days to perfect my chili recipe. I'm embarrassed that Everett left a full cart, so I drive across town to the other grocery store. I quickly find the things I need and hurry home.

I study the recipe and then mix the spices together with a beer as the recipe directs. Then I leave them to marinate and go upstairs to throw in a load of laundry. I gather Everett's shirts to take to the dry cleaners. He likes his shirts starched a certain way, and I've always been terrible at ironing. As I'm fishing them out of the hamper, I catch a scent of something tropical, maybe coconut. I hold his shirt to my face and inhale. I smell Everett, but something else. Is it a woman's perfume? I sink to the floor. He promised.

I allow myself to believe he is cheating, but only for a moment. I picture us getting a divorce. I'd go to live with Mama. His girlfriend would move in here. She'd be young and hip. Jenna would think she's cool. They'd become friends. And JT? He wouldn't understand. *Why would Daddy want another woman? He's married to you.*

I feel an ungodly pain press down on me. I can't do this. I go in the bedroom and dial Everett's number.

"Hey, babe," he answers. "What's up?"

I falter. How can I accuse him? He swore to me with tears in his eyes. He loves me. Just this morning he made love to me.

"Kate? You okay?"

"I'm fine. I just wanted to hear your voice," I tell him.

I hear the smile in his words as he says, "I love you, Kate. Did I ever tell you that?"

"You might have," I say.

"Well, then just to be certain, let me tell you again. I love you more than a man should be allowed to love. You complete me."

I know he's borrowed that last line from some movie, but it doesn't matter. He means it. I know he does.

As I drive back to Mama's, I try to decide how to bring up the subject of Cassie visiting. The more I've thought about it, the more I'm certain it's a good idea. Mama's bouts of depression are getting more frequent. Evelyn hasn't helped with this. She finds a reason to mention Frank every time she speaks to Mama. I'm hoping that Mama will have forgotten she was depressed this morning. Hopefully, the birds have cheered her. Thankfully, that tends to happen. The depression and comments about death come and go like bad weather. Most days I try to ignore them; it might just be a cry for help or it might be serious. How could I know when she never tells me what she's really thinking? Maybe she's just lonely. Cassie would be another trained professional who could help assess the situation.

I wish Everett would help, but there is no chance of that. He's so good with people; he can make anyone smile, from the meter maid to the surly teen bagging our groceries. But he's written Mama off, refusing to even set foot inside her house, let alone cheer her up.

If only I hadn't confided in Mama about Everett's affair. At the time, I felt like there wasn't anyone else to turn to. Mama said I should divorce Everett. Later, when I said we were working through it and Everett was sorry, Mama had laughed. "As if that's all it takes! 'Sorry' doesn't mean anything. Anybody can use the word."

And Everett isn't any better. He acts as if Mama doesn't exist. Sometimes it bothers me that Everett seems to have no capacity for forgiveness. Cross him once and he's done with you. There's no going back. That's why I worry so about Jenna's relationship with him. I can't believe he would write off his own daughter, though. I know Everett has a tender heart underneath his strong demeanor. He loves his daughter, but what if she pushes him too far? He still won't speak to Mama. I thought if enough time passed, they would let it go—for my sake at least—but last spring, Everett refused to go to Mama's house for her birthday dinner. We went without him, and when we got home, he wasn't there. He didn't come home that night until after midnight. When I asked him where he'd gone, he said, "Does it matter?"

"It does to me," I'd said.

"I'm sorry, Kate, I can't do it. She doesn't want me there. It'll just ruin the whole evening for you and the kids. It was better for me to not be there. I just went somewhere to take my mind off it."

I didn't ask where that was. Maybe I didn't want to know.

"I've brought you some of that chicken salad you love," I tell Mama now, setting a plate in front of her. A wind has kicked up, so Mama is eating in the kitchen.

"Sit and eat with me," she says.

"I will, just give me a minute to pour some iced tea."

"I'd prefer hot tea."

"That's probably a better idea," I agree, and put the kettle on before sitting down opposite her.

Mama's hands shake as she brings the sandwich to her mouth. I don't remember the shake being so pronounced.

"Is something bothering you, Mama?"

She chews her sandwich and says nothing. The teakettle whistles and I get up to make tea. I wish I knew how many of Mama's ailments are mental and how many are physical. I sit back down and watch her chew her sandwich slowly.

When she sees me looking, she says, "I've told you I'm not well."

"Yes, but do you have pain somewhere?"

She shakes her head.

"Maybe you need some new activities, some new friends," I say brightly.

She scowls. "I'm not a child."

"Jenna's befriended one of our neighbors. Cassie's a nurse like I was. Jenna's told her all about you. She'd like to meet you. Would it be all right if she stopped in for a visit?"

She looks at me skeptically and then asks, "Why?"

"She told Jenna she'd like to meet you."

"It doesn't matter, anyway. She's probably just saying that." Mama looks out the window. She wipes her mouth. I decide to take that as a yes. Maybe company is just what she needs.

"How about I invite her to come by tomorrow?"

Mama waves a fly away from her sandwich. "We'll see."

≈≈

When I pick up JT from school, he's very animated.

"I told Ms. Fall about the lady in the grocery store."

"You did? What did she say?"

"She said that I was a hero and the school should recognize me. She asked for the name of the grocery store."

"Did you tell her?"

JT nods.

"JT, do you understand why Daddy doesn't want people to know what you did?"

"No."

"It's not because he isn't proud of you. He is! He's extremely proud. I am, too, but he's worried that if the woman you helped doesn't live then maybe her husband might blame you."

"Why would he do that? I didn't touch her. I just told the other guy what to do. And I was right. It was exactly what you are supposed to do."

I don't say anything. I need to get home and call the teacher. When I do, I discover that I'm too late. She's already given JT's name to the store manager. They're

138

planning a special ceremony at the school to honor JT. The store manager and maybe the woman he'd helped will be there. The woman is fine, she tells me. She and her husband are so grateful to JT and the store employee who helped her; they just want to say thanks.

Maybe Everett won't find out. There's nothing I can do to stop it, and, besides, why shouldn't JT get some recognition? The woman is fine, so Everett's fears are for naught. When he comes home, I don't say anything about it. He seems very stressed anyway. He bickers with Jenna and she storms out. Later, I find her at Cassie's.

No one answers the front door, so I walk around to the back. Jenna's told me the cats live outside. Maybe she's there. "Knock, knock," I call when I spy her sitting on the back patio with Cassie and a crazy number of cats.

"Hello, Kate," says Cassie, and she gets up to unfold another chair from the stack leaning against the wall. "Join us. We're just having a conversation about Jane Austen. We were talking about which of the sisters in *Pride and Prejudice* we like best. I like Lizzie, but Jenna is partial to Mary."

"This could take some time," I say as I sit down. "Jenna's the expert, though; I can't keep them all straight."

"You saw the movie, too," says Jenna.

"It didn't stick with me like it did with you."

"No matter. Jenna, finish telling me why you like Mary so much. She always seemed such a dour and serious girl."

"She only seemed that way because she wasn't all boy-crazy and dress-crazy like the rest of them. She read books and played music and thought about serious stuff. I think she was ahead of her time."

"What time was that?" I ask, trying to join the conversation, although Jane Austen's books have always bored me to tears. I tried to read a few of them for Jenna's sake, but it was hopeless. They put me to sleep.

"Either 1813 or 1797, depending on your view," says Jenna.

Cassie smiles. "Most people say 1813, because that's when the final revision was made."

"Oh," I say, and listen as they debate this. None of it makes sense to me, but I enjoy listening to them. I had no idea Jenna could debate with someone so calmly, citing her facts and giving respectful opinions. There is never any of that Jenna involved in the arguments she has with her father. When they're finished and both are laughing, Cassie asks, "Did you come to collect Jenna or did you have something else on your mind?"

"I came to tell you that Mama would love to have you stop by sometime. I was kind of hoping you might have some time tomorrow. She's been pretty out of it lately."

"I'm actually in the office most of tomorrow catching up on records. I don't have any patients. I could stop by after lunch. Would that work?"

"That would be perfect."

"She's not your typical old person," says Jenna.

"How's that?" asks Cassie.

"She talks to birds. Most days she says she's dying, and sometimes she's really grouchy."

"That sounds about par for the course," says Cassie. "Believe me, I see many elderly people more eccentric than your grandmother."

"She is quite eccentric." That's a nice way of saying it. "And she's growing more so all the time. Lately she's had a few little bouts of depression."

"I'm not sure I'd call them little; I'd say they're more epic," says Jenna, rolling her eyes. "Gram wants to die."

"She is prone to exaggeration," I say.

"Gram or Jenna?" asks Cassie.

"Both," I say at the same time Jenna says, "Gram."

Cassie introduces me to her seven cats, letting Jenna fill in the names as they appear. After that, Jenna and I walk home.

"She's a nice lady," I say.

Jenna nods. "She's all right."

"I'm glad you can go there and talk to her."

"It's better than our house."

"I wish you didn't feel that way."

Jenna shrugs her shoulders. "Talk to Everett. He's the one being an asshole."

I hate when Jenna swears. And I wish she wouldn't call him by his first name, but I don't say anything. I've learned that there is no point to chastising Jenna for her language. It only builds walls between us. Besides, they're only words. The only power they have is the power you give them.

We walk the rest of the way in silence. When we reach the door, Jenna says, "I hope Gram likes Cassie."

"Me, too."

EVERETT

≈≈

I don't want to cheat on Kate. Every time I walk back down the rickety steps from Veronica's apartment, I say to myself, "That's it. That's the last time."

But then again, what man could resist a set up like this? Not a normal one. Not a man who likes sex in every variation. Veronica is creative and insatiable, and those are two qualities I find irresistible when it comes to women. It's like she spends her hours away from me thinking up new ways to turn me on. I know that's not the case, but I like to imagine it is. I like to imagine I'm the only guy she does this with, but I'm not stupid. I don't know what she does in her off hours, but it more than likely involves other men. Who am I to be jealous? Like I said, every time I leave I know it's the last time I'll be there.

When I married Kate, I made a commitment. I intend to keep it. I do. Even if I slip up sometimes. I only love Kate. No one else. She knows that. This is just sex. Nothing more.

I remember the first time I saw Kate. God, she was so classy and gorgeous. Not in a dressed up way, but real, deep-down beauty. She wasn't even wearing makeup, and her scrubs were old, worn out, and green, not flashy like the nurses wear now. Her eyes were so genuine—a hundred shades of blue. Her hair was soft, and when it caught the light, it shimmered like sunlight off the lake in the late afternoon. I don't know. What can I say—I was struck. It really did feel like that. There's no other way to explain it, except love at first sight. I had to have her.

Up until that point, I'd had plenty of girlfriends. I'm not a slacker in the looks department, and when you throw in a police uniform, most chicks just can't resist. I had my pick. And I picked Kate.

When I was with her, I felt like a good guy. I felt like that hero in the movies, the one who says the right thing and does the right thing. I used plenty of women, but never Kate. It was always real with her. I had no agenda except being with her forever.

When she was around, I could let my guard down; I could say anything. And she listened to me with eyes that seemed to look right into my soul. It was like she knew me before she knew me. That sounds crazy, but me and Kate have some kind of cosmic connection. No matter what happens, I'll always be hers.

Which is why I'm hurrying home right now. It's Friday and she wants to go the Braddingtons' stupid chili cook-off. Why she wants to go to their big house and have them turn their noses up at us in person—as opposed to from across the street, as they've always done—is beyond me. Way beyond. But I'm busting my tail to get there even though Veronica called and left a steamy message on my phone about meeting her tonight for what she called "vampire action." I can only imagine. Thinking about it now makes me hard. I drive past my mother-in-law's place and see Kate's car, so there's time to make it home and jerk off. Better than having a boner all night, knowing what's going on at Veronica's tonight.

When I walk in the door, I'm stunned to find Jenna home. She's never home anymore. I don't know whether to say hi or just ignore her. Every time I open my mouth around her anymore, she freaks out. It's like she can't stand the sight of me. I settle for a wave and make my way up to my room to change. Jerking off isn't necessary any more.

When Kate gets home, she's all worked up.

"Don't touch that!" she shrieks at me as I have my spoon poised above the Crock-Pot, ready to taste the chili.

"I was just gonna taste it."

"Sorry. I didn't mean to yell. I'm just frantic. Mama needed me to come deal with a bird that got trapped in her garage. How it got in there is anybody's guess. JT helped me, but now I'm way behind schedule. I've got to get a shower. Please don't touch the chili. If you're hungry, fix a sandwich."

She says all this as she's pulling off her shoes and her sweatshirt and running up the stairs.

"What about JT?" I call after her. "Should I fix him something?"

"He stayed at Mama's. She was real upset and he said he'd hang around there and watch his show. She seemed to want that."

Kate is standing at the top of the stairs now, looking down at me and unbuttoning her jeans. What's so amazing about her is she's so sexy and she doesn't even know it. Her standing there like that, about to peel off her pants and carrying on about her mother, is just as sexy as Veronica in a bunny outfit. Really.

"I wish we had a little time," I say to her. She knows what I mean.

"Not now, Everett! I've got to get ready!"

"We could be late," I say.

She turns and runs for the shower.

"You can't be late," says Jenna. She's standing right behind me and it makes me jump.

"Christ! Don't sneak up on me like that!"

"Chill, don't have a heart attack or something. JT's not here to tell me what to do."

She's such a smart-ass and I want to say a few choice things to her, but I don't. I think about Kate and what she said about Jenna's only power being her words. I'm not going to take the bait tonight. I shake my head at her, but say nothing. I fix a sandwich and click on the news.

And there's JT. He's standing with that goddamn store manager and the gangly guy with the pimples who did the CPR on that woman. There's an old guy there, too. That's the woman's husband. They're at JT's school and they're handing JT a medal and shaking his hand. He's smiling. Now the reporter is talking, telling about the incident in the grocery store. And behind him, I see Kate. She's smiling. What the fuck? Why did they not tell me about this?

"So, young man, how does it feel to be a hero?" asks the reporter.

"I was just doing a job," says JT. He sounds much older than he is. And I notice he's standing really tall, not slouched over like he's about to be hit, which is his usual stance. "In cases like this, you assume it's an MI, although it could be a CVA, so it's important to keep the heart pumping manually until someone can locate an AED or a doc."

The reporter smiles. He's impressed. I'm impressed. I never thought all that shit JT watches was really teaching him anything. I can tell the reporter doesn't know that an MI is a heart attack or a CVA is a stroke. Most people wouldn't. Unless you're a nurse or you spend plenty of time with one.

"Well, Mrs. Harkins sure was lucky you happened to be in the store when you were," says the reporter. "I think Mr. Harkins would like to say a few words to you, JT. Would that be okay?"

JT shrugs. He looks worried.

Mr. Harkins draws in a noisy breath. Let's hope he isn't the next to fall over. He looks at JT, not the camera. "JT, I owe you. You saved my Gertie's life. If I can ever do anything for you, son, *anything*, you let me know."

I can tell JT is thinking about this. He believes everything he hears, so he thinks the old geezer is ready to buy him the entire collection of *ER* on disc. Luckily, the reporter doesn't let him say anything because he's already wrapping it up and throwing it back to the anchor.

"Pretty cool," says Jenna. She's standing in the door-way of the kitchen watching. "I'm glad you decided to let everyone know what JT did."

I want to explode. I'm furious! I told Kate not to give JT's information out. Maybe we lucked out and the old man is not a nutcase. But what if he had been? And what if ole Gertie takes a turn for the worse? Then what? Then they might come after us. JT is just a kid. He could have been wrong.

But he wasn't.

I have an option here. I can give Kate a piece of my mind and refuse to go to the party. Go get JT, and let them all know how angry I am that no one listened to me. I told them to keep this quiet.

But my other option is to not react. Jenna hasn't said anything nice to me in almost a year. Maybe letting her think I gave the go-ahead for this shit is the best move. After all, it's done. I can't undo it. I can just hope to hell we don't have to pay for it in some way.

I go with my second option. I watch as Jenna opens the fridge and pulls out a bottle of water.

"Yeah, well, he did a good thing," I say.

≈≈

When Kate is ready, the three of us walk across the street to the Braddingtons' house. I'm carrying the Crock-Pot. Kate looks really nice. She's wearing a pretty pink skirt with a brown gauzy material covering it. Her tank top has shimmery fabric around the neckline and she's pulling a brown wrap around her shoulders. She smiles at me, just before she rings the bell. I really want tonight to go well for her sake, but I have a bad feeling about it. I've had it ever since the damn invitation came. I've had it every time I've looked at that invitation on the fridge. These are not our people. If they've invited us here, there's a reason. And it's not that they suddenly want to be cozy neighbors.

No one answers the bell, so Jenna pushes the door open and we follow her in. The place is packed with beautiful people wearing clothes like you see in magazines. I can see Kate begin to panic. She looks at me in my jeans and ironed shirt. I squeeze her hand. I knew we didn't belong here.

"You should probably put the Crock-Pot in the kitchen," Jenna says, nodding towards a doorway. How she knows her way around this house, I do not want to know.

JENNA
≈≈

It's totally embarrassing going anywhere with my parents. They are so clueless. It's like they're on drugs or something—they have no idea how not to look like idiots. Mom rings the doorbell, like someone's actually going to answer it and take our coats. We're thirty minutes late and the driveway and street are lined with cars. The party is already happening and no one cares whether we have arrived or not.

I open the door and lead them in, telling Everett to dump the Crock-Pot in the kitchen. I swear, they are so clueless. Mom looks terrified. I kind of feel bad for her. She's so out of her league with these women. It's kind of sad how much she wants to fit in. I know that feeling. I wore it all through elementary school, but then I gave up and stopped trying. Now I don't fit in and that's fine with me. How did she get to be a grown up and still care so much about fitting in?

I watch as Mrs. Braddington pretends to be all excited that Mom and Dad are there and listen as Mom tells her about the chili she brought. Mrs. Braddington takes it and places a card with fancy calligraphy on it labeling it *Chili # 11*. I notice it just says "Chili" as opposed to the other signs on the other pots that have clever names like, "Chili Chili Bang Bang" (stupid), and "Chiliardiac Arrest" (JT would appreciate that one), and "Beanies for Weanies" (lame). Everybody thinks they're a comedian. Guess Mom didn't know she was supposed to give it a dumb name. I kind of like that she named hers, "Chili."

Now she's explaining how the recipe is nothing special, as if she hasn't spent the entire week trying out different recipes. I've had chili for dinner for three straight nights. The last thing I want to do tonight is taste fifteen different types of chili with lame-ass names like "Chili of Destruction" and "Fire in the Hole."

I don't have time to read the rest of the names, because at this point Wells shows up, grabs me by the hand, and drags me downstairs to his dad's man cave. The walls are lined with plaques and there's a shelf going around the top of the room completely full of trophies. Guess Mr. Braddington likes himself. A lot.

I haven't seen Wells since the nose-licking incident. He's had to meet with the tutor his dad hired for him after school every day, and then his dad has been dragging him to the gym to work out. I had begun to think I only dreamed the nose-licking thing.

"Jesus, I hate this party every year," says Wells.

He pulls me to the sofa and we sit down, but he doesn't let go of my hand. I'm distracted by this fact. His hand feels really nice. It's heavy and completely covers mine.

"This is the first year we got invited," I say.

"Yeah, my mom only invited you because I said I wasn't coming if she didn't."

"Really?"

He laughs. "When I told her, she said, 'You mean that crazy girl across the street who broke into our garage?'"

"My mom was really excited to get the invitation. She's been dying to make friends with your mom."

He frowns. "I don't know why."

"She thinks that just because we're all neighbors, we should be these great friends."

"We should!" says Wells enthusiastically. "Where's your little brother? I heard he's some big hero."

149

I smile. It's cool that Wells heard about that. "He's at my gram's house. He doesn't do well with these kinds of things."

"My mom was all impressed with that. She was bragging about it to some of the other people who got here early. She acted like she actually knew him." He laughs. "She wouldn't recognize JT if she saw him on the street."

"He's hard to miss," I say. JT has this slightly bouncy walk and swings his arms awkwardly when he moves. He's never been very coordinated. When he was little, my dad made him play soccer, but everyone dreaded having him on their team. Whenever the ball came near him, Everett would yell at him to kick it and JT would grin and run around in circles waving his arms and squealing, but he never actually made contact with the ball.

"I missed hanging out with you this week," Wells says.

I missed him, too, but wouldn't say that out loud. In front of him. Jeez. "Maybe we should cut out of here and go do something."

"Nah," he says. "I have to hang around and help my mom count the ballots."

"The ballots?"

"For the chili. It's a cook-off, remember? Everybody tries all the chilis and then votes for their favorite. It's pretty hard-core. People go all out and concoct all kinds of crazy shit trying to win."

"My mom's chili is just chili. I guess she didn't know that."

He doesn't say anything, but he turns towards me and puts the hand that is not holding mine on my knee. My heart starts racing like crazy because I know that right now Wells Braddington is about to kiss me. Wells Braddington! I'm so nervous that I can't say anything, and right when he leans in to make contact, I start laughing. I can't help myself. I am SUCH A MORON. He looks hurt, but now I've got the giggles and they won't quit.

"I'm sorry!" I say. "I don't know why I'm laughing!"

He looks at me like I'm nuts and kind of smiles.

"Why is this funny?" he asks and the hurt in his voice stops my laughing.

"It's not," I say, shaking my head, and one last snort escapes. "Sometimes I laugh when I'm nervous."

"I make you nervous?" He looks surprised by this, as if his ridiculously good-lookingness doesn't make most girls nervous.

"No, not you, just you kissing me."

"Why?" he asks.

"I've never kissed anyone before," I tell him. I've decided that honesty is the best policy here. He'd figure it out as soon as he kissed me anyway.

He sits back. "Seriously?"

I nod.

"Wow. So this is gonna be, like, you're first kiss?"

I smile. "Only if you actually kiss me."

Now he smiles this goofy grin that almost starts me laughing again.

"Okay, then, I've got to get this right," he says, and he puts one hand up to my cheek, guiding me in for the kiss.

And then it happens. Wells Braddington kisses me. I feel like my insides are melting and a little sound escapes involuntarily. It sounds like the happy sound Marco makes when I rub his belly. Maybe this is what he feels like, too. All warm and happy and amazed.

And then the door to the upstairs opens and Mrs. Braddington calls down. "Wells? I need your help up here. It's almost time for the tasting!"

KATE

≈≈

Iwatch as one after another guest tastes my chili. I'm mortified that my chili is so plain. The other chilis are much fancier. Some have crab or shrimp or chicken in them. Some have exotic spices or large pieces of vegetables. There are several white chilis. And they all have clever names. I had no idea I was supposed to name my chili. When Susan asked me what I'd made, I said, "Chili." So that's what she wrote on the little gold-edged card propped up in front of my chili. I wish I'd thought to give my chili a funny name.

"That Gotta Gumbo Chili is really good," says Everett as he comes to stand beside me with another bowl of chili.

I don't say anything, but watch Everett eat his latest chili. I know he will spend most of the night in the bathroom after eating so many chilis. I can't bring myself to even try one. My stomach is in knots. We've been here for over an hour and no one has initiated any conversation with me. I've tried to talk to people, but I don't know what to say to them. I don't play golf. My kids go to public school. We have no exciting vacation plans. I haven't seen the latest hit shows on cable, and I don't even know who's running in the upcoming election. So now I'm leaning against the wall oven in the kitchen watching the chili tasting.

Susan Braddington starts to squeeze by, but then turns when she sees Everett and his chili.

"What do you think?" she asks him.

"It's really good," he says with his mouth full. There is sauce on his chin.

Susan starts to walk away and then stops. "You didn't bring your little hero with you?"

"What?" Everett asks, still with a mouthful of chili.

"JT is spending some time with his grandmother. She was having a tough day and needed company," I explain. No sense telling the woman that JT would have been apoplectic at the noise and the lack of pasta options at this party.

"Too bad. I know everyone would have loved to meet him," she says. "You must be very proud."

"We are," Everett and I say at the same time.

"I guess so," laughs Susan, and she continues on her tour of the kitchen, flirting with everyone as she goes.

"I don't know why you want to be friends with that woman," says Everett. "She seems awfully fake to me."

"You can't know that. She's probably very nice, but she's busy with the party." I know he's right and I don't know why I want to be friends with Susan. I just do. We're neighbors.

"How long do we have to stay?"

I ignore his question. "Have you seen Jenna?"

Everett scans the room. "I'll go look for her."

I put a hand on his arm. "No, you don't need to do that. I just wondered if she was having a good time."

"If she isn't, I'm sure she's already left. It's not like she does anything she doesn't want to do."

"I think she's becoming friends with the Braddingtons' son," I tell him, although I don't just think it, I know it. I've seen them walking on the street together.

"The tall one?"

"They only have one," I tell him. How could he not know this? We've lived across the street for years. He used to be a detective. He should be able to remember details.

"He plays football, right? Why would Jenna be interested in a football player?"

"I don't know, but I've seen them walking together after school."

"Doesn't he have practice?"

I shrug. He still has chili on his chin and I should tell him, but I don't. "I'm going to find a piece of cornbread." I leave him there eyeing the chili, and head for the dining room where the other food is. Out the floor-to-ceiling windows, I can see Jenna helping Wells clear dishes on the porch. They are laughing and talking. I watch them, forgetting why I've come into the room.

"Excuse me," says a man trying to move past me into the room. "I was looking for the macaroni and cheese. I heard there's some in here."

He is thin and has sharp features that soften when he smiles. He holds out his hand.

"I'm Phil. I just moved in. I live up at the other end, though, in the poor neighborhood." He laughs and I realize he is kidding. "Guess I shouldn't make jokes like that here, you might live on my end, too."

"Sorry! I'm Kate. We live across the street. My mother lives on your end, though. I think those houses are very quaint."

"Quaint is one way of saying 'small and cramped.' I live by myself, though, so I don't need a place like this."

"I guess not," I say. "What brought you to Pine Estates?"

"My wife died a few months ago."

"I'm sorry."

"It's okay. I probably shouldn't blurt it out like that since you don't even know me. I find my filter is not so great ever since she passed. I tend to be very forthright."

"That's okay. Can I ask how she passed?"

"She was sick for the last few years. I grew to be good friends with her hospice nurse during her last month. It was Cassandra who told me about the house for sale on this street. She lives in the neighborhood, too. I thought maybe she'd be here." He looks around.

"Cassie? I don't know if she's friends with the Brad-dingtons, but this is for neighbors so maybe she's here somewhere. It's a big party."

"So, you're friends with Susan, then?" he asks.

"Well, we've been neighbors for over ten years," I tell him. I don't want to lie and tell him we're friends, when probably we aren't.

"I've known Susan and Mark since college. Mark and I were in the same fraternity. Small world, me ending up on their street."

"I guess it is."

"What do you do?" he asks. It's an innocent question, but a question I hate to answer. I never know what to say. *I don't work* isn't exactly true. My days are full, start to finish, but it's impossible to make my days sound like they matter when all I do is keep people happy. Between making sure Mama has everything she needs and getting JT to and from school without incident, my days go by quickly, but I accomplish very little. Everett says I'm still nursing, but now I only have two patients.

"I used to be an ER nurse, but now my days are busy caring for my elderly mother. And I have two kids at home. My twelve-year-old son has Asperger's. I don't know if you've heard of that, but it sometimes makes our days challenging." I don't know why I'm blathering on about my days, but Phil's kind eyes are encouraging, so I keep talking. "Some days I find myself wondering what I did all day, even though by dinner hour, I'm exhausted."

"That sounds like quite a load. I'm familiar with Asperger's syndrome. I grew up with a brother who exhib-ited all the symptoms, but back then there wasn't a diag-nosis. My parents just thought he was eccentric. He's a world-renowned physicist now. Quite successful, but still has his quirks. Does your son exhibit the high ability in math and science that is characteristic of the condition?"

I'm stunned. Most people change the conversation when I mention Asperger's.

155

"He does. He's very good at both and has an incredible memory."

"And what are his obsessions right now? Dinosaurs? Space?"

I laugh. "We've been through a few. For the last year it's been emergency medicine."

"Really? You don't hear that one often."

"How do you know so much about Asperger's?"

"I'm a pediatrician. Comes with the territory. I've come to believe that every one of us is on the spectrum somewhere."

I've thought the very same thing.

"Are you in the blue house near Spruce?"

"I am! I moved in last month. It has a wonderful backyard. Some of those trees must be fifty years old or more."

"That's only two houses up from my mother."

"Maybe I'll see her when I'm out for my jogs."

"I doubt it. She keeps to herself, and for the last few years has refused to leave the house."

"That must make it hard on you."

I'm about to reply, when a cheer goes up in the kitchen.

"It must be the chili results! Excuse me," I say and hurry to the kitchen, although once I'm there I wish I'd stayed and continued my conversation with Phil. Susan Braddington is awarding prizes for the best chilis.

"And in fourth place we have a new entrant! It goes to Kate Turner for her entry, number eleven, called 'Chili'!" Half-hearted cheers go up and people return to their conversations as Susan continues. "Kate has won a spa vacation," she trills as she hands me a bottle of bubble bath and a sponge. She continues with the next three prizes, each entry winning more joke gifts. I wonder if they've always given away fourth place, or if Susan has done that because she feels sorry for me.

"Fourth place!" cries Everett, handing me a glass of champagne. "That's fantastic! And you worried no one would like your chili!"

156

I smile at him and hold up my "spa vacation."

"That woman is clever, isn't she?" Everett puts his arm around me. I can tell he is well on his way to being drunk.

"We should probably go pick up JT."

"It's still early," says Everett.

"I'm going to go find Jenna."

I wander through the rooms on the first floor, marveling at Susan Braddington's exquisite taste in decorating. How does she know what colors to use? I would never have the nerve to paint a wall burgundy, but in Susan's front room, it works perfectly. I wander through a side door onto a gorgeous sunporch. I can see our house from here. It looks dowdy and small in comparison. The beige siding is so plain and, in some places, the red shutters are fading. Even the mums outside are depressing in their fading rust-brown hue.

Just as I turn to go back and find Everett, I spot Jenna. She is sitting on a stone wall that surrounds the outdoor kitchen. Wells is sitting beside her. While I watch, he leans over and kisses her. I catch my breath—happy and scared for my little girl. Then, feeling as though I'm a peeping Tom, I hurry back to find Everett.

When I find Everett, he is in the kitchen talking up the young woman Susan Braddington hired to clean up. I take his arm. "Let's go. Jenna will come home when she's ready."

"What? Maybe we should help Delores here with the dishes." His words are beginning to slur. I smile at the woman hired to help at the party and guide Everett out of the kitchen. I need to get him home before anyone sees how drunk he is. I leave him next to the front door. "Wait here and I'll just go thank Susan."

"What about our Crock-Pot? I think Delores was going to wash it."

"Shit," I say. "I'll get it."

"Language," says Everett, laughing and opening the door. "I'll just wait on the stoop."

I retrieve our pot from the kitchen and find Susan in the living room.

"Thanks so much for inviting us," I say.

"You're leaving already? The party's just getting started!" Susan barely glances away from the cluster of equally well-clad women she is talking with as she says this.

"We have to pick up JT," I tell her. "But we had a really nice time."

Susan is laughing at something one of the other women says and nods, dismissing me.

JENNA
≈≈

It's so easy to talk to Wells. Isn't that funny? I've known him for years and always thought he was a stupid jock boy, but now there's no one else I like to talk to more.

After I help him stack all the dishes in the kitchen for the "party maid" as Wells calls her, we sneak outside and sit on the stone wall on their patio. He says his mom calls this the "outdoor kitchen" but they never use it. Wells lights one of the burners on the gas stove built right into the stonework.

"There, a campfire," he tells me, and then climbs up on the wall beside me and puts his arm around me.

I lean against his shoulder. Wells smells like grass and soap. I sniff his neck.

"What are you doing?" he asks.

"You smell good."

He smiles. Then he leans down and sniffs my neck, too, before he kisses it. This shoots all kinds of electricity through me. Is this what it feels like to be "hot" for someone? I turn towards him and kiss him on the lips.

"For a beginner, you're awfully good at this," he says when we come up for air.

"How many girls have you kissed?" I ask.

"I don't know."

"Then, a lot?"

"Yeah," he says, and then pulls me to him and kisses me again. I swear I could kiss him all night. While we're kissing this time, he reaches under my shirt and puts his hand on my side, sliding his hand up until his thumb is touching my bra, just rubbing back and forth. Again, I think I'm going to faint. I want him to touch me. I press myself against him.

"Maybe we should go somewhere else," he says.

"Like where?"

"Somebody's house. Somebody who's not home. Maybe someone who's at the party."

I laugh. "You're crazy."

"No, I'm not," he says, and stands up and takes my hand.

We walk up the street, waving to cars that pass us as they leave the party. I see my parents drive past on their way to get JT. Mom waves to me, but Dad looks passed out in the passenger seat. He was getting pretty loaded, last I saw him.

We pass Ms. Cassie's house and the lights are on. She's probably in her living room reading one of her Jane Austen novels. She's read all of them a million times. I think she's the only person I know who's read them more than me. I wish I'd lived back in that time, and then again I don't. I like the way they talked and I like that they rode horses everywhere. And the women wore dresses that look like nightgowns and cool boots that laced up. People spent their evenings reading and playing music. Not that I don't like television and Internet. They're okay, but they're overrated. The only thing that I wouldn't like, besides the occasional lack of indoor plumbing, is the fact that women were considered the property of men. I wouldn't want to be some man's property. Especially my father's. If he got to run my life, it'd be a nightmare. I'd hate to have to do what men told me to do.

Right now, though, I think I might be pretty happy to do what Wells tells me to do.

"How about that one?" Wells says.

We're a couple doors up from my gram's house. It's a blue rancher. Some guy just moved in there. It's dark, though, and it doesn't look like anyone's home. We peek in the window. It's wide open with just a screen. Guess the guy isn't worried about people breaking in. Wells starts to slide the window up when we hear a low growl. A big dog with blue eyes and stiff fur jumps at the window, snapping. Wells drops back to the ground beside me.

"Shit!" he says. "That scared me!"

"You're such a baby," I tell him. "It's just a dog."

"That's a big dog! And he was gonna bite me!"

I smack him. "Oh, c'mon, you're afraid of a dog?"

"I'm afraid of *that* dog," he says, pointing to the nose poking at the screen, still growling.

I stand up. "Hey, bud," I say in my sweet every-dog-likes-me voice. He quiets right down, his tail wagging. He's a cool-looking dog. Now that I'm closer, I can see that one of his eyes is half-blue and half-brown, split neatly down the middle. "What a good boy you are," I croon. "You're a good watch dog. You scared my wimpy friend here with your big growly voice."

Wells stands up behind me and the moment he does, the dog lunges for the screen again and goes into full-on kill mode. Wells takes off and I run after him, laughing. He stops when he gets to the playground. I'm still laughing.

"Holy shit! That dog wanted to kill me!" he says, but he's laughing now, too.

We sit on the old-fashioned merry-go-round. It's metal; the kind you can get spinning really fast. My mom never lets JT go on it. She said the metal merry-go-rounds are dangerous and the neighborhood association should have ours removed. It's fun to see how fast you can make it go, holding the bar and running hard on the worn path that circles it. It's easy to get it spinning fast. Then the trick is to jump on without getting hung up on the metal dividers between the sections.

"I'll spin ya," says Wells. I lie back on the merry-go-round with my head in the center of the circle while he gets the thing going really fast. I can hear his feet hitting the path and his breath panting fast as he runs. Then he yells, "All aboard!" and leaps onto the merry-go-round. He crawls to where I am in the middle and starts kissing me. It all feels unreal. The cool metal on my back, the stars above me, the force of the spinning merry-go-round that presses me to it, and Wells' lips on mine.

I'm happy. I don't think I remember ever feeling so happy.

KATE
≈≈

I can't sleep. I don't always wait up for Jenna to come in, but I can't shake the image of Jenna kissing the Braddington boy. Is it serious? How long has it been going on? I can't tell Everett about it. He would be furious. Besides, he's passed out on the couch in front of some late-night show. I wish I had someone to call. Someone to talk to about this. I think of Cassie. She seems like the kind of person who would understand how I could be so excited for Jenna, yet terrified at the same time.

I sit at the counter with a book, reading the same paragraph again and again while sipping a cup of herbal tea. I've already scrubbed the counters, cleaned out the fridge, and emptied the dishwasher. Finally, Jenna appears at the back door.

"Hey," she says as she comes in. There are leaves in her hair and her cheeks are flushed.

"Did you have a nice evening?" I ask. I want to ask so much more, but I know I have to tread carefully with Jenna. Sometimes she seems to want to talk, but other times it's as if the sound of my voice irritates her and she looks at me with such contempt.

Jenna opens the refrigerator and takes out the orange juice. She pours a glass and leans against the counter drinking it. I wait for her response. When she doesn't say anything, I get up and empty my teacup in the sink.

"I had a great night," says Jenna. She smiles at me and then puts her glass in the dishwasher. I watch in astonishment. It's the first time I've seen her voluntarily put anything in the dishwasher.

"I'm glad," I tell her. "What made it great?"

Jenna's smile vanishes. "Nothing," she says airily, and bounces out of the kitchen.

I remember being in love. I was about Jenna's age when I fell in love the first time. Jonathon was a football player, too. And so smart. I've seen on Facebook that he is a big shot for some chemical company now. He has a pretty wife and three pretty daughters. I wonder if he ever thinks of me.

I won't meddle in Jenna's relationship with Wells like my own mother meddled in my high school relationships. She teased me mercilessly and criticized Jonathon at every turn. He was too rich, too snotty, too full of himself, she'd said. But he'd just been a confident, happy boy who knew how good his future looked. I always wondered if I might have been part of that future if my mother had been different. By the time I was in high school, I'd heard Mama's lament on *men* too many times to count. They were all self-centered and only wanted one thing. Once they got it, they would leave you in a flash. When I was little, I thought my father's name was *That Louse*, as that was the only way I ever heard Mama refer to him.

Why don't I have a daddy like Erica? Her daddy taught her to ride a bike.

That Louse didn't stick around long enough to teach you to ride a bike.

How come you and Daddy don't live together anymore?

That Louse took off years ago. I'm glad he's gone.

She'd say that, but I wasn't too young to see that she wasn't glad he was gone.

Evelyn left me another message about Frank. She won't let it drop. This time she mentioned something about

164

paternity tests, which makes no sense. Unless she's worried he's not our father. That would put an end to this. I've avoided her calls. I don't need this. I've got enough to deal with between trying to get JT out of that awful classroom and hoping Jenna doesn't end up pregnant. Besides, the whole thing is obviously agitating Mama.

How could I have a father now? Fathers are for little girls. If he'd been around, maybe my life would have been different. Maybe I'd be married to Jonathon and live in a beautiful house like the Braddingtons'. Or maybe not. I fell hard for Everett. And I can't imagine any other life, not really. Besides, I'm happy . . . most of the time.

I lie in bed for over an hour rethinking the party. I keep going back over my conversations with all of the neighborhood women. Nothing we talked about went below the surface. The only meaningful conversation I had was with that man named Phil, the new neighbor. He was interesting and smart and he knew so much about Asperger's. I wonder where his medical practice is. JT's current doctor frustrates me. He has such low expectations for JT. He says things like, "You may need to consider what services JT will need long term," as if he doesn't think JT will ever be independent. Sometimes it feels like he's already written him off—as if JT's like every other kid with Asperger's, even though it varies widely in symptoms and prognosis. He always wants to defer to the school's wishes, saying, "They're in the best position to evaluate what JT's capable of," as if they would know better than me! Sometimes I feel so helpless. Instead of challenging him, they stick him in that classroom with all the other kids they aren't sure how to handle. I know he doesn't belong there, but maybe he doesn't belong in a regular classroom either. There has to be another option.

We don't have the money for private school. Everett keeps telling me that. He insists that I'm coddling JT. "The sooner he gets into a regular classroom; the sooner he will learn how to behave in a socially acceptable manner." Why does JT have to behave in a socially acceptable manner? Plenty of adults I know don't. And what's "socially accept-able" anyway? Tonight at that party, Susan Braddington treated me like I was some peasant come to worship the queen. Maybe I deserve that. For years, I've tried to be her friend. But after tonight, I think I don't want to be Susan's friend after all. Not someone like that.

I hope Susan Braddington's son is different. I hope he is genuine in his interest in Jenna. I hope my mother isn't right.

Everett stumbles into the bedroom. He kicks off his shoes and they bang against the wall. I hear him flip up the toilet seat. I never hear it bang back down. And then he crawls into the bed next to me. He is already naked. He reaches for me and I say, "Not tonight Ev, I'm really tired."

"Yes, tonight," he says. I allow him to pull down my panties and put his finger inside me. I know better than to fight him. Very early in our marriage I discovered that if I say no, Everett only becomes more turned on. He wants it more. One time I insisted that I meant no. I regretted that for weeks. It was summertime and I'd had to wear sleeves to cover the bruising on my arms.

As a nurse, I knew I'd been raped. But we were newly married. I couldn't bear the thought of moving back to Mama's house. It was easier to go along with him. After all, he was my husband. Why wouldn't I want to have sex with him? Most nights, I was as eager as he was, and after the kids came along, I learned what I needed to do and say to help him make it quick.

≈≈

Saturday morning I'm the first one up. JT is still sleeping. Usually he's an early riser, but lately he's begun sleeping later. Some mornings I have to wake him for school. I guess it's evidence that he is becoming a teenager. I know we won't see Jenna before noon, but I'm anxious to talk to her. I'm not as paranoid as my mother when it comes to boys and sex, but I need to be certain she isn't going to end up in trouble. I'll have to catch her before she disappears for the day.

I feed Marco and take him with me to walk to Mama's. No one pays attention to the poor old dog anymore. When he was a puppy, he'd been in the middle of everything. He was Jenna's best playmate, suffering through tea parties and "dog shows" and even leaping over the obstacles Jenna built for him in the backyard.

He waddles ahead now, happily sniffing at every mailbox we pass. When I reach Mama's, I leave Marco tied to the faucet on the side of the house. Mama doesn't like me to bring Marco over. She says he'll scare away the birds. I pat Marco on the head and he tramps out a circle in the leaves before lying down.

"Good morning, Mama!" I call as I open the front door.

"Is it?" she says. I find her sitting on her bed, holding a worn shoebox I haven't seen before. When I reach for it, she pulls it away.

"This is mine," she says, and holds it tightly to her side.

"I was just going to take it so you could get up."

"You don't need to," she says, hugging it to her.

I can't imagine what secrets she could have in an old shoebox.

"Just make my tea. I'll be out in a minute."

I line up her slippers next to the bed and set her walker nearby. Mama is usually in better spirits on Saturdays, especially when she knows Evelyn is coming for lunch, as she is today. Maybe she's forgotten. Or maybe she doesn't want to hear Evelyn talk about Frank. I don't either, but I don't plan to stick around.

"Did you forget that Evelyn is coming today?"

"I don't know why she bothers," she mutters.

"Because she loves you," I tell her and go to make her breakfast.

When she is settled on the porch, she says, "Maybe today isn't such a good day for Evelyn to visit."

"That's silly! She's probably already on her way."

I spoke briefly with Evelyn yesterday and she said she planned to come early. She was determined to get Mama out of the house. "Good luck with that," I told her.

"I think between the two of us, we can get her out."

"JT and I are going to the firefighter's museum."

"What? You won't be there? I thought we could make a day of it. All of us. The kids, too!"

I know that my sister thinks I have no life. She assumes the kids and I would be available to spend the day with her without any warning.

"Sorry, I promised JT. And Jenna already has plans with a friend." I have no idea what Jenna has planned, but after seeing her smile last night, I would assume her day will involve Wells.

"Oh, damn. Do you think you could rearrange things? It's only one day. Maybe Everett could come, too."

"You know how he feels about Mama. And no, I can't rearrange things. You're on your own with this. You know she won't go out of the house. Why don't you just bring her lunch and sit with her for the afternoon."

"I'm tired of that. The woman needs to get out!" she'd huffed and hung up.

I set Mama's tea and toast in front of her.

"She'll be here around ten. I think Evelyn has something special planned."

"I'm really not feeling well."

"That's awfully sudden; you'll have to make the best of it. Evelyn's coming to spend the day with you."

Mama looks confused for a moment and then says, "Fine."

I still haven't been able to talk to her about Frank. Every time I bring it up, she changes the subject or acts as if Evelyn hasn't told her.

"You're all set," I tell her after cleaning up her breakfast. "Evelyn should be here any moment. I'm going to go now."

"That's right, go on and leave me," says Mama.

I smile at her and give her shoulder a squeeze. "Try to have a good day, Mama." Then I lean down and kiss her on the cheek. On my way out, I peek in her bedroom hoping to take a quick look at the box she was so possessive of, but it's gone. She's obviously hiding something, but I don't have time to search for it. I've got to get home and talk to Jenna.

When I walk around to the side of the house to retrieve Marco, there's a man kneeling next to him.

"Oh!" I yelp before I realize it's Phil from last night.

He stands up quickly, smiling. "Sorry, I didn't mean to scare you. I just heard this little guy whining and brought him a treat. After our conversation last night, I figured this was your mother's house."

I unclip Marco's leash and he pulls towards the road. "It is. What made it so obvious?"

We begin walking up the street. I glance around. Everett wouldn't be happy to see me walking with another man, but, then again, Everett may not be in a place to complain. I wish I didn't think that.

"I've met most everyone else on this end. I walk every day with my dog. I'm surprised I've never run into her."

"You wouldn't." He looks confused, so I change the subject. I don't want to talk about Mama. "So you're a dog person?"

"I am. Sometimes I prefer them to people. Present company excepted, of course!"

He flashes a charming smile, and I laugh. "Well, thanks for checking in on Marco. He's usually good about waiting."

"He's a nice guy. Can't see much, though, can he?"

"He's getting old. We got him when my daughter was just a toddler. He's almost fourteen now."

"My guy's just five, but he still acts like a puppy. I better get back to him. This is me," he says, indicating the small blue house on the opposite side of the road. "We're headed out for a hike today. It's been a long week. Good to see you. And let your mother know I'm only a few doors down if she needs anything."

"Thanks!" I watch him walk away. He certainly is a nice man, so friendly and open. Everett can be that way, too, but lately he's guarded and skeptical, even with me. The other night, I asked him if he'd found out anything about Frank and he literally jumped at the mention of his name.

"Haven't had time," he said. "I'm sure there's nothing to find."

But he said it too quickly, like maybe there *is* something to find. I didn't get a chance to press him on it because he was gathering the trash and recycling to take to the curb, and by the time he came back, I was busy helping JT get ready for bed. After that, I simply forgot.

JENNA

≈≈

Here's how I know my mom knows about Wells. Today she came in my room, sat on my bed, and wanted to talk about sex. I about died. I just sat there and planned out the essay I have to write for American History in my head, nodding every now and then, while she went on and on about contraceptives and sexually transmitted diseases. I know she was a nurse and all that, but I'm not a little kid. I've heard all this before, and it's incredibly embarrassing to hear your mother say the word *penis*. I did my best to tune her out until she started talking about her first experience when she was young.

"Seeing your father the first time in his uniform, he was so handsome he made me swoon."

Swoon is not a word I use very often. It's a nice word. I like the way it sounds. It's kind of creepy to think of anyone swooning over Everett, but I can honestly say that Wells makes me sort of swoon. He's very swoonable.

"I just want to be sure you're being smart about all this," she's saying.

I look up at her, trying to gauge how much she knows. I haven't slept with Wells, but the idea is definitely not out of the question. It's simply a matter of time and place. We both know it, but does my mom know it, too? And how does she know it?

"I am," I tell her.

"Good," she says, and gets up to leave.

"Mom," I say, just as she reaches the door. "Why are we having this conversation today?"

She looks trapped. She does know something.

"Oh, I don't know. You're just at that age, I guess. I wanted to be extra sure you know all this stuff."

"I do," I assure her. "I'm good." I give her a thumbs-up and she finally leaves. I flop back against my pillow and grab my phone from the charger next to the bed.

I text Wells.

Today?

He texts back, *Working out with the f-team*

Lucky you.

Ya

When I finally get up, the house is quiet. Mom went to some fireman's museum with JT. He's talked about it all week. My dad is watching football. I walk to the Ashers' house to feed their fish. They're away for the weekend. I stay to work on my essay.

Just after lunch, Wells shows up.

"You're here," I say, stating the obvious, which is stupid. I find myself doing that more and more around Wells. It's like I have to talk just to talk. I hate when people do that.

"I am," he says. I hold the door and he walks past me to the kitchen.

"Do they have any food?"

"They do, but you can't eat it," I tell him.

"Why not?" he asks as he pulls out a carton of milk and starts to drink from it. I yank it out of his hand and put it back in the fridge.

"Because they know I'm watching the fish this weekend. They're paying me. If food disappears, they'll know it was me."

"So?" he says, looking hurt.

"You'd make a terrible criminal," I tell him.

He laughs and puts his arms around me. He leans close, but doesn't kiss me (which makes me nuts). "Why?" he asks.

I've already forgotten what we are talking about. I'm preoccupied with his lips being so very close to mine.

He laughs. I think he can read my mind sometimes. "Why would I make a terrible criminal?"

"First rule is that you have to be trustworthy."

"That makes no sense."

"Yes, it does," I tell him and pull away. I can't be that close and not kiss him. "If people trust you, they won't ever think you'll do anything criminal. They'll be blind to it."

"Hmmm," he says, and jumps up on the counter. "Makes sense. I'm pretty trustworthy."

"Are you?" I ask. I'm kind of serious. My gram is always saying you can never trust a man. I think I trust Wells, though.

"C'mere and I'll show you," he says, raising his eyebrows.

I know that today we will go much further than kissing and him putting his thumb on my breast, but I don't want it to happen too fast. It's not that I think my gram is right and Wells only wants one thing. I don't. I just don't want Wells to think I'm an easy lay. He's a football player so that's probably what he's used to. I'm pretty certain I'm going to sleep with Wells Braddington eventually, just not today. But he doesn't have to know that.

"I'm just gonna wait for you to prove it," I tell him and pack up my notes.

"Where are we going?" he asks, following me.

"Depends," I say.

"On what?"

"When do you have to be home?"

He frowns. "Four. My mom is making us go to a stupid dinner at her club. Her golf team played in some big tournament today."

"Fun," I say.

"It could be if you went with me." His face lights up; I can tell he just thought of this.

"I don't think your parents would be too excited to have me as their guest at the club."

"Why wouldn't they be?"

"Oh, c'mon. I'm not exactly the girl they're hoping you'll bring home for dinner."

"So?" I'm kind of hurt that he doesn't argue with me on this point. I know I don't look like Marcia Brady, but that's not the point.

"Let's go," I say.

He puts his hand on my waist. "We could stay here."

Five minutes ago, that would have totally been my plan, but now I'm annoyed. For no reason. I hate that.

"I thought you were hungry," I say.

"I am."

"Then let's go find a house with food."

≈≈

We wander the neighborhood looking for an empty house, but everyone seems to be home today. Go figure. Finally, we end up at Ms. Cassie's house.

"Good morning, young people!" she calls out as Wells and I come around the corner of the house. Ms. Cassie is working in her flower garden. The cats swarm us. They know I'm usually good for an extra can of tuna.

"Hey, Ms. Cassie. This is my friend Wells." I want to say boyfriend, but I don't know if I can call him that yet.

"Welcome!" she says, standing up and holding her hand out to Wells. He shakes it and gives her one of his killer grins.

"Are you here to visit me or the kitties?" asks Cassie.

I shrug. "We were bored."

"Ah, I see how I rate, then. When there's nothing else to do, go visit the crazy old lady with the cats." She winks at me, but I feel bad. I didn't mean it that way.

"You're not old!" I say.

She laughs. "But I am crazy and I do have too many cats."

"I like your cats," says Wells. I want to kick him because now he's made it clear that I've brought him here before. Remember the rule about criminals being people you can trust? Here he goes busting it all over again.

"Let me introduce you," I say, scooping up Doc. "This is Doc." Ms. Cassie's listening, too, because she can't ever keep them straight.

"These two are Sneezy and Dopey," I nod towards the two rubbing against my legs. They're the major pigs in the bunch and probably won't quit until I feed them something.

"Let's see," I say, walking towards the patio. "That's Grumpy on the chair and Bashful standing by the door. Sleepy is lying over there on the wall." I point to the low stone wall at the edge of Ms. Cassie's yard. "And I don't see Happy. He's probably out hunting. He's the best at that."

"I don't know how you keep them straight," says Ms. Cassie. "Would you like a glass of iced tea?" She glances at her watch. "Oh, it's after lunchtime! Hungry?"

I smile at Wells. See? I want to say. Never let it be said I don't know how to find free food.

We spend another hour or so at Ms. Cassie's. Wells is fascinated that she's a hospice nurse. He asks a lot of the same questions I asked about dead people. It's wild how Ms. Cassie can talk about it like it's nothing. Like death is as natural as anything. Which is the point she's always trying to make.

"So, I met your grandmother," she says to me.

"Oh yeah, I forgot about that. How'd that go?"

"She's funny."

Okay, now, I've heard my gram called many things, but funny is not one of them.

"Really?"

She nods. She's opening a bag of Oreos and I can see Wells is nearly salivating. She pulls the tab, exposing all the yummy chocolateness. They're Double Stufs, my favorite. She hands the package to Wells.

"Sure. She told me all kinds of stories about the birds in her backyard."

"And you thought that was funny?"

"I did. Don't you?"

"I don't listen when she starts up like that. It makes her seems nuts."

"But that's her world," insists Ms. Cassie. "She knows those birds the way you know my cats."

I think about this. Could Gram actually be able to tell them apart? I frown at Ms. Cassie. "I think she makes all that shit up. She imagines it."

"Don't be so sure. What else does she have to do all day? She chooses not to leave her house. She spends entire days watching those birds. Of course she knows them. When you pay great attention to anything, you pick up on details the rest of us miss. We don't take the time to notice the tiny differences between one chickadee and another, but she does. It's like my cats. I see two gray ones, a fat orange one, two with long hair, a black-and-white one, and one with patches, but I don't know much else about them. I don't know their personalities. You don't even live here, but you know who's who and which one likes to sleep on the chaise lounge and which one is shy and which one is the best hunter. I don't know those details because I choose not to pay attention to them. It's all about what you pay attention to."

I lick the icing out of a Double Stuf and think about this. I catch Wells watching me lick my cookie. He's grinning again and suddenly I just want to kiss him so bad. I stand up.

"I'm glad you liked her. Not many people do," I say.

"I'd like to meet her," says Wells, taking a handful of Oreos for the road.

"We gotta split. Thanks for the food," I tell Ms. Cassie.

176

"Any time. It's nice to have company." She closes the Oreo pack. I notice she didn't eat any. "Thanks for coming by."

"Sure," I say, and we take off.

When we're walking towards Wells' house, he says, "I meant that. I'd like to meet your crazy grandmother."

"She's not crazy," I say, irritated again. "And she wouldn't like you."

He laughs. "How do you know that? Most people do."

"She's not most people."

"You aren't either, but you like me," he says. I look at him and he gives me that amazing smile. The one that makes all girls melt, including me right now. I grab his hand and pull him towards a little grove of trees that hide the run-off pond on the only vacant lot on this end of Pine Road. Once we're under cover, I reach up and I kiss him. He kisses me back and before I know it, we're kneeling in the pine needles and still kissing. He lays me down on my back and lies down beside me. He kisses me more and pulls me towards him, slipping his hands under my sweatshirt.

My heart is racing so fast and I press myself against Wells. I want this and I don't. I feel a little out of control. He stops kissing me and props his head up on his elbow. His hand under my sweatshirt rests on my stomach. It tickles and I let out a giggle, rolling towards him to get out from under his hand. He pulls his hand back out and touches my cheek.

"I really like you," he says, but he says it like he's surprised.

I look at him, really stare into his eyes. Does any of this matter to him? Am I just another girl who falls for him because he's so crazy hot? I don't want to be just another girl to him. Is he someone I can trust or just another louse like Gram would say. I want to trust him. He's done nothing to make me not trust him. At least not recently. When we were in elementary school, he told me I smelled bad the one time we had to sit next to each other on the bus for the field trip to the state capitol. Most of the rest of our childhood, he's just ignored me, but once in middle school, during field day, he told me I ran like a girl. We had just gotten off the bus and I was actually feeling kind of happy. I'd gotten third place in the four-hundred-meter dash.

"Do you think people are mostly good or mostly bad?"

He makes a face. "How would I know?"

I roll onto my back and look up at the tree branches above. They're beautiful. "Do you think we all start out good and learn to be bad or are some people just inherently good and others bad?"

He lies back next to me and holds my hand. "I think it depends on how people treat us. Most people are nice to little kids, but as you get older, they aren't so nice. They usually want something from you."

"What do they want?"

"I don't know. Depends. Most people want me to make them laugh or be good at sports or, in my dad's case, get into Harvard. How nice they are to you depends on how much you live up to their expectations."

I think about this for a minute. There seems to be some truth to this, but then I can think of plenty of exceptions.

"I don't think that's always the way it is. Maybe with parents, but like, Ms. Cassie, she's nice to me and I don't do anything for her except eat her food and feed her cats."

"But you're nice to her, right?"

I shrug. I don't know if breaking in to her house and feeding her tuna to her cats would be considered nice, but she doesn't seem to hold it against me.

"Everybody wants something," says Wells.

He's right, but I don't want to think about that. I don't want to think that Wells is one of those people who wants something from me.

"I want something," I say.

"You do?" he says with a smile in his voice.

"Yup," I say, and sit up. His eyes are closed, but he's smiling. It's not his girl-winning smile; it's different. It's a contented smile.

"What do you want?" he asks, opening his eyes and looking at me.

"I want to beat you to your mailbox!" I jump up and start running, and I can hear him scramble to follow me. I've got a big head start, but, of course, he's a football player and a jock and he's got at least six inches on me, so he passes me, laughing as he does.

"You still run like a girl!" he yells. I can't believe he remembers his snarky comment from middle school. And then, just before he gets to the mailbox, he starts running in slow motion, letting me catch up and beat him.

I blast past him and tag the mailbox. Then I throw my arms in the air. I start singing that Queen song, only I sing, "I am the champion, my friend . . ."

He laughs and pulls me into a hug. Then he kisses me. Just then we hear his dad call, "Wells!" He's standing on the front porch. "We have to leave in twenty minutes!"

Wells lets go of me instantly. He scowls at his dad. "Guess I gotta run," he says.

"Yeah, have fun at the club," I tell him, and squeeze his hand.

"I wish you were going to be there."

"I don't," I say, and this makes him smile.

"You never know. You might like the place. Lots of phony people who want stuff."

"Then you better go give it to them," I tell him and turn to go.

"What are you doing tomorrow?"

"My history essay."

"Well, text me if you want to get together. I'm supposed to play golf with my dad, but I can always skip it."

I look up at his dad, who is still standing on the porch watching us. I wave and take off across the road.

"See ya," I call. "Wouldn't want to be ya!"

EVERETT

≈≈

I wasn't going to go to Veronica's today. Kate and JT went to that boring-ass museum and I was going to stay home and get things done around the house. Evelyn called me on her way to Mildred's, wanting an update on Frank. I stalled her since I haven't even talked to Kate about it or figured out what any of it means. It's hard to say what the fuck really happened forty years ago, but something in the story ain't right. That's pretty damn clear. When I talked to Evelyn earlier in the week, I suggested she get a paternity test to be certain Frank is who he says he is, 'cause nothing I'm finding out is making sense.

I did get a few things done. I cut the grass, hopefully for the last time until spring, and I fixed the side door that was sticking. Now we won't hear Jenna when she comes in late because the door no longer screeches when it finally gives. Then I caught a little of the game. Jenna was nowhere to be found. I don't know where the hell she goes these days. I think she's spending time with that single woman down the street. I'm pretty sure she's a lesbian. Kate says she's a nurse, too. Not sure why she'd want to hang out with a sixteen-year-old.

Christ, I can't believe Jenna is sixteen. I guess one of us is going to have to teach her to drive soon. She can't stand the sight of me, so it'll have to be Kate. One more thing for Kate to deal with. I feel bad that she does so much. She's always tired. That's why I was trying to help out around here today. I straightened up the kitchen, even mopped the floor. But all the time I'm thinking about Veronica and her message about the vampires.

Finally, I can't stand it anymore and I text her. *Sorry about last night. Do the vampires come out to play in the daytime, too?*

She texts right back. *Working. Done at 4. Vampires always available for you.*

I look at the clock. It's two. I pull out the vacuum and do the whole first floor. Then I shower and shave and I'm about to walk out the door. Jenna is in the kitchen with a cup of tea. She looks almost like Kate sitting there, swirling her tea bag around in her cup.

"Oh, you're here," I say.

She just looks at me. Says nothing.

"Well, I've got to run in to work for a few hours," I say.

She rolls her eyes.

"Can you take Marco out?" I ask. I forgot about the damn dog. He hasn't been out all day. He's sitting at Jenna's feet, watching her. That dog has always loved her. Follows her everywhere.

She looks down at Marco. "You smell awfully nice for an empty office," she says without looking at me.

"I'm meeting with a client," I tell her, but I don't know why I have to explain myself to my kid. I turn to go to the garage door, grab my keys off the key rack, and I'm almost out the door when I hear her say, "I'm sure she'll appreciate it." I freeze. Every part of me wants to go back in there and smack some sense into this kid. She has no respect. But I think about where I'm going. Why would she have any respect? I sigh, picture Veronica with fangs and fishnet stockings, and bolt out the door.

KATE
≈≈

Ican't get JT out of the museum until nearly closing. When we get home, it's five thirty. The house is dark. Jenna is in her room working at her desk. Marco perches on her bed, watching her every move.

"Hey, we're home," I say from the doorway. "Hungry?"

"Uh-huh," says Jenna without looking up.

"Where's your dad?"

"I don't know. He said something about having to go in to work for a few hours."

Great. I don't want to think where he might really be. Maybe he is at work. He told me they have an important client visiting this week. I just wish he'd mentioned that this morning. The house looks great, though, so he must have felt guilty about having to go to work. He even cut the grass.

"Well, I'm going to make JT's pasta and then maybe we could order in some Chinese. Would you like that?"

"That'd be great," says Jenna. She still doesn't look at me.

After dinner, JT and Jenna sit at the counter playing Jenga.

"And the oldest thing they had was a pumper from 1806," JT tells Jenna. I'm amazed at how patient Jenna is, listening to all the details from the museum. The place was nearly deserted. The only other people walking through the exhibits were a pair of elderly men—former firefighters. They regaled JT with stories about some of the machines on display. I was grateful, as by that point I was bored out of my skull. Plus, I was distracted trying not to think about what Evelyn might be telling Mama about our father. Thanksgiving is coming up fast and Evelyn is still determined we have a family holiday together, "*all* of us." She doesn't seem to realize how difficult that could be for everyone. It's like she's editing our lives to fit to an ideal that can never be. She wants some kind of happy ending, but how can we be a family now? We were never one to begin with.

I watch JT and Jenna at the counter. I love that they get along so well. Jenna can be difficult at times, but she loves her little brother.

"Cool," says Jenna. "Did they have an old ambulance?"

"Nah, it was all fire stuff."

"But you liked it?"

"Yeah, most EMTs these days get certified in firefighting also. They have to because jobs are hard to find. I think I could be an excellent firefighter. It's all about understanding how a fire behaves."

"How can you know how a fire behaves?"

"Science. Air flow, heat, fuel. It's basic really."

Jenna glances up at me. I know what she's thinking. "Firefighting's dangerous, JT," she says. I shake my head and shrug. We both know that once JT gets fixated on something, it's best to just ride it out.

"You only have to be fourteen to start training to be a junior firefighter," he says.

"Is that so?"

"And you have to have your parent's permission."

"Well, that's still two years away."

JT nods. He concentrates on pulling out a Jenga block. The tower tilts, sways, but holds.

"Good one," says Jenna.

I watch as Jenna works out her next block. "Did your father say when he would be home?"

Jenna shakes her head. Her block breaks free. The tower sways and then tumbles to the table with a crash.

"I win!" cries JT.

"And now it's time for bath and bed," I tell him.

≈≈

When I come back downstairs from saying goodnight to JT, Everett still isn't home. Jenna makes us both a cup of tea. I can't remember my daughter being quite so thoughtful since she was a little girl, younger than JT. When she was little, Jenna was sweet and precocious. She charmed everyone from old ladies at the supermarket to the furnace repairman, but once the tween and then teen years began, she grew angry and distant. She was deeply upset by Everett's affair. That was the low point for all of us.

Jenna and Everett were so tight when Jenna was younger. She followed him everywhere, practically worshipped him. When she found out about the affair, she'd been furious, pelting him with her anger. The therapist said it would take time for her to learn to trust her father again. But what stunned me most was how angry she was with me. Sometimes it seemed like she thought it was my fault that Everett had strayed.

Recently, she's begun to soften. She doesn't bolt from the room every time I sit down with my cup of tea or glass of wine and book.

"Thanks," I say, accepting the cup of tea she offers now.

"You wanna watch a movie?" she asks.

"Let me guess—*Pride and Prejudice*?" It still amazes me that Jenna loves the Jane Austen stories so much. It's such an incongruous passion for a girl who is campaigning for a tattoo her father will never let her have.

"*Sense and Sensibility*?"

"Sounds good," I say, following her into the living room. My phone rings. Evelyn.

"Hold on," I tell her. "I've got to take this. Your Aunt Evelyn took care of Mama today. Go ahead and start the movie. I've seen it plenty of times."

I answer the phone in the kitchen.

"How'd it go?"

"Not so great," says Evelyn.

"What happened?"

"Oh, she was more off her rocker than usual. I tried to talk to her about Dad, but she acted like she didn't know who I was talking about. And you know she does. She might not remember what she had for lunch, but she remembers every tiny detail of her husband abandoning her with two small children."

"Maybe it's too painful for her. I don't understand why you insist on talking to her about him."

"Because she needs to face the truth! And I want the truth. Nothing she says matches what Dad says. He didn't want to leave. She made him leave. He wants to make things right and she won't give him a chance."

"Why do we have to drag all this up now? We're grownups, Ev. This is ancient history. It doesn't change anything. Why is it so important to you that she talk about it? Obviously, she doesn't want to, so why can't you let it be?"

"Because I can't. She's fucked up so many lives. She should have to own up to that fact instead of being allowed to pretend she doesn't remember anything. And you know she remembers! That's the whole problem. She's never forgotten or forgiven anything! How can you be so blind? You've always done everything she asks and believed every word she said."

"You're not being fair. She was a wonderful mother. She loves us."

"Oh, c'mon, Kate! She was not a *wonderful mother*! If she was, she would have at least let us see a father who wanted to see us! And now she's trying to destroy your

185

marriage as well. She won't allow your own husband in her house!"

"That's not true. She's never told Everett he can't come to her house. He chooses not to go there. Besides, my marriage has nothing to do with this."

"Sure it does. It's her way of making sure you'll always be there to take care of her. If she can drive you apart, she'll have you all to herself."

"You've watched too many episodes of Geraldo. You're imagining this stuff. Everett and I are fine. Mama has nothing to do with us."

"Great! If everything's so hunky-dory, you can deal with her. I'm not going to keep spending my Saturdays with her."

"That's not fair! I take care of her every other day of the week."

"Then let's get her in a home. I'll pay for it. We can find her a really nice place. I've actually been in touch with several. I left the brochures with Mama."

"Great. I'm sure she loved that."

"She ignored me, but she knows they're there. I was hoping maybe you could talk to her. It really is time. You need your life back and she's growing worse all the time."

"She isn't any worse," I insist, although I know that isn't true. She's become even more forgetful and is sleeping longer and longer.

"Have you given any thought to meeting Dad?"

Every time I hear Evelyn refer to him as "Dad," it grates on my soul. How can she so easily give him that title when he's been anything but a father to us all these years? And why is she so intent on pulling our family together? She didn't even have the patience for a husband.

"Honestly, I haven't had time, but I still see no reason to."

"I'm sure your kids want to meet him. He's their grandfather."

"In name only."

"It's a start. He's gotten his ticket. He's coming for Thanksgiving. I'll host dinner at my house. It'll be fine, you'll see."

"What about Mama?"

"I want her to come. Dad says he'd like to see her."

"She won't come. You know that, right? She isn't well enough to deal with any of this."

"She's playing with you, Kate. Can't you see that? She's always been able to fool you. I don't think she's as feeble as she pretends. And you want to believe she's this loving mother, but she's never been that."

"Yes, she has. You're the one who holds a grudge. He left! She didn't!" I glance towards the living room, the lights are off and I can hear the movie starting.

"Fine. Stay in your make-believe world, but I'm having our father here for Thanksgiving and I'd really like it if we could all be there. You, Everett, the kids, *and* Mama. Speaking of Everett. Tell him I got the DNA sample he needs."

"What DNA sample?"

"Don't you talk to your own husband? He's got some crazy idea that Dad isn't who he says he is. He wanted a DNA sample from Mama and from me."

Now she's truly making no sense. Why wouldn't Everett tell me this? I glance at the clock. It's after nine and Everett is still not home and hasn't called.

"I have to go. I'm in the middle of a movie with Jenna." I hang up before Evelyn can protest and then I text Everett. *Where are you?*

I stare at the tiny screen. Nothing. Sighing, I pick up my tea and join Jenna in the living room.

"Everything cool with Gram?" asks Jenna.

"What? Oh, yes. She's fine. Evelyn just wanted to update me on how the day went."

I stare at the screen numbly. I'd much rather have the problems of the Dashwood sisters than the ones weighing on my own heart tonight. Jenna is rapt, twirling the end of her hair that is finally growing back. If only life could be as simple as it was in Jane Austen's time.

"Love is complicated," I say. I didn't mean to say it out loud; it just slipped out.

"What?" asks Jenna, not taking her eyes from the screen.

I turn back to the movie. Hugh Grant looks so young and charming and fake. Maybe times haven't changed at all.

"Nothing," I say.

JENNA
≈≈

Wells wasn't on the bus today. I texted him and got no response. Weird. Maybe he was sick. Which means I could get sick, too, since I kissed him Saturday. I'm still kind of shocked at the thought. I look around at the people in my homeroom. They would all freak out if they knew that I had kissed Wells Braddington. I smile to myself. My secret. For now.

I spot Wells at the end of the hall just before lunch. He's at his locker joking around with his jock friends. I don't know if I should say anything. If he doesn't make the first move, I'll walk right past him.

"Hey, Jenna," he calls, running to catch up with me. He slips his hand in mine. I shiver and glance around nervously. He laughs at me and then pulls me into a doorway. He kisses me quickly. "Sorry, my dad took my phone."

"Why? I thought your grade in English was better."

"I shouldn't tell you because you already think my parents are pricks, which they are."

"What?"

He sighs. "Don't be mad because this doesn't change anything with us."

As if I could be mad at Wells about anything when he's holding my hand IN SCHOOL and he just kissed me IN SCHOOL. "I won't be," I promise.

"They said they want me to concentrate on school and that hanging out with you is a distraction I don't need."

"Oh," I say. "In other words, they don't want you spending time with the crazy girl across the street who broke into their garage."

He smiles. I melt. "Something like that," he says. The bell rings. "Meet me after school."

"I can't," I tell him. I want to meet him, but today I have to be home to keep an eye on JT. Mom has some doctor's appointment to go to. The kid is twelve. He is fine at home. In fact, if something terrible happened, JT would be the one helping me and not vice versa. But I promised. Mom looked pretty shell-shocked this morning when she asked. Dad didn't get home until after midnight, and he was drunk.

"Later?" he asks as he's walking away.

"I'll text you," I say, then remember his phone.

"No worries. I'll find you!" he calls as he's rounding the corner. I turn to hurry to class and see several cheerleader girls watching me go. I smile. They saw Wells kiss me.

≈≈

Mom still isn't home at five. I wonder what's up. As if she can read my mind even when she's not here, my phone rings.

"Hey," I say.

"I'm at Gram's. I'll be home in about an hour. I need to fix her dinner and she's pretty agitated."

"Okay."

"Can you make JT's noodles?"

"Yeah. Do you want me to make them for the rest of us, too?"

"Sure, that would be great."

"Bye."

"Jenna?"

"Yeah?"

190

"Thank you. I really appreciate your help."

"No problem. I might go out after I eat. I want to check in with Ms. Cassie's cats just in case she isn't home yet."

"Okay."

Mom sounds a little zoned. Maybe she's just tired. Or maybe she finally called Everett on his bullshit. I wish she would. I think. Sometimes it's easier to pretend things are fine instead of dealing with shit. Like Gram. Nothing matters in her little world except the birds. 'Course, she's pretty miserable mostly. I don't know, maybe being an adult sucks.

JT eats his noodles while telling me more of the stuff he learned about firefighting at the museum.

"Did you know that Benjamin Franklin was a firefighter? He started the first volunteer firefighters. And George Washington, Samuel Adams, and Thomas Jefferson. They were firefighters, too."

"Wow. Cool. I'm learning about them in American History but no one mentioned they were firemen."

JT smiles. He loves it when he teaches me something. He takes another bite of his noodles. I sprinkle some more parmesan on mine and then reach for the crushed red pepper. How can he eat this bland shit every day?

"Those will burn your tongue," he tells me, looking at the pepper shaker.

"I like that."

"Milk will cool it."

"Thanks. I'll keep that in mind."

"Women can be firefighters, too."

"No shit."

"Really. The first woman firefighter was Molly Williams. She was a slave and lived in New York City about two hundred years ago."

"Great." I can tell this firefighter shit might be way more boring than the emergency medicine stuff. JT tends to obsess over stuff. He learns every tiny, boring detail. But sometimes there's funny shit, too. Like when he was telling

191

me some of the funny slang terms that EMTs use. When JT explains them all seriously, it's even funnier. Like UBI, which is an Unexplained Beer Injury. As in, a patient shows up at the ER with an injury sustained while intoxicated that he can't explain. Or terms they use on their charts like PITA (pain in the ass) or ATFO (Asked to Fuck Off) or CAH (Crazy as Hell). It cracks me up to think that these guys in uniform who seem like the white-knight types are actually pretty funny and all. I wouldn't want a job where you had to deal with crazy people all the time. Sane people are hard enough.

I hear the garage door open. Everett is home. Mom always parks her car in the driveway. Everett tells her to so people will think someone's home. 'Course, I know that's not always the case. In fact, there is usually at least one car home when everyone's out because if a family isn't home then they went out together in one car. The big car. The convertible will still be sitting in the driveway. At least that's the way it works in this neighborhood.

"Hey, kiddo, I gotta go check on the cats. Dad's here. I'll see you in the morning."

"Okay," he says. JT still loves Everett. He has no idea.

≈≈

Ms. Cassie isn't home when I get to her place. The cats are happy to see me. I give them some tuna and after they're all chomping, I lie down in the grass to look at the stars. It's crystal clear, like it can be in the fall. The grass is growing damp, but I don't mind.

I wonder if Wells will ask me to homecoming and I wonder if I'll go. I touch my hair. It's growing out. I shaved it last spring and then dyed it jet black in July. Mom freaked out a little and Everett told me I looked like a drug addict. The color is fading. I used one of those do-it-yourself jobs. I had planned to dye it purple, but now I don't know. It's too long to spike with the gel, so lately I've just let it be its wild self, which is curly and messy. Maybe I won't do anything to it.

I hear a noise at the side of the house. Maybe Wells has found me. But it isn't Wells. It's a cat I haven't seen before. A big tomcat. He's brown and black with long hair. I think he's a raccoon at first, but then he sidles up next to Sneezy and shares her bowl. He keeps looking at me, and when I sit up, he takes off.

I see the lights of Ms. Cassie's car bounce off the trees at the side of the house. In a minute, she flips on the patio light and comes outside.

"Jenna?" she calls. She can't see me because of the light. I look at her. She's kind of pretty. I wonder why she isn't married. Everett thinks she's a lesbian, but he thinks that about every attractive woman who isn't married.

"Hey," I say. "Did you know there's a new cat hanging out with the dwarfs?"

"Yeah. I've seen him. He's a big coon cat."

"He was just here."

"You want to come inside? I'm starved."

"Sure," I say. "I already ate, though, so you don't have to feed me."

I watch as she whips up a quick stir-fry. It's amazing to me how she can cook without a recipe. My mom can hardly boil water without one of her little cards. Well, that's not fair. She does boil water every day to make JT's noodles. But Everett doesn't like "gourmet crap" as he calls it, so other than that, we mostly eat burgers and chicken nuggets.

"How was work?" I ask. Ms. Cassie is the only adult who has a job I find the least bit interesting. And it's not that I'd like to be a hospice nurse; it's just so cool that she is.

She sets her plate down and finds a napkin. She uses real cloth napkins. That's another weird thing she does.

"I have a new patient. He's in a tough situation."

"How so?"

She takes a bite and chews. Then she closes her eyes and sighs. "I was so hungry," she says. She takes another bite and when she finishes, she sips from her glass of wine. "The patient is Michael. He's been dying for several years. And one of his dying wishes is to find the son he fathered as a teenager."

"He lost him?"

"No. He was young and he and his girlfriend gave the baby up for adoption. Back then adoptions were closed, so he never knew what happened to the baby. His wife has been trying to find the child for him. And she finally did, but now she's jealous of the relationship the son has with his father. Jeremy, the baby he gave up who is now in his fifties, was so happy to meet Michael. He's there almost every day. It's like they're trying to catch each other up on a lifetime and the days are running out. Phyllis understands that it's important to Michael, but she'd like to have Michael more to herself. It's hard. She's a good person, but sometimes when it gets close like this, when I'm called in, people become desperate."

She takes another sip of her wine. "People have a whole lifetime together, but it's not until they know it's ending that they really cherish their time together." She shrugs. "I do believe having the opportunity to say good-bye is a blessing, but in some ways, at least for some people, it might be easier to get hit by a bus."

"That's harsh."

"Maybe. I'm probably just tired."

I take my cue and get up. "I gotta work on some math homework. I'll see you around."

She nods, but doesn't say anything. She goes back to her meal and I sneak out quietly, hoping to catch another glimpse of the new cat. He's sitting at the edge of the yard and Dopey and Sneezy are lying near him.

I wave and he runs.

When I get home, it's quiet. Mom is home, but she must be upstairs with JT. Everett is watching television. Some stupid reality show. I grab Marco's leash and head back out with him. I don't spend enough time with Marco. Honestly, sometimes I forget he's there. He's so quiet these days. He used to be so hyper, but now he's old. I feel bad that I don't pay more attention to him.

"C'mon bud," I say softly. I don't want Everett to notice me. I can barely look at him. I wish he were different. I wish he were like he used to be.

Marco and I head out.

KATE
≈≈

My yearly physical reveals that I am perfectly healthy. When I tell the doctor how tired I've been feeling, he says I need more rest and less stress. Is it crazy that I almost wished he'd found some kind of health issue? Something that would put me in a hospital where I could rest and be taken care of instead of taking care of everyone else. Somewhere I could go so I wouldn't have to face Everett and ask him where he was yesterday until after midnight. He came in drunk and smelling of someone's cheap perfume. I've never worn perfume. Mama always said it makes a woman too obvious.

If I was laid up in a hospital somewhere, I wouldn't have to fix her tea and wonder if she's faking her confusion whenever I mention Evelyn or Frank. I wouldn't have to worry if she's serious when she talks about wanting to die. Maybe Evelyn's right; maybe Frank's story *is* the real one. Maybe he didn't leave us; maybe she did kick him out. But what good would it do bringing that up now? At this point, who cares why we grew up without a dad? The fact is we did. You can't change facts. Maybe that's why JT finds them so comforting.

If I was sick, I wouldn't have to go into JT's school and continue to argue that he's being babysat and not taught. He deserves better. He's probably smarter than that silly woman who runs the special ed room. If only we could afford a private school like the one Phil mentioned.

If I was hospitalized, maybe Jenna would come and sit by my side and be the sweet girl who watched a movie with

196

me on Saturday and not the sarcastic teen who calls her father by his first name and kisses the neighbor boy.

I shake my head and put the car in gear. I stow the slip with the order for lab work in the glove compartment. I don't know when I'll have time to get it done. The doctor said there's no rush. It's standard tests and he doesn't expect to find anything out of the ordinary. "You're one of my healthiest patients," he told me.

When I reach Mama's house, Phil is standing on the stoop ringing the bell. He's holding a loaf of bread. He smiles when he sees me and comes down the walk to meet my car.

"Hey! I was hoping I might catch you," he says.

"You were?"

He nods, holding up a foil-wrapped package. "I made this for your mother. Orange cranberry bread."

He holds the still-warm loaf out and I take it. It smells delicious and makes my stomach growl. I haven't had anything since breakfast.

"You bake?"

"I'm a closet baker."

"Thanks," I say, and glance towards the house. I'm sure I see a curtain move. Was Mama watching?

"Is your mother home? I'd love to introduce myself."

"She's probably napping. I just came by to wake her up and make her dinner."

Phil looks at me expectantly. I realize he's waiting for an invitation. I hate that he'll be disappointed by Mama. She doesn't like strangers, especially men, and she's already tolerated Cassie coming to visit.

"She's not much for company."

"I won't stay long. Here, let me help you."

He reaches for the grocery bags I pull from the back seat. I lead him around to the side door and through the garage. When we get to the house door, I pause.

"I hate to ask this, but could you wait here so I can make sure she's okay with company?"

"Certainly," says Phil.

I open the door and set down the bag I'm carrying, then reach for Phil's bag. I smile at him as he stands there in the smelly garage with Mama's old Chrysler that has probably leaked out all its oil by now. It was supposed to be Jenna's car to drive, but somehow her sixteenth birthday came and went and there it still sits.

I close the door behind me.

"Who's that?" asks Mama, making me jump.

She is standing in the doorway between the kitchen and the living room. So she *had* been watching.

"That's Phil. He's your new neighbor. He'd like to meet you."

"Why would I want to meet him?"

"He's a doctor. He's very nice."

"I don't need a doctor."

"Mama, please do this for me. Just say hello to the man. Look—he baked orange cranberry bread."

"I hate cranberries."

"You do not."

Mama reaches for the chair and I instinctively go to her and guide her to her seat.

"There, now I'll just bring him in for a quick visit."

"There's no point," she says. "I don't know why you insist on parading all these strangers through my house."

"Cassie isn't a stranger. She's my friend. She's Jenna's friend. And you enjoyed your visit with her."

"That doesn't mean I'll enjoy this one." Mama sets her mouth in a frown and looks away from the door like a stubborn child. Maybe that's what she has become.

I open the door.

"Come in, Phil. Mama is delighted to meet you!"

Phil smiles at Mama and holds out a hand, which she ignores. He doesn't miss a beat, taking the seat opposite her.

"It's so nice to meet you, Mildred. I've just moved in a few doors up."

She looks at him. I pray she will be nice.

"Good for you," she says finally.

"Yes, it has been. It's a great street. I've taken my dog on long walks and met quite a few nice people. Everyone's so friendly."

I'm surprised by this comment. I've never found the people on this street to be friendly in any way. Maybe it's because he's a man. Or maybe it's because he's a doctor. Or maybe he's the one who's friendly. That seems more like it.

"I hope your dog won't disturb my birds," says Mama, and my heart sinks. Couldn't she be nice, just this once?

"Oh! What kind of birds do you have?" Phil looks around, straining to see a birdcage.

"Mama is talking about the birds in the backyard. She's grown very fond of them."

"They love me more than my own family!" she insists, glaring at me.

"I can hardly believe that," says Phil. "Kate speaks so highly of you, and I know she's here all the time taking care of you. She must love you very much."

Mama softens a little at this. I see it. She refocuses on Phil, probably trying to size up his intentions.

"What did you say your name was?"

"Phil."

"That short for Philip?"

"It is."

"I know a blue jay named Philip. He visits every morning. Faithfully. *Unlike* my family. The thing is, Philip, you don't know my family. They'd as soon stab me in the back. My daughter Evelyn told me this past Saturday that she wants to stick me in a home. She can't be bothered with her own mother! And my grandchildren! They wouldn't recognize me on the street!"

I giggle. I can't help myself. It isn't funny. Mama's nonsense and anger is suddenly more than I can take. Phil is sitting here so nicely. He's taken time out of his day and is patiently listening to her nonsense, still smiling. He even baked her bread, for God's sake. He looks at me now, not sure how to react to my laughter and my mother's anger.

"I'm sorry," I say, covering my mouth. "It's not funny. I'm just over-tired."

"Sure, sorry I intruded," says Phil, getting up. "It was very nice to meet you, Mildred. Please don't hesitate to call on me if you need anything at all."

"I'm fine. I've got Katie." She raises her eyebrows at me.

"You sure do," I say. I open the door for Phil and then follow him out through the garage.

"I'm sorry about that. She's not very good with new people, especially men."

"Why is that?" Phil stops and turns to me. His question is sincere and he looks at me with curious eyes. He doesn't seem offended by Mama at all. His kindness is embarrassing and I look away, but his response compels my honesty.

"I don't know for sure. My father left us when I was just a kid and Mama's always been angry about that. As she's gotten older, she's only gotten angrier. And he turned up again recently. He talked to my sister. His story doesn't match up with Mama's. Evelyn believes him, though, and she keeps trying to talk to Mama about it."

"Is that why your mother is so upset with her?"

"Evelyn has this crazy idea that we should all welcome Frank, my father, back into our family. She wants Mama to admit that she made him leave and he didn't want to leave like she's always told us."

"And what do you think? Is there truth to your father's side of the story?"

I hesitate. Why am I telling a stranger all of this? "I haven't actually talked to him. Only Evelyn has. I don't know what to think, but it was a long time ago. I'm not sure it matters anymore."

"It probably does to your father."

"Maybe, but either way the bottom line is that he left and didn't come back."

"It's not my business, but maybe you need to hear him out."

"Maybe. Anyway, thanks for the bread."

"Sure," he says, and starts to go, but stops. "Kate?"

"Yes?"

"I don't think your mother is as confused as she lets on. That's just my medical opinion. I know I didn't spend much time with her, but she doesn't seem like the typical elderly person with dementia. She can't even be that old. How old is she?"

"Seventy-one."

"It's probably as much mental as physical. That happens sometimes. Let me know if I can help in any way." Phil turns to go. "Good to see you again."

"Yes, you too." I watch him walk up the street. *What a helpful person.* And then I hear Everett's voice asking, *What's in it for him?* I shake my head. *Sometimes people are just nice.*

When I get back inside, Mama is still seated at the table. "I'd like to go back outside and check on my birds," she says.

"It's growing dark. Maybe it would be better to stay in for the night."

"I want to see my birds!" she says forcefully.

"Okay, okay, let me help you."

I watch her from the kitchen window as I prepare soup for dinner. Is she pretending to be confused like Evelyn, and now Phil, say? She watches the birds and I can see her lips moving, but whatever she's saying is too quiet for me to hear. It is so hard to know what is going on in someone else's heart. Can honesty be relative?

I call Jenna and ask her to start JT's dinner, then I take the steaming soup to Mama on the porch and sit opposite her.

"Did you like Phil?"

201

She scowls. "Why does that matter? Have you taken up with him?" She shakes her head. "Can't say that I blame you, living with that louse Everett."

"What? No! He's just a new neighbor. I met him at the Braddingtons' party. I think it's nice that he took an interest in you."

"I don't know why he bothers. I'm old and dying."

"You're not really that old, and I don't think you're dying."

"You don't live in this body."

"Plenty of people your age are still living well."

"Plenty of people aren't me."

I watch her spoon the soup to her mouth.

"I think you're only pretending. I think you're just upset because Evelyn is talking to Frank." There, I said it.

Mama says nothing, just shovels the soup into her mouth slowly, robotically.

"Maybe going to Thanksgiving at Evelyn's would be good for this family. We could finally put the past behind us. Evelyn says that's all Frank wants."

She looks at me suddenly, the pain in her eyes so raw I have to look away.

"That's not all he wants," she says quietly.

"What else could he want?"

"Your father is a louse."

"You've said that before, but Evelyn says he only left because you kicked him out. She says you threatened to tell the police his mistress was underage if he didn't leave."

"What?" She looks at me with honest confusion. "That's not what happened."

"Then tell me what happened."

She spoons more soup into her mouth, but says nothing.

"All my life, you've called him a louse. But really, other than leaving, why is he a louse?"

She turns and looks at me, her hazel-gray eyes clear as they bear down on me. There is pain, but there is also determination. For a moment, I think she's going to finally tell me. Explain what he did that left her lost in her own small, bitter world. She sighs. Looks at her hands. When she speaks, it is quiet, defeated. "I only called him a louse because I was angry and didn't want to say curse words in front of you girls. He was a lot of other things; louse may have been the wrong word." She sets her spoon down and wipes her mouth.

"You have to talk to us about this. Evelyn isn't going to stop until you do. It was a long time ago. You were young and hurt. But now you have an opportunity to fix it."

"It is not something that can be *fixed*. Now, I want to go to bed," Mama says as she gets up. She holds the table, but she is shaking so badly that I have to reach out to steady her.

"I just don't know what to do. I wish you could tell me what happened all those years ago. I think you owe me that. He's my father."

She looks at me again with the intense focus that has been missing for months, maybe years. "He isn't your father. Now, I want to go to bed." She turns and reaches out for the wall, but I step beneath her arm and guide her.

I get her settled in her bed and wait until I hear her snoring before leaving. I climb in the car, but don't start the engine. My head is spinning, overloaded. What did she mean, *"He isn't your father"*? Is he not our father because he's never been one to me or because he really isn't our father? I need to ask Everett about all this DNA nonsense. Why did he need Mama's DNA and Evelyn's, but not mine? I also need to tell him about Jenna and the Braddington boy before he figures it out himself and does something rash. He's never home anymore, and even if he is tonight, JT will need me and want to tell me about his day and all he learned about firefighters. I put my head down on the steering wheel. I can't do this. Is it terrible that what I really wish right now, more than anything else, is for a glass of wine and some peace and quiet? Phil is probably home in his quiet house. Maybe he likes wine. I start the car.

EVERETT

≈≈

"You're sure?" I ask my guy at the lab.
"No relation to the other samples."
"And the other two?"
"A match on maternity, but not on paternity. They've definitely got different fathers."
"Huh. Thanks Gordo. I owe ya. I'm good for a round or two at Pike's."
"I'm gonna hold you to it. You need your samples back?"
"Nah, but could you fax me the results?"
"Already did."
"Great. I'll see ya soon."
"Sure."

I grab the fax from the machine before nosy Elaine can ask about it. Frank's story is definitely not right, but neither is Mildred's. I can't give Evelyn any of this until I sort it out, but there's not time now. I shove the report in my desk. I need to focus on work and not Kate's messed up family.

It's been two days and she still hasn't said one word about the other night. I know I was shit-faced when I got home. Probably shouldn't have been driving. I just can't resist Veronica. It's like a sickness. And it's growing worse. I want to be there all the time. I feel awful about it. And Kate must know something. Otherwise, why hasn't she grilled me? I should probably say something first. Head her off at the pass. Make up some shit about an emergency at work and going out with Ronnie afterwards. I use that one too much. Ronnie doesn't even work here anymore. If we go to the Christmas party, she'll figure that out fast.

Maybe I should come clean with Kate. Maybe if she knew, that would give me the strength to say no when Veronica calls. I've got a meeting in a half-hour and I've got to give a presentation. I need to pull my shit together. I open my drawer to get my reading glasses and there are Veronica's panties. The purple ones. She gave them to me so I'd think of her. The woman is killing me. I hold the panties up to my nose and take a breath. Just then my door opens and bossman walks in. I shove the panties in my drawer. I'm too late, though, I catch his smile.

"So, how's Kate?" he asks, pulling up my extra chair.

"She's fine. How's Joanne?"

"Doing great."

He winks at me. I know he's got a girl on the side, too. It's cool though. We don't talk about it.

"You ready for the presentation?" he asks, taking out his phone and scanning the screen.

"Yeah. I got this."

In no way have I "got this" but I'll figure it out. I'm good at pulling off crap like this. I should have been an actor.

"Well, let me know if you need me to take over. This is a big client. You need to land them."

"I will."

He looks at me carefully, like he's studying me. He narrows his eyes. "Look, man, I know we go back, but Elaine is worried about you. Says you've been leaving early a lot and taking long lunches. I'm no saint, here, you know that, but you can't come back to the office with liquor on your breath."

That cunt. I have never come back drunk. Sure, I've been a little lit, but that only makes me better at my job. I'm more relaxed, more creative.

I shake my head. "I'm fine, Duncan. Really. I got this."

He stands up. "Can I tell her not to worry? You'll clean up your act."

I'm pissed. I'm mean really pissed. Elaine has been with me for years. Christ, I gave her that damn Bloom of the Month shit for Christmas last year. Cost a fortune, but Kate said it would remind her how much I appreciate her every month all year.

"Sure. Tell her not to worry."

He leaves. I text Veronica, *Want to do lunch?* She knows what I mean when I say "do."

JENNA

≈≈

O n Thursday, Wells finds me just before third period.
    "Hey, let's cut out of here at lunch."

"What?"

"I mean it. I want to see you. My parents are controlling every single second of my life outside of school, but they have no idea what I'm doing during school. We can go somewhere."

We both have an English test fifth period. But I haven't seen Wells except in English class all week. He always meets me at my locker and walks me to class. He holds my hand. We don't sit together at lunch because he's with his football guys and I don't go to lunch. I go to the library. It's my chance to get away from the animals. That, and I don't have anyone to sit with. I have a couple sort-of friends, but they aren't in my lunch so, outside of sitting by myself at the loser table, the library is much better.

"We have a test," I remind him.

"We can make it up."

"Where would we go?"

"I don't know. We could find some house nearby. You could get us in." His eyes light up. He likes the breaking in a little too much.

"I can't do that. Our neighborhood is easy. I know most of the systems because Everett put them in."

"Then this will be a challenge."

I hesitate. He reaches for my waist and pulls me close. "C'mon. I really want to see you."

What do I care about English? Nothing. But Wells should. If he doesn't pull his English grade out of the toilet, his parents will never let him off the leash.

"I can't miss the test. You can't either. Let's meet tonight."

He lets go of me. Hurt. "We can't. My parents have me on lockdown."

"Locks have never kept me out before."

"They'll be home. You don't do houses with people home."

"There's a first for everything."

He smiles. "I'll call you. Maybe I can sneak out."

When he smiles, it just kills me. Completely. I put my arm around his neck, and he leans down to kiss me. Right there. In the hallway of our stupid high school with all the stupid people walking past. Wells Braddington. Me. Kissing.

≈≈

At dinner, there is a veil of silence enveloping my parents. They don't talk to each other. Mom fusses over JT, asking about all the firefighter shit. Everett stares at his phone like there's something really important there and he's not just playing some dumb game. I eat and split.

"Where are you going?" calls my mom.

"Out," I say.

No one asks where. What would be the point? It's not like I'm going to tell them the truth. I walk over to the Braddingtons' place. I can see the whole family sitting around the dining room table like a Norman Rockwell painting. Who does that? I go to the other side of the house and slip in the garage. It's much easier getting in when the alarm's not set. I pull the door open a crack and listen. I can hear

Mrs. B droning on about some golf match. Mr. B asks Tiffany to pass the rolls.

I step in and close the door behind me. It's a very good thing that the Braddingtons don't have a dog. A dog could ruin this for me. All I have to do is walk through the laundry to the back stairs. The Bs have back stairs for the maid to use. Only they don't have a maid; they have a cleaning service. Their house is custom built and Wells told me it's based on an old southern plantation where his mother grew up.

I make it to Wells' bedroom undetected. It is so clearly his room. Lots of trophies, posters of football players, and a Harvard pennant. I'm surprised he hasn't torn that down. I look through his bookshelf. Typical boy stuff—*Lord of the Rings*, *Hobbit*, all the *Harry Potter* books in hardback, plus a bunch of football biographies. I open his closet. There's a bookcase in there too, but this one has all kinds of weird shit. A homemade butterfly collection, some creatures in jars, books on biology, and even a nasty, petrified dissected frog with the tags and notations still attached.

I decide to read ahead in English. I pull his textbook out of his backpack and a note falls out. It's some kind of frilly stationery. Who writes notes anymore?

Dear Wells,

Since you aren't answering my texts, I guess you're playing hard-to-get.

I've missed you and I know you've missed me. I don't know why you're slumming with that goth chick.

Am I the goth chick? I've never tried to be goth. Just because I have black hair and wear a lot of black clothes does not make me goth. It simply means I like black. I keep reading.

I know you're trying to make me jealous. And it worked! I M crazy hot for U! I'm going to buy the sexiest dress for homecoming you've ever laid eyes (or hands!) on.

C U Saturday at the club. Maybe we can sneak down to the caddie shack and catch up.

XOXOXOXOXO,
Amber

Whatever. If he wants to bang Amber Blevins that's fine with me. I shove the letter in my pocket and try to read the next chapter in English. It's a short story set in medieval times. I can't concentrate. I wish I could leave, but now I hear the family moving around the house. I'm stuck here. This was a dumb idea. My phone lights up with a text. It's Wells. Guess he got his phone back.

Hey. Stuck here. Ps are watching my every move.

I smile. Maybe he doesn't want to fuck Amber Blevins in the caddie shack.

Maybe you should just go to your room and study, I text back.

Probably. See you tomorrow. Sorry about tonight.

No problem. I close the English book and wait.

A few minutes later, the door opens and Wells comes in. He doesn't see me at first, but then he does a double take and slams his door.

"Holy shit! You're here!"

"Shhhh!" I tell him. "Don't screw it up!"

He is grinning ear to ear and the risk was worth it. I just want to kiss that smile. He grabs my hand and pulls me over to his bed, shoving the crap piled on it to the floor. We sit there and kiss for what feels like forever.

When we finally stop, he says, "I probably taste like lasagna."

"You do, but I don't care," I tell him, and pull him back for more. He lays me back on his bed and pulls up my T-shirt. I don't know where this is going and, for the moment, I don't care. I let him unhook my bra. I think things would have gone much, much further, except Tiffany walks in.

"Shit!" yells Wells, and he jumps up. "You can't knock?"

"What's she doing here?" asks Tiffany. Wells reaches behind her and slams his door. I sit up and reattach my bra.

"None of your business."

She raises her eyebrows. "Oh, really? So if I just go down the hall to where Mom is reading in the loft and mention that you have a whore in your bed, it's not a problem."

"Shut the fuck up!" says Wells. I'm still processing the fact that little freshman shit Tiffany has labeled me a whore. Tiffany used to beg me to play with her when we were in elementary school. I gave her smiley face stickers on the bus and she put them all over her backpack.

"What do you want?" he asks, grabbing my hand and pulling me up beside him.

"I was only going to ask if we could leave a little early for school tomorrow and stop at the donut place, since you got your car back."

"You did?" I ask.

He nods. "Dad checked on my grades today. I aced the English test."

"That's awesome!" I tell him.

"Hello? I asked you a question," says Tiffany.

"Yeah, I'll take you to the donut shop. Just don't mention this to Mom."

"Of course not," says Tiffany. "Bye Jenna!" she says loudly as she exits.

"Shit!" says Wells, and he shoves me into his closet. "Stay there."

I can see him through the crack between the doors. A moment later, his mom appears. "Wells? Is somebody here? Did I hear Tiff talking to someone?"

He looks up from his desk, where he's pretending to study. From here, I can see that his textbook is upside down. Hopefully his mom is as nearsighted as mine.

"Nope. I was just talking on the speaker phone."

"Oh," she says, glancing around. She spots the pile of shit Wells shoved off the bed.

"I would appreciate it if you'd put those clean clothes away. I didn't fold them for my health." She turns and leaves.

When the door closes, Wells laughs quietly and opens the closet door. "That was fuckin' awesome!" he says. We resume our activities on his bed. This time, I pull off my shirt myself and the sharp intake of breath he emits emboldens me to remove my bra, too. I'm saving him the trouble, but at the same time I just want to see his reaction. The guy drives me crazy.

"No sex, though," I tell him, and he gives me a look like a wounded puppy dog. "Not here."

We mess around for another couple hours, sometimes kissing, sometimes exploring, but talking a lot, too. I don't say anything about Amber's note. He can do what he wants, right? Around eleven, he helps me sneak back out. When we're outside, he kisses me one last time. Then he says, "I know dances aren't your thing, but want to go with me to homecoming?"

I die. Okay, I don't die. But I feel like I could. Maybe I swoon. I always say I hate dances, but they're my favorite scenes in every Jane Austen book I read. I love those scenes in the movies, too. Everyone looks so much better than they do in real life. And the dresses! I love the dresses. Maybe Mom will buy me a new dress just for homecoming.

"Yes! Wells Braddington, I would love to go to homecoming with you." He looks surprised, but pleased.

"Great!" he says. Guess he better break the news to Amber Blevins before she spends too much on her sexy dress.

I'm floating the whole way down the driveway, but my mood is completely ruined when I see the garage door go up at our house and Everett leave. Where the fuck is he going at this hour of night?

KATE

≈≈

Jenna is just about to go out the door to the bus when she says, "Hey, I need to go shopping for a homecoming dress."

I look up, startled. I haven't seen my daughter in a dress since she was probably eight years old and we went to a wedding for one of Everett's coworkers.

"Really?" I ask.

"Why would I say that if I didn't need to go shopping for a dress?" Jenna says, impatiently adjusting the straps of her backpack.

She is wearing a long gray T-shirt with the words *We're all chemicals* printed on the front, over a pair of leopard-print leggings in black and pink. Evelyn gave her that T-shirt last year for Christmas. Jenna loved it and I've never been able to figure out what's so funny or why Evelyn gave it to her.

"We can go tonight after your father gets home."

"Cool," she says just before she shuts the door behind her.

I start JT's oatmeal, measuring the water and salt. JT likes his oatmeal the same way every day. Any slight change in the saltiness or texture could set him off. It's going to rain, and the wind is already blowing. Leaves shower down outside the window, covering the backyard in a blanket of yellow and gold. I have a meeting later this morning with JT's IEP team. His individual education plan is not working. At least it isn't working for me. I asked

Everett to attend the meeting and was surprised when he said, "I'll try."

Normally, Everett gets angry whenever I approach the school with any kind of complaint about JT's education. Everett has never been able to understand why JT isn't in a regular classroom. "He's smart. Why should he be with the retards?" he'll ask. Every time, I have to explain that the special ed room isn't for retarded children. Then I remind Everett that people don't use the term "retard" anymore, and Everett will say something like, "I know that, but everyone knows that's what they are," as if we're talking about animals and not children.

Everett has been tiptoeing around me for the last few days. I know he's guilty of something, but right now I don't want to know what. I've got enough to worry about between Evelyn's endless drama, Frank's impending visit, Mama's failing mind, JT's school situation, and Jenna possibly sleeping with Wells. I'm tired of trying to save our marriage. It's easier to ignore it. Besides, Everett is much nicer to me and the kids lately. Whatever it is he's feeling guilty about does make the house more peaceful.

"Hello Mom-Unit," says JT, sliding onto a stool at the counter and smiling at me. He's wearing his firefighter badge Everett dug out for him. Everett trained to be a firefighter before he was accepted into the police academy. This gives him near-God status in JT's world right now.

"Hello, yourself," I say, and place the oatmeal on the counter. I set the containers of brown sugar and dried apple pieces in front of him and then pour myself more tea. I know I should eat, but lately breakfast just doesn't appeal to me. The food sticks in my throat. Yesterday, I found a pair of Jenna's jeans she no longer wears; "too geeky," she'd said. They fit me better than any of my own, so I'm wearing them again today. Everett complimented me last night, telling me that he's the only guy whose wife is thinner now than at their wedding.

"We need to leave a few minutes early this morning," I tell JT. I'm actually planning to leave more than a few minutes early, just in case he has difficulty with the change to our morning routine.

He looks up, wrinkles his brow. "Why?"

"I have a meeting with your IEP team."

"Are you going to tell them I want to take that calculus class?"

"Among other things."

"Will Tucker get to take it, too?"

"I don't know."

"He wants to."

"I know."

I smile at him and push the hair out of his eyes. I wish he'd let me cut it. He wants to grow his hair long enough to put in a ponytail. So far, I've refused, knowing that Everett would never stand for that. Plus, JT stands out enough already. Kids have plenty to tease him about. No sense adding to it. Jenna is on his side; she says that kids will think he's cool if he has long hair.

"Maybe after school, we could stop by the barber shop and get your hair tidied up."

"Did you know that there's a natural gas vent in Iraq that has been burning continuously for over four thousand years?"

"I didn't." I find a notepad and search in the junk drawer for a pen. I'm still struggling with how to word my request at the meeting this morning. Maybe writing it down will help.

JT squints at me, skeptically. "You didn't?"

"No."

"Then why did you nod?"

"I nodded?"

"You did, and Mrs. Fall says that when someone is nodding at me, they are agreeing with me." He smiles proudly. One of the goals this year was for JT to watch other people when they speak and pay attention to their body language. Normally, he's so focused on sharing his own thoughts that he barely looks at the other person at all. He isn't comfortable with eye contact and he struggles to understand nonverbal responses.

"I'm sorry. My mind was elsewhere."

He frowns, but then continues. "It's called the Eternal Fire and it's been mentioned by Herodotus, Plutarch, and even in the Bible."

"Wow," I say, feigning enthusiasm, while trying to decide whether my question about the calculus class should really be a question. Maybe I should simply tell them I want JT placed in the class. "I've got to go get ready for my meeting. When you finish your oatmeal, can you take Marco out for a quick walk?"

"I can," says JT.

"Thanks."

I change my clothes three times, trying to find something that fits right. I hate the way my collarbone protrudes. Finally, I settle on a sweater set and scarf. If Everett is there, maybe we can go out for coffee afterwards. I'll eat something then. Something fattening, like a big cinnamon bun from that place he loves so much.

≈≈

I say good-bye to JT in his classroom and head back to the office to wait for our meeting. I'm early, but the principal is delayed and I have to wait almost thirty minutes. It's enough time to lose most of the nerve I thought I had. Finally, the secretary calls my name. I'm about to follow her back to the conference room when Everett appears at the entrance. I can see him on the monitor at the secretary's desk. All the schools have installed new security at the entrances. Everett's company bid on the job, but didn't get it. The secretary makes him show ID before she buzzes him in. His face isn't familiar to her. I never have to produce ID since I am probably too familiar to them.

I look at Everett now on the monitor, smiling and holding up his license for the camera to take a picture. He is still handsome. He hasn't aged at all. Well, maybe he's put on a few pounds and his shoulders aren't as muscled as they'd been when he worked on the force, but women still notice him. When he arrives in the office, I watch the secretary's demeanor change. She is softer, smiling. Everett has some kind of magical power over women. He takes my hand and squeezes it before kissing me on the cheek.

The members of the team are seated at a table when we arrive. It seems like they've been meeting for some time already. Empty coffee cups and crumbs from some kind of breakfast snack are scattered on the table. The principal, guidance counselor, special ed teacher, school psychologist, math specialist, and one of the aids who works in JT's classroom are all there. Everett and I sit at the far end of the table. I move my chair closer to Everett, who sets his hand on my knee.

"So Mr. and Mrs. Turner, we're glad you could meet with us this morning," says the principal. "Mrs. Fall has been filling me in on JT's progress and your request. I'll let her explain our thinking on this."

I glance at the aide, Ms. Michaels—she looks uncomfortable. JT doesn't like Ms. Michaels. He says she talks to him like he's a baby. It frustrates me that so many people do this, but I hadn't expected it of someone who is supposed to be a trained professional. JT may be socially awkward and prone to tantrums when he's frustrated, but he has a brilliant mind and he's generally smarter than most of the adults around him.

"We've seen some progress with JT this year. He's working very hard to make consistent eye contact and to listen actively to others," said Mrs. Fall. "But he still has a long way to go. It's our opinion," and here she gestures to

Ms. Michaels, "that he would struggle if we put him in a regular classroom for math."

"It wasn't a regular classroom that I requested," I say, trying to keep my voice calm. "It's the honors pre-calculus class."

"Yes, well that class is at the high school," says the principal. "That would require special transportation."

"Which I am willing to provide," I tell them, and Everett nods.

"It's just not a good idea for so many reasons. I'm sorry," says Mrs. Fall, as if she is concluding the discussion.

I feel Everett tense up beside me. He drops his hand from my knee. "Mrs. Fall, may I call you Cathy?" I wonder how Everett knows her first name is Cathy. I didn't even know it was.

Mrs. Fall smiles at him. "Of course."

"Cathy, I haven't been to one of these meetings before. I'm wondering if you couldn't walk me through some of the reasons that make it not such a good idea for JT to attend a class at the high school."

Mrs. Fall cocks her head to the side, like a puppy. She smiles again. "I'm sure your wife has shared those with you."

"Actually, it would be really helpful to hear them from you."

"I'm not sure we have time to go into all of it, but I've outlined it all in the report recommendations."

The guidance counselor breaks in, "I have that report right here. We just need your signatures on it."

"Super," says Everett, still smiling. "I'd love to read all of it and then after we understand your reasoning, we can sign it."

I can't help but smile. The other members of the team look stunned, except the math specialist who is smiling.

"Could I say something right here?" the math specialist asks, looking to the principal for approval.

"Go ahead."

"I think that sending JT to the high school for a class might be very helpful, not just for him, but for the other students and for all of us. We will never know what a student with JT's abilities is capable of until we explore them."

I could kiss her! She gets it. My heart is racing as the woman continues.

"Honestly, I've never seen a child of JT's age with such an ability in math. There's very little we can offer him in terms of math education here at the middle school. I wouldn't be surprised if he knows more than any of us."

I watch as Mrs. Fall's expression goes from frustration to anger.

"I really believe he would struggle in that environment," Mrs. Fall says. "And I don't think that's what you want for your son." She directs her comment to Everett, not making eye contact with me.

"We will never know that if we don't try, now will we?" says Everett. "Maybe we need to give JT this shot. See how he does. If it's a disaster, then okay, we learned something here. He's not ready."

"But Mr. Turner," she begins.

"So, this seems like a good plan," says Everett, placing both hands on the table as if everything is decided now and he can go. He smiles at all of them. "That's what I love about this school. You're always ready to do what's right for the student, even if it means breaking a little protocol now and again."

I look at the stunned faces. No one says anything; they look to Mr. Brice, the principal, who smiles at Everett.

"Well, Mr. Turner, if you're on board with this idea, then I guess we can move it forward. We'll give JT an opportunity to take the class at the high school and then we'll evaluate in, say, six weeks? See if we all agree it's working or whether we need to make another adjustment."

"Great! I'll just leave this report with you then, so you can make the changes and then Kate can sign it when she picks up JT later," says Everett, getting to his feet and holding out his hand to shake Mrs. Fall's hand.

≈≈

In the parking lot, I hug Everett. Sometimes I forget how amazing he can be. How he can command a room and just fill it up with his confidence. At this moment, I love him hard. "You were wonderful," I gush. I can't help myself; I'm as bad as that secretary. "I don't know how you do it."

"You just have to know how to play people," says Everett. "You take your idea and make it their idea."

I shake my head and kiss him on the cheek. "I wish you'd come to JT's meetings before. They listened to you."

"Oh, they'd listen to you, too, if you just assert yourself more."

"I try, but it's not easy for me like it is for you."

"I've had a lot of practice," he says.

"Let's celebrate! We can go to that coffee shop near the hospital. The one with the huge sticky buns. We haven't been there in years."

"I should get back to work."

"Please?" I can see Everett hesitating. He probably has important meetings to attend to. "It'll be like a little date. We haven't spent any time together in so long."

"Okay, but real quick. I do have to get back to work."

I follow him to the coffee shop in my car. He holds my hand as we walk across the parking lot. The woman behind the counter smiles at Everett. "Well, isn't it good to see you," she says. "It's been too long." The way she says it makes it sound like it *hasn't* been too long since she saw Everett. I look at her dyed-blond hair with black roots, her huge chest, and her painted-on face. Do I know her from my days at the hospital when Everett and I used to make

221

out in the corner booth after his shift? That was nearly twenty years go. She's too young to have worked here then.

Everett steers me to the very same corner booth. The Formica tabletop is worn and scarred—most likely it's the same table, too.

"I remember this table," I say.

"If only it could talk," he says, squeezing in beside me.

The woman from behind the counter appears. "Isn't this cozy," she says, handing us menus and winking.

I read her tag: *Veronica*. I don't know any Veronicas, except the one in *Scooby Doo*, and this one certainly doesn't look like *that* Veronica. The woman fills two coffee cups. "Anything else?" she asks.

"I'd like one of those huge sticky buns in the case," I tell her.

"Nothing for me," says Everett.

"You sure, darling? There's some delicious options here." She winks again and smiles at Everett.

I watch her walk away. Her uniform stretches taught across her hips, and the height of her heels is surprising for a waitress. Like nurses, waitresses are on their feet a lot; you'd think she'd wear something more practical. A clip peeks out from beneath her short skirt where it holds up thigh-high stockings with a seam down the back. I didn't know anyone wore stockings like that anymore, except hookers.

EVERETT
≈≈

Christ, what a morning! I went to that meeting at JT's school. Kate's always after me to attend. They keep JT in a classroom for retards. He shouldn't be there. I went today because Kate was finally fighting to get him in a regular classroom instead of just a different curriculum. It's crazy that those people spend entire days with the kid and don't realize how smart he is. Sometimes people see what they want to see. That's half the problem.

Kate still hasn't said anything. But she knows. She knows I've been screwing around. I'm sure of it.

When she insisted we go to the place where Veronica works, I thought all holy hell was going to break loose. But she was just trying to be romantic. She didn't know who Veronica was. We sat in the old booth where I used to feel her up after her shift at the hospital. It was part of our routine. We'd go there for coffee and breakfast and, by the time we left, I'd be so hot for her, we'd sometimes have to do it in the car before we got to my place. Those were the days. I don't know where that Kate went. If she'd stuck around, maybe I'd be able to resist women like Veronica.

It was crazy sitting there watching Veronica while Kate was sitting beside me. She kept making up reasons to stop by our booth just to drive me crazy. She even came out from behind the counter to wait on us, instead of letting Josie do it. I tried not to look at her, but what man wouldn't? Even with Kate there beside me, I couldn't help myself.

223

My phone lights up with a text. *You can't tease me like that. Now you have to meet me after my shift.*

Last night I told Veronica I couldn't meet her today. I shouldn't have been there last night, but I couldn't stay away. She said some guy kept calling her, and wanted me to come over in case he came by. I know she was making that shit up, but when she said she'd make it worth my while, I knew what that meant. Kate had been in bed for hours. I was in the car before I knew what I was doing. But I told her when I left, no more. We were seeing each other too much. And I know Kate is on to us.

It has to be quick, I text back.

That's entirely up to you.

I know what that means. It means she'll have some crazy new shit planned that will make me want to stay.

God, you kill me.

Then she texts back a bunch of those stupid smiley faces whose expressions I can't see without my glasses, so I put the phone down and turn on my computer. I'm going to have to crank out some work so I can get out of here early. Hopefully, the boss won't be in. He's out more than I am.

JENNA
≈≈

Shopping with my mom sucks because she brings JT along. Dad had to work late, and she wouldn't leave him home alone. I asked why she couldn't just leave him with Gram, and she said that Gram hasn't been feeling well lately. No shit. When has Gram ever been feeling well?

She takes me to the department store she loves. All they have are old-lady dresses. I don't want a long dress.

"Look at this! It's beautiful!" She's holding up a shiny blue dress with poufy sleeves and a poufy skirt. It's awful. Looks like something a flower girl in a wedding would wear. I glare at her and she puts it back.

"There's nothing here I like," I tell her.

"How do you know? You haven't even looked."

"I can tell."

JT is sitting on a bench reading a book Mom bought him about the chemistry of fire. Not sure what she's thinking here. The way he is, tomorrow he'll be wanting to try out the chemistry of fire and he'll burn down the whole neighborhood.

"Can't you just drop me at the mall with your credit card?"

"I really want to help you find a dress," she says. "This is your first dance."

"It's not a big deal," I tell her.

"Yes, it is! It's your first dance and your first date and Wells is such a nice boy."

She has no idea what kind of boy Wells is. I wish there was some way this dance could happen without her knowing it. I don't know why I told her. But then again, she's so genuinely happy for me, it's kind of nice. I wish it didn't irritate me when she talks about Wells.

"I remember my first dance. I went with a boy named Jonathon." She gets a dreamy look on her face. "He was my first love."

"I thought Dad was your first love."

"He was the first man I loved. Jonathon was the first boy I was *in* love with."

"There's a difference?"

"Yes!"

"I don't love Wells." I say this, but part of me does love him. Or at least is *in love* with him. It has to be that, otherwise why am I shopping with my mother for a dress to go to a dance? Why do I think about Wells 24/7? Why do I want to kiss him whenever I see him?

We gather up JT, who makes us stand there and wait for him to finish his page before leaving. At the mall, Mom says she'll wait in the food court with JT and I can text her when I find a dress. Fair.

As I'm walking by the store where everyone buys their dresses, I see Tiffany and a gaggle of her friends inside. I walk past. I find a store called Urban Chic. The dresses are all dark and some are pretty daring. My store. I try on three dresses that I know my mother will never buy and then find a black halter dress that fits me tightly and has a built in pushup bra. There's a rhinestone trim around the top that connects with a rhinestone encrusted ribbon that goes around the neck, kind of like a necklace, but actually it helps keep the dress from slipping down. There's a rhinestone-covered princess seam, just like the dresses from Jane's day, although this dress hits me mid-thigh and that is decidedly *not* Jane's era. The back is bare all the way down to the waist, with two rhinestone-covered ribbons across the middle to keep the front from falling down. Hot. That's what this dress is. It's hot. It's also $198. Mom said our budget is $100. I text her and tell her I've found my dress and I'll pay for half. I have a pile of money from pet sitting and housesitting for the Ashers and Ms. Cassie.

When Mom sees the dress, she says, "I don't know about this, Jenna. It seems pretty revealing."

"That's the point."

"I thought the point was to look beautiful at the dance. I'm not sure you could dance in this dress."

"Sure I can," I tell her, which is true. I *could* dance in this dress if I knew *how* to dance.

"I don't think your father will approve."

"So?"

She sighs. "You do look beautiful." She walks around me. She sighs again. "But so grown up."

"Hello? I am grown up. I'm sixteen."

"Maybe we could buy a wrap that you could wear with it."

A wrap could work. That would keep hypocritical Everett from spazzing out on me. "Okay," I tell her.

We have to go to another store to find a wrap. I let Mom pick it and act like I like it when it doesn't really matter since I'm going to take it off the second I leave the house. We also pick out a pair of black heels with tiny rhinestones trimmed around the top. I will be hot. Wells will be blown away. Mom says she has a necklace and ear-rings I can wear, too.

This happy mother-daughter moment would be perfect, except, as we're paying, we both hear JT. We left him on a bench just outside the store. He's yelling, "STAY AWAY FROM ME! DON'T TOUCH ME!"

"I'll go," I tell her, and run out of the store while she is signing her credit card receipt.

JT is standing against a wall, next to a fire extinguisher box that is open. There are two security guys reaching for him and, whenever they do, he kicks them.

"JT!" I call. "Are you okay?"

"JENNA! THEY WON'T GO AWAY! MAKE THEM GO AWAY! I PUT IT BACK!"

I stand between JT and the officers. "JT, look at me!" I get right up in his face, but don't touch him. I know when he is freaking like this, if anyone touches him, he might hit them. I've gotten a bunch of black eyes courtesy of JT, so I don't touch him. I just block his view.

"Hey, chill," I say. "We can explain this to the officers, but you have to chill right now. Don't hit anyone. Don't hit me."

"Okay," he says, but he doesn't move.

"Here, sit next to me." I sit down on the floor, with my back against the wall. Mom arrives at this point and starts talking with the security officers. I look up, and there is Tiffany with her gang. She waves and then walks off giggling.

"So what happened?" I ask JT.

"I was just looking at it. I wanted to see if it was a stored-pressured extinguisher or a cartridge-operated extinguisher. They work very differently, you know." He continues to talk his mumbo-jumbo fire extinguisher factoids, but I watch Tiffany walk down the mall. How can Wells be related to someone like that?

Mom comes back and says, "JT, you need to tell the officers that you're sorry you opened the box and you won't do it again."

"But I'm not."

She glances behind her to see if the officers are listening. They're not. They're talking to the guy who works in the store that we're sitting in front of.

"I know you're not sorry you opened the box, but you can be sorry that you didn't know you weren't allowed to open the box."

He thinks about this. "Okay. I am sorry I'm not allowed to open it."

She smiles. "Good. Come with me."

I wait while JT does his penance and then we split. When I get home, I text Wells. *Got a dress. Hope you were serious about homecoming.*

He texts right back. *Completely. Is it hot?*

No, it's kind of cold out right now. I smile to myself and shut down my phone. I love messing with him.

KATE
≈≈

The next week, I drive JT to the high school for his pre-calculus class. Since the class is first period, JT will start his day at the high school. This means while he's in class, I have only fifty minutes to get back to Mama's house, make her breakfast, and get her situated before racing back to the high school to pick up JT and drive him over to the middle school for the rest of his day. It took a week for the new IEP (individual education plan) to be written, presented to the high school principal and calculus teacher, and then be signed by everyone involved, including Everett who, for the first time, actually read JT's IEP.

"I like what they're doing for math. Why does he still stay in the class with the crazy kids for everything else?"

"They're not crazy kids," I remind him.

Everett waves his hand in the air like he's shooing a bug. "I know, I know, but why is he still in there?"

"The new IEP only addressed his math, nothing else changed. He does still need some services. Mrs. Fall is making progress with his social skills."

"Waste of time. JT just needs to understand that he can't cry like a baby whenever he doesn't get what he wants. The high school kids would teach him that pretty quick."

"It's not that simple."

"I believe it is, but what do I know? I'm the idiot around here."

"Everett, please don't be like that."

Every conversation we've had about JT's Asperger's always ends with Everett shutting down and refusing to talk about it. That conversation was no different.

After I drop JT and Jenna at the high school, I hurry to Mama's. Thankfully, Jenna agreed to walk JT in and then be sure he found his pre-calculus class. It took a little convincing to get the school to allow Jenna to be late for homeroom during this first week, but I know it will make all the difference for JT. He'll arrive in the classroom safely and not upset. We can deal with next week when the time comes and he has to do it on his own. First, we have to get that far.

"Mama? I'm a little early, like I warned you," I call. The house is dark and there's no sound from the bedroom. The curtains stapled to the windows are effectively black-out curtains. It could be any time of day or night in the living room or bedrooms. At least the kitchen windows and sliding door aren't covered.

Mama is asleep, so I gently shake her. She opens her eyes and then begins screaming, "What? What is it? Is it a fire? What's happened?"

"No, Mama, it's me. JT started his new math at the high school today. Remember, I told you I'd be here earlier to make your breakfast."

"Oh," she says, sitting up. "I don't remember that at all. That just won't do. I can't have you waking me up and scaring the bejeezus out of me every morning."

"Sorry, but it's my only option."

Mama continues to grumble as I help her to her feet and she shuffles to the bathroom. I leave her there and go prepare her breakfast. Mama has steadfastly refused help in the bathroom. I worry that she will slip, but the room is tiny and she can reach a wall at all times, so she insists she doesn't need help. "I'm not a baby. No diapers, yet."

Mama has fallen twice, and both falls set her back tremendously—making her seem much older than her years.

She's broken a hip and a shoulder within five years. Still, she's not ready to be in a home, as Evelyn wants. It's not always easy taking care of her though, and certainly not getting easier. She's a lot like JT. She has her routines and is only happy when they're followed. Mess with them in any way and there will be hell to pay. It promises to be a rough week getting her used to the new routine.

"Okay, now you're all set. If you need anything before I'm back to help with lunch, just call me. Your walker is right here if you need to go anywhere." Mama is sitting in the kitchen in front of the sliding glass door where she can watch her birds.

She scowls at her walker. "I hate that thing," she mutters.

"I know you do, but it's better to be safe than sorry, right?" I tell her. "And remember Cassie is coming by today after lunch. That'll be fun."

Mama says nothing, just stares at her birds.

≈≈

I wait just outside the office for JT to return from his math class and spot him walking down the hall with Jenna. He is smiling and talking excitedly. He must have loved the class. They are still a long way off when I see Wells catch up with them. He gives JT a high five and then holds Jenna's hand as they walk up the hall. JT in front, Jenna and Wells behind. When did Wells become friends with JT? JT doesn't touch just anyone. That high five means he knows Wells and likes him.

When Jenna sees me, she whispers something to Wells, who drops her hand and heads off down another corridor. JT sees me and runs down the hall.

"How was it?" I ask.

"Great!"

"See ya, JT," says Jenna.

"See ya, Sister-Unit!" he says, and laughs.

"Thanks, Jenna." I smile at her and reach out to touch her arm, but she moves away.

"No prob," she says. I watch her go. She is changing, and I wonder if she's in love.

≈≈

That afternoon, I've just finished Mama's dishes when Cassie knocks at the door.

"Who's that?" asks Mama, scowling.

"Remember, Mama, it's Cassie. She said she'd come by." I open the door for Cassie and whisper, "She's in a bit of a grumpy mood."

"Me, too," says Cassie. She sets her coat on a chair and follows me into the kitchen.

"Hello, Mildred!"

Mama nods. "Did you bring it?"

Cassie smiles. "I did!"

"What?" I ask.

"Mildred told me that she is also a fan of Jane Austen, like Jenna and I, so I brought my copy of *Sense and Sensibility* to watch."

"Oh," I say. "Haven't you watched that one with Jenna?"

"Not in a long time," says Mama. Then she says to Cassie, "Jenna doesn't come by much anymore. She thinks I'm nuts."

"Oh, I don't think that's the case. She does worry about you though. She gets upset when you talk about dying."

"What? I *am* dying."

"We're all dying, I'm afraid," says Cassie. "It's a chronic problem." She chuckles at her own joke as she helps Mama to her feet and guides her to the living room to watch their film. Mama is much more animated, almost happy, around Cassie.

"I think I might head home for a bit," I say.

"You go ahead," says Cassie. "I'll keep an eye on her."

"I really appreciate this." I feel unexpected tears well up. It is such a relief to have someone else in charge of Mama, even for just a few hours.

"I'll walk you to your car," says Cassie. "I wanted to ask you about something."

When she shuts the door behind us, Cassie says, "I think your mother is depressed."

"No, she's always been like this."

"I've run across a lot of depressed elderly people in my work and she fits the bill. I think it might be good for her to be evaluated. The right medicine could change her life."

"I can't get her to leave the house at all anymore, not even for doctor's visits."

"What if a doctor came to her?"

"I don't know."

"Phil agrees," says Cassie. When I look surprised, she says, "He said he'd met you and Mildred."

"He said he was a friend of yours. He's a nice man."

It makes sense now. Phil must be interested in Cassie. Why else would he have moved to Pine Estates? Cassie is beautiful and interesting and available. It's tragic, but not surprising that they would find their way to each other.

"Phil's awesome. I worked with his late wife."

"He said you encouraged him to move to Pine Estates."

"I knew the house was up for sale and he wanted a fresh start and a smaller place."

"Are the two of you an item?"

"Excuse me?"

"I mean, it's been quite a while since his wife passed and you'd spent a lot of time with him, so naturally it makes sense that you would grow close."

"Me and Phil? No! That's funny," says Cassie, laughing. "Kate, I'm gay."

I can't help myself; I'm shocked and I know my face gives me away. It's not that I have an issue with it. I'm just honestly shocked. I don't want her to think I'm being judgmental; I'm not. It's fine with me if someone is gay. I'm embarrassed at my relief that Cassie is not dating Phil. *Why?* I don't know what to say and stutter, "I didn't know. I just assumed, I mean, I guess I assumed wrong."

"Phil's a great guy. If I were into guys, yeah, I think I might like him. But I'm not."

"No, I guess not," I say, wincing at how awkward that sounds.

"So, about your mother, what do you think? I have a friend who's a family doc, but she has a lot of geriatric patients and I'm sure she'd make a house call."

"Really?"

Cassie nods. "Do you want me to talk to her about it?"

"That would be great. Thanks."

"Happy to do it," she says. "I like your mom."

At home, I intend to do some cleaning, but find myself sitting idly on the porch swing. Evelyn is still calling and I am still stalling her. Everett doesn't say much. When I asked him when it first came up if he thinks I should agree to go to talk to Frank, he said, "He's not really your father." Did he mean that literally? I've never felt like I had a father, but I've always known that Frank was my father. I can't imagine all of us going there for Thanksgiving, having never even talked to the man. Evelyn called the other night on the house phone and Everett answered and talked to her, at length, before coming to find me. Evelyn seemed agitated when we finally spoke.

"So, I need your answer. Frank has purchased his plane ticket. He'll be here on the Wednesday morning before Thanksgiving. Maybe you'd consider meeting him at the airport with me."

"No!" This is not some happy family reunion, and I don't think I could stomach watching her pretend it is. I need to ask Everett what it is that he and Evelyn were talking about for such a long time, but things have been better lately and I don't want to change that by bringing up the situation with Frank. It's as if our relationship is a live grenade and, if I touch it, everything might explode. It's been easier to tiptoe around it. The last time I asked him about Mama and Frank, he said, "I'm working on it. I wish you and your sister would stay off my case."

"Well, when do you want to meet him then?" Evelyn is speaking, insisting that I meet this stranger who is not our father in possibly more ways than one.

"I don't know."

"We could meet you for a drink, later."

"The kids still have school that day and I'll have to take care of Mama. Why does it have to be over a holiday? Can't he come the next week, instead?"

"Thanksgiving is about family. I want my family all together. You can't tell me you haven't wished for the same thing all your life."

"He's the one who chose not to be a part of our family."

"That's her version, not his. There's more to it than meets the eye."

"Meaning what?"

Evelyn lets out a long sigh. "Jesus, Kate, do you always have to be like her? Can't you let this go? He's not the enemy."

"But he's not exactly family, either."

In the end, I agree to meet them Thanksgiving morning. It will make the day even crazier, but it would be better than waiting until the big dinner. I know she wants it to be some kind of Hallmark moment; I just don't want it to be a disaster.

JENNA
≈≈

"I'm so fucking sick of my parents controlling my life," says Wells. He's lying in the grass in Cassie's backyard. The new cat, Prince Charming, is lying on his stomach and Sneezy and Dopey are crashed out right next to him. All the cats love Wells and want to be near him. I know how they feel.

"That's their job, right? I mean their lives are so incredibly boring, they have to try to make ours just as bad."

"Maybe. I think my dad's just a dick."

"I know my dad is."

"That's true." I've filled Wells in on Everett's affairs. He's still fucking some woman named Veronica who has huge tits and works as a waitress. The gross emails are piled there in his history for anyone to see, although Mom wouldn't have a clue. Sometimes I think about showing them to her, but she's so wrapped up in JT's school shit and Gram's helpless shit that I feel sorry for her. Besides, she has to know. I mean the jerk goes out so many nights and works late all the time and he's super nice to her when he's around. He brought her flowers the other day for no reason. No reason except he's a guilty asshole who's cheating on his wife. That's all. Still, it's their deal, not mine.

Wells crawls over to where I'm sitting, working on my calculus homework. His cat entourage follows. He lays his head in my lap and looks up at me. Now how do I resist that? I laugh and climb over and pin him to the ground.

237

Then I kiss him. Serious kiss. The kind that makes him hard against me and makes me think this is going places I'm not ready to go.

I sink down against him, matching my body to his, still kissing him. "God," he says while I'm still kissing him. "You kill me. Let's go somewhere."

By "somewhere" he means somewhere we can finally have sex. We've gotten really close, but every time we do, I stop things. I don't even know why. Maybe I'm afraid once we really do it, he won't want me anymore. I know that's crazy because Wells and I are meant to be. We are. I've never known someone the way I know Wells.

I don't have a chance to answer because we both hear Ms. Cassie's car come in and sit up quick. Wells grabs my calc notebook and puts it over his lap and I laugh. Prince Charming takes off. He's still afraid of everything. You have to let him come to you. So far, he's only let me touch him once, but he's all over Wells. Wells has the magic touch. Ahem. I'd have to agree.

"Hey kids! Put your pants on!" calls Ms. Cassie, and Wells and I burst out laughing. She thinks it's a joke when it very nearly was completely true.

"How are things with the pussies?" she asks when she comes outside. This also causes Wells and me to erupt. "Juvenile," she says, but she laughs, too. She picks up Sleepy and cuddles her under her chin. "How goes life in the land of young love?"

"It's good," I say, and Wells grins.

"I was just at your grandmother's house. We watched *Sense and Sensibility* while I tried to talk some sense into her."

"She loves that movie."

"I know," says Ms. Cassie, and she sets down Sleepy and picks up Doc.

"And did you talk any sense into her?"

"I tried, but she's a hard nut to crack."

"Really, she's just a nut," I assure her.

"I don't think so. I think she's depressed and the right medicine and therapy might help her."

"You think so?" I ask. I've never considered Gram might have a problem other than being a bitter old person. She's never gotten over my grandpa running off. She hates all men on principle. I don't see her much anymore, but I would never tell her about Wells. She'd say mean shit about him and I would have to argue with her.

"I do. I'd like her to let me bring a doctor over to check her out."

"She'll never go for that. She hates people, especially men."

"There are women doctors."

"That would be better, but I still don't think she'd go for it. She's really stubborn. And pretty mean."

"What do you think, Wells?" asks Cassie.

"I've never met her," says Wells.

"Really? Jenna, you should introduce him."

"No way. Gram hates guys."

"Women like me; I keep telling you that," says Wells.

"For good reason," agrees Cassie.

"Ain't gonna happen," I tell them both.

≈≈

"I do want to meet your grandmother," says Wells when we're walking home.

"Why?"

He shrugs his shoulders. "Because she's related to you."

"You've never met Everett." Wells has met my mom a couple times now. We've been watching JT for her on Saturdays when she's at Gram's.

"I'll meet him this weekend."

"True." Homecoming is this weekend. I will put on my smokin' hot dress (and my wrap) and pose for pictures with

Wells in my backyard before we go to his house for pictures and then to the dance. That's the plan. What will happen after the dance is still being negotiated.

"Okay, well maybe I'll introduce you one of these days."

We're at my mailbox. This is where he always says good-bye. He presses against me and kisses me gently. "I can't wait for Saturday," he says.

"Me either." Saturday is only two days away.

"You sure you won't go to the game Friday night with me?"

"I'm sure," I tell him. Everyone at school knows we're together now, but I'm not ready to sit with his dad and all the other popular kids at the football game. Besides, I hate football. Stupid way to ruin your brain.

"Okay, then see ya in school."

"Not if I see ya first," I tell him. I say this just to see him grin. Which he does. Damn. The boy is killing me, too.

≈≈

Later, I walk Marco. I look up at Wells' bedroom. I haven't snuck in there again. His parents relaxed their grip on him once his grades started to rebound. His mom must be pissed that he's taking me to homecoming. He says she isn't, but when I tell him he's lying, he says he doesn't care what she thinks. Guess I'll see for myself on Saturday when we go there for pictures with Tiffany and her date.

The light is still on in Wells' room. I think about texting him, but don't. Instead, I watch his silhouette. I can see him moving around in his room. He pulls off his T-shirt and then the light goes out.

"Sweet dreams," I say out loud. Life sure changes quickly. "I am one lucky girl," I tell Marco. He can't hear me, but he thumps his tail. He thinks so, too.

KATE
≈≈

When Cassie arrives with her doctor friend, Phil is there, too. I hadn't expected him. That's too many people for Mama, so I hurry outside to intercept them. It's a beautiful day and Mama is in the backyard talking with her birds.

Cassie introduces her doctor friend, whose name is Laura. They seem very close. I wonder for a moment if she's Cassie's girlfriend, and then chastise myself for fixating on Cassie's sexual preference. I've never been friends with a lesbian before. I don't know what to expect. Why do I expect anything?

I smile at Phil. "I didn't know you would be here today."

"I thought maybe Phil could keep you company while we visit with Mildred," says Cassie.

"I should probably be there," I say.

"It's better if you're not," says Laura. "Sometimes it's hard for older people, especially parents, to admit they're struggling in front of family. I brought some materials I had on hand about depression to show you. And Phil can answer any questions you have."

"Or, maybe we could take a walk with Cooper. He's very good company," says Phil. Cooper is sitting at his feet, gazing up with what could only be describe as adoration. He has an enormous head, and his tongue hangs almost to

241

his knees as he pants in the sun. I reach down and give him a pat. He seems to smile at me, so I smile back.

"I don't know," I tell them. "Mama might be confused if I'm not there."

"Why don't you go in with Cassie and Laura and introduce Laura, and I'll just wait out here," suggests Phil.

Maybe it *would* be better if I'm not there. Mama barely agreed to this visit in the first place and she's been angry all day knowing it was coming. Besides, a walk with a pleasant, not unattractive man and his dog might be nice. "I'll just come in and introduce Laura, and then I'll be right back."

Mama smiles when she sees Cassie, but is not happy to meet Laura.

"I don't need a shrink," she says. "I'm fine."

"Well, then, this will be easy," says Laura. "I'm not a shrink."

"I'm just going to go take care of a few things," I tell her, and step away before she can protest.

Outside with Phil, I feel a sudden sense of freedom, as if I've just been given a reprieve. The air seems fresher. I feel lighter. I smile at him, but there is a lump in my throat and tears threatening. It feels good to set down the burden of my mother—to know I'm not alone. Kindness is powerful and yet such a simple thing.

"She's lucky to have you," he says.

"My sister wants to put her in a home. I can't do that, but lately it's been a lot for me." I don't know why I'm sharing too much with this man who is virtually a stranger to me. His concern is disarming. I change the subject.

As we set off up the street, I ask Phil about his practice. He explains that he only works three days a week now. After watching his wife battle cancer, he realized he didn't want to spend so much of his time working. He wanted to spend more of it living.

"I wish my own husband felt that way," I say.

"Does he work a lot?"

"He works long hours, and he goes back in on a lot of nights and weekends. They don't pay him for those hours, but if his phone rings, he goes."

"I know that life. My patients got more of me than my wife did for a lot of years. I regret that it took cancer to teach me how backward that was."

I don't know what to say. I can't imagine losing Everett. We walk in silence, except for the dog's steady panting. We stop to let him investigate the smells surrounding a cluster of mailboxes.

"Do you plan to ever go back to nursing?" asks Phil.

The question surprises me. I'd forgotten I told him I was a nurse. It doesn't really matter what my plans are, though. There will always be JT and Mama. "My certification is outdated now."

"That's not an impossible thing to remedy."

"I'd like to, but between Mama and JT, I don't know how I ever could."

"How is JT?"

"He's doing well. He's taking a math class at the high school. I wish the situation was different at the middle school, but it's better than nothing."

"Maybe. Do you know about the Independent School?"

"What's that?"

"It's a private school for kids who need a less traditional education."

"I'm sure we couldn't afford it."

"I think they have a sliding scale on tuition. You might consider looking into it."

"Everett, he's my husband, isn't a big fan of private schools. He thinks our tax dollars are paying for JT's education already, but lately he's gotten more involved. He was the one who insisted JT take the math course at the high school."

"Parents have to be their children's advocates. No one else will do it."

We arrive back at Mama's house. I sit on the stoop and watch as Phil throws a ball for Cooper. He asks me about my work in the ER and coaxes a few stories out. He's a good listener, and I find myself enjoying the memories.

The door behind us opens and Laura comes out.

"Cassie's with your mom."

"So, what did you think?"

"Cooper and I have to run," says Phil. I appreciate his discretion and watch him saunter down the driveway. He has an athlete's walk with a little hitch in his knee. I wonder if he's had a knee injury.

"Your mother is a tough woman." Laura interrupts my thoughts.

"Don't I know it."

"She's been fighting this depression for almost a lifetime."

"Really? Are you sure?"

"I deal with this a lot. She's from a generation who don't medicate their pain. They push through it."

"Did she agree to treatment?"

"Cassie's going to continue to work on her about that. I wrote a prescription and left it there for her. You should fill it, just in case she changes her mind. It's a very mild anti-anxiety medication that should help take the edge off enough that she might be able to start venturing beyond her home. Walks would be good for her, and more visits with family and friends. Hopefully, it will help her see her life more clearly. At any rate, it's a process, and if this med isn't the right one, we'll find the one that is. I left information for you about what to look for in terms of side effects."

"What about her dementia?"

"I didn't really see it. I think it's another symptom of her underlying problem. Medication isn't the only answer. Ideally, she'd agree to therapy, but she was very resistant. Maybe once she's on the medication, she'll be more open to it."

"She's complicated," I say, not knowing how to begin to explain Mama's story.

"We all are," says Laura. "Tell Cassie I'm going to walk back to her place. I'll meet her there when she's finished."

"Thank you, Laura. How do we pay you?"

She waves. "You owe me nothing. Cassie's told me how much of a help your daughter has been to her. That's payment enough."

When I go inside, Mama and Cassie are at the kitchen table. Cassie is making supper, following Mama's instructions. "Don't let the onions fry!" she cries. "Cook them slowly, and then add the garlic."

"You're cooking!" Mama hasn't cooked anything in years. She used to be a wonderful cook.

"I'm not cooking. Cassie's cooking. I'm just sitting here yelling at her," says Mama, but I can see something different in her eyes. She seems a little more there.

EVERETT
≈≈

Jenna is cooking noodles for JT, but I told her we'd order pizza for us. Kate's got some doctor talked into visiting her mother at her house. Don't know what that's gonna cost me and don't know what the point is. The woman is nuts. Nothing you can do about nuts. Or maybe she isn't. Maybe she wants us all to think she's nuts. One thing I know, there's more to her story with Frank than she's told us. I'm still collecting information, but I've got enough now to know that Kate and Evelyn are the adopted children of Mildred and Frank, not biological as they've believed all their lives.

Now, that could mean a lot of things. Maybe they just never wanted to tell them, but maybe it's more than an adoptive parent's paranoia. Frank gave up custody of them when Kate was four and Evelyn was two, but it's not really clear why. I was a cop long enough to know that a parent doesn't give up a child simply because they decide they don't want to be a parent anymore. Something must have happened, and it has to be more than he ran off with a bimbo, as Mildred's always said. But I can find no record of anything. In fact, Frank's history was spotless; not even a speeding ticket.

I'm trying to find out what happened to the birth mother. She'd be the one with the answers. The same woman is listed for both girls, and the DNA does show they really are sisters—half sisters, at least. Evelyn knows I know something, but I'm not giving her the heads up until

246

I've got it all sorted out and that might take a little while. She even went so far as to try and bribe me the other night. Ridiculous. The bottom line is that their father skipped out on them, so why she's so keen to have him back or why he's suddenly appearing is the real question.

I watch Jenna grating the cheese for JT's noodles. There's a smile playing on her lips, except when she glances up and sees me watching, then her scowl returns. She isn't speaking to me much these days. That's fine, because whenever we talk, it never ends well.

I don't remember being like that as a teen. She's so disrespectful. My dad would have smacked me across the room if I'd talked to him like she talks to us. I don't know what we did wrong. Kate's too soft on both of them. But that's her nature.

"So, homecoming's tomorrow," I say, trying to make conversation.

Jenna nods and pulls the pot off the stove, balancing it on the edge of the sink while she grabs a strainer from the cabinet beside it. I'd point out that she should have gotten the strainer before she brought the pot over but I've learned that Jenna doesn't want my advice on anything anymore.

"So, I hear you're going to the dance with the Braddington boy. How come we haven't seen him around here before?" I still haven't figured out why she'd want to go with the kid. Family has more money than they know what to do with, and I'm guessing the boy is after one thing. I know I was when I was seventeen.

She holds the strainer up until the water has run out and then dumps the noodles in the bowl.

"Mom's met him. She likes him," she says, and then she yells, "JT!"

JT is watching some series about firefighters. That's his new thing. The kid obsesses over one thing after another. I think firefighting is a little better than emergency medicine, all of which is way better than dinosaurs or space. Those obsessions lasted for years, and talk about useless information. What good will it do him down the road that he can name all seven hundred gazillion kinds of dinosaurs? I mean, who really cares unless you're on some game show?

Jenna puts the bowl on the table for JT and pours herself a glass of milk.

"Nice of you to help your mom out and make dinner for JT," I say.

"Well, you're rarely here to do it."

She looks at me with those light-green eyes of hers. I remember the first time I looked into those eyes at the hospital when she was first born. They seemed to know something already. I knew she was smart then. But now she's not just smart, she's gorgeous. I don't know why she does all that crazy shit with her hair. At least now it's almost back to its normal color and she's stopped styling it in weird spikes. It's actually grown out a little and looks really pretty. Kate says it's because of the Braddington boy. Maybe she should have kept the spikes. That scared off most of the boys.

"What's that mean? I'm here every day."

"At least you still sleep here," she says, and before I can react, she's out the door. It slams behind her and Marco whines as he watches her go.

"Hey, Dad-Unit," says JT.

"Hey, yourself, Son-Unit."

JT laughs at my lame joke. It's our routine. He tells me about the latest firefighting facts he's gathered. I know most of them since I worked with a lot of firefighters when I was a cop. This impresses JT. Maybe he'll fixate on police work next.

When Kate gets home later, she's not hungry, so I eat leftover pizza.

"How'd it go with the doctor and your mother?" I ask. I'm afraid to ask what it's gonna cost. That would make it seem like I didn't think it was a good idea in the first place, which I didn't.

"She thinks Mama's depressed."

"Depressed?"

"Yes. She said it often goes undiagnosed or misdiagnosed in elderly people. It's probably been growing worse since her falls."

"I don't know. Your mother doesn't strike me as the kind of person to get depressed. I think she's just still bitter about whatever it is that made your father take off. She's spent her whole life being pissed off."

"Maybe she's been depressed that long."

This all strikes me as people making excuses for Mildred. She's just a bitter old windbag as far as I'm concerned. And now I'm fairly certain she's hiding something. Frank turning up is only making her panic. I should probably go over there and ask her about it. I haven't talked to her in over a year. Not since she wouldn't quit with all the shit about Charlene. Woman hates me. Can't say it isn't reciprocal.

"What about all the talking with the birds and the fact that she won't set foot out of her house? Isn't it more likely that she's losing it?"

Kate shakes her head. "No. Social phobia is a symptom of depression in older people. They didn't know what to make of the birds other than the fact that she's very fond of them and she has little else in her world right now."

"So do they think she should see a shrink?" God knows what that'll cost me.

Kate nods. "Yes, but she's, of course, unwilling. They also prescribed some medication."

"Will she take it?" I'm counting on Mildred to be a stubborn cuss and refuse the meds, thereby saving me some money.

"Cassie's working on it. She thinks she might. I asked Evelyn to speak with her tomorrow about it."

"I thought Evelyn had stopped coming down on Saturdays."

"I called her and told her what the doctor said, and she's going to try to get Mama to agree to try the meds."

"Maybe I should talk to her," I offer. I'd like to ask Mildred a question or two about what I discovered in the DNA analysis.

"Ha. This isn't really something to joke about."

"I wasn't joking. Maybe if we all press her, like an intervention, she'll give in."

We've been sitting at the table, and Kate reaches across and takes my hand. "That's really sweet, babe, but I don't think there's anything you can do with this."

I love when she calls me babe. I don't remember the last time. I pull her hand to my lips and give it a kiss. She really is way too good for me. I've got to stop seeing Veronica.

"Maybe she's just upset about seeing Frank again."

Kate nods, but she doesn't say anything. Her eyes have gone all soft and I wish I could take her to bed right now. Make up for everything.

"Well, if I know Mildred, she'll figure out a way to stop that from happening. She's not one to do something she doesn't want to do."

Kate sighs. The mood is broken. She hates it when I say stuff like this. I feel the phone vibrate in my pocket. That'll be Veronica. Not tonight. Tonight I'm going to stay here with my wife. I told her that this morning when I stopped in for a quickie before work. The woman is insatiable. She said she bought me a sexy cop uniform. I saw a show once about sex addiction. I remember thinking that's pretty much a permanent condition in men, but these guys were over the top. Now I'm thinking maybe Veronica is the one with a sex addiction. I can barely keep up. Not complaining, here, though.

"Evelyn is really pushing about Thanksgiving. She's insistent that we all come."

"All of us? Even your mother?"

Kate nods. Evelyn is a fucking control freak. And she's a drama queen. Her theatrics in court are legendary. I know prosecutors who are terrified to go up against her. I can only imagine the circus the holiday will be.

"Frank and Mildred? At the same table?"

"That's what she says. She says Frank really wants to see Mama. That he's not bitter, he just wants to know his family."

"Huh." I don't know what to say. I still don't know what Frank is up to, but I've got to sort it out before Thanksgiving. 'Course, I've always figured Frank was glad to get the hell out of Dodge. I would have been if I'd been married to Mildred. But why come back?

I open a bottle of wine. Pour Kate a glass. Dry white wine is her only vice.

"How about I take care of tucking JT in tonight. You enjoy your wine."

She looks at me surprised. We haven't exactly been on the same page much lately.

"That would be nice," she says.

Putting JT to bed is never an easy thing. He has these routines he has to follow. Sometimes I get impatient. I mean, Jesus Christ, the boy is gonna be a teenager soon. Shouldn't he be able to put himself to bed? I wait on the edge of his bed while he brushes his teeth. When he comes in, he says, "Where's the Mom-Unit?"

"She's really tired."

He looks at me. I worry he's gonna have a fit, but then he says, "Okay."

We talk for a few minutes. He tells me five things he's learned today. Kate started this little tradition when he could barely talk. I complain about his rituals, but I do appreciate JT's mind—he could win millions on Jeopardy. He tells me four boring firefighting facts and then he says, "And Jenna's going to have sex with Wells."

"What? Where'd you learn that?"

"I heard them talking."

"Today?"

He nods. "They were kissing on the couch behind me when I was watching my show after school."

"What did you hear?"

"Wells: Are we ever going to have sex? Jenna: Yes, but it's not like I can schedule it. Wells: Why not? Jenna: I want it to be right. Wells: It will be, but it's gonna happen, right? Jenna: Yes."

That's the thing about JT, he's not making this up. He has perfect auditory memory. That's what the doc called it. He can remember anything he hears, word for word. I stumble through the rest of the routine and hurry back down to Kate.

"You're not going to believe what JT just told me in his five facts."

She laughs. "I know he's really finding some bizarre fire facts. Did he tell you that cotton will catch fire if you apply super glue to it? 'Cause I don't think that's really true. I told him he needed to check his source."

"He told me that Jenna is going to have sex with Wells."

"What? How does he know that? It hasn't happened yet, right?"

"What do you mean, it hasn't happened *yet*? Did you think it had?"

"No, but I figured it was gonna come up. The boy is almost eighteen. Jenna's very mature. They've been seeing a lot of each other, unsupervised."

"They have? And why is it I don't know this? This dance is the first I've heard of the boy."

Kate takes a sip of her wine. I know she wants to say something. I've been out so much, spending too much time with Veronica. And this is what happens. I've got to quit her. As if she senses this, my phone vibrates with what I'm sure is another text. Hopefully it's not one with pictures. I've got to turn this situation around.

"I'm sorry. I know I've been working too much. I didn't realize things were moving along so quickly with this boy. What should we do about it?" I go to the fridge and open another beer.

"I don't think we can do anything about it," she says.

She may think that, but it isn't so. I don't want to fight with her now, though. I'll deal with Jenna tomorrow.

"Come, sit with me. I'll build a fire," I say, and take her hand and lead her to the living room. I move JT's books and we sit on the couch.

When I start to get up, she says, "It's not cold enough for a fire. Just sit with me." She puts her head on my shoulder and says, "I've missed this."

My phone vibrates again. I pull it out and shut it off without looking at it. I set it on the coffee table and pull Kate onto my lap. She's so little. That's one of the things I loved about her when we were first dating. I could pick her up so easily. She seems even lighter now.

"Do you remember our first time?" I ask.

"It was my first," she says.

"I know. It was mine, too."

"No it wasn't," she says, smiling.

She knows what I'm going to say next, but I say it anyway. "I'd had sex before, but it was the first time I *made love*."

Between Veronica's texts and Kate on my lap, I'm pretty turned on.

"Why don't we go upstairs and see if we can recreate that moment," I say, and nuzzle her neck. I feel the muscles in her jaw smile. She turns her head and kisses my forehead. It's like a healing balm. It's all I want. Kate is all I've ever wanted. I don't know how I strayed from this. If we'd never had kids, if Mildred lived a thousand miles away, if I'd kept my job on the force and Kate was still a nurse, I wonder if everything would be different—if we would be enough.

JENNA
≈≈

I know that Wells is at the game. His whole house is dark. I open the garage door and have twenty seconds to punch in the number. Wells told me they changed the number after I broke into their garage, but he also told me they had to hide a piece of paper with the number on it because Tiffany can't ever remember it. The girl isn't so bright. It's probably all that hairspray—wrecked her memory. I open the garage fridge where Mr. B keeps all his fancy beers and find the number in the egg holder.

I grab a beer from the fridge, go inside, and then re-alarm the house. I don't even like beer, but I'm thinking if I drink it, I might have a little more nerve. Wells has really been dropping the hints about sleeping with him. I want to. I plan to, but now we've put it off so long it's become like this thing hanging over us. We both know it's going to happen, but now I have all these expectations. He does, too. This won't be his first time. I wish it wasn't mine. I wish I knew what to do.

I drink the beer while I read his American History essay, marking grammar mistakes and writing funny comments in the margins. The beer tastes terrible. Not as terrible as the cheap beer my dad buys, but still pretty bitter. It does make me feel warm inside.

It's almost eleven when I hear the garage door open. I wonder if the whole family went to the game. Tiffany was on the homecoming court as a freshman princess, so they

254

probably did. I pull off my jeans and slide into Wells' bed. I leave them hanging on his chair.

I hear them downstairs in the kitchen laughing. Then there are feet on the stairs. His door opens and the light comes on. I roll over to see him, and it's not him. It's his mom! Shit. She's holding a laundry basket. She stares at me. Then she backs out of the room and slams the door.

Shit. Shit. Shit. Now what? The door reopens, and there she is without the laundry basket.

"Are you dressed?" she asks.

"Mostly," I say.

"Get out of that bed and out of my house."

I nod. Crawl out of bed. It's really weird that she stands there and watches me put on my jeans. She holds the door open and waves me out. Wells is coming up the stairs as I exit his room. I'm so freakin' embarrassed.

"Jenna!" He looks at me, then at his mom.

I hurry past him and he says, "What the fu—" but doesn't finish his question, which is obvious. I'm thinking the same thing. What the fuck have I just done? I rush out the side door of their house and past the outdoor kitchen. When I'm sprinting down the hill, I hear Wells behind me. "Jenna! Wait up!" I won't. I can't. I'm just so fucking embarrassed. I run all the way home. I hear him gaining on me, but I win. I run in our backdoor and almost trip over Marco, who is faithfully waiting for me. I start for the stairs, but Wells walks right in behind me.

"Wait! Jenna!" he calls.

"Shhhh!" I turn and wave him back.

"Then come talk to me," he says, and reaches for my hand. He pulls me back outside.

"What happened?"

"What do you think happened?"

He smiles. Then he starts laughing.

"It's not funny!" I say, smacking him across the chest and dropping his hand.

"Oh, c'mon, it is funny!"

"No, it isn't," I say, and then I start crying. Now I'm even more embarrassed. Why the fuck am I crying?

He pulls me to the bench swing under the oak tree in the side yard. He kisses my face, kisses my cheeks. "Stop crying. It's okay."

I shake my head. "No, it's not. Now your mom hates me."

"Wait! Are you under the mistaken assumption that my mom liked you before tonight?"

I smile, but I don't want to.

"C'mon, give her more credit. You are still that crazy girl across the street who broke into our garage."

I wipe my nose. "Great, now I'm that crazy girl across the street who she found naked in your bed."

"You were naked?" Wells sounds pretty happy about that.

"Not really, but she'll probably say that."

"What were you wearing?"

Leave it to him. "My underwear and a T-shirt."

"God, why didn't I put my dirty clothes in the laundry room myself? Then she wouldn't have gone in there."

"Good question."

"Can we pretend she never caught you and sneak back over there?"

"Somehow I doubt that your parents are asleep right now."

"Yeah, you're probably right. Next time you should text me that you're going to be there."

"What? And ruin the surprise?"

"Were we going to do it tonight?" he asks. I can see his wheels spinning.

"Maybe."

He smiles. "I'm getting closer."

A light goes on upstairs in my house. A minute later, I see my mom in the kitchen.

"You better go," I say.

"You sure?" he says.

I nod and get up. He starts walking away, but stops and comes back. He kisses me and then he whispers, "Just so you know, I'm gonna have fantasies about finding you in my bed naked now."

I smack him. "I wasn't naked!" I hiss.

"That's not what my mom said!" He laughs, and starts running home.

I really, really, really like that boy.

KATE
≈≈

When Jenna comes in the door, she's flushed. I'm in the kitchen making a cup of tea. I can never sleep until I know Jenna is safe at home.

"Hey," she says. She picks a banana out of the bowl on the counter and peels it.

"Hi. Were you with Wells?"

Jenna nods, chewing.

I'm not sure how to broach the subject of sex again, but I need to warn Jenna that her father may be aware of her plans.

"I'm not sure how to ask this, and it's really not my business, but . . . are you sleeping with Wells?"

Jenna smiles, and I assume the answer is yes.

"No," she says.

"No, you don't plan to, or no, not yet?"

"Do I have to answer? Didn't you just say it wasn't your business?"

"You're right; it isn't. I just want to warn you that your father is concerned."

Jenna snorts. "About what?"

Jenna and Everett barely speak anymore. Jenna seems to have lost respect for him ever since the Charlene incident. I so wish that Jenna hadn't answered the door that morning.

It was a cold day, and Everett had gone to the hardware store to buy more wood for the woodstove. He loved to keep it burning in the winter.

The doorbell rang and Jenna called, "I'll get it!"

I followed behind her, wondering who it could possibly be. We so rarely get visitors. I could hear Everett's voice in my head. *You don't have to answer the door just because someone knocks.* By the time I reached the front hall, Jenna had opened the door to find a woman in four-inch heels wearing more makeup than a Saturday morning warranted, giant hoop earrings, and skin-tight leather pants. Her hair was dyed badly blond and she wore a black leather jacket. She smelled of cigarettes and a faintly familiar perfume.

"You must be Evy's little girl," she said to Jenna.

I asked, "Who are you?"

The woman smiled. "I'm the woman who's been fucking your husband. I just thought you'd want to know." And then she laughed and turned around. She wobbled once on the step off the porch and then retreated to a beat-up Honda.

"Mom," said Jenna. She was fifteen then. Of course, she knew what the woman was talking about. "Dad's cheating on you."

"We don't know that," I snapped, but then I stumbled to my room and crawled back in bed, and when Everett came home, I wouldn't speak to him. Jenna had been the one to tell him what happened, word for word.

"So what's he concerned about?" asks Jenna now, scowling.

"He's your father. You're his little girl."

"So?" Jenna gets up and drops her banana peel in the garbage.

"JT told him you planned to have sex with Wells."

"What? How did JT know that?"

"It doesn't matter," I say. "But now your father is a bit upset."

"Oh, great. As if he has any right to be upset."

Jenna starts to leave and I reach out and stop her. Jenna is bigger than me now and certainly outweighs me. I wish

I could wrap my arms around her. I wish she was still my little girl.

"Honey, I know your father isn't perfect. None of us are. Just be careful."

"With Everett or with Wells?"

"Both."

≈≈

In the morning, after fixing Mama's tea, I wait outside for Evelyn's car. I want to intercept her before she barges in and starts bossing Mama around. While I'm sitting on the step, Phil happens by.

"Good morning!" he calls. "Everything all right?"

I get up and walk down the driveway to speak to him.

"Cooper and I are just heading off on our walk. Would you like to join us?"

"I can't. I'm waiting for my sister."

"Everything go all right yesterday with Laura?"

"Yes, thank you. It seems my mother is a bit depressed."

"Oh, there's plenty of treatment for that. What route is she going to take?"

"Well, so far, none. She's very resistant."

Phil frowns. I'm touched that he seems sincerely concerned.

"That's too bad."

"It is. I'm hoping between Evelyn and me, we can convince her to try something."

"Some older people are very resistant to therapy and medication. Their generation sees it as some kind of weakness instead of the disease it is. If she had diabetes, she'd treat it, but depression still has a stigma for a lot of people."

I see Evelyn's car turn onto the street. I wish I could set off on a walk with this pleasant man and his dog instead of spending my day with my sister and mother.

"Well, good luck," says Phil, and he smiles before loping off with his dog.

When Evelyn gets out of the car, she says, "Who was that?"

"A neighbor," I tell her. "He's a doctor."

"He is?" Evelyn squints down the road after him. "Kind of cute, too."

"I thought you'd sworn off men." Evelyn hasn't dated seriously since her divorce.

"Not permanently," says Evelyn. "Just until I make it."

"I'd say you already have." Evelyn has an enormous house in the best part of town and more money than she knows what to do with. Her practice is thriving, yet she works endless hours. I really don't know what she's working towards. But I've never understood my sister. It's hard to believe we're related. I've never understood why she cast aside such a wonderful man like Josh. Sure, he wasn't as driven as Evelyn, but he was a lot of fun. Maybe it was all those years as a divorce attorney; maybe she couldn't resist practicing what she preached. And I never spent that much time with them. You can't know what's going on in someone else's marriage. Take mine for instance.

"How is she? What kind of drugs did they put her on?"

"None yet. I have the prescription, but Mama refuses to even try it."

"Why?"

"She says she isn't depressed, just dying."

Evelyn scoffs. "That's ridiculous. Can't we just put the drugs in her tea?"

"I asked. That's illegal."

"Is it?" asks Evelyn. I can see the wheels turning. Evelyn is already trying to think of a legal way to drug our mother.

"I was hoping if we approached her together, carefully, she might consider taking the medication on her own—if not for her, then for us."

Evelyn frowns. "Unlikely. She doesn't do anything for other people. Has she said anything about Thanksgiving? It's only three weeks away."

"Whenever I bring it up, she ignores me or changes the subject."

"I think Everett has found more information on our father. Has he said anything to you about it?"

"No, but maybe now is not the time to talk about Frank. Let's just deal with this depression first."

"There will never be a good time to talk about Frank for Mama. You know that."

I love my sister, but I'm so tired of Evelyn's agenda always coming first. Maybe it's because she's the youngest. Everything's always about her.

"Mama has brainwashed us both into believing her story and not Dad's."

"Up until recently, I didn't know Frank had a story."

"What she did isn't right!"

"We don't know what really happened. You, of all people, know how complicated relationships can be. Can you imagine being left alone with two kids to raise and no job?"

"This isn't about me!"

"Yes it is! It's always about you!"

Just then, the front door opens, surprising us both. Mama stands in the doorway, shakily holding the door frame.

"Stop fighting! I can hear you, and so can the whole neighborhood!"

I haven't seen my mother open her front door voluntarily in years. I rush up the walk and help her back inside.

"I'm sorry, Mama."

Evelyn follows. She sets an elaborate tray of food on the counter. Mama inspects it.

"Looks like there's enough here for the whole neighborhood!"

I pull out a chair for her and she sits.

Evelyn shrugs. "Everything looked good, so I bought it."

"Maybe you've been doing that too much lately," says Mama, pointedly looking at Evelyn. Evelyn has always struggled with her weight, but lately she seems to have given up the battle.

"I'm working a lot," she says.

"Doesn't mean you have to get as big as a boat," says Mama.

"So great to be here, Mama," says Evelyn, and kisses her cheek.

"So I was telling Evelyn about the doctor's visit yesterday."

Mama sits up taller and crosses her arms. Evelyn sits down beside her. Just then her phone chirps and she gets back up. "Be right back!" she says, and disappears into the living room.

"I don't want to talk about yesterday," says Mama.

"We need to."

"We do not."

"Well, this morning I filled your prescription." I pull out the vial of pills and set it on the table in front of her. "You are to take one each day with food. You should take it at the same time every day, so I think breakfast makes the most sense. I'm always here at breakfast time and can help you remember."

"You say this as if it's already decided. I don't need drugs. I'm not crazy, I'm just dying."

"You are not dying!" says Evelyn as she comes back in the room. "I'm so tired of hearing that! You're depressed, Mama! Maybe if you start taking the medicine, you'll feel happier and then maybe you can rejoin the land of the living."

Mama snorts and looks out the window, stubborn pain etched in her expression.

I take her hand. "This could be a really good thing. Laura said that it's very common for people your age, especially women, to become depressed. Don't you want to feel better?"

She looks at me. "Why can't you just leave me alone? You with the medicine and Ev wanting to dredge up the past!"

Evelyn and I exchange looks, and she takes the opening.

"Sometimes we all remember things differently. Frank remembers the divorce differently than you do. He wants to meet his grandchildren."

"He probably just wants your money!"

"He doesn't want my money!"

"Then what's he want? He wants to make you all hate me! He wants to rewrite the past! I loved you. I had to protect you. You don't know what he did!"

Mama gasps and tears start running down her face.

"Evelyn, leave her alone!" I say, and pull my chair closer, putting my arms around her protectively.

"Protect us from what? A father who loved us? This doesn't have to be a big scene. He's not angry. He doesn't want anything. He just wants to know his family. Why is that too much to ask?" says Evelyn.

"It's not that simple," says Mama quietly. I'm not sure Evelyn even hears her.

"I can't be here," says Evelyn, and she grabs her purse and leaves.

I watch her go, but make no move to stop her.

I hand Mama a tissue and she dabs her eyes. "I want to go outside now. I need to be with my birds."

"Okay, but first I'm going to give you your medicine."

"I don't want it."

"I know that, but I need you to take it."

Mama stares at my outstretched hand holding the pill. She looks at me, then her shoulders sag, they lose their authoritative stiffness. "I'll take the damn pill, but don't treat me like a child. I can take it without you nagging me." She grabs the pill and puts it in her mouth, swallowing it with a sip of tea.

"Thank you," I say, but I don't feel as though I've won.

"Leave the bottle on the counter. It's my medicine. I'll be the one who decides when to take it." Mama stands shakily and reaches for her walker. I move to help her.

"I don't need your help," she says. I watch her shuffle outside.

I don't need your help. If only that were true. I can't imagine my life without the daily care of my mother. Even before she'd fallen and broken her hip, I had been the one to drive her where she needed to go, to help her with her grocery shopping, to deal with doctors. Everett had taken care of the house, the yard, and even met with her lawyer for her. I can't remember her having friends, but she must have had some over the years. Where are they now? And why did I never know how lonely my own mother must have been?

I take the cordless phone outside and set it beside her. "I'm going to go home. Give me a call if you'd like company for lunch."

Mama doesn't say anything. She just stares at the birds by the feeder.

"Tonight is the homecoming dance, and I want to help Jenna get ready."

This gets her attention. "Jenna's going to a dance?"

"Yes."

"With a boy?"

I nod.

"Why didn't she tell me this?"

"I don't know. It's kind of recent."

"That's why she never has time for me anymore," says Mama. "Some boy?"

"I don't think that's it. She's busy." I know Jenna rarely pops in to see her grandmother like she used to. When I asked her if she'd seen Gram recently, she said, "Every time I go over there she just talks about the birds. I think she's losing it."

I'm glad Jenna hasn't shared her news about Wells. Mama would have nothing nice to say about him anyway. I grew up listening to her tales of the dangers of men. "They all want the same thing," she'd say. "You can't trust them." I've heard her story of my father walking out so many times, I can picture it. Mama says he left at night. I have a vision of watching him leave from my window, but I don't know if I made it up or not. I think I see him—wearing a suit, carrying a duffel bag. He turned and looked at me. He was crying as he lifted his hand and pressed it to his heart. It was probably my child's mind filling in the blanks, but it was a memory that grew true in my mind.

I give Mama a kiss on the forehead. "See you later. I'm glad you're going to take the medicine. I know it will help."

She says nothing, just tosses some sunflower seeds from the jar on the table.

JENNA
≈≈

Today is homecoming. I still can't believe I'm going. It's really not the kind of thing I do. But Wells isn't the kind of guy I ever thought I'd be so shit-crazy in love with. There, I said it. I'm in love with Wells Braddington.

I can't sleep, so I get up early and take Marco for a walk. We make it as far as the playground. That's generally his limit. After that, he'll just sit down and refuse to move his sweet little beagle self. At that point, I have to turn around for home or carry him if I want to keep going.

When we get to the playground, Marco lies down in the sand around the swings, panting. I take a seat on a swing and text Wells.

Wake up.

Already did that.

Where R U?

Lifting with Dad.

Did ur mom freak out?

Depends on def of freak out. Gotta go. Ready to dance?

No, I'm not ready to dance. In fact, that is the one thing that has me the most weirded out about tonight. I've never danced. Well, that's not technically true. When I was little, my mom put me in ballet classes. Reportedly, I loved the tutus and costumes. I have very little memory of that period of my life. I do love to watch the dance scenes in the Jane Austen movies. But I'm thinking there won't be any waltzes in the band's repertoire tonight. Marco and I watch the sun get itself settled in the sky. Then he nudges my knee. He's ready for breakfast.

I decide to go see Ms. Cassie. Maybe she knows how to dance. I drop Marco at home. The cats at Ms. Cassie's are not fans of Marco. I fill up his bowl with kibble and run some water over it to soften it. Then I place one piece of American cheese on the top before I set it down for him. Mom doesn't like me to give him people food, but it's a special day.

"Enjoy your fancy breakfast, little buddy," I tell him, and head for Ms. Cassie's.

She is sitting on the back patio surrounded by cats, but she is not alone. There's another woman there.

"Hey," I say, walking around the side of the house.

"Jenna!" says Ms. Cassie. I love that's she always happy to see me. As if me showing up has made her day. "Come meet my friend Laura."

"Hi," I say, and shake Laura's hand.

"Great to meet you. I met your mom and grandmother yesterday."

"You did?" This makes no sense. Gram hates people.

"Laura is a doctor. She stopped in to see your gram."

"Is something wrong with her?" Why do I have to ask a stranger this question? Couldn't my own mother be bothered to tell me that Gram was sick?

"I think she may be depressed."

"Like suicidal?" I ask. "Because Gram has been saying she's going to die for years. It's like her little pity thing. She's kind of nutso."

Laura smiles. "I don't think she's nuts; I think she's clinically depressed."

"Wow," I say, and drop down in the grass near them to gather cats. Three immediately jump in my lap. It's like a cat blanket.

"So, tonight's the night," says Ms. Cassie, and then to Laura, "Jenna's going to a homecoming dance with Wells, my other young neighbor and cat aficionado."

"He's more like a cat whisperer."

Ms. Cassie laughs. "So what does your dress look like?"

I tell her about my super-hot dress that will make Wells drool.

"Wish I could see it," she says.

"You can! We can stop here before we go."

"You don't have to do that!"

"Wells won't mind, and anything I can do to delay the actual dance is a good thing."

"I thought you wanted to go to the dance."

"I do! I just don't want to dance at the dance."

She makes a face.

"I don't know how!" I explain.

"I thought that these days, you just move your body along with the music in any which way you feel," says Laura.

"I don't know how to do that," I tell her. "I was kind of hoping Ms. Cassie might have some ideas."

They both laugh now, as if I've said something funny.

"C'mon, Cass, let's get our groove on," says Laura. "Put on some music. This girl is in need of our help!"

Ms. Cassie is still laughing, but she goes into the house and brings out her iPod speaker. She finds some music and then holds her hand out to Laura. It's kind of like a guy would do when asking someone to dance. Laura bats her eyes and takes her hand, and then the two of them are dancing all over the patio. They look kind of funny and they scatter the cats. When the song ends, they collapse back in their chairs.

"I don't think that's how people will be dancing at the homecoming dance tonight," I tell them, and they both erupt in laughter again.

"How do you know each other?" I ask Ms. Cassie when they've recovered. They seem like really good friends, but Ms. Cassie hasn't mentioned Laura before.

"We're dating," says Ms. Cassie.

It takes me a minute to wrap my mind around this. I didn't realize that Ms. Cassie was gay. I've heard Everett say it, but he says it like it's a bad thing, like it's a derogatory thing. I don't know if Everett is a homophobe or if he's just threatened by women who don't flirt with him.

"Oh," I say. "How long?"

They look at each other. "Maybe a month or so, but we've known each other much longer."

"Laura was married," Ms. Cassie says by way of explanation. Gay marriage is only recently legal in this state, so I guess she must have married somewhere else. I don't want to be a nosy pain in the ass, so I drop it. They seem really happy together. This makes me think of Wells. I hate that I have to wait another five hours to see him. He's picking me up at four.

They're smiling at each other. I can tell when three's a crowd, so I tell them good-bye and go home to obsess over my hair for the remainder of the day.

"We'll come by sometime after four," I tell them, and Ms. Cassie says she'll be here so I guess no one is dying today.

EVERETT

≈≈

I spend the whole afternoon watching *Backdraft* with JT and trying to figure out how not to beat the snot out of the Braddington kid when he comes by later to pick up Jenna for homecoming.

The movie ends and JT goes upstairs to the computer to research it. He likes to do that—find out every last goddamn detail about a movie. It'll keep him busy for another hour. I've been sending dirty texts back and forth with Veronica while she's at work.

Kate took Jenna to a hairdresser. I was kind of surprised Jenna went for that. She's not a traditional kind of girl. Usually, she takes care of her own hair—dying it crazy colors and occasionally shaving the whole mess off. Kate came home from her mother's in a great mood. Apparently, Mildred's agreed to take the drugs the doctor prescribed. Kate thinks that all this time she's been depressed, not just a bitch. I kept quiet. She doesn't want to hear what I think.

My friend in records did find the birth mother—Kimberly Patowski. So I guess that means Kate's Polish, not English like her mother. Problem is, Kimberly Patowski is dead and, oddly, the date is only one year after Evelyn was born. There's no father listed for Kate, but the real kicker is that the father listed for Evelyn is a name I know. In fact, it's a name Kate and Evelyn know, too.

When Kate and Jenna walk in the door, Jenna is laughing. I swear I haven't heard her laugh in years. Not like that, not the laugh of my little girl, the one who still wore high-tops and pigtails. I smile at them from where I'm sitting at the counter, and Jenna's expression changes instantly. Back to the angry teenager who hates her father. I glance at Veronica's latest text and shut my phone off.

"Wow, you look gorgeous!" I tell Jenna, and I mean it. The hairdresser has done some kind of thing where all her hair is piled on top of her head, disguising the fact that one side is short and one is long. There are sparkly jewels poking out everywhere. Jenna can't help but smile, even though she hates me.

"I know!" says Kate. "I love it! Doesn't she look like a princess?" Now Jenna rolls her eyes and vacates the kitchen.

"I'm going to put my dress on. DO NOT let Wells in. You can't talk to him without me," she says, glaring at me. Kate must have told her what JT told me. Well, what does she expect? She's too damn young to be having sex with anyone, let alone the goddamn football player next door who has probably shagged the whole cheerleading squad.

"Did you have fun?" I ask Kate, and pull her in for a hug.

She leans against me and says, "I did. It was great. I think Wells is good for her."

"I think I'm going to have a few words with the boy when he gets here."

She immediately pulls away and looks at me like I'm the one in the wrong here. "No, you are not!" she says. "You are going to stay out of this. You are going to trust your daughter to be smart."

"She's not the one I don't trust!"

"They're kids," says Kate, opening the fridge and putting the boutonniere on the shelf to stay fresh. It's hot pink. I wonder if a football player will be okay with a hot pink flower on his chest.

"Exactly, so I know what he's got on his mind. And it's not dancing."

"You can't know that. Maybe all boys aren't like that. Maybe he really likes our daughter."

"I'm not saying he doesn't. I'm just saying he's a seventeen-year-old boy, and that means he has only one thing on his mind."

"Just because you did, doesn't mean he does. You sound like my mother."

"Well, for once, we agree."

The doorbell rings and I move towards it, but we both hear Jenna pounding down the stairs.

"Don't answer it!" she yells. And I can't because I am struck still by the sight of my daughter. She is breathtaking. The dress hugs her body and reveals more than clearly that she is no little girl anymore. No goddamn way is she going out of my house dressed like that.

She's almost to the door, when I yell, "Hold on a minute!"

She freezes and turns to look at me, a cat with claws out. I backtrack. I know better than to talk like this to a woman, and right now, at this moment, that's what she is.

"Honey, before you let him in, let us have a moment to admire you."

She stops, softens, and walks back towards the kitchen.

"Where's the wrap we bought?" says Kate. Then to me, "She's got a cover-up that goes with the dress."

"Oh yeah, it's upstairs. I'll get it before we go."

"No, you'll get it right now," I tell her. I can't help myself. I have to protect her. I smile, touch her bare arm. "It's cold outside."

She looks at me carefully. I know she's deciding whether I'm playing her. My daughter is smart. Too smart.

"Right," she says, but I don't miss the look in her eyes before she heads upstairs. The look that says, *I'm playing along with you right now to keep everything copacetic, but don't fuck with me.* I know that look. I use it all the time at work.

As soon as she turns the corner, I stride to the door.

"Ev!" says Kate. "She asked us not to open the door!"

"We can't leave the poor boy standing out there in the cold." I open the door, and there stands the boy who intends to take my daughter's virginity. He's bigger than I am; at least taller. Obviously he works out. I thrust out my hand and he shakes it. Firm grip. Confident for a kid.

"Mr. Turner, nice to see you," he says.

"Wells? Right?"

"And Mrs. Turner, good to see you, too." He's still standing on the stoop. I don't really want to let him in my house, but Kate pushes me aside.

"Come in, Wells. Jenna just went to find her wrap."

He walks in, and only takes two steps before he freezes in his tracks.

"Wow," he says. And then again, "Wow." He's staring at Jenna, who has just come into the hall. This time she has a black wrap over her bare shoulders and back, but it's not enough to hide the rest of her. The kid's jaw is on the ground.

"You like?" asks Jenna, spinning around in her high heels.

"Wow," he says once more. The boy is smooth.

"Okay, we gotta go," says Jenna, grabbing his arm.

"Wait!" says Kate. "Pictures! Everett, go get the camera."

I go look for the camera while Wells tries to pin a corsage on Jenna. The corsage is also hot pink. When I come back, they've given up and are laughing. Kate shows them how it has a wristband, and Jenna slides it over her wrist. She pins the boutonniere on Wells' lapel. It's a nice suit. Probably cost more than any suit I own.

We go outside and snap a few pictures. Then I say, "Wells? Could I have a few words with you?"

Jenna says, "No!" but Wells smiles. "Sure," he says, and I take his arm and walk him around to the side of the house.

"So you like Jenna?" I ask him.

He nods. "She's great."

"She is."

He waits for me to say something else. I can see Jenna and Kate have followed us and are watching from the front yard.

"Look. My daughter is a class act."

"I know that, sir."

He gets points for the "sir."

"So I just want to be sure you're not planning to . . . uh . . . that your intentions are good." God, I don't know what the fuck is wrong with me. I sound like a Hallmark movie. This is not how I wanted this to go.

"I'm not sure I follow," says Wells.

I take a deep breath, I look him in the eye, and then I say, "Keep everything in your pants. That's all I'm saying."

He laughs nervously. "Oh, of course. No worries."

I don't know what that means, but I let it go because Jenna is marching towards us with Kate right behind.

"We have to go now! We're going to be late," she says, and takes Wells' hand.

I watch them walk across the yard to the driveway. Wells helps her into his car. It's a loaded beamer—his dad's. He backs out carefully and then drives across the street and up his drive. Kate says they have to take pictures with his family, too.

JENNA
≈≈

"Christ! I thought we'd never get out of there," I tell Wells. "What did Everett say to you?"

He's creeping up his driveway slowly, but he stops and puts the car in park. He looks at me. I'm thinking, *Shit, did Everett threaten to kill him?*

He starts laughing. "He told me to keep everything in my pants!"

"No, he didn't!" I scream. Then we are both laughing our heads off.

"Holy shit. I thought he was gonna tell me he had a gun with my name on it. He was so serious. Like the fucking mafia!"

I'm laughing, but a teeny tiny part of me kind of likes that Everett is worried about me. Crazy that he thinks he has to protect my honor. He must think all guys are like him.

Wells shifts the car back into drive and I remember where we are headed. I put my hands over my face and sink down in the seat. "I can't go in there," I tell Wells.

"Sure, you can. Just act like nothing happened."

"Right! I can't look at your mom."

"Tiffany and her date are already there. We have to give them a ride."

"We do?"

"As of this morning, that's the plan. I guess my parents figure you won't take your clothes off if Tiffany's there."

276

I smack him.

"OW!" he says.

He parks the car and starts to get out, but I grab his arm. "I can't go in there!"

He smiles, closes his door, and reaches for me.

"You can do this. I'll be right there. I promise she'll be on her best behavior."

"Right, like my dad was."

He laughs again. "C'mon, let's get this over with."

Wells opens my door and helps me out. "'Course she might take you to the side yard and tell you to keep your pants on!" I smack him again and he laughs and puts his arm around me. He kisses the top of my head and then says, "I really haven't had a chance to tell you how smokin' hot you look."

I smile at him. "Really?"

"Crazy hot," he says, and shakes his head. "Really." He kisses me again, but this time it lasts much longer. He tastes like mouthwash.

We walk around to the back patio where Tiffany and her date, Jeffrey, are already posed for pictures.

"There you are!" says his mom, beaming at Wells and not looking at me. She positions Wells and Tiffany in the center with me and Jeffrey on the wings. She still hasn't even said hello to me.

We do a few more poses. When we're finally finished, Mr. Braddington walks with us around to the car.

"Jenna, may I say you look simply gorgeous and all grown up?"

"Thanks," I tell him.

Mrs. Braddington trails behind, and after we are in the car, she starts snapping pictures again.

"Christ! What took you so long?" asks Tiffany. "We were stuck there with them for hours."

"Sucks for you," says Wells. "We've got one more stop."

"What?" whines Tiffany as Wells pulls into Ms. Cassie's driveway.

"You kids be good," he says, and helps me out of the car. Ms. Cassie and Laura gush over us.

"Wow! Jenna, you are stunning," says Ms. Cassie.

"Like a model," says Laura. Then she turns to Wells, "You aren't so bad yourself, you lucky dog."

He grins. He loves this stuff, I can tell.

"You clean up pretty good," says Ms. Cassie. "Let me grab a picture."

"With the cats!" suggests Wells.

We troop outside and pose for a picture with six of the cats. Prince Charming and Happy are missing.

"Maybe they already left for the ball," jokes Ms. Cassie.

≈≈

When we get to the country club where the dance is being held, Tiffany and Jeffrey take off. "You kids have fun!" calls Wells. Tiffany gives him the finger. Class act, that one.

"Do we have to take them home, too?" I ask.

"Nope. Jeffrey's parents are handling that shift, much to my mother's dismay." He takes my hand and pulls me across the parking lot to a garden with tables.

"Aren't we going in?" I ask.

"I want to talk to you first."

"Okay," I say. We stop and he takes my hands in his.

"What?" I ask. Now I'm getting worried. Is he too embarrassed to go in with me?

"It's just . . . I want this to be a great night. I want you to have a good time."

"I will, but we have to go inside for that to happen."

"Wait. I have to warn you about something."

"What?"

He sighs. He looks at me, frowns. It's not fair that he can look so good even when he's frowning.

278

"Some of my football friends may not be happy to see you."

"Why? What'd I do to them?"

He shakes his head. "Nothing. They just think I'm not trying to get back on the team because of you."

"That's crazy," I tell him.

"Actually, it's not."

"I'm the reason you aren't on the team?"

He hangs his head now.

"You're the main reason, but it's more complicated than that. I'm sick of it. I'm sick of my father's obsession with it. I don't even enjoy the game anymore."

"So you purposefully failed to get kicked off the team?"

"No! But when it happened and I realized how much better I felt, I didn't want to go back. And then I started hanging out with you, and Christ, Jenna, I'd rather be with you than a bunch of smelly jocks."

"I'm flattered."

He tilts his head, looks at me with those eyes, those crazy, gorgeous melt-me eyes.

"I am," I tell him, and I kiss him.

"Let's get out of here," he says.

"I want to go in," I say, because I do. I want to walk into the homecoming dance on the arm of Wells Braddington.

"Really?" he says.

"Really," I tell him.

As we're headed to the door, I stop. "Wait," I pull off my shawl.

He whistles. "Now I really don't want to go in," he says. "I want to keep you all to myself."

"C'mon," I say, and pull him along.

The dance is okay. People do stare, and Wells ends up arguing with a drunk football buddy who eventually gets thrown out of the dance. I love that girls stare at me. They're probably trying to figure out who I am. We stay for an hour and dance one slow song. As we're twirling around the floor, Wells says, "Did we stay long enough? Can we leave now?"

I kiss his neck, even though I know a teacher will probably separate us for PDA. When the song ends, Wells leads me to our table to collect my wrap and say good-bye to a couple kids we were sitting with. I don't remember their names, but they seemed all right. Later, when I tell Wells I liked his friends at our table, he says, "I have no idea who they were. I thought they were your friends."

Wells drives us to another entrance to the club. It's for the people who work here. He parks in their lot. His car stands out against the rusted older model sedans and motorcycles.

"Where are we going?" I ask.

He holds his finger to his lips, shushing me. I follow him to a small building with lockers and benches. In the back, there's a lounge. This must be the caddie shack that Amber Blevins was referring to. I'm annoyed. This is where he takes everyone he has sex with.

"What is this place?" I ask, even though I know.

"It's the caddie shack. No one will be here until morning."

"Is this where you take all the girls?"

He smiles. "Some of them."

I don't know why this bothers me. He's here with me, not some other girl. Wells Braddington. Me. Here to have sex. This was the plan, right?

He pulls me to him, but when he leans in to kiss me, I turn my head.

"What?" he says. "Is something wrong?"

I shake my head. He turns my face to him and starts to kiss me.

"I can't," I say, breaking away.

"You can't kiss me?"

"I can't do this here."

He looks around. "I don't understand. What's wrong? I thought this was what we wanted."

"I do want this. Just not here."

He sighs. "Why not?"

"I don't want to have sex with you in the place where you have had sex with half the high school."

"I haven't had sex in here with half the high school."

"Whatever."

"Jenna, you make no sense."

"Yes, I do!" I know I do. I know that this thing we have going is special. It's special to him, too. "Having sex in here with you makes us like all the others. This," I point to him and me, "is not like all the others. We're more."

He looks at me but says nothing. He reaches for my hand and laces his fingers through mine. He pulls it to his lips and kisses it. I am such an idiot. All I want is this boy. Right now. Just not in the caddie shack.

"Okay," he says, and pulls me to him. We sit like that, me leaning on his chest, our fingers intertwined, for what seems like a long time.

"I know what we should do," he says finally.

"What?" I ask.

"We should go bowling."

"Bowling? Are you nuts?"

"You look so gorgeous. I want to show you off. Let's go bowling!"

I laugh, but let him drag me out. And that's what we do on homecoming night with me in my smokin' hot dress. We go bowling. And Wells kept it in his pants. Everett would be impressed.

KATE

≈≈

Mama has been taking the pills for two weeks, according to my calculations, but she doesn't seem any different. Each morning, when she's not looking, I check the bottle in her bathroom and count the pills to make sure she hasn't missed one. They go down steadily, one a day, but when I study Mama for signs that the medication is having some effect, I see nothing.

Thanksgiving is now only about a week away, and every time I bring up the idea of going to Evelyn's for dinner with Frank, she says, "What dinner?"

Evelyn calls every few days, pressuring me. She seems almost desperate for some kind of crazy family reunion. Sometimes I wonder if she is doing this simply out of spite, to hurt Mama for not being what she wanted her to be. When she calls again today, I tell her I've decided to stay home with Mama.

"Just make Mama a nice Thanksgiving lunch and then come."

"I can't do that," I tell her. "She'll be hurt. Everett can come and bring the kids."

"You have to be there. She'll survive a holiday without you," she says.

"I can't do that, but I'll still meet you and Frank that morning. That's about all I can probably handle anyway. Everett can represent us. He's good with stressful situations."

"I wish you'd change your mind. Please, just think about it."

"I will," I tell her, knowing full well that I won't.

On Sunday afternoon, the house is quiet and for once I have nowhere I have to be, so I decide to take a bubble bath. I used to take them all the time, but these days there's never time, and in the evenings I'm too exhausted to wait for the tub to fill. Cassie is spending the afternoon with Mama and I'm grateful for the break.

I don't know where Everett is. Sometimes on Sunday afternoons he likes to catch up on paperwork in his office. That's probably where he is since it's Thanksgiving week and he's already told me work is so busy he can only spare the day Thursday, but not Friday. He works so hard, I worry about him. Sometimes my imagination gets the best of me and I can't help but worry that he's involved with Charlene again.

He's come home a few times smelling of alcohol and women's perfume. He says the perfume is from his new secretary who sprays it around her desk. When I ask about the alcohol, he apologizes. "I was just too keyed up to come straight home, so I stopped for a beer on the way. I don't want to come home and bite your head off about something that's irritating me at work. That wouldn't be fair."

Maybe what we need is to have a date night. While I was waiting for JT, I overheard one of the high school secretaries telling the others about how she and her husband have a date night every Friday. Maybe then we could recapture some of the romance we used to have. I miss those days.

In those early years, it was like a bubble existed around the two of us. We were so happy together. We couldn't keep our hands off each other. I smile just thinking about how Everett used to ask me to put on my nurse's uniform— the white one Mama gave me when I graduated, not the scrubs I normally wore. He even came home one night ng Normal

with a nurse's cap for me and white fishnet stockings. That was quite the night.

I finish shaving my legs and notice a funny rash on my feet. It reminds me of the strange rash I used to see on patients in the ER. The red spots are penny-sized but they don't itch. A chill goes through me and I shake my head. I look at the rash again. It isn't possible. When I treated prostitutes for syphilis in the ER, I saw spots like those on the women's palms and the soles of their feet. I look at my own palms. Was that redness at the base of my thumb?

I get out of the tub and dry off. Still wearing a towel, I look up "syphilis" on the computer. Funny, it pops up right away, as if the computer knew I'd be looking for it. I've never liked using a computer and don't understand how Everett can spend hours with the machine. On the Web MD site, I read:

> According to the CDC, the rate of new cases of syphilis had plummeted in the 1990s, and in the year 2000, it reached an all-time low since reporting began in 1941. However, new cases of syphilis doubled between 2005 and 2013 from 8,724 to 16,663.

There's only one way I could have syphilis. I haven't had sex with anyone other than Everett.

JENNA

≈≈

"This is it," Wells tells me. We're standing in front of a two-story house just four houses up from my Gram's house.

"It doesn't look empty," I say.

"It is," says Wells.

"How do you know?"

"My mom says the woman who lives here is engaged to the golf pro at the club. She already put the house on the market."

"That doesn't mean she isn't here."

"She's on a cruise. My mom was telling my dad all about it. It's some kind of golf cruise she wants him to take her on for their anniversary."

I look at the house. I've been inside before, but that was years ago. Back when I decided to break in to every house on the street. I almost did it, too. Just couldn't get in to the Solomon's place. They moved here from New York and have like five locks on their doors. Plus, they've got a trained guard dog, a Rottweiler. They must be more paranoid than Everett. I can't remember how I got in to the house in front of us.

I follow Wells around to the back. "Can you tell if she has an alarm?" he asks.

I look at a garage window and see the magnetic sensor. I pull out a fridge magnet I brought just in case and place it on the sensor, then I slip the window open. Too easy. Why doesn't anyone lock their garage windows? Probably so they can break in to their own home if they forget their key.

Wells and I climb through the window and close it again. I look at the security box next to the door. The light is flashing. You've got to be kidding. But then I realize it's not the window I opened. It's blinking because the system has a short. Such luck. Maybe this is meant to be. I turn around and Wells is right behind me. So close I could kiss him, so I do.

"Good house, right?" he says.

"Good house," I agree. Then we case the garage and find what we're looking for—a spare key. It's in an empty can of tennis balls.

Once we get inside, Wells immediately heads to the fridge. He's always hungry. I walk through the first floor. Spotless. There is a stack of wedding presents in the living room, unopened. How could anyone leave presents unopened?

Wells reappears eating a protein bar and takes my hand. He leads me upstairs where we find three bedrooms.

"Let's pretend this is like the Three Bears' house," he says. And we do. We lie down on the bed in each room and decide we like the green bedroom best. The bed is firm and there is an old quilt on it that's faded and pilled, but soft like Marco's ears.

I know we came here to have sex, but it seems weird now. I look at Wells and he smiles. He takes my hand and holds it. Then he moves closer and kisses me. Slowly, without taking his lips from mine, he takes off my jean jacket. Just then his phone buzzes. He pulls it out of his pocket and throws it across the room without looking at it. I laugh. Then he stands up. I watch him take off his shoes and I kick my own off.

Wells scoops me up and sets me in the center of the bed. I'm not gonna describe what happens next. It's private.

Later, after we've done it, we lie there next to each other naked. We talk about what Wells really wants to do after he

Cara Sue Achterberg

graduates. He wants to study biology. His dad wants him to be a lawyer. I tell him about my Aunt Evelyn's obsession with us meeting our grandfather, and how the woman my dad is sleeping with has huge tits and is the exact opposite of my mom. He tells me that he's pretty sure his own mom has something going with the owner of the club. We kiss a lot and he can't seem to stop touching my breasts. I like that.

"I'm starving," Wells says. "I'm gonna go find more food."

I watch his naked butt walk out the bedroom door and I giggle to think he's walking around down in the kitchen naked. I sit up. I can see the street. I watch a few cars go by. I see my mom headed to Gram's house. If only she knew. Actually, I kind of think Mom would understand. I don't know why I think that, but I do. Dad would flip out, and then he would probably kill Wells.

Wells reappears and climbs back in the bed. He's brought a box of crackers. He feeds them to me and then we have sex again. It's his last condom, so that'll be it for the day. He takes everything slower and I like it even more this time.

I think this is my favorite day.

EVERETT

≈≈

So JT thinks I am the best dad in the world. He told me so. I brought home an old scanner for him to listen to the fire calls. We sit in his room and I interpret the coded language for him. He loves it. He's always had a big thing for languages. Kate wants him to take French at the middle school, but they can't fit it in his schedule because of all the social skills classes he has to take. That, and it would mean putting him in a regular classroom. She's sure he would pick it up quickly.

Some days it feels like I really know what I'm doing as a dad. Some days I get it right. They're pretty rare nowadays, but I sure do appreciate it when it happens. I watch JT as he sits next to the scanner, listening intently. I wish it could always be this easy to make the kid happy.

I leave him to it. Kate is at her mother's, so I take a shower. I spent the entire afternoon in Veronica's bed and I know I smell like her. I brush my teeth and even shave. It's been a good day, all in all. I hope Kate has something nice planned for dinner.

KATE

≈≈

When I get to Mama's, she and Cassie are eating an early supper in the backyard. Mama is introducing Cassie to some of the birds, and Cassie seems truly interested.

"It's a bit late and many of them have already gone in for the night," Mama apologizes.

"Still, it's nice to meet these few," says Cassie, and she waves at me. "We finished our movie early, so I ordered Chinese."

"Chinese?" I can't remember my mother ever eating Chinese food. "That's new."

"It's salty," complains Mama, but I see she's eaten most of it anyway.

When Cassie gets up to go, I follow her out.

"Can I talk to you?" I ask.

"Sure," she says. "I have nowhere to be. I just have a little paperwork to finish tonight, but the day is mine."

We sit on Mama's front steps. "It must be hard working in hospice."

"It can be," Cassie says. "But it suits me. I always know how it's going to end."

I smile hesitantly, but then Cassie laughs. "Sorry. Gallows humor is best used within hospice not outside it."

I laugh, too. "We used to joke like that about the work in the ER."

"Funny. I can't picture you in an ER. You seem too normal," says Cassie. "Don't take that the wrong way!"

"I loved it," I tell her.

"Then you should go back to it."

"I should, but I have Mama and JT to consider."

"And Jenna," adds Cassie.

"Oh, Jenna usually takes care of herself."

"I don't know if that's the best thing for her, though."

"Why? Is she getting into trouble?"

Cassie laughs. "Jenna? I can't imagine she isn't, but that's not why I say that. Most kids need their moms around even when they act all grown up."

She's right. I know that.

"But that's not what you wanted to talk about, is it?"

"No. I'm not sure I can even say it, but I don't know who else to ask and you *are* a nurse."

"I am."

I take a deep breath. Then I close my eyes and say, "I think I may have syphilis."

Cassie looks startled. "Now, *that* I did not see coming."

"I'm not certain. I haven't had any symptoms, just this weird rash." I hold up my palm and show her the red circle near my thumb. Since my bath, it's become even more pronounced.

"It's been a long time since my OB/GYN rotation, but that looks like it," says Cassie.

I'm relieved that she doesn't ask where I got it.

"I was hoping you could ask your friend Laura to write me a scrip for penicillin."

"I could, but she'd probably want to see you herself."

"Oh."

"I can give you her number and tell her you'll be calling. I'm sure she'd fit you in tomorrow."

"Thanks," I say, but I'm disappointed that I'll have to go in for an exam. There's no time this week.

"Not a problem," says Cassie.

After Cassie scrawls out Laura's number, I watch her walk back up the street and realize that this means I will have to stop pretending that I don't know what Everett has been up to. I wanted so badly to believe in him. I need one thing in my life to be normal.

When I get home, Everett is watching football and I can hear a scanner coming from JT's room.

"You bought him a scanner?" I ask.

"Yeah, got it from a buddy who just got a new one. He loves it!"

I can't look at him, so I hurry to the kitchen to start dinner.

"Hey, what's for dinner, babe?" calls Everett.

Babe. I am not his babe. Someone else is his babe. Someone who has syphilis.

I go through the motions of making JT's noodles and fixing tuna casserole for Everett. I know I will not be able to eat anything myself. I pull my cardigan closer around me. I'm cold from the inside out.

Just then, Jenna walks through the door.

"Hi, Mom!" she calls. She looks flushed and happy. I can't help but smile.

"How was your day with Wells?" I ask.

"It was awesome," says Jenna. "I'm gonna grab a shower." I watch her disappear up the stairs. She is so beautiful.

JENNA
≈≈

Today in school, JT freaked out. I knew it was a matter of time. There's just too much chaos in the building. He doesn't do well with chaos.

A couple of upperclassmen were making fun of him, walking behind him, imitating the bouncy way he walks. I saw them, but didn't say anything. JT probably didn't notice. But then the guys were irritated that JT didn't notice, so they ran around him and dumped his books as they passed. JT stopped to pick them up but was shoved along in the busy hallway. He tried to get back to his books. I did, too, but the bell rang and people hurried even faster. I saw the panic spread across his face, but before I could get to him, he collapsed and began screaming.

Everyone backed away and there he was, my little brother, lying on the floor of the high school, screaming and rocking.

I grabbed for his books and Wells appeared, taking them from me. I sat down next to JT but didn't touch him. You can't touch him when he's like this. I try to say this to the assistant principal when he turns up, but he either ignores me or can't hear me over JT's screaming and he reaches for JT's arm. JT kicks out and catches him in the face. Square on. Mr. Melbur goes flying backward. He's angry now and on his phone calling security.

"Just don't touch him," I say. "He'll calm down. I know what to do."

"You need to get to class," he says to me.

"She's his sister," Wells explains.

Mr. Melbur looks up and sees Wells, star football player and National Honor Society member, and he looks relieved.

"Can you help me move him to the nurse's office?" he asks.

Wells shakes his head. "No. Listen to what Jenna's saying. You can't move him right now. You have to give him time to calm down."

Thank you, Wells. Mr. Melbur stares at him, but he listens, and when the security guards show up, he waves them away.

JT's howls are softer now and he's letting me touch his back. Finally, he stops and he looks at me.

"They made me drop my books," he says.

"I know," I tell him. "I saw them."

We walk JT to the office to wait for Mom, but she doesn't show up. I miss my next class. I don't know what to do, but finally the guidance counselor says that I have to leave. She'll sit with JT until Mom gets here. She's not answering her phone. I don't want to leave, but I have to.

After school, instead of going to the golf pro's fiancée's house as Wells and I had planned, I go home. I want to be sure JT is okay.

KATE
≈≈

They're behind schedule at the doctor's office. The waiting room is crowded. There's a woman next to me reading to her toddler. It's *Go, Dog, Go*. I remember how much Jenna loved that book. I mouth the words along with her. *It's a dog party . . .*

I glance at my phone. Twenty minutes before I need to pick up JT. I feel helpless, like I'm in someone else's nightmare. What am I doing here? But I can't leave now.

If I'm late, JT can work on his math homework in the office. He won't be missing much at the middle school. I stare at the door, willing it to open. Finally, the nurse calls me back. She takes my weight and height, then blood pressure and temperature. Not surprisingly, my pressure is high.

I look at my phone. Ten minutes.

"You'll have to turn that off in here, ma'am. It's policy," says the nurse.

I switch off the phone and drop it in my purse. Give her a tight smile.

When Laura finally comes in, she apologizes.

"It's okay," I say. "I know how things can get."

"That's right. You're a nurse, aren't you?"

I nod.

"So, Cassie tells me you think you might have syphilis."

"Yes." I look away. I'm embarrassed. I should have gone to a different doctor. Someone who doesn't know me. Doesn't know I'm not the kind of person who would contract syphilis.

"What are your symptoms?"

I hold up my hands and then say, "It's much worse on my feet."

She asks me to pull off my socks. Then she puts on rubber gloves and looks at my feet.

"But nothing else? No sores in your mouth or on your genitals?"

I shake my head.

"How about your weight? You seem very thin. Is the weight loss recent?"

"I'm not sure. I just haven't felt hungry. I've been so tired and things have been, well, they've been complicated."

Laura makes a note. Then she looks in my mouth. She listens to my heart and breath sounds.

"Well, it does look like syphilis, I'm afraid."

I nod. I knew it was. I read everything I could find on the Internet and in my old textbooks. There was plenty of information.

"Do you know how you contracted it?" asks Laura.

I know the answer to this question, too, and my face blazes red.

"From my husband."

"Does he know?"

I haven't been able to tell Everett. I even held his hand last night, examining it and finding no rash. I couldn't have caught it from anyone else. I can only assume he is in the latent stage of syphilis. He needs to be treated or the consequences could be life threatening.

"You'll need to tell him. He'll need to be tested along with any partners he's had."

I blanch at the word *partners*. I hadn't considered there could be more than one.

Laura writes out a prescription for penicillin. "This should clear it up," she says. "But let me know if you experience any other symptoms."

I thank her and hurry out of the office.

I drive aimlessly, eventually finding myself in the parking lot of Everett's work. His truck is there. I stare at it for a long time. I find a tube of lipstick in my purse. I walk to the truck, not caring if anyone is watching. I scrawl the word *louse* on the windshield. Then I get back in my car and drive to the high school to pick up JT.

EVERETT

≈≈

I know I shouldn't go. I spent all afternoon with Veronica yesterday. She's like a sickness. I'm addicted. Lunchtime rolls around and I can't help myself. She's working a late shift today so this is my only chance. I tell Elaine I'm going out for lunch and she says, "Right." I know she knows, but you know what? She doesn't matter. She's the most self-righteous bitch I know.

I'm strolling to my truck when I notice Pete and Ray standing next to it. They're laughing. They see me and scatter. There on the windshield, in bright pink lipstick, it says *louse*. There's only one woman in this world who calls me a louse and she can't drive a car. I look around for Kate, but don't see her car. I know that this should make me swear off Veronica and hurry home to apologize, but instead it makes me even hotter to get to her apartment and bang her brains out. Maybe I know it will be the last time. Maybe I'm too much of a louse to face up to Kate. I don't know. All I know is I'm in such a hurry to get to her place, I don't even bother wiping off the graffiti, and when a cop pulls me over for speeding, he says, "Guess that was written by a fan?"

Everybody's a comedian.

KATE
≈≈

JT is too upset to go back to the middle school, so I take him with me to Mama's. I check the medicine bottle and note that she has taken her meds. At least one thing in my life is going as it should. JT tells his grandmother about the scanner Everett brought home. In only a day he seems to have mastered the language that always sounded like gobbledygook to me back in the days when we had one in our apartment. Back when Everett was on the force. Back before Everett was catching syphilis from a hooker.

I set lunch out for the three of us.

"So, Mama, how are you feeling?"

"Same as I always feel."

"No better?"

"I've told you that I'm dying, but you don't seem to believe me. I feel horrible today, just like yesterday and the day before. No little pill is going to change that."

I'm frustrated that the medicine hasn't seemed to have had any effect, but I know I can't call Laura about it. Not now.

When JT goes to check the TV for one of his shows, I broach the subject of Thanksgiving, which is only three days away now.

"Have you given any thought to joining us at Evelyn's on Thursday?"

"What's Thursday?"

"You know what Thursday is. It's Thanksgiving. Evelyn would like you to be there."

"You know I don't like going anywhere."

"I know that, but this way we can all be together."

"I think I'll stay here."

"Please, Mama! For once it would be nice to spend the holiday together as a family. It's time to put the past in the past."

She doesn't say anything. She wipes her mouth with her napkin and meticulously folds it and puts it under her plate.

"Frank says he'd really like to see you. He isn't angry."

Mama flinches when I mention Frank's name. She sips her tea and turns to watch the birds out the window. "That cardinal is so striking this time of year."

"I hate to think of you having Thanksgiving here, all alone."

"I'll go," I think I hear her say, but it's so quiet, and in a voice I hardly recognize.

"You will?" I ask. I can't believe it. I'd already resigned myself to having two Thanksgiving dinners—one early with Mama, and one later with Evelyn. "You really mean it?"

"Stop carrying on, or I'll change my mind. I just want you to stop bugging me about it."

I get up and kiss her cheek. "I'm so glad, Mama."

Finally, the meds are working!

≈≈

I fill my penicillin prescription and take it, but say nothing to Everett. I know I should tell him, but something stops me.

We are polite with each other. I see him looking at me as if he is waiting for me to say something. But I say nothing. He washed his windshield, but I can still see several splotches of pink lipstick he missed. I know I have to talk to him about the syphilis, but first I have to get through Thanksgiving.

JENNA
≈≈

Wells and I keep ending up here. I know it's a cliché, but we can't get enough of each other. He got some flavored condoms and we experimented with those. I never thought I'd be doing the things I've read about in smut magazines, but then I also never thought I'd be in love with Wells Braddington.

His parents have given up on forcing him to apply to Harvard. Football season ended and the team didn't even make regionals, let alone states. Wells took a lot of shit from his buddies for that. He promised he'd be back next year. I don't know how I'll feel about seeing him bashing his head in on some stupid football field, but it's a long way off. Still, I know we'll be together. We are meant to be together. I know, I know, everyone says stuff like that about the first person they sleep with, but this is real. We love each other. We do. But we haven't said it yet.

Yesterday we were walking Marco and I said, "I like you."

He said, "I double-like you."

And then I said, "I triple-like you."

To which he replied, "I centuple-like you."

I smiled. Then I kissed him. I like having a boyfriend who knows what centuple means.

≈≈

On Thursday morning, I meet Wells at our house. That's what we call it, "our house."

300

We are having our own Thanksgiving before we have to suffer through our family Thanksgivings. He brought the fixings for eggs Benedict.

"You really know how to make eggs Benedict?" I ask.

He smiles at me and points to a chair. I sit down and watch him cook. I have the most amazing boyfriend. I do know this.

The eggs Benedict isn't the best I've ever had, but the sex afterwards is pretty good. We're cleaning up the kitchen and I'm just closing the dishwasher when we hear the sirens. They're close. Wells goes to the front window to see how close.

"Shit!" he says. "I think they're at your grandmother's house!"

"What?" I ask, racing to the window. "Christ!" I yell and yank on my boots and coat. I run full speed to Gram's with Wells right behind me. I have a really bad feeling about this. Everything's been off-kilter in my house, including the plan for a happy everybody-all-together Thanksgiving. I about shit when Mom said Gram had agreed to Thanksgiving at Aunt Evelyn's with my grandfather.

When we get to the house, we can see flames coming out of the roof. JT is there. A really big fireman has ahold of him, but he's struggling and I can see he's scratched the poor guy's face really bad. He's wailing and crying and shaking his head. He can't see me.

"Is Gram inside?" I ask him.

"Do you know this kid?" asks the fireman.

"He's my brother. Is my grandma in there?"

"We got her out," says the fireman, and I feel like I should collapse on the ground. My heart is beating so hard. "They're loading her up now." There's an ambulance at the end of the driveway. The attendants are closing the doors. I run towards them, but the ambulance pulls away.

"Where are Mom and Dad?" I ask JT, who is no longer fighting the fireman. He's standing very still for once, staring after the ambulance.

"It was on the scanner. I heard the call. I could've gotten her out." He says all this in his robo-tone. I know he's shutting down, so I get right up in his face.

"Where are Mom and Dad? Why aren't they here?" They never leave JT alone. Never.

"I'll get my car," says Wells.

EVERETT
≈≈

O f all days, Thanksgiving. But she's persistent. I've
stayed away all week, ever since the lipstick on my
windshield afternoon. I figure I deserve this. Later I've got
to go to Evelyn's house with Mildred, which is bad enough,
but with Kate's father there, I think Mildred might have
a coronary or maybe she'll drown on all the bile she'll be
spewing. I guess those happy pills are doing their trick
because I never imagined I'd ever see her and Frank in
the same room, let alone at the same table. Maybe we'll
finally get some answers. I haven't told Evelyn or Kate
what I found out about them being adopted. The family
is screwed up enough, but I'm curious to see what Frank
will do. I'm guessing he's turned up for a reason and that
reason might be the names on those birth certificates.

Kate's been in a tizzy about Thanksgiving for the last
two days, ever since Mildred said she'd go. I've been grateful for the distraction. I know Kate is the one who wrote
louse on my truck, but for now, she's keeping mum. Hasn't
asked me anything.

In light of the afternoon ahead, I think I deserve a little
Veronica this morning. Kate's rushed off to the grocery
store with a list a mile long, and JT is happily monitoring
the scanner. There should be plenty of car crashes to keep
him entertained, what with the holiday traffic. I'll be quick
and Kate will be home any minute.

Things don't go quickly, but fuck, they are good. This woman is the kinkiest chick I've ever known. I know I've got to put an end to this, but she's making that really hard, so to speak.

I linger as long as possible. My phone's been buzzing nonstop, so I know Kate is probably home and wondering where I am. I told her I might pop in to work this morning. I watch Veronica putting on her makeup. She's getting all dolled up to work the Thanksgiving shift at the diner. Tips will be good. I ask her why she isn't with her family and she laughs. She doesn't have any kids and her mom is in Palm Beach. I wonder why I didn't know that already. I mean I knew she didn't have kids, but I just assumed she had family somewhere. Everybody's got family. My folks are in Toledo. They live in a retirement village. They'll spend Thanksgiving with my sister, like always. We see them at Easter. Mildred and my mom get along great. They're both complainers, so it's like the bitch Olympics.

Finally, I take a quick shower. I've started keeping some stuff here. I know Kate gets suspicious when I come home smelling like Veronica. The woman smells like sex, no two ways around it. I pull on my clothes and tell V good-bye. She slips her hand in my pants as we kiss, but I'm whooped, so that goes nowhere. Time to leave Thanksgiving Heaven for Turkey Hell.

KATE
≈≈

Itold Everett I had a few more items to pick up at the grocery store, but really I'm meeting Cassie for coffee before I meet Evelyn and my father. My father. Will I really meet him today? I didn't have a chance to tell Everett I would be meeting Frank with Evelyn this morning. Whenever he's in the room, a static buzz starts up in my head. I can't think clearly, and have to concentrate really hard just to do simple things like put dishes in the dishwasher or tuck JT in for bed. I can't look Everett in the eye and I shy from his touch.

I've been out of my mind, immobilized by this entire nightmare. But I need to talk to someone, and since Cassie already knows about the syphilis, I figure she's a safe bet. Plus, I like her. I asked to meet at a coffee shop instead of her house because I don't want Everett to know what I'm doing. Explaining why I'm meeting Cassie for coffee on Thanksgiving morning would have been impossible, plus I don't have a lot of time if I'm going to meet Evelyn at eleven.

"Thanks for meeting me," I say when Cassie arrives. I'm twenty minutes early. I've already finished my coffee and even managed to eat a sticky bun, which is now lodged in my stomach like a brick. Are my lack of appetite and weight loss symptoms of the syphilis or my out-of-control life?

"No problem. I know family can be tricky, especially at the holidays."

"What are your holiday plans?" I ask.

"I'm going with a friend to her family's house this evening."

"Oh, that sounds nice. Do you like her family?"

"I haven't met them yet."

I wait while Cassie orders her coffee. When she sits back down, she asks, "So, I assume this has something to do with your appointment with Laura?"

"It does. She confirmed that I do have syphilis."

"I'm kind of afraid to ask from whom," says Cassie, taking a sip of tea. "I'm assuming your husband doesn't know."

She thinks I got it from someone else? I laugh, but tears follow quickly and I dig in my purse for a tissue. "No, he doesn't know, but he's the one I got it from."

Now it's Cassie's turn to be surprised. "Oh, that's even trickier."

"It is. Honestly, I don't know what to do."

"You have to tell him. And then you have to ask him who the hell he got it from."

"Could he be a carrier? Could he have gotten it from someone he had sex with a few years ago?"

Cassie thinks about this as she sips her coffee and I blow my nose. "Possibly, but he'd probably have some kind of symptoms by now. I'm not sure how long the latent stage lasts, but if he's had it that long, he could have serious complications."

I nod. "I've read about them."

Cassie smiles. "Should be an interesting holiday for you." She takes another sip of her coffee and says, "I don't know you that well, but from what I do know, I think it's time you stood up for yourself."

"What do you mean?"

She shrugs. "You let your mom push you around, your daughter run wild, and, obviously, your husband cheat on you. You must have known he was up to something."

"He was working a lot of late hours, even going in on weekends, but I thought—or maybe I wanted to think—he was just trying to get ahead. And he and Jenna are at odds most of the time. Plus, JT can be a lot to handle."

"It sounds like you make excuses for him. You're dealing with the same stresses, plus your mother, and I take it *you* aren't getting anything on the side?"

I know she's right. Tears start again. "I've made a mess of things."

"I think maybe Everett is the one who has made a mess of things. But it's nothing you can't fix."

"I don't see how," I say. "My mother was right."

"What was Mildred right about?"

"She said Everett was a louse, like all men."

"That's a bit of an unfair generalization. Even as a lesbian, I know that all men aren't louses." Cassie smiles.

"Today I'm supposed to meet my father for the first time."

"You've never met him?"

"No. He left when I was four. My mother says he walked out and never came back. But somehow he's back, and I'm supposed to meet him in an hour."

"What does he want?"

"I'm not sure. Everett thinks he wants money. Evelyn says he only wants to know us."

"How does Mildred feel about this?"

"I have no idea. For months, she's either acted like she has no idea what I'm talking about or said she'll have nothing to do with him. But then two days ago, she suddenly changed course. Said she would go with us to Evelyn's for Thanksgiving dinner. Frank will be there."

"That's peculiar, even for her. Maybe the meds are finally kicking in."

"It was such an abrupt change of heart, though. I can't help but wonder if, when we show up to get her, she'll back out or pretend she can't remember she agreed to go."

"Wow. And I thought my dinner would be nerve wracking."

I look at Cassie. Is she my friend? This feels like friendship. I don't know why I invited her for coffee. Maybe I just needed to say all this out loud. There is nothing she can do for me anyway. I get up.

"I better go. I'm sorry I dragged you out on a holiday morning."

"It's fine. I wasn't doing anything, really. I have to go check on a couple patients at lunchtime, but right now I have plenty of time. Sit back down. I don't know that I can help, but I can listen."

I sit back down.

"Will you confront Everett today?" she asks.

Can I? Today?

"I don't know. There probably won't be an opportunity."

"You really can't wait any longer, you know. He needs to get tested and treated."

"Is it awful that I hope it's too late and he'll have all the horrible complications of untreated syphilis?"

Cassie laughs.

"Oh, I don't mean that!" I say. I love Everett. I do. I just hate that my mother is right. "I'm so tired of my mother being right." I think of my mother and the day ahead. It will not be easy for either of us. She must be terrified. It's crazy for Evelyn, and now me, to make her do this. If she loved Frank even a fraction of how much I love Everett, this day will tear her apart. Maybe I should refuse to take her.

"She's not always right," says Cassie, interrupting my thoughts. "She's a cantankerous old bitch, if you want my opinion."

I love the honesty of this woman. "Then why have you spent time with her?"

"I like cantankerous old bitches," says Cassie. "Plus, I really like Jenna, and she seems genuinely worried about her."

Jenna. My beautiful daughter. "I think Jenna's sleeping with her boyfriend."

"She is," says Cassie.

"How do you know?"

"It's obvious from the way they act together. They've definitely been intimate."

"So you've met Wells?"

"He's great. He and Jenna like to hang out with my cats."

"I'm glad she's had a place to go. She and her father fight all the time, and she's had to be responsible for JT more than she should. He adores Jenna, though."

"What about you and Jenna?"

"We're getting better. I feel bad that I spend most of my time with JT, but she doesn't need me so much. She's always been independent."

"I don't know. She probably needs you more than you think."

"She was such a sweet toddler and child. She adored her father, followed him everywhere. It breaks my heart to see the way they fight these days. She's so disrespectful; it drives him nuts."

"Is he respectful of her?"

"He's her father."

"That doesn't mean he respects her. That's all most kids want."

I search my purse for my phone. I want to show Cassie the pictures I have on it of Everett and Jenna a few years ago, before Jenna became so cynical and angry. Before Everett betrayed me.

"What's the matter?" asks Cassie.

"I can't find my phone. I must have left it at home on the charger. I should probably go. I have so much to do to get ready for dinner at Evelyn's." I'm supposed to meet Evelyn and my father, but now I can only think of my mother and what today will be for her. I'm not going to meet Evelyn. If

I had my phone I could let her know, but I'll call her from Mama's. I stand to leave and Cassie stands, too.

"Thanks for trusting me with all this," she says.

"I don't mean to dump it all on you."

"It's fine. Let me know if I can help. I'm sure you'll sort it all out. One thing at a time."

If only it was one thing at a time. "I will," I tell her.

As I walk to the car, I realize my life is a lot like the ER at this present moment. One crisis after another. But I'm good with crisis. In fact, sometimes I think I'm better in crisis than in real life. It's all about prioritizing the injuries and, right now, it's become clear to me that my mother's is by far the most pressing pain.

JENNA
≈≈

Wells drives JT and me to the hospital, but no one will tell us anything. They sit us in a waiting room with plastic chairs and outdated copies of *People* magazine and tell us to stay here until our parents arrive. I call Mom, and her phone rings and rings with no answer. JT says she probably left it at home on the charger when she went to the grocery store. Everett's phone goes right to voicemail. JT tells me he left after Mom did, but didn't say where he was going. Really? He's visiting his hooker on Thanksgiving? I leave him a message.

"I don't know where the fuck you are. We're at the hospital. Gram's house caught on fire and they brought her here, but they won't let us see her. As usual, you're useless."

"Harsh," says Wells when I hang up.

"Where's Mom?" JT asks for like the millionth time. Whenever he's freaked like this, he always wants her.

"She'll be here," I tell him. He rocks in his seat like he used to when he was really little. He doesn't rock so much anymore. It helps him not look like a freak. But today he does. The other people in the waiting room eye him suspiciously, like he might explode or something. He might. I glare at their scared faces. I can't wait for him to grow up and surprise the world by curing cancer or something.

"Gram could be dead," he says.

"What?"

"Smoke inhalation. She's old; it could kill her fast. That's probably why they won't let us see her."

311

I get up and go back out to the nurse's station. Wells follows.

"Can I help you?" asks a new nurse. She wasn't here when we came in over an hour ago.

"Is my grandmother dead?"

"Who is your grandmother?"

"Mildred Watts."

She looks at some charts and then says, "I'll be right back." Only she doesn't come back for like ten minutes. Wells buys a Reese's from the vending machine and gives half of it to me. I love Reese's. It makes sense, what JT said. I can't imagine Gram dead. I mean she's always talking about dying. I guess she'd be happy, though. It's what she wants.

When we were little, I liked going to Gram's. She wasn't always so obsessed with birds. Well, actually she kind of was, but in a normal way. Before she broke her hip, she used to take me birdwatching with her. We'd sit in the bushes in some park, sucking on Jolly Ranchers, waiting. She could tell you what birds were around just by the songs they sang. She could spot a bird's nest way up in a tree. I could never find them, but she would patiently point them out to me. She'd crouch behind me, put her chin on my shoulder, and take my pointing finger in her hand, moving it until it was pointing right at the nest. Then I'd see it.

She never liked my dad, so I know she's not as senile as he says she is. She knew he was a louse long before I did. I was as shocked as anyone when I heard she was going to Aunt Evelyn's today for Thanksgiving dinner. It'll be weird to meet a grandpa I never thought I had. Mom's not too happy about it, but JT is excited. He likes relatives. They have to like him, even if he freaks out. It's gonna be one big happy family reunion. Or not. If Gram is dead, that'll kind of screw up the whole dinner.

The nurse comes back. "We're still trying to reach your parents. Do you need anything? Can I get you a soda?"

"No, I don't want a soda. I just want to know what happened to my gram. Is she dead?"

"I'm sorry. I don't have that information, but I can try to find someone to come talk to you."

"Yeah. That'd be great," I say.

"Sure I can't get you a soda?" she asks again.

Wells takes my arm and leads me back to our room. JT is gone.

"Shit!" I say. "This is all I need."

Wells and I look for him all over the friggin' hospital. We get shooed off one floor after another and pretend like we're just lost. Finally, I hear him. We're near the ER, and he's doing his wailing noise. The one he makes when he's really freaked out. Not just falling on the floor nuts, but hurting himself crazy. I start to run; Wells does too. He passes me and gets to him first.

JT is cornered in a curtained off area. Gram is lying on the bed. She's a blue-grayish tint. Several hospital security guys are trying to talk JT down. A nurse standing near the bed sees us and pulls the sheet over Gram. That's how I know she's dead.

JT keeps smacking the wall, and whenever a guard moves towards him, he kicks out hard. They're trying to be nice because they know he just found his dead grand-mother, but he can't hear them. So I push past them and start singing the *Winnie the Pooh* song. I know I look pyscho, but this is the song my mom sang to us when we were little. I'm singing pretty loud because I want JT to hear me over his wail. I'm halfway through the second verse when he stops wailing and looks at me. I keep singing, but softer. I don't reach for him; I wait for him to come to me, and he does.

"Gram is dead," he says. "She died of smoke inhala-tion. That's why she's a funny color. They'll have to do a blood test to confirm it, but they can probably scope her and see the damage."

The security guard and the nurse are still standing there listening. I look to the nurse.

"He's right, isn't he?" I ask her.

She nods and then backs out, waving the security guards to follow. "Take all the time you need," she says.

We sit with Gram for a while. JT pulls the sheet back and looks at her closely. "I don't think she's in there," he says.

"No, she's not," I agree.

"I bet she's happy where she is," he says.

"Yeah, probably."

"Do you think she started the fire?" JT asks.

I shrug. Gram was nuts, but probably not that nuts.

"She did almost burn her house down that other time," he points out.

"True," I say.

Wells leaves after a while. He wants to stay, but his mom keeps calling and I don't want her to hate me any more than she does.

"Don't tell her about Gram," I tell him. I don't want the whole neighborhood to know before Mom does.

KATE

≈≈

When I pull onto our street, I see firetrucks parked in front of Mama's house. They're blocking the street. I slam the car in park and start running.

I try to run past the firemen, into the house, but a heavyset guy nearly tackles me and pulls me back. The damage isn't terrible; the fire is pretty much out. There's a hole in the roof, but the front of the house looks fine.

"We got her out," says the fireman, and for a moment I'm hopeful that this means Mama is alive.

"Old lady didn't make it," says another. "Did you know her?"

"She was my mother."

"Shit," says the first fireman.

"Sorry," says the other. "They took her to Mercy. You want a ride?"

I shake my head and walk back to my car. I drive on autopilot, hoping the fireman is wrong. There were plenty of people who arrived in the ER mostly dead who we were able to revive. He's probably wrong. Only I know he isn't. Somehow I know. The world feels different to me. More foreign, and at the same time more real.

When I reach the hospital parking lot, I see Everett running across the lot. I watch him. He doesn't know yet, I think. Or maybe he does and he's rushing to my side. I should call the kids. I should go in and see to Mama's body. Instead, I sit in the car watching people come and go.

A young couple comes out the doors with their newborn baby. The husband carries the infant in a blue plastic car seat with a bright plaid cover. The wife holds a balloon, a bouquet of flowers, and a lime-green diaper bag. I can't take my eyes from them. *They don't know.*

Finally, I get out of the car. I enter the hospital through the ER with its familiar smells. I can feel the energy of the place, and long to pull on scrubs and go back to my life the way it was when it was just me and my mother. Mama loved to hear my stories from work. She was so proud that I was a nurse. When Everett came into my life, Mama changed. She began to doubt me. She never trusted Everett. Maybe she knew then. But I never wanted to believe her. I wanted to believe in Everett instead. He would be my hero. So now what?

I find a payphone and call Evelyn.

"What?" she screams when I tell her. "How? Did it have to happen today?"

It's probably unfair, but I imagine Evelyn is angrier that her dinner is ruined, and she won't get to see Mama's expression when she sees Frank for the first time in almost forty years, than she is upset that her mother is dead. All that drama and build up wasted. I've never understood why Evelyn has always been so angry with Mama. She did the best she could. *Isn't that what we all do?*

"I have power of attorney, so don't make any decisions about anything without me. I'll be there as soon as I can," says Evelyn. I hang up while she's still talking.

At the information desk, I ask where I can find my mother. The volunteer is flustered because Mama has not been admitted, but she makes a call and finds that they've already moved Mama's body to the morgue.

I know the way. I wheeled a few bodies down to the morgue when I worked in the ER. Not everyone made it.

I'm surprised to find Everett standing outside the door to the morgue, talking on his phone. When he sees me, he says, "She's here now," and hangs up. He looks at me and I can tell that his heart is breaking for me. Even if he hated Mama, which he did, I don't doubt the pain I see on his face. He loves me. *But what does that mean?*

He takes me in his arms and holds me while I cry. I don't know if I'm crying for Mama or for me. I love the strength of his embrace. His chest swallows me up. I've always felt safe when I'm in his arms. How will I ever feel safe if he's gone?

"They said she died quickly from the smoke."

I nod into his shoulder.

"The fire started in the kitchen, but it wasn't the stove like last time. The chief said they'll have to do more investigation. We can't get in the house until they're finished."

I nod again. I close my eyes and breathe him in. I will miss him. I will miss the feel of him, the smell of his cologne.

"Mom?" says JT, coming out of the morgue doors.

I pull away from Everett. "JT," I say, reaching for him. He's stiff as I hug him, as he always is.

"Gram died from smoke inhalation," he says.

"I know," I say. "I'm sorry."

"Do you think she started the fire?" he asks.

"I don't know," I tell him, truthfully. "I hope not."

Jenna comes out next and I pull her into our circle, hugging her tightly. Everett puts his big arms around all of us. It only lasts a moment, and then Jenna pulls away.

"JT wanted to see the morgue," she explains. "It's cold down here. Can we go?"

"Take the kids home. I'll just be a few minutes. I need to say good-bye."

"She's already gone," says JT.

"C'mon," says Jenna, leading the way.

"I can stay," Everett offers.

"I don't need you," I tell him. His eyes hold mine and I know that I mean it. Maybe he does, too.

When I enter the room where Mama's body is, I don't feel the way I probably should. I can tell she isn't here, but I wish she were. I wish she could tell me what I should do. Oh, I know she'd tell me to divorce Everett, but it's really not that simple. I love him. All of him. Even the bad parts. I need her to tell me how I do this—how I keep going by myself. I'm not sure I can do this without her *and* without Everett. How dare she go. How dare she leave me to figure this out. To face my father. To face my husband.

Mama has always been so strong. That's how I think of her, even now as she lies here on this table, gray and gone. When I was little, I trusted that strength. I wanted to be like her. Maybe that's why I became a nurse. And now—am I to become her? Will I spend the rest of my days angry at Everett? Angry at the world? Finding my only solace in my children, who will feel as smothered as I felt most of the time?

"Mama," I say, and my voice bounces around the metal room. "How dare you?" It's all I can say. I pull the sheet back that is covering her. I stare at the wrinkles around her eyes and the slight bend to her nose. Did she break it once? She never told me. I follow the path of age spots dotting her chest and see the bruising where the paramedics performed CPR. I put my hand to her cheek. She is cold to my touch. I pull the sheet back over her head. She isn't here.

There's a commotion in the hall. Evelyn has arrived. For once, I am grateful.

JENNA

≈≈

D ad drives me and JT home and then goes back to the hospital. He says Thanksgiving will be postponed. I'm okay with that. Not much in the mood for celebrating now. It's weird that Gram is dead. I feel bad that I had pretty much stopped hanging out with her. She was such a downer lately and I outgrew the bird stuff. Guess you have to be into that shit. It got kind of boring. I think the Gram I loved when I was younger was gone long before this day. Or maybe I only imagined that she was nicer then. I do remember she kept lollipops in her apron and always asked me what I was reading. Once, when I spent the night at her house while my parents were with JT at some clinic three hours away, she let me stay up late and we chased lightning bugs. We trapped them in a jar, covered it with plastic, and poked holes in the top. I didn't want to let them go; I wanted to take them to school for show and tell. But when it was time for me to go to bed, Gram said, "They'll die if you leave them closed up in there. You have to let them go." Maybe Gram felt like that these last few years— closed up in there.

In a weird way, I'm glad for her, but I feel bad for Mom. I wonder what she'll do with all her time now that she doesn't have to go over to Gram's every day. I think I feel more badly for Mom than anything else. I am sad about Gram, though. Seems like a horrible way to die. Even if you wanted to die.

There's nothing else to do, so I settle on the couch to binge-watch *ER* with JT. Happy Thanksgiving.

319

EVERETT

≈≈

We're at the hospital for hours. Kate is weirdly calm. She keeps touching me, like she's afraid I'll disappear. Evelyn, of course, takes charge. That's what she likes to do and she seems almost giddy as she signs forms and gives orders for moving Mildred's body.

After that, we meet with the police and fire chief. They have to finish their investigation, but the fire appears to have been intentional, so that should fuck up things with insurance. Kate doesn't act surprised. Apparently Mildred very carefully placed a bunch of books and papers and pictures in a metal trashcan in the middle of the kitchen floor and set it aflame at approximately nine this morning. Then she sat down in her bird watching chair and waited to die.

They think she might have taken an overdose of something. Kate says there was no medication in the house, only her anti-depression meds. Mildred had insisted on taking them herself and Kate was sure she was, but the detective asked if it was possible she was only pretending to take them. The doctors say she wouldn't have died from the drugs, but it would have put her out enough that the smoke inhalation wouldn't have been painful, and she was probably dead before the fire could have gotten to her. Luckily it didn't, thanks to an observant neighbor. Some guy named Phil who was walking his dog. Kate knew him. Said he had been very nice to Mildred. The toxicology report takes weeks, so we may not know for a while.

320

It's almost eight when we finally go home. Mildred's body won't be moved until tomorrow, what with the holiday and all. Evelyn says we can postpone Thanksgiving. Frank is still at his hotel and Evelyn will meet him now for dinner. She invites us, but Kate says no. So we go home.

The kids are watching one of JT's TV shows, so I order pizza and the three of us eat it in front of the tube. Kate takes a glass of wine and goes to bed. Later, when I climb in bed with her, we make love. It's not until we finish that I realize she's crying.

"I'm sorry about your mom," I tell her.

"That's not it," she says. She sits up and pulls on her panties and a T-shirt. She turns on the light. She's gotten so skinny lately. I don't know if it's some new diet or what, but the bones in her shoulders protrude.

"I want you to leave," she says. She says it so quietly, I'm not sure I hear her right.

"What?" I ask.

"I want you to leave, now."

"I don't understand," I say, but I do. I understand and I don't blame her. But at the same time, I can't bear the thought of leaving her. Kate is everything good about me. Without her, I'm nothing. I'm just some schmuck who sells fear for a living.

"You should also go get a test for syphilis because you have it."

"What the fuck?" I say. Now I'm freaked. I have fucking syphilis? Did I get it from her? Is she boning somebody else? "How the hell do you know that? Did you give it to me?"

She shakes her head calmly. Tears still spilling down her cheeks. "I got it from you. It's a sexually transmitted disease."

"I know what it is! I was a cop, remember? All the hookers used to get it. You didn't get it from me!"

"I've never had sex with anyone except you, Everett." She looks at me when she says my name. It's like a knife in my heart. I used to love to hear her say my name. I'd beg her to say it when we made love. It sounded so much better on her lips. Now it sounds dirty the way she says it. Like she is disgusted with my name. With me.

I don't know who I got it from. Could be any number of women. I had a few odd symptoms a while back, but they cleared up, so I figured it was nothing. And I always ask chicks if they're clean before we do it. I don't like to use condoms. It messes up the whole experience for me.

"Please, go," she says again. She's sitting on the bed with her bony knees pulled up to her chest. The polish on her toenails is half worn off. She's become so tiny; she looks like a little girl.

"I'm sorry," I tell her.

"Don't," she says.

She won't look at me, even flinches when I reach out to touch her. I'm certain if she'll just let me back in the bed, we can make this right.

I pull on my clothes. "I don't know where you expect me to go. It's Thanksgiving night."

"I'm sure you can find a bed," she says.

And she's right. I can find a bed, but for once I don't want to go to Veronica's bed.

"I'll sleep on the couch," I say, and go downstairs. I'm not leaving. This is my house.

JENNA

≈≈

It's been a crazy couple of days. I haven't seen Wells
except at the funeral. His dad and mom came, too. That
was strange. They never met Gram. A lot of the neighbors
came. Ms. Cassie and Laura were there, too. I was glad to
see them. Evelyn gave the eulogy. Mom said she couldn't. I
didn't know a lot of the stuff she said about Gram.

I didn't know that her life book was up to almost two
hundred birds. She only had about 150 the last time I went
with her, and considering the last few years she hardly left
her house, that's pretty huge. I didn't know that she had
been a nurse, too, like Mom. She was a nurse in the army
before she married my grandfather.

Speaking of which, I met him! That was the weirdest
thing about the funeral. He sat in the second row, right
behind Evelyn. My mom was polite to him, but you'd
never think they were related. He liked JT. They talked
about Central America, which is where he's been all these
years. He's some kind of minister or monk or something.
Now he lives in Florida. Mom says we might finally have
Thanksgiving dinner with him later this week.

Okay, but here's the big news. Mom finally called Dad
on all his shit. He's been sleeping in the living room, but
he's moving into Gram's eventually. It's all covered in
plastic from the damage, but he's going to fix it up so they
can sell it. Or he might live there, Mom says. I'm amazed
how at peace Mom seems to be with this. I'd be going all

323

ape-shit on his ass. But she's just sad. I guess she wishes he weren't such a louse. Even now, I can hear Gram saying, "I told you so!" from her grave.

The golf-pro's fiancée is back, so we lost our house. Wells picks me up and we drive to the reservoir. It's an oddly warm day for November. Wells brings a blanket and we stretch out in the sun. It's nice to be somewhere quiet with no family drama. He sits up, tossing rocks into the water, and I lie down next to him wishing he would kiss me. He runs out of rocks and goes to get more.

When he sits back down, I ask, "So what's going to happen to us?"

"What do you mean?" he asks, and throws another rock. I watch it plop in the water, scattering circles.

"Are we going to get tired of each other eventually?"

He leans back on the blanket next to me, resting on his elbow. "I don't know."

I like that he's honest.

"I don't know either," I tell him.

He kisses me, and I stop thinking about death and cheaters and complicated families and grandfathers I never knew.

KATE
≈≈

Walking through Mama's house, I'm struck by how different it seems. It's not the smell or the charred wall in the kitchen, it's the quiet. I pick up the broken bits of drywall that lie on the floor and carry them to the trashcan. The empty tea box sits on top of the trash where I placed it that morning after I'd made Mama's tea. Did I rush her that morning? I was preoccupied, anxious to meet Cassie and worried about meeting Evelyn and Frank.

It's not nearly as bad as I expected. JT explained to me that the firemen didn't use water because the fire was small enough to put out with extinguishers. The tile floor hadn't ignited, so it was only Mama's bonfire and a few cabinets and part of the ceiling and roof above that actually burned.

The house smells like smoke, so I open all the windows. Cold air blows through the house as I gather the few things I want from this place. In Mama's closet, there is an old army trunk. Inside I find her birding life book and a framed picture of me at graduation in my nurse's uniform. Also, my mother's uniform and gear. JT might enjoy looking at everything in here, including the books on triage in the field. Mama was an army nurse.

I find a big black contractor's trash bag in the garage and shovel the remnant of Mama's bonfire into it. It's almost comical how neat she was in her preparations before setting the fire. She used the metal trashcan that we store birdseed in. It was nearly empty because I'd forgotten

325

to pick up more birdseed. Usually she reminds me about things like that, but this week she didn't.

When I pick it up, the bottom falls out, along with what's left of the wedding album and scrapbooks she'd attempted to burn. The fire licked up the wall quickly and caught the curtains and then ceiling, and seemingly abandoned Mama's pile at the bottom of the can. JT could probably explain why it behaved like that if I asked him. I push a few things aside, and then I spy Mama's shoebox—the one I found her with right after she found out Frank was coming.

The top is browned and the edges burned, but it's intact. Inside, there is a ribbon-wrapped pile of letters. I untie the ribbon and slide a letter out. It's a love letter from my father. There are at least thirty of them, written while she was serving in the army overseas. I sink down on the floor and read. I get up once for a glass of water and to wiggle my foot when it falls asleep, but otherwise I just sit and read through all of them. I have to know if Mama loved Frank the way I loved Everett. The letters are beautiful, funny, honest, searing. They are written by a man whose world revolved around her. How could he have ever left?

I carefully stack the letters. Some are worn thin. I can see smudges of fingerprints along the sides where she traced his words.

What did she write back? What did she say to this man who adored her beyond reason? Who claimed his heart beat only because she was in this world? Who looked at the stars every night and was jealous because he knew they'd seen her?

Discovering that he had slept with another person must have rocked her world the same way mine is swaying now. How could someone love you so completely and still make love to another person? Was it possible to touch another woman and not feel the betrayal beneath your fingertips?

All the years of listening to Mama call my father a louse makes sense to me now. If a man could love a woman the way Frank had loved Mildred and then walk away for forty years, then nothing could be trusted.

But Frank didn't seem like a louse.

He seemed like an ordinary man. Maybe that was the mistake. Believing that a man is infallible; that love will protect you. Love can have holes in it, but does that mean it isn't love?

Did Everett mean all the words he has said to me? Words written on my heart as clearly as these on the delicate paper I'm holding. He is begging me to give him another chance. With all my heart, I want to give him that chance. I want to believe in him.

Did Mama wait all these years, hoping Frank would come back? Is that why she shunned other men? But why would she kill herself now? Was it that she couldn't bear to see him? *Oh, Mama, I wish you were here. I wish you could have explained this kind of love to me. What do I do now?*

I look at my watch. It's time for the kids to get home. Wells is driving both Jenna and JT home. JT was excited about it. Every school day, all his life, I have picked him up from school, but when Wells offered, I couldn't resist the excitement in JT's eyes. So I said yes, and wrote the note giving permission.

When I get home, JT, Wells, and Jenna are in the kitchen having a snack.

"Hey Mom-Unit!" calls JT. "I made it home alive!"

I laugh. "I never doubted it for a second. Thanks, Wells."

"No problem, Mrs. T, happy to do it."

I watch Jenna with Wells. They are so natural and happy.

Later, I find Jenna doing her homework in the living room. I sit down on the sofa next to Marco, who is sprawled out faithfully watching Jenna. I scratch his ears and he rolls over for a full tummy rub.

"So, amidst all the chaos of the past week, I haven't had a chance to ask you how things are going with Wells."

Jenna sets down her book and pen. She smiles. "It's good."

"You really like him?"

Jenna nods.

"Is it serious?"

She laughs. "Depends on how you define serious. If you're asking me if I've slept with him, then, yes, I have."

"And you're being careful?"

"Duh, I'm not stupid."

"Do you think you'll marry him?"

Jenna lets out another laugh. "Wells? I doubt it. We still have to go to college. And his country club family is definitely not in my fan club. I don't even know if I'll get married."

I'm relieved. At least one woman in this family knows how to keep perspective around men.

"Everything else okay?"

Jenna picks up her book again. "I'm fine, Mom, don't worry about me. You've got enough to deal with."

I feel tears prick at my eyes. When did she grow into such an amazing young woman?

"I'm going to run over to Cassie's, but your father is here if you need anything."

"Got it."

≈≈

"So, he's still in the house?" asks Cassie. "I thought you were going to kick him out?"

"I did, but he had no place to go."

"What about his girlfriend's?"

"He broke up with her."

"Sure he did."

"I believe him."

"That's the entire problem," says Cassie. A longhaired white cat jumps up on her lap. I can feel another cat swirling around my feet. I don't understand people with all their cats. Dogs make more sense. Much more loyal. I cross my legs to discourage the brown cat circling me from jumping onto my lap.

"How did it go clearing out Mildred's house?" asks Cassie.

"There wasn't much there. She was militant about throwing away unnecessary things, but I did find something."

"What?"

"Dozens of love letters from my father. He'd written them while she was serving a tour in the army. She was stationed in Korea for about six months."

"And she kept them? I thought she hated your father."

"I thought so, too. When I was growing up, she couldn't even say his name. She called him *the louse.*"

Cassie laughs. "Mildred was something. What was in the letters?"

"Long descriptions of how he pictured her, a few poems, even song lyrics. They were beautiful. He really worshipped her. I can see why she kept them."

"Why keep love letters from a man who walked out on you?"

"Maybe she thought he'd come back."

"He did."

"And she killed herself on the very day that she was going to see him again."

"Seems like a Shakespearean tragedy."

"Or true love."

"That's where you get it," says Cassie, looking intently at me.

"What?"

"Your romantic delusion."

"My what?"

"Your delusion that just because someone says they love you that means they do."

"How else would you know?"

"They show you."

I don't say anything. I know she's talking about Everett. I sip my wine. I know she's got more to say. I've come to Cassie's almost every night this week to sip wine on her patio. Tonight it's chilly, but Cassie likes to spend time with the cats when she gets home. I have trouble reconciling Cassie's sunny disposition with her depressing job, but she insists it isn't depressing. Quite the opposite, she says.

"Love isn't romance. It's a grind. It's being there every day, even when you don't want to be. I see it all the time. I watch these people who sit with their dying spouse or friend or parent. They clean up their shit, spoon feed them their dinner, bathe them, read to them, take care of them—because they *love* them. It's the most romantic thing I've ever seen, but it's not something you'd ever find in a romance novel. Love isn't some grand thing that you luck into; there's not magic chemistry involved. It's a decision. A conscious decision. You have to decide you're going to love someone and then you have to make that decision every day, every hour, again and again. Even when it sucks."

"You don't think Everett loved me?"

"He loved the idea of you, but he sure as shit wasn't making the decision to love you when he shacked up with the bimbo who gave you both syphilis."

I think about Cassie's words long after I get home. I'm wiping down the counters when Everett creeps into the kitchen. He sits at the counter and reaches for my hand. I let him hold it.

"How can I make this right?" he asks.

"You can't."

"There has to be a way."

I look at his earnest face. I love that face. I long to reach out and stroke his cheek, feel his lips against my palm. Will I ever love like this again?

"It's time for you to move to Mama's. I've taken everything I want out of it. You can make the house your own."

"Kate, don't do this," says Everett, rising and coming around the counter to meet me. He places a hand on my waist. "I've never loved anyone like I love you. "

"I know that," I say, and turn to go, out of his reach. In the doorway, I stop and look at him. "Please move your things tomorrow."

EVERETT
≈≈

I can't believe how I've seriously fucked up everything. And I've got syphilis. I don't know how my life went from pretty damn good a week ago to totally screwed.

For now, I'm sleeping on the futon in the office. Kate is eerily calm about everything, but then again she's not a screamer. She seems very settled on the idea of me moving out. I'm hoping she just needs some time. I know I fucked up, but I'm gonna make it right. I already broke things off with Veronica. Or actually, she broke it off with me before I had the chance to. When I told her about the syphilis, she starting yelling at me and throwing shit. Saved me the drama of breaking things off with her.

I offered to work on Mildred's house for Kate and Evelyn. It's not really that bad, mostly smoke damage. I've got to replace a lot of dry wall. Kate suggested I just live there while I'm doing the work, so I guess I'm gonna do that. I'm sticking close for now, though. I know she's gotta be pretty freaked out about meeting her pop. Hard to believe he's still around. Especially now that I know his story doesn't check out. I'd bet he's just after Ev's money. She's got a truckload of it. He met the kids at the funeral, but we haven't seen him since.

JT says he's nice, but JT likes everyone. The kid passes no judgment. More people should be like him. I'm spending a lot of time with JT since he's the only person living here who will talk to me. I like listening to stuff on the

332

scanner with him. A couple times, we've jumped in the car and gone to check out a fire. Except for the not touching people thing, JT would make a great cop. He sees things very clearly in black and white. But he's so frickin' smart, he should be a scientist or something.

Jenna won't even look at me. I know she's sleeping with Wells. I can tell by the way she arrives home late, all disheveled and rosy cheeked. It kills me that I can't do anything about it. I'm glad she keeps that sonofabitch away from here.

KATE

≈≈

On the way to Evelyn's, I try to apologize to the kids. "Okay, I know it's been a really hard week. I wouldn't even make you go through with this except that Frank . . ." I pause. It feels weird to say his name to the kids. I take a breath and continue, "Your grandfather is still here and your aunt really wants us to have the belated Thanksgiving she planned."

"It's okay Mom-Unit. I like him. I want to go."

"Yeah, it's cool. I'm kind of curious, too."

"Well, don't feel like you have to hug him or anything like that. I understand that it might be awkward."

When we arrive, they climb out of the car and start up the long stone walk. It's already dark and through the lighted windows, I can see my father. I hardly looked at him at the funeral. I stop to study him. He is tan and trim. He's intently talking with Evelyn in the living room. I'm surprised at the anger I feel. All along, I thought that meeting Frank didn't matter to me. He wasn't a part of my life. But seeing him with Evelyn, watching him lean in and laugh at something she says, I feel cheated. What might my life have been if I'd had a father? What if he'd been the kind of man who loved his wife and didn't cheat on her? A man who stuck around.

"Mom? You okay?" asks Jenna.

She stands on the stair behind me with JT beside her. I turn and see her face lit up by the walk light. She's stopped wearing the harsh makeup she's hidden behind for the last few years. She is beautiful.

I take Jenna's hand and JT's. "I haven't thanked you for being so helpful to me this week. I couldn't have survived it without you."

"No biggie. We didn't do anything," says Jenna.

"I know things will be different from now on, with Gram gone and your father moved out, but I love you very much. You need to remember that above everything else."

Jenna hugs me. "I love you, too." It is a balm to hear those words from her.

"Can we go in now?" asks JT.

I take a deep breath. "Yes, let's do this," I say.

≈≈

Evelyn opens the door. Frank is standing there. He's smiling. And behind him, wearing a suit and freshly shaven, is Everett. What's he doing here? He moved into Mama's house yesterday and I never mentioned this dinner. Evelyn. Why the hell didn't my sister tell me she invited him?

"I'm grateful that you came," says Frank. I'm surprised to hear a slight Hispanic accent. The funeral was a blur; I never spoke with him. Never acknowledged him. Still don't want to. I shake his hand, but I can't stop looking at Everett. He is smiling at me. Jenna and JT shake Frank's hand and there is an awkward moment before Evelyn says, "JT, my computer's been acting up. Do you think you could take a look at it?"

"I could," he says.

"You know where to find it?"

"I do," he says, and heads off to Evelyn's home office. He's always enjoyed visiting here because Evelyn has all kinds of fancy computers and TVs and gaming systems and other gadgets I don't understand. The kids come home complaining that we don't have whatever the latest thing is.

"Let's sit down in the living room and have a glass of wine before we eat," says Evelyn. "Jenna, I've got a fancy cranberry fizz soda for you, too, or you can have wine if your mom allows it."

She looks at me, eyebrows raised, and I shake my head.

Evelyn leads Frank into the living room and Jenna follows.

Everett doesn't move.

"Why are you here?" I ask.

"Evelyn invited me," he says, and holds out his arm as if I should take it. I walk past him and sit in the newly upholstered chair across from where Frank has seated himself on the sofa. He's holding a drink, swirling the ice cubes as he examines it. Everett stands behind me. He sets a hand on my shoulder. I know he means to comfort me, but his touch feels like a branding iron. Evelyn sits beside Frank. Jenna mills around the sideboard where Evelyn has set out some food.

Frank asks, "How are you holding up? Losing your mother so suddenly must have been quite a shock."

I wonder how much he knows. Did Evelyn tell him that Mama most likely committed suicide? Has he thought about the fact that she did it on the very day she was to see him? All along, I thought she was growing well from the medication. But she'd only been playing me, manipulating me as she's done all her life. As I've let her do. I look at Frank; I wonder if he even knows what he's done.

I want to ask him so many things. I'd planned to, but now, sitting here looking at him, I can't speak. He's only an old man. He doesn't seem like the monster who betrayed my mother. I thought I'd feel more when I actually spoke to him, but I don't feel much of anything. He seems so ordinary.

"Where's Waldo?" asks Jenna, suddenly. She loves Evelyn's cat.

"Probably somewhere upstairs," says Evelyn, shrugging.

Jenna looks at me and I say, "Go, you don't need to sit through this."

After she is gone, Evelyn says, "So I thought maybe if we were all here together, Everett could tell us what he's discovered."

Everett looks surprised; almost drops his drink. Frank sits up, as if startled awake. The ice cubes rattle in his glass. I see a smile pass over Evelyn's lips. She loves this.

"Maybe not now, Evelyn. This might not be the place," says Everett.

"I think it's the perfect time," she says as she pours herself another glass of wine and leans back on the sofa. "We're all here."

"In light of all that's happened, maybe we should save this for another time"

"Nonsense. I'd like to know what you found out," she says.

I can tell Evelyn knows something. Whenever there's a scene to be made, she'll make it. I take a deep drink of the wine I've been holding since she placed it in my hand. It's a rich red. I usually stick to white wine, but tonight this red wine fortifies me. Obviously, I'm here for a show.

"Well," begins Everett. "The only thing I know for sure is that you were both adopted and Mildred wasn't your mother."

I drop my glass, red wine spilling over my skirt and onto the coffee table.

"Shit!" yells Evelyn, and I'm not sure if it's because of the wine or Everett's announcement. She runs to the kitchen for towels and returns, throwing them at me. She turns to Everett, "And this matters because?"

She knew. She knew we were adopted and never told me?

"It doesn't really matter that you were adopted. What matters is who your father is."

"Why does that matter?" she asks. I mop the wine on the table, but some of it runs on the floor, so I kneel down on the carpet. It will stain. It seems easier to focus on the wine than on what Everett is saying.

"You have the same birth mother, but different birth fathers," he says, and looks at Frank. "You want to take it from here?"

I pause, holding the dripping towel, and look at Frank. He looks stricken, white as a sheet. He sets his highball glass on the coffee table, and I can see that he is shaking.

When he doesn't speak, Everett continues. "I haven't figured it all out. I was hoping Frank might fill in a few blanks. Your birth mother died about six months after you were born, Evelyn. It was a drug overdose, but the police thought it might have been more. The investigation dried up, but the detectives on the case were never completely convinced it was accidental. They were pretty sure she wasn't alone when it happened." He looks at Frank. Raises his eyebrows.

"She was alone," Frank says. There are tears in his eyes. "She was a drug addict. Mildred met her at the ER. She was tiny. Mildred thought she was fragile as a little bird. Kimberly. That was her name. Your mother took to her, tried to help her dry out for the sake of the baby she was carrying."

He reaches for his glass, raises it to his lips, then realizes it's empty and sets it back on the table.

"When you were born, Kate, Kimberly asked us to take you. We had tried for years to have our own children, but couldn't. Mildred wanted a baby so badly. I never understood it. I always told her that she was enough." He shakes his head, looks in his empty glass.

Evelyn gets up and gets the bottle of scotch from the sideboard. She pours his glass half full.

"If she was enough, then why would you leave?" I ask. The words are out before I can stop them. "Why would you sleep with another woman if you loved her so much?"

He shakes his head. "It was different than that. I did it for her. That makes no sense, I know that now, but at the time I only wanted her to have everything she dreamed of.

She wanted children. That's all that mattered. I messed up. I know that. But I never stopped loving her. I never wanted to leave."

He nods at Evelyn, thanking her for the drink. Then lifts the glass to his lips and drinks it unsteadily. I don't know if he's drunk or nervous or has arthritis. I don't know him at all, I realize. He's not even my real father. He's no one.

"Wait!" says Evelyn, holding her hand up like a traffic cop. "What about me? You said we had the same mother. Did Kimberly get pregnant again?"

"She did," says Everett. "You want to tell her who her father is, Frank?"

He shakes his head. "I know it doesn't make sense now, but she wanted another baby so badly. It was something I could give her and Kimberly wanted to do it for Mildred. That's what she said. I didn't love Kimberly; I loved Mildred. But Kimberly and I could give her a baby."

I'm trying to wrap my mind around what he is saying, trying to make it not sound crazy. "So, she was your surrogate?"

"Not exactly," says Frank.

"Frank is your father, Evelyn. He slept with Kimberly. That's how she got pregnant." Everett says this quietly. I wonder if he's only now figuring it out or if he's known all along.

"I never loved her," Frank says.

"As if that makes it better," says Evelyn.

"You were there," says Everett, standing up suddenly.

"What?" Evelyn and I say at the same time.

"You were with Kimberly! You helped her overdose!"

"I had nothing to do with it. She did it to herself," Frank insists.

"Mildred found out you were the father," says Everett. "Didn't she?"

Tears are streaming down Frank's face now. He looks at Evelyn. "I think she knew the moment you were born, but she never said so. It wasn't until Kimberly said she wanted to take you away. She wanted me to marry her and for us to raise you together. I never meant for it to be like that. I only wanted to give Mildred another baby. I had no idea Kimberly would want to marry me. What was I to do? I couldn't take you from Mildred. She couldn't bear it. I didn't know what else to do. I swear I didn't make her take those drugs. She wanted them."

"You never need to make an addict do anything," says Everett.

"So, if Kimberly died, why did you leave?" I ask.

"Because she threw me out. She was so angry. She kept saying, 'You killed their mother!' but I didn't. I didn't. And besides, *she* was your mother! Don't you see that?" He is crying, slumped back against the couch. "She was your mother," he whispers between his tears.

For a moment, no one speaks.

"Why didn't you come back?" Evelyn asks.

"I couldn't. When I called Mildred and asked her to take me back, she said she'd turn me in to the authorities. They knew someone else was with Kimberly when she died. And more than that, Kimberly was underage. Mildred said she'd have me locked up for statutory rape. I didn't know what else to do. My heart was broken. I left. I found solace in the only place I could."

"God," says Evelyn.

"Horseshit," says Everett. "If you had nothing to do with her death, there was nothing the cops could do. And if the sex was consensual, even that wouldn't have been enough to lock you up. Kimberly was seventeen and she'd already had a baby for Christ's sake."

"I didn't know any of that. I was scared." Frank wiped a tear and set down his empty glass. "And besides, if Mildred didn't want me, what was the point?"

"The point?" I can't help myself. "The point is that you had two little girls who had no daddy. Two little girls who thought their father left them and never came back.

Who thought their father never loved them enough to stick around! Is that not enough point for you?"

"I'm sorry, Kate. I am. That's why I'm here now. I wanted to tell you that I never stopped thinking of you."

"It's a little too late," I tell him, getting up. I'm finished here. I don't want to spend another second in this house with a man who could never be my father and a man who has never been a husband.

"Jenna? JT?" I yell, and they both come clomping down the stairs instantly. They head right out the front door. Most likely they've heard it all from the top of the stairs. I'm about to follow them, but I have one more question for Frank. I turn back to the living room, where he and Evelyn are still sitting, shell-shocked. Everett is pouring another glass of wine.

"Then why would Mama kill herself? What was she so afraid of?"

"I don't know," Franks says. "I guess she thought I'd tell you girls that you were adopted. She never wanted you to know. She was adamant about that. You were hers. No one else's."

"Certainly, not yours," I say, and turn to go.

Evelyn gets up and rushes out after me.

"Don't leave!" she pleads.

"This is what you wanted, Evelyn! He's here! *Your* father—what a prince!"

"This isn't what I wanted. You know that. But we can't change things. Can't you stay and talk?"

"I'll leave that to you."

Everett appears in the doorway. "I'll call you," he says, but I don't say anything because I have nothing to say.

≈≈

Later, it's Evelyn who calls. I don't want to answer, but I figure she might be as upset as I am. Maybe more so, since he's her real father.

341

"Hey," I say.

"That was something," says Evelyn, and I can tell she's already trying to spin the whole evening. "How are you doing?"

"I'm okay."

"You aren't going to say anything to anyone about Frank and what happened with our birth mother, are you?"

"Who would I tell?"

"I don't know. The police?"

"What would be the point?"

"I just figured you'd be mad and want to blame someone."

"He's not to blame, right? He said so himself. Don't you believe him?"

"I do, I do."

In all honesty, I do think that Frank should pay for the death of the teenager who gave birth to us, but I have enough to deal with in my own life. Besides, Everett's right—there's no way to prove it. I have to believe that he has already paid a price by losing my mother. After reading the letters in her box, I know he believed he loved her. It just wasn't enough. Or maybe it was too much and it ate them alive.

"Where is he now?"

"He went back to his hotel. He's leaving in the morning."

"Why? I thought he was staying?"

"I told him to leave."

"You did?" Sometimes my sister surprises me. Rarely. But it does happen.

"Kate, I don't want it to be like this. You're my only family now."

"I don't want it to be like this either," I tell her. I'm not sure how else it could be, though.

"Good," she says. "We need to talk about what we're going to do with Mama's house."

"Everett is going to clean it up. He moved in there yesterday. That's where he's going to live."

"He said you're only separated. I'm sure you'll work things out. After he gets it cleaned up, we can talk about selling it."

"We'll see."

"You sound like Mama," she says.

I smile. That was Mama's favorite answer. Whenever either of us girls suggested we do something that would very likely never happen like go to Disney World or buy a new car or ever meet our father, she'd always said, "We'll see."

EVERETT
≈≈

I've been living in Mildred's house for four months. It still smells like smoke. I took down the damn fencing in the backyard and threw out the birdfeeders. I even took a sledgehammer to her concrete birdbath one night when I got drunk. She poisoned Kate. She's the reason I'm alone.

Kate got a lawyer. I'm sure she's someone Evelyn recommended. I haven't gotten one because I don't need one. I don't want a divorce.

Yesterday, I saw her walking down the street with that doctor who lives in the blue house. He has a big, funny-looking dog who growls at me when he walks by. I've gotten the house in perfect shape; even put in a flower garden out front. Kate always wanted flower gardens. I think gardens invite strangers. They always want to comment on your flowers or ask what you're growing. People are too goddamn nosy.

Jenna still isn't talking to me, but I got her an internship at FABSO. She knows the systems really well and is doing a great job as a salesperson. Clients love it when she shows them how easy it is to break in to their place. They buy everything she's selling. She's saving money for college next year.

She's still seeing that kid up the street. They drive past in his fancy Corvette. Sweet ride. He always waves and smiles. She won't even look my way. She'll come around, though. She's a softy, like her mom, even though she acts all tough.

JT spends a lot of weekends here. I helped him fix up his own room and bought him a new scanner and computer. He's moved on to neuroscience, but he still likes to listen to the calls. He already knows more about what's going on inside the brain than any shrink I've met. He's gonna start at the high school in the fall. Just a few classes. The rest he'll do online through the local college. Kate wants him to take his GED this summer. I don't know. I just want him to be normal.

Really, that's all I want for any of us.

JENNA
≈≈

I got Wells a microscope for his birthday. It's not the best one. I couldn't afford a better one, but it's still pretty cool. It comes with all these slides that show what stuff really looks like. You think a hair is just a really thin string, but it's actually more like a cable with all these fibers. I like that he wants to know what's beneath the surface. He loved it. Kept shaking his head and saying, "You're amazing," like the dumb thing was a really big deal when it was only about a hundred bucks on Amazon.

I tell Cassie and Laura about the microscope.

"You guys are getting pretty serious, aren't you?" asks Cassie.

I shrug. "Maybe." I can't help myself and I smile. I hate that thinking of Wells makes me grin like an idiot. But he makes me happy.

"What about you guys?" I ask. They seem to find my relationship with Wells so amusing, but they've been spending a lot of time together lately. Laura is almost always here. Makes breaking in pointless.

They smile and then they both hold up their hands. Matching rings.

"That's awesome!" I tell them. "When?"

"Next Valentine's Day," says Cassie. "Only because Laura is a hopeless romantic. You and Wells are invited."

"Cool," I say.

Later, when Wells shows up, Cassie, Laura, and I are playing hearts.

"Good, a fourth!" says Laura.

"Cards?" he says, and wrinkles his nose. "I just came to say good-bye to Jenna." Wells and his family are leaving for a cruise in the morning. It's spring break.

We walk up the street together.

"I wish I wasn't going away."

"You'll be back," I say in a *Terminator* voice.

Wells laughs.

Life will be so boring here without him. I'll probably put in a lot more hours at FABSO. They love me there. Only downside is seeing Everett, but that's getting a little bit better. Our relationship will never be what you'd call normal, but, then again, nothing is.

"I'll miss you," I say, because I will.

Wells says, "Same," and then he stops and takes my hands. He kisses me really slowly, so slowly that I almost giggle because it's weird. I look up into his crazy gorgeous eyes. He kisses me one more time, and then he says, "I think I love you."

"Same," I tell him. Because I do think I love Wells Braddington. And for now, that's enough.

KATE
≈≈

I've been walking almost every day with Phil. He's a nice
man. I like his dog, too. Cassie says to be careful with
him, like he's a piece of china. But I understand that fragil-
ity. I feel it, too. My heart doesn't feel very sturdy anymore.
Maybe it's worn out. Or maybe Everett took it with him. It
doesn't matter. I enjoy Phil's company. I'm not expecting
anything. That's why, when he suggests I come for dinner,
I'm surprised.

"Me?"

He laughs. Looks around. "Is there anybody else here?"

I laugh, too, but I don't answer him. I just keep walking.
I've brought Marco along this time. He's already huffing,
but seems determined to keep up with Phil's dog, Cooper.
JT is home alone. He told me recently that I don't need to
babysit him all the time.

Lately, JT's fascinated with the brain. I'm not sure if
he's trying to figure out his own or if he's trying to unscram-
ble what went so haywire in his grandmother's brain that
she would kill herself. I'd like to know, too, but I have my
theories. I don't think it was her brain as much as her heart.

I think she loved my father too much. She lived her
whole life in the shadow of her disappointment and cob-
bled together a fragile existence that only worked without
him. Seeing him brought back everything—the cost of
motherhood, the betrayal of a man whose love defined
her, the truth—that our family was a sham built on the

348

grave of our birth mother. It's more than one heart could hold. I understand now why she had no room for others in our lives. She needed to create a world she could contain. Frank coming back now would expose all of it. And her heart was exhausted from the effort of a lifetime.

We come to the cul-de-sac at the end of the road. I turn to go, saying, "C'mon, Marco. Time to go back."

I know Phil is still waiting for an answer to his question. He's a nice man. I wonder what it would be like to be with a man so normal. Phil is not exciting like Everett. He is not as handsome or charming. I doubt he would bring home fishnet stockings for me, but you never know. Maybe normal could be good. Maybe normal is relative.

ACKNOWLEDGMENTS
≈≈

I have to first acknowledge the Downhillers—Ann, Paul, Dahna, Andy, Dave, Tommy, Lisbeth and, most especially, Linda. Thanks for the endless games of kickball, wiffleball, two-hand touch, kick-the-can, and Mulocks, the hours spent at the bus stop, the kamikaze sledding, and for teaching me the meaning of neighborhood. Writing this story brought back so many memories of those early years in Montgomery Woods, and it made me oh-so-grateful for all of you and the influence you had on my life.

A debt of gratitude to my early readers—Lisa Weigard, Gina Moltz, Margot Tillitson, Candace Shaffer, Marcia Bates, and Pat Hazlebeck. You are dear friends who indulge me and read the gobbledygook when it is barely formed. I am blessed to have you.

Also thanks to Crystal Mueller, Kirstin Myers, and Shelby Fizer for making sure I got JT right. Thanks also to Crystal for the inspiration behind the math specialist.

One Foot In Heaven: Journey of a Hospice Nurse by Heide Telpner (Julia Barrett) was a fascinating and touching read that helped me understand what a hospice nurse goes through, and Julia's gracious (and fast!) reading of my manuscript helped me fix many of the details. Anything that doesn't ring true is totally on me.

Thanks to Lou Aronica, whose patient editing has made me a better writer. Thanks for always being so respectful when you tell me I've got it all wrong, and for your faithful belief in my abilities.

Once again, much thanks to Nora Tomada for fixing all my commas and making me sound much better than I am. Someday I hope to buy you a glass of wine and apologize. A second shout out to Candace Shaffer, who lent her amazing editorial abilities to this manuscript free of charge and who brainstormed with me for three days straight, first over a bottle of wine with Gina and then via endless text messages which helped me finally come up with a title!

A special thanks to my kids, Brady, Adelaide, and Ian. While you are none of the young people in this story, your habits and hearts have informed them. Being your mom is always my greatest privilege in life.

Big thanks to the guy who pays the bills, indulges my writing habit, tolerates my moods, puts up with the foster puppies, and makes my world complete. I love you, Nicholas.

We are all just practicing normal.

ABOUT THE AUTHOR
≈≈

Cara Sue Achterberg is a writer and blogger who lives in New Freedom, PA with her family and an embarrassing number of animals. Her first novel, *I'm Not Her*, was a national bestseller, as was her second, *Girls' Weekend*. Cara's nonfiction book, *Live Intentionally*, is a guide to the organic life filled with ideas, recipes, and inspiration for living a more intentional life. Cara is a prolific blogger, occasional cowgirl, and busy mom whose essays and articles have been published in numerous anthologies, magazines, and websites. Links to her blogs, news about upcoming publications, and pictures of her foster dogs can be found at CaraWrites.com.